Hearts
Made Whole

Books by Jody Hedlund

The Preacher's Bride
The Doctor's Lady
Unending Devotion
A Noble Groom
Rebellious Heart
Captured by Love

BEACONS OF HOPE

Out of the Storm: A BEACONS OF HOPE Novella
Love Unexpected
Hearts Made Whole
Undaunted Hope

ORPHAN TRAIN

An Awakened Heart: An ORPHAN TRAIN Novella
With You Always
Together Forever
Searching for You

BEACONS OF HOPE ⟶ BOOK TWO

Hearts Made Whole

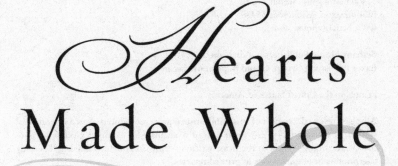

JODY HEDLUND

BETHANYHOUSE
a division of Baker Publishing Group
Minneapolis, Minnesota

© 2015 by Jody Hedlund

Published by Bethany House Publishers
11400 Hampshire Avenue South
Bloomington, Minnesota 55438
www.bethanyhouse.com

Bethany House Publishers is a division of
Baker Publishing Group, Grand Rapids, Michigan

Printed in the United States of America

Library of Congress Cataloging-in-Publication Data
Hedlund, Jody.
    Hearts made whole / Jody Hedlund.
        pages ; cm. — (Beacons of hope ; book 2)
    Summary: "In 1865, Caroline has tended the Windmill Point Lighthouse in Michigan since her father's death, but her home and livelihood are threatened when a wounded Civil War veteran arrives to take her place"—Provided by publisher.
        ISBN 978-0-7642-1238-3 (softcover)
        1. Lighthouses—Michigan—Fiction. 2. Man-woman relationships—Fiction. 3. United States—History—Civil War, 1861–1865—Veterans—Fiction. I. Title.
    PS3608.E333H43 2015
    813'.6—dc23   2014046625

Scripture quotations are from the King James Version of the Bible.

This is a work of historical reconstruction; the appearances of certain historical figures are therefore inevitable. All other characters, however, are products of the author's imagination, and any resemblance to actual persons, living or dead, is coincidental.

Cover design by Jennifer Parker
Cover photography by Mike Habermann Photography, LLC

To all the women who worked in lighthouses

Thank you for your courage and for showing
that women are capable of doing anything.

Chapter 1

A distant flash of lightning crisscrossed the darkening skies of the west, followed by the call of a nearby loon. "I don't think you should set out." Caroline Taylor clutched her shawl tighter against a cool gust that wrestled with it. "The storm's coming fast."

Her father shoved the rowboat across the gravelly shore of Lake St. Clair. "We'll be fine," he said over his broad shoulder. "We'll beat the storm. Besides, I've crossed this lake in more storms than I can count."

The old doctor already waited on a bench inside the cutter, clasping his top hat and fighting with the wind to keep it on his head. "I can't stay any longer, Caroline," the doctor said. "I've done all I can for your sister."

She wanted to blurt out that she knew that. That she'd been

7

in Sarah's room when he'd examined her and made his dismal prognosis. That they'd all known Sarah wasn't getting better. That no matter how much they'd hoped and prayed over the winter, Sarah had only gotten worse. But instead of saying anything, Caroline merely nodded.

"Unfortunately I've got too many other patients needing my attention." Beneath the brim of the doctor's hat, deep grooves etched his forehead and seemed to grow deeper with each visit. "Too many young men ripped apart from limb to limb."

With General Lee's surrender at Appomattox a month ago, some of the fighting men had begun to return home. If reports were true, many of the soldiers who had made it out of the bloody war were injured, maimed, and only half alive.

Caroline's father gave one last heave, and the boat screeched against the rocks as though in protest of having to leave. Holding on to the bowline, her father limped on stiff legs into the murky water. His rheumatism was always worse when the weather was about to change.

Caroline glanced at the sky again, to the piles of dark clouds gathering in heaps on the horizon. Her lungs pinched. "Father . . ." she began but quelled her protest by nibbling on her bottom lip.

The waves slapped high against his rubber boots and doused his trousers at the knees. His blue eyes, so much like her own, reached across to her tenderly. "Cast your cares on Him, honey."

His gentle admonition loosened the tightness in her chest only a little. They both knew she was prone to worry. It wasn't something she was proud of. But there were times when anxiety crowded into her head like a thick, heavy fog, blinding and choking her.

He glanced toward the keeper's cottage, where her siblings

stood. "Mind Caroline while I'm gone!" he shouted above the wind.

Tessa stood on the step in front of the weathered house, her beautiful, dark wavy hair flowing like ravens taking flight. She had her arms around the twins, anchoring the wiry boys to the spot, as Caroline had instructed her.

Even though ten-year-old Harold and Hugh squirmed, anxious to be set free to get into their usual trouble, they were obeying Tessa and staying by her side—at least for the time being.

"We'll be good," one of the boys called, peering from beneath his scraggly brown hair that was overdue for a haircut. But Tessa didn't say anything. From the downward slant of her lips, Caroline could tell Tessa wasn't pleased with their father's admonition. At seventeen she'd made no secret that she was ready for her independence.

Her father nodded at the boys, his smile lingering over each of them. He'd already said his good-byes when they'd been gathered in Sarah's room earlier. He'd already told each of them he loved them, that he was blessed by God to have five fine children. There was no need to linger now and say the good-byes again. Not with the storm coming.

"If you must go," Caroline said, "then you'd best be on your way."

The boat was jerking up and down in the rapidly churning waves. Another flash of lightning lit up the western sky.

Her father took a backward step toward the bow, but then hesitated. "You know I have no choice in going. I have to find medicine for Sarah." Helpless anguish shadowed his face for the briefest moment, giving Caroline a glimpse of his inner turmoil at having to watch his sweet young daughter suffer day in and day out.

"I'll be praying you find something," she said, knowing he would need all the prayers they could offer. Medicine of any kind was in short supply due to the demands of the war. The closest town to their isolated lighthouse, Grosse Pointe, had run out of even the most basic medicine long ago. And her father had been forced to search the backstreets of Detroit on more than one occasion in recent months.

The war may have ended, but their battles were far from over.

"I love you, Caroline," her father said, the lump in his throat moving up and down. "Thank you for all your help. I don't know how I'd get by without you."

She shooed him with a flutter of her hands. "I'm sure you'd do just fine." Although she didn't know how he'd manage either, especially the light. When his rheumatism was bothering him—which seemed to be most days lately—he couldn't get his legs to work to climb the tower stairway. And she'd taken over lighting the lantern on all but a rare day.

He heaved himself over the edge of the boat, the strength in his arms making up for the weakness of his legs. He settled himself at the oars, his muscles bulging through the seams of his jacket.

She had to remember he was an experienced lightkeeper and sailor, that he knew the lakes better than most. If anyone could traverse Lake St. Clair in a storm, he could likely do it with his eyes closed.

Even so, the airways in her lungs constricted again.

He dug the oars into the water and pressed the boat back against the waves. "Remember what I always say," he called to her with another of his kind smiles. "God is good—"

"All the time," she said, finishing the sentence for him.

He strained against the waves, pushing the boat in small

but steady increments away from the shore. His smile was just as steady.

The waves crashed higher, sending water in a rushing cascade toward her boots and forcing her to retreat from the shoreline. She drew in a deep breath, the brisk wind bringing the scent of the wet arrow grass and cattail that grew along the lake and overpowering the aroma of the newly bloomed Indian paintbrush.

If only she didn't worry so much . . .

But in the years since her mother had died, as the oldest child she'd fallen into a motherly role with her family. As her father's joints had continued to stiffen with pain, she'd gradually shouldered his work too.

She hadn't minded. In fact, she loved taking care of the lighthouse for her father. It was one of the many duties she relished.

Yet there were times when she half agreed with her father that perhaps she'd had to bear too much too soon in her short life. At twenty, she couldn't remember a time when she'd ever had the freedom to be a child, to play, to experience life without worries—like the twins did.

With each stroke of the oars her father propelled the boat farther out on the lake, steering it toward the wide mouth of the Detroit River where hopefully he would meet calmer passage.

She cast another glance at the ominous black clouds. Even though it was only midday, the descending darkness was like that of eventide. She would need to climb the tower steps and crank up the lantern during the storm. The light would not only help her father but all the many vessels sailing across Lake St. Clair in their journey from Lake Huron to Lake Erie.

For a long moment, however, she remained motionless on the shore, her eyes fixed upon the tiny boat bouncing against the whitecaps.

She watched and waited . . .

Until finally her father lifted his hand and waved.

Warmth stole into her heart. She rose to her tiptoes and stretched her arm in a wave back to him. In spite of her worry, she smiled at their tradition, one that she'd shared with her father since she'd been a little girl just learning to walk.

With a long last wave she forced herself to spin around. The keeper's dwelling and the tower stood less than fifty feet from the shore and would have made a picturesque sight any other spring day with all of her flowers blooming around it. But with the gray chill, she was reminded once again of the harsh Michigan winter that had only recently passed.

"I'm going up to light the lantern," she called to Tessa, who'd released her grip on the twins. The boys had already darted toward the shore to watch their father until he was out of sight. "Keep an eye on the boys. I don't want them running off to play during the storm."

Tessa gave an exasperated sigh, as if keeping track of the twins was life's greatest hardship. With their energy and penchant for mischief, the boys were a handful. But Caroline knew that Tessa enjoyed taking care of them, almost as much as she herself loved overseeing the lantern.

Caroline strode across the grassy knoll. Even though the green was lush and thick from the warm, sunny days they'd had lately, the vegetation and her flower gardens could use the coming rain.

If only it would hold off until her father and the doctor made it across the lake to the river. She reached the enclosed walkway that connected the tower to the house, and a burst of wind ripped at her shawl, wrenching it from her shoulders and plastering it against the peeling white paint of the stone tower.

Behind her one of the boys shouted, rapidly followed by the other twin's cry. The urgency sent a charge through Caroline's nerves.

She spun only to find them both ankle-deep in water, staring with openmouthed horror into the distance . . . south, in the direction Father had rowed.

Her breathing ceased when she caught sight of her father's rowboat turned upside down. A scream ripped from her lips. "Father!"

She ran back across the grassy embankment toward the shore. Her feet felt wooden and heavy. Her skirt tangled in her legs, causing her to stumble. She careened forward until she stood next to the boys near the crashing waves, her heart pounding, her breath coming in wheezes.

"Father!" she screamed again.

As if responding to her frantic call, a head popped through the waves. Her father's broad shoulders appeared at the rounded hull. He was gripping the doctor's arm, clearly attempting to keep the man afloat in the churning waves.

He wrapped his free arm over the boat and clung to the keel.

"Hold on!" she cried. "Pull yourself up!"

The twins mimicked her call, yelling across the lake at the top of their voices. Tessa joined them at the water's edge and added her shouting.

Caroline knew that Father wouldn't be able to hear them, and that nothing they could say would help him. But she couldn't stop yelling instructions anyway. Every limb of her body shook like the branches of the nearby willow that draped over the lake.

A crashing wave swept against her father and the doctor and then over the boat, plunging them both completely underwater again.

"No!" She lunged into the water, heedless of her shoes and skirt. She had to save them. She had to get to them and assist them.

"You can't go out there!" Tessa called, splashing after her. She reached for Caroline's arm and jerked her to a stop. "You'll only drown yourself."

The waves splashed up to Caroline's knees, already weighing her skirt down. Her mind told her that Tessa was right, that she couldn't swim out into the lake under the current conditions, that to do so would only send her to a watery grave.

But she struggled against her sister's hold nevertheless. "I have to go to him!"

Her father's head appeared again, and he flung his arm over the boat once more, still tightly gripping the doctor with his other. She wanted to yell at him to let go of the old man, to save himself. But she couldn't. She knew he wouldn't. She knew he'd die first before he let go.

His flimsy grip slipped as the waves came up to choke him again.

Panic swelled in Caroline's stomach, and she found herself screaming again. Even from the distance, she could see that he was weakening. That he wouldn't be able to hold on to the boat with one hand. That he wouldn't be able to crawl on top of it either. And even if he did, how would he be able to stay there? Not with the waves and wind beating against him.

"Hold on!" she shouted again.

He held on by the tips of his fingers. But the weight of the doctor was dragging him down. Like most people, the doctor probably couldn't swim. And even if he could have, they were too far out and the water too furious to be able to swim back to the shore.

A gust of wind sent more high waves against the boat and the men. Her father lost his grasp again and disappeared beneath the water.

For several long, agonizing moments, she waited for him to reappear as he had the last time. She strained to see him and the boat. But when she caught sight of the hull again, he wasn't there. The underside of the boat was barren, and the water surrounding it empty, except for the doctor's tall black hat bobbing on the waves.

She stared at the spot. "Come on. Come on. Please surface!"

Next to her, Tessa had begun to pray.

The wind whipped at them. And for an interminable minute, they all stood silently holding their breaths, eyes trained on the spot they'd last seen Father.

A sudden crack of thunder caused Caroline's nerves to jump and warned her that the storm was only minutes from hitting. She had to find a way to save Father and the doctor before the storm unleashed even more fury.

"The canoe!" she said, then turned and started sloshing back toward the small boathouse and the old canoe tipped over on its side next to it. She'd take the canoe out to rescue the men. She could paddle by herself. She'd done so hundreds of times in the past.

Again Tessa dragged her to a halt. "No, Caroline!"

Caroline yanked her arm, but Tessa dug in her fingers.

"Don't you dare try to stop me!" Caroline yelled at her sister.

Tessa's beautiful eyes flashed with fury even as tears ran down her cheeks. "What makes you think you can make it if Father couldn't?"

The logic of Tessa's words sent frustration roaring through Caroline. "We can't just leave them out there to die."

Tessa pressed her lips together. But Caroline could sense her unspoken words. She ceased struggling and stared at a glistening tear that dripped from the tip of Tessa's nose, seeing in her sister's tears what she didn't want to accept . . .

It was too late. There was absolutely nothing they could do to save Father now. There never had been anything they could do. They were completely helpless.

Caroline spun and looked out over the turbulent lake. Emptiness filled her vision. Silent screams flooded her chest and expanded until the pressure reached her throat. But her airways were too tight to let the screams pass.

The wind battered her, and the first icy drops of rain sliced into her.

Even then, she stood mutely, frozen.

One of the twins slipped a small, warm hand into her stiff one.

Lightning zigzagged across the sky, opening it, unleashing a deluge of rain. It pounded Caroline's head. When it began to run in rivulets down her cheeks, she finally let her tears flow.

Chapter 2

*Y*ou have one week to vacate the premises," Mr. Finick said matter-of-factly as he penned another note in his record-keeping book.

Caroline slipped off the step stool, her heart landing on the ground along with her feet. Surely she hadn't heard the district lighthouse inspector clearly. "One week? That can't be right."

Mr. Finick paused in his slow, meticulous note-taking to pick at a loose thread on his too-tight, white-and-gray plaid trousers that coordinated with his white coat and gray silk vest. "You heard me, Miss Taylor. You have exactly one week to pack your belongings and leave the lighthouse."

The shade of the tall tower on the cool September morning

17

left Caroline chilled through her shawl, down to her bones. "That's absurd, Mr. Finick—"

His sharp gaze cut off her protest before he tipped his head back and peered up and down the tower several times. Then he bent his head again and added another note in his book. His white derby hid his perpetual frown, the frown he wore every time he came to Windmill Point for an inspection.

Caroline glanced up the height of the forty-four-foot tower. The white paint had peeled away from the stone in numerous places, revealing large gray patches. The bright sunshine of the fall morning only highlighted the dilapidated condition, particularly the low crack she was about to repair when she'd heard the approach of a horse and realized Mr. Finick was nearly upon her for one of his infamous surprise inspections.

"I meant to paint the tower over the summer," she hurried to explain, "but time got away from me."

"You know women are not allowed to paint the tower, Miss Taylor. Lighthouse regulations strictly forbid it."

She opened her mouth to object, but then quickly clamped her lips closed. She'd painted the tower in years past, and she'd never had any trouble. But she knew her experience wasn't the issue. The real trouble was that she was a woman. And women were prevented from painting the tower because they wore skirts.

Of course, she agreed that standing on a ladder in a skirt was inappropriate and immodest. But she couldn't tell Mr. Finick that she always changed into a pair of her father's trousers when she painted. Mr. Finick would likely fall over with a heart attack if she even hinted that she donned men's clothes.

Besides, she already had enough trouble pleasing Mr. Finick whenever he made one of his surprise visits. She didn't need to earn any further disapproval, especially with his news about her needing to leave the light.

"The superintendent of Detroit Lighthouses named me as acting keeper," she started.

"You are being replaced."

"But he told me I could stay."

"He did it out of sympathy." Mr. Finick's tone rose, and his perfectly groomed black mustache twitched like an irritated cat's tail. "At the time, there were no other men available to take your father's spot."

Caroline glanced out to the calm blue waters of Lake St. Clair in the direction where her father had disappeared that horrible day four months ago. Sometimes she could still picture him desperately grasping at the hull, fighting against the spray of waves, his muscles straining beyond endurance to save himself and the doctor.

But on calm sunny days like the one that stretched before her, it was difficult to understand why he'd died, not when the lake was so peaceful, calm enough that even a toddler could dog-paddle to shore.

Eventually the lighthouse boat had washed up onshore a mile down at the mouth of the Detroit River. It had been wrecked beyond repair from the ferocity of the storm.

But they'd never recovered the bodies of either her father or the doctor.

She'd resigned herself to the fact that his grave was at the bottom of the lake. That he'd gone home to heaven. Maybe now he was rowing the celestial lakes next to his beautiful wife, who'd met her end in very much the same way, by drowning when they'd lived at the lighthouse in Massachusetts. Mother had gone out to help rescue several drowning sailors and had ended up drowning with them.

"Now that all of our Union men have been discharged from duty," Mr. Finick said, "we have plenty of qualified applicants who can take over the position here as head keeper."

He snapped his notebook closed and spun away from the tower. Without waiting for Caroline's response, he strode with his quick but jerky steps toward the walkway that connected the keeper's dwelling to the tower.

Caroline scrambled to make sense of what Mr. Finick was telling her. The news was the worst she could possibly get, and she refused to believe he could be serious.

"I don't know why you'd need to replace me." She bolted after him. "I'm qualified to run this light. I've been doing it for quite some time without any problems, haven't I?"

Mr. Finick didn't stop to knock at the walkway door. He swung it open and proceeded inside as though the home belonged to him. She raced through after him and found herself almost crashing into his backside. She pulled herself up short just in time to avoid offending the man further.

He'd stopped abruptly in the middle of the passageway and was running his fingers along the edge of the desk where she kept her logbooks. He lifted his pointer finger and, at the sight of dust on his lily-white glove, scowled. "When is the last time you've cleaned the inside of this watching room?"

"I clean once a week, Mr. Finick," she said, her chest starting to tighten. "It's due for another cleaning on the morrow."

He lifted his nose and sniffed. "What's that awful smell?" He snuffled into the air like a dog on a hunt. It took him only a few seconds to trace the source of the aroma. The jar of purple loosestrife she'd picked earlier in the week from the marshy meadows of Windmill Point. The narrow reddish-purple flowers had begun to droop, shedding petals and leaves in a light coating across the wood floor.

Caroline swiped up the broom propped next to the door and whisked the mess toward the door.

"The condition of this room is deplorable," Mr. Finick said. "Absolutely deplorable."

Caroline sighed inwardly. She knew it would do no good to argue with the man. From past experience she'd learned he expected perfection. Anything less was unacceptable. He wouldn't care what she'd done right. He'd only see the wrong.

"This is exactly why you may not stay on as keeper," he continued, opening his ledger and removing the pencil. "You're too busy doing men's work to have time to keep up with the duties God has assigned you as a woman—the upkeep and maintenance of the home."

"I don't think God expects me to keep a perfect home," she said, unable to hold back her caustic retort.

He bent his head to make a note in his book. "He does require you to mind your place as a woman and stick to the work He's given you, which is being a keeper of your home, not of the light."

She'd heard his protests before. In the two years he'd been the inspector, he'd never approved of her helping her father with the lighthouse duties, had always said it was "man's work." Her father, being an honest man, had never hid from Mr. Finick the fact that he relied upon his daughter, especially when his rheumatism had made it all but impossible to climb the tower stairs that last winter and spring.

When Mr. Finick had visited after her father died, he'd wanted her to leave then too. But when the superintendent of

Detroit Lighthouses had suggested that she keep the vigil, Mr. Finick had grumbled but finally assented.

"There's no need to change your mind about me now," she said.

"I'm not changing my mind. I've never approved of your taking over the position."

"I'm more than qualified to take care of the lighthouse."

"You're qualified to get married, bear children, and manage your household." His words had a clipped finality to them that made the muscles in her arms tense.

He pivoted abruptly toward the door that would lead into the cottage. His immaculately polished black shoes tapped against the floor as he made his way out of the passageway and into the storage area and washroom of the keeper's cottage.

"Don't you want to check my logbooks?" She followed after him. "The records are in perfect order." She'd done a meticulous job recording the daily weather, the number and types of vessels that passed through, a summary of daily activities, visitors at the station, and any local happenings of note. If Mr. Finick examined the books, he'd see for himself how well she was doing as lightkeeper.

Mr. Finick paused to scrutinize the shelves that she'd recently replenished with the tomatoes, beans, and pickles she and Tessa had preserved in preparation for the coming winter. The tang of dill lingered in the air.

He traced a finger along the edge of a shelf, pulled it back, and then held it out for her inspection. "Do you see that, Miss Taylor?"

She squinted through the meager light in the back room coming from the open doors on either end. "More dust?" she guessed.

"Precisely."

"But what is a little dust when I haven't failed a single time to light the lantern these many months?"

"You know the rules, Miss Taylor." He bent his head to write another note in his ledger. "The official lighthouse guidebook for keepers states that you must keep the light and the house clean. And that includes dust."

"A little dust doesn't disqualify me from continuing my position here."

"The undeniable fact that you are a woman disqualifies you." He gave a pointed glare at her hair falling in disarray about her shoulders.

She combed back the strands of her straight dark brown hair. There wasn't an ounce of life to the strands, not even a wave. Not like Tessa's. Sometimes she thought when God had made her, He hadn't quite stamped hard enough. The imprint He'd made on her was faded, thin, and inconsequential next to Tessa's vibrant and curvy beauty.

Perhaps God had thought to give her father a firstborn son, but at the last minute had changed His mind. It was too bad He hadn't gone through with His original plan. Being a woman seemed to offer so few benefits compared to those of men.

If she'd been a man she'd have no problems getting a job so that she could provide for her siblings. Who would take care of them if not her? And how would she be able to provide for them if she lost the keeper job? Where would they live?

More important, how would she take care of Sarah and afford her increasingly expensive medicine if she lost the keeper job? Caroline's breath pinched within her chest. She had to do something. She couldn't stand back and let Mr. Finick drive her from the only source of employment she knew.

He clomped down the hallway past the two bedrooms. As he passed Sarah's room, he didn't even give the girl a cursory glance. In fact, he looked in the opposite direction, into the bedroom her father had once occupied but that Caroline was now using.

The man obviously had no pity on a poor sick girl. And was calloused to the fact that if he evicted them from the house, Sarah would become homeless.

As Mr. Finick strode into the kitchen, Caroline paused at Sarah's doorway, trying to keep the dejection from bending her shoulders.

From her mound of pillows and the colorful cushions Tessa had sewn, Sarah was like a pale trillium among a bouquet of striking cardinal flowers. Even though she had the vibrancy of Tessa's darker hair and green eyes, the rest of her body was translucent and lifeless.

The bed was positioned so that Sarah could look directly out the window into the sprawling flower garden that Caroline had planted at the back of the house. Though many of the plants had already lost their blossoms, Caroline had made sure to include some varieties that bloomed in late summer and fall just so Sarah would have a beautiful view for as long as possible.

Sarah gave Caroline a smile that rivaled the bright morning sun. "I see Mr. Finick is here," she whispered in her raspy voice.

Caroline tried to push down the worry that was drawing its noose tighter about her chest. She couldn't burden Sarah with Mr. Finick's attempt to evict her from their home. Instead, she returned Sarah's smile and tried to lighten her voice. "As usual, he's finding every speck of dust."

Sarah's smile dimmed and turned infinitely gentle, reminding

Caroline of her father and the way he used to smile at her. The ache in Caroline's heart gave an unexpected pulse.

"Don't worry, Caroline," Sarah said, her lips tinged with the usual blue. "We'll be fine, so long as we're all still together."

Caroline's shoulders slumped. Had Sarah managed to hear everything Mr. Finick had spoken? In the little one-and-a-half-story cottage, the sounds often carried to all parts of the house.

The glimmer in the girl's eyes told Caroline that she knew everything, and so much more. Sarah might only be thirteen, but she had the insight of one much older and wiser.

Silently Caroline berated herself for not being more careful with her conversation with the inspector so that Sarah wouldn't hear. Now she had no choice but to go to the man, fall on her knees before him, and beg him to let her stay. Perhaps if she started weeping and pleading and using some of Tessa's dramatic flair, Mr. Finick would have pity on her and change his mind.

She peered down the hallway into the kitchen, where he stood next to the table taking more notes.

Her entire body revolted at the thought of bowing and scraping to him. But she closed the door, hoping to protect Sarah from the words she must exchange with Mr. Finick. Then she took a deep breath and forced one foot after the other down the hallway until she entered the kitchen.

Thankfully, Tessa had walked the mile and a half with the twins to school in Grosse Pointe that morning and had planned to stay and sell some of the apple butter they'd canned over the past few days. No one but Sarah would be there to witness her utter humiliation.

The cheerfulness of the room, from the bright blue curtains in the window to the potted plants she kept on the windowsill, did nothing to assuage the swarm of bees that began to buzz in the pit of her stomach.

"Mr. Finick," she began in a loud whisper, "I sincerely ask that you reconsider your decision. This is my only job, my only means of providing for my family."

He removed a shiny gold watch from his vest pocket. Its brilliance only served to remind Caroline that she hadn't been paid for her lighthouse duties since early in the summer. The proprietor at the Grosse Pointe General Store had begun to complain to Tessa about the size of their long-overdue tab.

Mr. Finick glanced at the watch and then quickly tucked it back in his pocket. "I don't have time to listen to your whining, Miss Taylor. I suggest that instead of wasting both of our time with needless complaints, that you instead put your effort into packing your belongings and securing your future."

"But what future do I have if not working in a lighthouse?" She hated the desperation in her voice. "That's all I know how to do."

"Get married." He stepped to the window, rubbed a finger against the glass, then bent to make a note in his book. "Find a husband to take care of you. That's what most women your age do. And quite frankly, it's what you should be doing too."

She had no response to give Mr. Finick that would keep her from embarrassing herself even further. She hardly knew any single men. With so many having enlisted in the army, there had been very few unmarried men left behind. And living so far out of town at the lighthouse didn't exactly afford the opportunity to socialize with men.

Besides, even if there had been an eligible pool of men who'd wanted to come courting, the truth was she didn't have time for that kind of frivolity. She was too busy trying to take care of her family and the light.

"Surely there are other women acting as keepers at other lighthouses," she said. "Why must it be a man?"

"Men are much more capable of handling the rigors of the work. If a woman is in a lighthouse, it is strictly to act as a helpmate to her husband."

Most people would agree with Mr. Finick that women shouldn't be doing men's work. She'd never questioned it herself, had always just accepted the different roles assigned to men and women. But such a division of labor didn't seem quite fair. Not when she was as equally qualified to handle the lighthouse as any man.

Mr. Finick snapped his book closed and proceeded across the kitchen.

She swallowed her mounting frustration and chased after him. She had to do her begging now, before it was too late.

Without allowing herself to think twice, she grabbed his coat sleeve and pulled him to a halt. Then ignoring his murmurs of disapproval, she fell to her knees before him and grasped his free hand. He scowled at her hand touching his and immediately yanked it free of her grip.

"Please, Mr. Finick. I'll work harder to keep the house and tower just the way you like them. I'll take a pay cut. I'll do anything you want. Just please let me stay."

He reached inside his white coat and drew out a crisply folded handkerchief. He unfolded it one corner at a time and then proceeded to first dab his sleeve where she'd touched him and then finally to wipe the gloved hand she'd held.

She stayed on her knees before him even though everything within her heart rose up in protest of having to degrade herself simply because of her gender.

"I never liked your father," he said in a clipped tone. "He was always causing too many problems with the locals."

The only problem her father had experienced with "the locals" was with Mr. Simmons and his illegal smuggling. Father had confronted the man, had even threatened to get the law involved to stop him. But since she'd taken over the light, she'd turned a blind eye to Mr. Simmons's illegal activities. Though there were times when she felt guilty about it and knew her father would have done more, she used the excuse that she just didn't have the energy or time to fight that battle right now.

"I'm not having any trouble," she stated. "Ask anyone. They'll tell you I'm doing a good job."

"It's too late, Miss Taylor." Mr. Finick's sharp footsteps echoed against the whitewashed walls as he started toward the sitting room. "Even if I wanted to consider your request—which I don't—I've already found your replacement. And he'll be here at the end of the week."

"My replacement?"

"Yes. A war veteran. The Lighthouse Board is providing some keeper positions to veterans in gratefulness for their fighting during the war of rebellion."

"But will he know anything about how to operate a lighthouse?"

"He knows enough." With that, Mr. Finick stepped into the sitting room.

"But I know everything!" she called after him. "I'm much more qualified and experienced than a war veteran."

"You have until the end of the week, Miss Taylor," he replied, his voice ringing with finality. "That's all I'm going to say on the matter."

Caroline sat back on her heels, the urge to fight oozing out of her. Her body sagged into a puddle on the kitchen floor, and she dropped her face into her hands.

Helplessness crashed over her, just like that stormy day four months ago when she'd stood on the shore and had to watch her father drown without being able to do a thing to save him.

By the end of the week she'd be jobless and homeless. And there wasn't a single person left in the world who would care.

Chapter 3

Ryan Chambers cradled his head in his palm. The pounding in his temples was as deafening as cannon blasts, growing steadily louder since he'd entered the Roadside Inn a short while ago.

"Would you like another shot of rum?" A giant of a man behind the bar held up a dark flask and sloshed it. The man's bald head glistened too brightly even in the shadowed interior of the tavern. His arms bulged. And his broad girth appeared to be solid muscle. For such an imposing man, his voice was surprisingly cultured and soft-spoken.

Ryan peered through glazed eyes at the empty beer glass before him. Even though he was tempted to nod and ask for another, he pushed back from the bar before he gave in to the all-too-easy temptation.

For one thing, his pockets were nearly empty. And for another, he needed to make it to a bed before he passed out.

He slid off the stool, dug in his pocket, and retrieved a few coins. He slapped them on the bar with his good hand, nodded his thanks to the proprietor, and turned to leave.

31

He swayed and grabbed a nearby table to keep from falling. The stickiness of spilled beer met his grip—the grip of the two fingers that remained. Unbearable pain shot up his arm into his shoulder and then his head. Quickly he shoved the mangled hand back into his pocket where he kept it. He bit back a cry of anguish and silently berated himself for using his injured hand.

"So you're returning from the war?" The giant paused in wiping down the bar's polished walnut, staring at the pocket where Ryan had stuffed his hand.

Ryan wanted to tell the big man to mind his own business. But if he was going to be living in the area, he couldn't afford to make an enemy of this man.

"Aye," he said, forcing out the word. "I was discharged at the end of July."

The only other customers in the tavern, two old men at a corner table, lifted their heads from the newspaper they'd been sharing. And the young man who'd been sweeping the floor paused in his work to stare openmouthed, his nose running and his big ears red.

Ryan's mouth went dry, and his throat parched just like when he'd been sprawled in a bloody field, breathing in the dust and smoke of the battle raging around him. He needed another drink to quench his thirst.

"What unit you from, son?" one of the old men asked.

Except for the ticking of a clock on the mantel behind the bar, the room grew silent.

Bile swirled in Ryan's gut. He should be used to the questions by now. He'd faced them enough over the past month and a half since he'd arrived back in Michigan. Everywhere he'd gone, everyone he met had peppered him with unwanted questions about the war.

He knew most were waiting on news of loved ones. They wanted some word on their son, grandson, brother, or cousin who hadn't yet returned. They wanted to discover what had happened and cling to the hope that somehow the loved one had survived against the odds.

But the sorry truth was that most of the Billy Yanks weren't coming back, especially from his company. And the more time that elapsed, the less hope there was for the waiting families.

He couldn't blame the old men for asking him. He might be their only link to a lost son or grandson.

"You ever heard of Jeb Williams?" the other man asked, his aging eyes crinkled at the edges with worry. "He was in the infantry, Eleventh Regiment."

Ryan shook his head. "Nay. I was in the Twenty-Fourth, I Company."

"Ah, the Iron Brigade," said the other, his face lighting up with wide-eyed admiration. "We're mighty proud of you boys. Heard about your bravery and hard fighting."

The bile in Ryan's stomach roiled faster. If the man only knew some of the things his company had done in the name of war and survival, he wouldn't be so proud then.

The stuffy interior of the tavern began to close in on Ryan. The sickly sweet scent of beer and tobacco that was ingrained into every fiber of the room swirled around him. Ryan took several steps toward the door, but then staggered to a stop.

He had no idea where he was going. Wasn't that why he'd stopped at the Roadside Inn in the first place? To ask for directions?

His head pounded again, and his eyes ached with the need to close in slumber.

"I'm looking for Windmill Point Lighthouse," he said to no

33

one in particular. "I'd be obliged if you could tell me how to get there."

"What business do you have at the light?" The big man behind the bar frowned, his voice turning steely.

"I'm the new keeper. Ryan Chambers."

For a long moment, the giant glared at him, taking in his civilian apparel—his new trousers in sore need of laundering, his wrinkled shirt, and his coat, likely stained from liquor or vomit or both. He wore a leather satchel over one shoulder that strapped across his chest. And even though he had avoided looking into the big mirror on the wall behind the bar, Ryan could guess just how badly he needed a shave, haircut, and washing.

He'd burned the tattered rags that remained of his army uniform the day he'd mustered out. He'd never wanted to see the uniform again. At the time he hadn't counted on only being able to afford one new outfit. But he hadn't been able to hold down a job for more than a couple of days. And now it showed.

He half expected the giant to barrel around the bar, pick him up by his coat, and toss him out the door.

But surprisingly the man's scowl disappeared and was replaced instead by a slow grin. "So you're the new keeper." His voice was smooth once more, all traces of anger gone.

"Aye."

"Looks to me like you're just the sort of man we need taking care of the light."

Ryan arched his brow. Was this man half blind?

"Mr. Finick passed through here earlier today and said you wouldn't be here until the week's end."

Finick. Was that the uptight man who'd hired him down in Detroit yesterday? Ryan couldn't think past the haze that floated through his mind. All he could remember about the interview was that after too many questions a finely dressed man with a long black mustache had told him he could have the keeper position at Windmill Point.

Ryan had been both relieved and surprised. He didn't have any experience as a keeper. But his sister was an assistant keeper, and she'd taught him a thing or two during his visits to Presque Isle over the past years. It hadn't been much. But apparently it had been enough to get the job.

"I'm here now," Ryan said, hoping the keeper's dwelling had a bed. He hadn't slept in one since August of 1862, over three years ago. "If you'll point me in the right direction, I'll be on my way."

"I'm Stephen Simmons." The giant finally sidled around the bar, wiping his hands on a clean apron tied around his waist. He held a hand out to Ryan.

But it was the wrong hand. Ryan would have to take his injured hand out to complete the introduction. And taking it out once was enough. He held out his other hand instead.

A flicker of something passed through Mr. Simmons's eyes. But it was gone before Ryan could name it. Instead the man shifted hands and clasped Ryan's in a gentle, almost womanly grasp. His skin was soft and free of the usual calluses of a workingman.

"Welcome to Grosse Pointe," Mr. Simmons said with another grin. "Mr. Finick said you'd be the sort of man we'd be able to work with. And I do believe he was correct."

"I hope so," Ryan replied, not quite certain what kind of work he'd need to do with Mr. Simmons. He'd applied for the lighthouse job because he hadn't wanted to be bothered, had wanted to be left alone in the isolation that light keeping usually afforded.

There was something about Mr. Simmons's grin that seemed slightly off-kilter. But Ryan couldn't be sure since the room seemed to tilt every now and then too.

"The old keeper sure gave me a hassle," Mr. Simmons said. "I haven't had too many problems since he's been gone and his daughter took over. But the fact is, she's as uncooperative as her father, and it's well past time to get someone new at the light."

Mr. Simmons gave the young man holding the broom a sly smile. "My son Arnie there has been ogling that girl forever. I told him now's his chance to propose marriage to her when she's desperate and won't be able to turn him down."

Arnie rapidly bent his head and began to sweep again, his ears turning a brighter red than before. He swiped his sleeve across his dripping nose without breaking stride in his sweeping. With his smooth boyish face and slight of height, Arnie looked too young to be thinking of courting. If not for the receding hairline, Ryan wouldn't have believed him old enough.

"All the same, we're glad you're here," Mr. Simmons said, returning to the bar and picking up a small bottle of fine-looking whiskey. He held it out to Ryan. "Here's a home-warming gift."

Ryan reached for it, trying not to appear too eager.

As he grasped it, Mr. Simmons didn't relinquish the bottle but held tightly to one end. "I'm kind to my friends. Especially to helpful friends." The giant's eyes hardened and held Ryan's.

For a moment, Ryan struggled through the haze in his mind to make sense of the message the man was obviously trying to send him. "I'm a helpful guy," Ryan offered, and hoped it was the right response.

"That's good to hear." Mr. Simmons's smile widened and he let go of the whiskey.

Ryan flipped open his satchel and stashed the bottle inside

next to his supply of pills. He backed toward the door as he closed and latched the leather case.

Mr. Simmons followed him across the room. "Do you like prizefighting, Chambers?"

"Depends." Ryan made his way outside, staggering against the brilliant sunlight that was a shocking change from the dimly lit interior of the tavern. Pain rose at the backs of his eyes. And he could only hope that the ride out to the lighthouse was a short one.

"I run the best cockfighting in the entire Detroit area," Mr. Simmons said.

Ryan strained to untie his horse's lead rope from the post in front of the inn. But it was difficult to do with one hand, especially when someone was watching him. He shifted his body to shield his cumbersome efforts.

"I've got some of the best conditioned and trained game-cocks this side of the Mississippi," Mr. Simmons continued. "Of course, I usually have to bring them in by way of the Canadian border on Lake St. Clair." He then paused as if waiting for a response.

Ryan shrugged. "I don't have any money to bet." And even if he'd had the spare change, he wasn't a betting man. He wasn't too keen on watching animals fight to the death either. But he didn't suppose that was what Mr. Simmons wanted to hear at that moment.

"Don't you worry about money," Mr. Simmons said. He clamped Ryan's shoulder and squeezed. Fortunately it was his uninjured arm or Ryan might have spun and punched him. "Like I said, I take good care of my friends."

"Then I'll be sure to nurture our friendship."

Mr. Simmons laughed, let go of him, and started back to the open tavern door. "I think I'm going to like you, Chambers."

Ryan fumbled with the rope, drawing the knot tighter with his ineptness. The sun beat against his black hat and made his head itch as sweat beads formed across his forehead. All he wanted to do was find a place where he could be alone, take one of his pills, and escape into oblivion.

After several minutes, he was finally on his way east on Big Marsh Road. Mr. Simmons said it was less than a mile from the tavern out to the lighthouse, through bogs and marsh. He claimed the road was hardly passable at certain times of the year, but was apparently dry enough in autumn.

The wind blew mournfully through the few willows and poplars that stood in clusters around the prairie-like marsh. It whispered through withered reed stalks and rusty sea grass that grew in abundance around stale sloughs.

As tired as Ryan was, and as much as the jarring of the horse pained his arm and shoulder, he couldn't neglect appreciating the quiet beauty of the area. The coarse marsh grass muted the clomping of the horse so that he could hear the buzzing of dragonflies and the humming of cicadas. The gentle sounds, combined with the heat of the afternoon sun, made him drowsy, and he half slept the last quarter mile.

When the horse pulled up short, Ryan jerked straight in the saddle, and his eyes flew open to the sight of a conical tower rising above a few lone poplars. The lighthouse wasn't very tall. And it seemed to be in some disrepair. But at least it was connected to the brick dwelling. The passageway would make his life easier during storms and the colder days of autumn that would soon arrive in Michigan.

He slid from his horse and led her to a spot of shade underneath one of the trees. As he worked to remove her saddle and bridle, he took in the landscape, the tower and house rather quaint against the backdrop of the endless blue of Lake St. Clair.

The shore beyond the lighthouse was a leveled mixture of sand, pebbles, and stones that led to a grassy embankment. And flowers. There were flowers of every kind. And what appeared to be the remains of a vegetable garden.

For a fraction of an instant he allowed himself to feel hope. Hope that he might actually find peace here, that he might be able to hold down a job, that he might start earning the money he desperately needed in order to repay the debt he owed.

He couldn't mess things up this time. He had to prove that he could do the work. And then maybe finally his demons would stop chasing him.

He pulled his hand from his pocket and forced himself to look at the red, mangled skin that had finally grown back over the spot where he'd lost half his hand that awful day in July of '63 at Gettysburg. A shudder ripped through his body, and the movement nearly sent him to his knees with pain. He'd long since guessed he still had a piece of shrapnel embedded in his arm somewhere that caused him these bouts of pain. The surgeon had claimed he'd gotten it all out, but Ryan had seen how overworked and sleep-deprived most of the doctors had been. He'd seen the extent of his injuries and knew that even a well-rested doctor would have had trouble fixing him.

And now that his flesh had closed around the shrapnel wounds, he tried to get by the way he had during the last months of the war, by dulling the pain.

He patted his leather satchel, exhausted beyond endurance. For a moment he almost considered dropping into the shade with his horse. But the stillness of the house beckoned him. Along with the fact that it had been so long since he'd found comfort in a real bed.

Finding the front door unlocked, he stumbled inside. For a moment he was taken aback by the cozy furnishings, the pastel painting on the wall, the colorful knitted afghan draped across the rocker, the brightly woven rug in front of a couch.

If he didn't know better, he'd almost believe someone still lived here. But the man who'd hired him had assured him the occupants would be gone when he arrived. Besides, didn't most keepers' dwellings come furnished?

He pulled off his boots and discarded them by the door before plodding silently across the room and tossing his cap onto the couch. He dug through his satchel for one of his treasured pain pills and popped it into his mouth. Not only would it dull the pain in his hand and arm, but it would help him sleep without the nightmares that had become all too common since that fateful night when he'd sold his soul for food.

With a weary sigh he shrugged out of his suspenders, untucked his shirt, and slipped his good arm out of the sleeve before carefully sliding it off his injured arm. He dropped it in the hallway and at the same time let his trousers fall down and pool at his feet. He kicked them aside and jerked off first one dirty sock, then the other.

Finally down to his muslin undershirt and drawers, he glanced at the two doorways on either side of the hallway. One was closed, but the other was open a crack, revealing a bedroom. Though the room was darkened from thick curtains, he could see the outline of a double bed.

Every muscle in his body ached for the comfort the bed would afford. Without another thought, he pushed open the door, trudged to the bed, lowered himself carefully to the edge, and then sank into the mattress with a low moan of contentment.

His mind blurred, blocking out everything and everyone just

the way he liked. He shifted only slightly and threw his arm across a mound of soft pillows next to him.

To his surprise, the mound moved. In fact, it rose like an apparition.

There was a gasp. Then a long, terrified scream, followed by a hard thump against his face and head, almost as if the pillow next to him had decided to have a pillow fight.

Or kill him.

Chapter 4

Terror pummeled through Caroline. All she could think to do to defend herself was thwack her attacker with her pillow over and over as hard as she could.

When finally the person lay motionless, Caroline scrambled off the opposite side of the bed, her breath coming in gasps. She held the pillow above her head ready to defend herself again if necessary, although she knew she ought to open the bottom dresser drawer and locate her father's pistol instead. But fear rose in her chest and paralyzed her, so that she could only stand and stare at the bed.

Through the darkened room she made out the lanky form of a man. Her muscles twitched with the desire to bring the pillow back down on him, but when he didn't move she hesitated. For a long moment she held her breath.

"Caroline?" came Sarah's faint call from her bedroom across the hallway. "Is everything all right?"

"Everything's fine," she called back. At least everything would be fine in just a few moments when she'd driven the intruder from her home.

At the sound of her voice, the intruder sat up so fast that Caroline jumped at the bed again and brought her pillow down against the man's head.

"What in the name of all that's holy?" came a muffled voice.

"Get out of my house," she demanded in a low voice.

The man bolted out of the bed and in the process tangled himself in the covers, tripped off the side, and tumbled to the floor. He groaned, not making a move to rise.

Holding her pillow above her head in readiness, Caroline inched toward the curtain. When she reached the window, she yanked open the thick coverings she'd made for her father long ago so that he could sleep during the days in some semblance of darkness.

Sunlight cascaded into the room at an angle that told her it was midafternoon and that she hadn't slept nearly long enough, especially since she'd had such a difficult time clearing her mind of her worries when she'd first lain down after Mr. Finick had ridden off.

The brightness fell across the bed and onto the bent head of the man in her bedroom. His sandy-blond hair was tousled and bore the ring of his hat. He gave another moan before pushing himself up slowly, as if each slight movement cost him dearly.

When he finally stood, Caroline gripped her pillow tighter and lifted it higher, ready to whack him again if he took even the tiniest step toward her. "Get out now," she said again, this time louder.

The man lifted his head, and brown eyes peered out from behind strands of overlong hair that dipped over his eyebrows. Surprise radiated from a handsome face shadowed in a layer of dusty whiskers. He was staring back at her, speechless, and there was something sad, almost haunted in the depths of his

44

eyes. There was also a vulnerability in his expression that told her he was no criminal intent on hurting her. He seemed almost as bewildered by her presence in the room as she was by his.

"What are you doing here?" she asked, still holding up her pillow in defense.

He gave his head a slight shake to shift the hair out of his eyes. "I could ask the same of you."

"I live here. And this is my bedroom."

Confusion flickered through his eyes. "This is Windmill Point Lighthouse, isn't it?"

She nodded. "Of course it is."

"Then I live here."

"No, you don't," she stated adamantly. "I've lived here for the past seven years with my family—" She stopped. Understanding began to thread its way through her mind. "I suppose you're the veteran Mr. Finick hired?" she asked, studying his face. The strong lines along his jaw and around his mouth hinted at an aging beyond his years. The war had done that, had caused them all to grow up too soon.

"Aye. I'm Ryan Chambers. Who are you?"

"I'm Caroline Taylor. The keeper of this light." She knew her answer was a tad boastful and not completely true. The superintendent of Detroit Lighthouses had only named her as *acting* keeper. Nevertheless, she couldn't resist making sure this man knew she was experienced enough to run the light by herself.

Without responding, he glanced around the room, first to the mussed bed, then to the partly open dresser drawers, and finally to the heap of clothes on the bedside chair. Her clothes.

His attention shifted back to her, to her body clad only in a nightdress. With her arms still above her head holding the pillow, and the sunlight seeping through the flimsy linen, she could only imagine the view she afforded him.

Heat rushed through her, and she rapidly lowered her arms and shielded the front of her body with the pillow. At the same time she took in his grayish-colored underclothes and the loose linen of his knee-length drawers, the top button undone, revealing a spot of his muscled stomach. His undershirt was loose too, testifying to the days and weeks of hunger he'd faced or the ravages of disease that had left him a shell of the man he'd likely once been.

At her stare at his own unclad body, he flushed, averted his eyes, and fumbled at the bedcover. Using only one hand, he tore the top quilt off the bed and tossed it to her. "Please forgive me. I didn't realize . . . I didn't mean to invade your privacy."

She wrapped the quilt around herself, shrouding her nightgown and protecting her modesty. Meanwhile, he retreated from the room into the hallway. He bent over and picked up a discarded pair of trousers and made quick work of jerking them on over his drawers, still only using one hand, which made the movements awkward and slow.

"I had no idea you were in the bed." His voice was tight with pain or embarrassment—she couldn't tell. "Who sleeps in the middle of the day anyway?"

"I could ask the same of you."

He ducked his head and reached for a shirt. And that was when she saw his hand, the hand he'd been trying to hide. It was mangled, three fingers were missing, and his wrist and lower arm were laced with white scars that stood out against his sun-bronzed skin.

When he saw where her attention was directed, he wrapped

his shirt around the wound, grabbed a pair of dirt-streaked socks from off the floor, and stumbled down the hallway away from her.

"Caroline?" Sarah called again from the other bedroom.

"Everything's fine," Caroline assured. Actually *nothing* was fine, but she couldn't worry Sarah. Instead she followed Ryan into the kitchen.

He stopped at the table, swayed, then grabbed onto a chair to steady himself.

She wanted to ask how he'd been injured, but she guessed he'd already gotten enough questions from everyone else he met and didn't need any more from her.

His back stiffened, and he seemed to be waiting for her barrage of questions about the war. She stood silently, forcing herself not to look at his injured hand wrapped in his shirt.

His knuckles were white where he gripped the chair. After a few minutes, he glanced at her sideways. She met his gaze head on. She wouldn't let this awkward situation intimidate her.

He cleared his throat. "I should have knocked. Or at the very least I should have made sure the bed was empty."

"That would have been helpful."

He straightened and turned to face her. In the bright light streaming in the kitchen window, she could see even more clearly that he'd been a handsome man at one time, that with a haircut, shave, and the addition of several pounds, he'd be a striking man again.

"I hope you'll forgive me," he said, his eyes pleading with her.

"Of course." Maybe she could forgive him for crawling into her bed with her, but she wasn't sure she'd be able to forgive him for barging into her life and taking away her job.

"You sure do pack a punch with your pillow." He glanced

at the pillow she was still holding. "I hope you're not planning to hit me again."

Exactly how many times had she whacked him? Embarrassment seeped through her. She started to lower the pillow to her side, but a teasing glimmer in his eyes stopped her.

"I suppose I should be grateful you didn't reach for a shoe," he added with a half smile.

From the sadness swimming in the deep brown of his eyes, she had the feeling he hadn't had much to smile about lately. She offered a tentative smile in return. "I've been known to pack a good punch with an oar."

"An oar?" His grin inched higher on one side.

"Once, my father startled me when I was in the boathouse putting away supplies." Her smile widened at the memory. "I should have put the oar down before turning."

"Ouch."

"Yes, I knocked him flat on his back."

"I'll have to remember to stay away from you when you're handling an oar."

Her smile faded. He wouldn't have to remember to stay away from her. He wouldn't have to remember anything about her. Not when she was being forced to leave.

As if sensing her thoughts, he glanced away, first to the wood-burning stove in one corner, then to the tall cupboard along the wall, and finally settling back on the long oval table with its mismatching of wooden chairs.

"Where's your father now?" he asked, shifting awkwardly.

"At the bottom of Lake St. Clair." She said the words flatly without emotion.

His eyes jerked up, the haze in them disappearing for a moment and filling with genuine remorse.

She waited for him to give her the usual platitudes that members of the community had given her, the trite "I'm sorry" that did nothing to ease the ache in her heart.

But instead of words, his expression filled with tenderness and understanding that reached across the room and enveloped her. It was the empathy of someone who had lost a loved one too, the kind of look that said he knew her pain, had felt it himself, and that she wasn't alone.

It was too tender, and she had to look away to the tin washtub and the stiffly dried towels hanging over the edge to hide a sudden surge of tears—tears she'd thought were long gone.

How dare this stranger come into her home and be so entirely likable and sweet?

She didn't want to like him. In fact, she wanted to be angry at him for being the one to take her job and home away. But she couldn't muster any anger, not even slight irritation. It wasn't his fault that she was losing everything. It wasn't his fault that she was being forced from her home—simply because she was a woman and not a man.

"I wasn't expecting you to arrive today," she finally said, hugging the quilt around her shoulders and pinching it closed up to her chin.

"Aye, that's clear enough."

"Mr. Finick said you'd be here by the end of the week."

"I take full responsibility for any mix-up." He leaned heavily against the table. "I have no doubt I misunderstood his instructions. I'm not always thinking clearly these days."

"Then you'll allow me to stay here at the light a few more days so that I can pack?" She held her breath, praying he would be agreeable.

"I have no problem with that." Weariness had settled on his

face like a haggard mask. He glanced with longing down the hallway toward the bedroom.

If he insisted on staying in the house, she'd have to move out right away. It wouldn't be appropriate for her to be under the same roof with an unmarried man—if he was unmarried.

"I suppose you'll be wanting to move your family in?" she asked, pushing for some clue to his situation.

He gave a short laugh. "It's just me. Thank goodness."

Her mind whirled as it had since Mr. Finick had made his visit earlier that day. What would she do with Sarah? She and Tessa and the boys could make do for a few days, but she couldn't move out Sarah until she located a place to stay. "I could pitch a tent outside or stay in the boathouse."

At her suggestion, his brows rose.

Her heart quavered, and she rushed to finish before he told her no. "I don't mind for myself, not in the least. But my sister . . ." She nodded toward Sarah's bedroom. "If you'd let her stay inside until we leave . . ."

He regarded her with wide eyes for a long moment, confusion playing across his features. The haziness in the brown reminded her of Sarah's eyes when she was under the full effect of her pain-killer medicine, which she didn't have often enough lately.

The sourness of alcohol wafting around him told her that he was likely under the influence of more than just pain-killers.

"Please let Sarah stay in her room," she whispered.

Before Ryan could say anything, the front door of the dwelling banged open, and the patter of footsteps echoed on the hardwood floor of the other room.

"We're home!" called one of the twins.

"I'm hungry," called another.

"Take off your muddy shoes first" came Tessa's voice, scolding her brothers.

Ryan spun and stared through the doorway that led into the living room. His brows disappeared altogether under his shaggy hair.

We're home. Home. Home. Her brother's innocent greeting jarred Caroline all the way to her bones. All she could think was that her brother wasn't home. This was no longer home.

And somehow she was going to have to break the news to them that they were now homeless.

Chapter 5

*R*yan stared at the boys, certain his medication was causing him to see double. He blinked hard. Then blinked again. But two identical brown heads and two identical pairs of blue eyes stared back at him. Their hair was sun-streaked, their faces bronzed, and their noses sprinkled with too many freckles to count, the obvious sign of boys who spent a great deal of time outdoors.

At the sight of him standing in the kitchen doorway, their ready smiles dimmed, replaced by curiosity.

For a long staggering moment, Ryan's vision clouded with another boyish face, with wide innocent eyes, filled with curiosity . . . at first. But then the face had grown angrier and more incensed as the soldiers ransacked his home. Ryan had wanted to shout out a warning to the boy. At the very least he should have stopped his comrades. But like a coward he'd stood back and done nothing.

Ryan shook his head and focused again on the twins. But the boyish face flashed before him again, only this time it was pale with lifeless eyes staring at nothing.

With a gasp, Ryan took a step back into the kitchen, his forehead breaking out into a sweat, his head pounding with enough ferocity to weaken his knees. He needed the bed. He needed to escape the torturous memories that wouldn't let him go.

He looked around the kitchen frantically. Where had he discarded his leather satchel? His throat burned for a sip of whiskey from the flask the tavern owner had given him.

Caroline had moved past him into the sitting room with the children. He prayed she would take them away, get them out of his sight.

"Caroline," their childish voices chorused, "who is he? Why is he here?"

Ryan leaned against the wall near the door, the coolness of the plaster seeping through his undershirt and reminding him he was only half dressed. How must that look to the new arrivals? To find both he and Caroline undressed?

"His name is Mr. Chambers," Caroline replied. "And he's here . . . he's come to . . ."

There was desperation in her tone. She apparently hadn't expected him to arrive today. She wasn't ready to move out. She hadn't even begun to pack, which would account for the homey feel of the cottage.

"Exactly why is there a strange man in the house?" asked the young woman who had arrived with the twins.

"Mr. Finick visited this morning," Caroline started again, "and he brought some bad news."

Ryan tensed, and he lifted his head. So she'd only just received the news about having to leave the lighthouse earlier that day? No wonder she'd been surprised to see him.

"He's found a new keeper," she added. "Mr. Chambers."

Her voice was drowned by a chorus of "That's not fair" from the boys and "It's about time" from the young woman.

"I did my best to convince Mr. Finick to let me stay," Caroline said louder above their voices, "but he wouldn't listen to me. He thinks the lightkeeper needs to be a man."

"No one should be a lightkeeper," said the young woman, "except for crazy people who don't care about whether they live or die."

"Tessa!" Caroline's voice was sharp and commanding. It brought the sitting room to silence and told him exactly who was in charge. If her father had died, he guessed the other children were her siblings and that she was the oldest and responsible for their care.

For a long moment no one said anything. Only the distant yodeling cry of a pair of loons echoed through the open kitchen window.

"I thought we had until the end of the week to move out," Caroline finally said, breaking the silence. "But as you can see, the new keeper arrived today."

"Where will we go?" asked one of the boys.

"What will we do?" asked the other.

"Why don't we move to Detroit?" Tessa said. "Surely you can find normal work there."

The questions came in rapid fire. They shot through Ryan's muddled brain and his heart, opening old wounds.

He stared at the center of the kitchen table, at a jar filled with fresh-cut flowers. His eyes moved to the aprons hung neatly on a peg in the wall, then to a corner shelf unit lined with an assortment of blue dishes.

This was their home.

"I don't know where we'll go yet." Caroline's voice rose

again above the clamoring. "But Mr. Chambers has agreed to let us stay here for a few more days so that I can pack and find a new place for us to live."

The questions the others had raised ricocheted around Ryan's mind. Where would she go? And what work would she find to support her siblings?

"We'll camp outside for a few days," Caroline continued with forced cheerfulness. "I know how much you boys like sleeping in a tent. So you can help me fashion a tent in the yard. And Tessa and I will sleep in the boathouse."

The twins' response was enthusiastic, while Tessa gave a cry of protest. "Surely you're jesting. I'm not sleeping in the boathouse."

"Be grateful he's allowing us to stay a few extra days."

"I *am* grateful. To be going," Tessa retorted indignantly. "But I won't stand for being thrown out like trash."

"That's enough, Tessa—"

"And what about Sarah? You're not proposing to make her sleep in the boathouse too, are you?" Tessa's pitch rose with each word she spoke. "It would kill her."

There was a pause. Ryan peered down the hallway to the closed door. Who was Sarah? And what was wrong with her?

"I'll do my best to persuade Mr. Chambers to let Sarah stay in her room."

Ryan pushed away from the wall, a low growl welling up in his chest and spilling out. He'd listened to enough, and he couldn't take any more.

"She can stay," he said, ducking through the doorway into the sitting room.

The four grew silent and turned hard eyes upon him. Accusing, angry eyes. For a moment the face of that other boy flashed before him with the same accusing and angry eyes. Quickly, Ryan shoved the memory aside. He had to focus on what was happening here and now and not let his pain and problems distract him.

"Sarah can stay," he repeated, though he had no idea who Sarah was. "In fact, you can all stay." Maybe the war had turned him into a monster, but he wasn't the kind of man who would kick a family out of their home—not without them having somewhere to go.

Caroline stared at him with wide eyes, which were an interesting shade of light blue, the color of the summer sky in the full heat of day with the smoke from campfires casting a haze. They didn't contain anger, only resignation and worry.

He hadn't paid attention to her features in the bedroom, but here in the brightly lit sitting room that overlooked the lake, he had a clear view of the heart shape of her face and the sleekness of her cheeks that only highlighted her pretty lips. Her straight hair was a warm honey brown. It fell in tousled disarray across her shoulders and dangled halfway down her back.

The quilt had slipped from one of her shoulders, revealing a slender neck and the dip of her thin nightgown. Although he hadn't meant to look in the bedroom earlier, he'd seen enough before he'd averted his eyes to know she was slender yet womanly in all the right places.

Embarrassed, he shifted his attention to his bare toes. It had obviously been too long since he'd been around a pretty woman.

As if sensing the direction of his thoughts, she tugged the quilt back up and tightened her grip. "I don't understand. You're letting us stay?"

"I'll sleep in the boathouse," he said.

"You will?"

He nodded. "I'm used to sleeping wherever I can find a dry place. Been doing it for the past few years. So several more nights bedding on the ground won't bother me."

She released a long breath. "Thank you."

He met her gaze then. And the gratefulness in the clear blue of her eyes made him want to do more for her.

"Stay the whole week," he offered.

The twins regarded him with suspicion, and Tessa eyed him with open curiosity.

Caroline cocked her head, and her hair slid forward over the side of her face. She peered at him through the loose strands as if trying to assess his true motives.

"If Mr. Finick said you have until the end of the week," he said, "then I can wait to move in until then."

"We won't need a week since we're anxious to go," Tessa said.

"We're not anxious to go." Caroline shot Tessa a look of warning. The younger girl ignored it and instead bent to pick up a haversack she'd discarded near the door. "We'll be thankful for every day that we have here."

Ryan stepped aside as Tessa brushed past him into the kitchen, leaving him alone with Caroline and the two boys, who were still staring at him.

If he didn't escape them, he had the feeling they would bombard him with unwanted questions, especially if they caught sight of his injured hand.

"Can we talk somewhere privately?" he asked Caroline. "Maybe outside?"

She nodded and then said to the twins, "Go wash up and Tessa will give you a snack."

They gave Ryan one last disparaging glance before obeying their sister and padding across the room into the kitchen.

Ryan headed out the front door, down the stone steps, and onto the thick grass that spread out in front of the dwelling. It felt cool and soft beneath his bare feet, with the breeze coming off the lake equally soothing.

Surprisingly, the weight of his earlier exhaustion had lifted. He was still tired, the alcohol and the pain-killers both made him sleepy, yet for the first time in a long while his mind was clear and the perpetual need to sleep gone.

The door banged closed behind him, and then Caroline joined him in the yard. She peered across the lake to a distant steamer passing to the south, likely on its way to Detroit laden with the harvest of northern farms. The sharpness in her eyes told him she was experienced with seafaring vessels and their navigation—probably much more than he was.

"Listen," he began, not exactly sure what he wanted to say but knowing he had to say something. "I didn't know all this would happen when I rode up here today."

She shrugged and turned her attention to the swarms of black and orange fluttering along the shoreline. "The monarchs are here." For a few seconds a smile transformed her face and chased away the lines of concern.

He was tempted to simply watch the delight playing across her face, but when she peeked at him sideways, he rapidly shifted his sights to the hordes of butterflies along the shore to the north.

"They usually stop here at Lake St. Clair each year while migrating to Mexico for the winter." She spoke softly, almost reverently. "Sometimes we see large groups of hummingbirds migrating too."

Against the backdrop of the blue lake, the monarchs were a majestic display of color, along with the fading russet grass and yellowing poplars.

It was all so beautiful. He drew in a breath and then released the tension that had found a permanent home in his shoulders. After weeks of restlessness he could finally find peace here, couldn't he?

Next to him, Caroline shifted, her toes poking out from the tattered edges of the quilt.

The fleeting peace evaporated, and guilt tightened his muscles again. Apparently his peace was to come at this woman's expense. "After you leave here, where will you go?"

Her eyes clouded, covering all traces of delight. She glanced over her shoulder at the door before responding. "I haven't had the time to locate a place to stay."

"Do you have family you can live with?"

"I might have an uncle or aunt back east," she said quietly. "But even if I could travel that far with Sarah—which I can't—I wouldn't want to burden them with her care."

"Sarah?" Though he'd heard her name several times now, he'd yet to make sense of who she was.

"My youngest sister," Caroline explained, worry lines creasing her forehead. "The doctors don't really know what's wrong with her, except that she has some kind of muscular disease where she just keeps getting weaker."

"I've heard of the disease," he said. And from what he'd heard, the prognosis wasn't good. The muscular degeneration only continued until the lungs were too weak for breathing or the heart too flimsy for beating.

"Sarah can't get out of bed anymore," Caroline said with a sadness in her voice that tugged at him. "Unless we carry her . . ."

"How long has she had the disease?"

"It started coming on a couple of years ago, about the same

time my father's rheumatism worsened." She stared at a distant spot far away in the lake. Was that where her father was buried?

He swallowed the question. She likely resented the prying about her heartaches as much as he did. From what he'd been able to piece together, she'd lost her father not too long ago, she was losing her sister, and now she was losing her job and home.

Was it possible someone else was in as much or more pain than he?

During the past months, since he'd mustered out of the army, he'd only thought of himself, his nightmares, and the debt he owed. But now, standing next to this pretty young woman at the edge of the lake, with the lighthouse towering behind them, he couldn't keep from thinking about her plight and wishing he could help her come up with a solution.

He wanted to tell her to stay here. That she didn't need to move her family out of their home for him. That he would go back to Detroit and find another job. That she could keep hers.

But he couldn't squeeze the words past the burden weighing upon his chest.

He needed the job too desperately. He'd failed at everything else he'd done so far. With the condition of his hand and the recurring pain in his arm, he hadn't lasted but a couple of days out fishing with the company he'd worked with before the war. And he hadn't even made it past a week in the Detroit fisheries doing women's work. He'd tried a dozen other things over the summer, but all of them had required the use of two good hands and the brawn behind two strong arms.

The truth was he was crippled now. And he always would be.

When he'd heard the Lighthouse Board was hiring war veterans, he realized work at the light was his last option to earn the money he needed. He hadn't really expected the Board would give him a full keeper's job, not with his disability. Apparently, though, his connection with his sister and her husband at the Presque Isle Lighthouse was enough to get the job.

He'd assumed the keeper at Windmill Point Lighthouse *needed* replacing. But now he wasn't quite sure why Mr. Finick had hired him so quickly. Not when Caroline had been handling the light fine these many months. Or had she?

"I don't understand why Mr. Finick hired me to take your place," he said.

Her features hardened. "He's never liked our family being here," she said bitterly. "And ever since my father died, he's been looking for a way to replace me."

"Why?"

The blue of her eyes turned the color of an icicle. "Because I'm a woman."

Ryan shook his head. "What difference does that make?"

"It doesn't. I've been running this light for months without any trouble. Every vessel and captain that passes through these waters can attest to my efficiency."

Ryan glanced at his injured hand, his shirt still wound around it. Would he be able to do the same? Could he run the light as efficiently? Of course, he'd told Mr. Finick about his injury and the loss of his fingers, even if he had kept his hand squarely in his pocket during the entire meeting. But the man hadn't seemed to think it would impede with his keeper duties.

"I'm sorry it's come to this," Ryan offered. He wished he didn't have to be the one to displace her and her family. But the job was his now, and he couldn't just let it go.

A wave of weariness rippled over him, and once again all he could think about was sleeping. He needed to find a spot where he could lie down and let himself escape into the oblivion where he wouldn't have to think about all the nameless people he'd hurt. And where he could forget about how he was now hurting another family, including this beautiful woman.

He spied a small shed near the keeper's dwelling. The boards were gray and warped, long overdue for a coat of paint that could protect them from the weather that blew in from the sea. Several shingles on the roof were crooked or missing. And with the door hanging open, he could see the interior was packed with an assortment of equipment: oars, life jackets, buoys, ropes, barrels, and crates.

How would he find space to sleep in there? Maybe it would be easier to pitch a makeshift tent.

She had followed his gaze to the boathouse. "Thank you for letting us stay in the house for the week," she said softly. The breeze rippled the edges of the quilt, revealing the white linen of her nightgown and flattening it against her legs.

"Don't thank me." Agony swirled through him. "I'm obviously not good for much other than causing trouble for everyone I come across."

At his harsh words, her eyes widened. But before she could say anything, a horse and rider came trotting around the house.

Ryan couldn't keep from reaching for his side, for the revolver that was no longer there. After months of living on edge, of not knowing who was friend or foe, he couldn't shake the foreboding he felt every time he was startled.

Caroline offered a warm smile to the newcomer. From the boyish clean-shaven face, childlike eyes, and blushing cheeks, at first Ryan thought perhaps a friend of the twins had arrived to play.

But when the young man dismounted and removed his bowler, Ryan recognized the receding hairline and big ears. It was Arnie, the tavern owner's son, the one who'd been sweeping the floor and hiding in the shadows at the Roadside Inn. Upon closer examination, Ryan could see aging lines around Arnie's eyes and guessed him to be at least twenty-five, if not thirty years old.

Arnie took several quick steps toward them before stopping and clutching his hat in front of him. He rolled the brim in shaking fingers and looked at Caroline.

Ryan caught sight of pure adoration shining in Arnie's eyes before the man lowered them and continued to fidget with his hat.

"Hi, Arnie," Caroline said kindly. "How are you doing this afternoon?"

"I-I'm fine," he stuttered, his cheeks and ears flamed a bright red. He stood a head shorter than Ryan. He was even smaller than Caroline by a couple of inches. Obviously the man's giant of a father hadn't passed along to his son any of his impressive height and strength.

"What brings you out to the light?" Caroline asked, almost as if she were speaking to a child rather than a full-grown man.

Arnie folded and unfolded the brim of his hat and stammered for several seconds. Finally he got his words out. "I came to ask you to . . . to marry me."

Chapter 6

"Marry you?" Caroline almost burst into laughter. The thought of marrying Arnold Simmons was about as silly an idea as marrying the uptight Mr. Finick, or the grumpy Jacques Poupard, the old hunchbacked Frenchman who lived on the marsh beyond the ruins of the windmill. Even though Monsieur Poupard was their nearest neighbor, Caroline knew he wouldn't shed a tear to see them leave.

Yet Arnie's expression was entirely too serious and his face too red for him to be joking. Besides, Arnie wasn't one to say things without his meaning it, especially since almost every word he spoke took incredible effort.

"Why, Arnie," she said, forcing down her humor at his earnest proposal, "you're very sweet to make such an offer."

Next to her, Ryan snorted.

She was tempted to elbow him as she would Tessa, but she held herself back from the overly familiar gesture, considering she had just met the man.

"Since you have to . . . m-move from here," Arnie said

hurriedly, which only caused him to stutter all the more, "I c-can give you a . . . a home now."

What kind of home? she wanted to ask. *A room above his father's tavern?* She could only imagine such a life. The noise, the raucous laughter, and the constant coming and going of patrons. Not to mention the cockfighting, which turned her stomach every time she thought about the poor roosters bloodied and battered and fighting to the death.

On top of it all, her father and Mr. Simmons had never gotten along. It was no secret that the tavern owner brought over his cocks, alcohol, and even drugs by way of the Canadian border that ran through the middle of Lake St. Clair. Mr. Simmons had asked her father to turn off the light on several occasions so that he could do his smuggling in the dark without fear of detection. But of course her father had always refused, had in fact threatened to alert the sheriff.

Her father's refusals and threats had always angered Mr. Simmons. And everyone knew what a bully Mr. Simmons was when he was angered. He'd roughed up her father, thankfully nothing beyond a few bloody noses and black eyes. But even if Arnie's father hadn't been a brute, the fact remained that she didn't love Arnie—not romantically, not in the least.

Arnie's inky eyes lifted to meet hers finally, but only for a second before dropping again in shyness. But it was glimpse enough to see the sincerity of his proposal, his affection, and dare she say *attraction?*

Her heart gave a disquieted lurch. She hadn't known his feelings for her went so deep. She'd assumed that he considered her a friend, just as she did him. Most of her kindness to the young man had stemmed from the fact that no one else regarded him with any respect, least of all his father. She hadn't been able to bear the cruel and calloused way so many people treated him. And she'd gone out of her way to make sure he felt safe and welcomed whenever he visited the lighthouse.

But what if in her kindness she'd led him to believe she cared about him beyond friendship?

She swallowed hard before she could speak. "You're very thoughtful for thinking of me, Arnie."

He dipped his head bashfully.

She was being truthful. Arnie had always been considerate of her needs, especially since her father had died. On more than one occasion he'd brought her sacks of food when her supplies had run low. He'd given her chickens, and she'd even found skinned possum and muskrat on the front step once in a while.

But just because Arnie was thoughtful and caring didn't mean she should consider marrying him. Even though he was a couple of years older than her, he was like a little brother to her.

"Oh, Arnie," she said, releasing a long sigh. "I appreciate your offer, but I can't leave my family to fend for themselves. I have to stay with them and take care of them. They need me now more than ever."

He lifted his head. His expression was earnest, almost pleading. "They c-can come too. I'll build you a . . . a house b-behind the inn. They can . . . live with us there."

His statement stopped her ready reply. She straightened and stared at him. "You'd build me a house?"

He nodded and gave her one of his lopsided grins. "I'll give you the b-best. I've been s-saving for it."

"What about Sarah?" she asked. Arnie had a big heart, but taking in Sarah was too much to ask of any man.

"You can p-plant another garden for her at . . . at our n-new house."

Caroline was drawn by the earnestness lining Arnie's boyish face. Even as her heart protested the thought of uniting herself in marriage with someone she didn't love, she knew she couldn't spurn him, not when it meant she'd only have to move Sarah a mile or so. After all, many people married for convenience and not love. Why shouldn't she?

"You can't seriously be considering his offer," Ryan whispered, his brown eyes wide with disbelief.

Arnie's ears were apparently big enough to hear Ryan's muffled words. The young man glanced up at Ryan, and for the first time he seemed to notice that Ryan was unclad down to his suspenders and undershirt, and that Caroline was wearing nothing but a quilt and nightgown. A rush of fresh red crawled up Arnie's neck and ears.

Caroline hugged the quilt closer, inwardly berating herself for not having the foresight to put her clothes back on before stepping outside with Ryan. She hastily retreated to the stone steps of the house. "I'll *seriously* consider your offer, Arnie," she told him over her shoulder, though she was looking at Ryan rather than Arnie.

Ryan's brows shot up.

"You're a sweet man for caring what becomes of me and my family." Her attention flitted back to Arnie. He stared at Ryan again, and this time there was the glint of a knife blade in his eyes. The hostility flashed for only an instant before getting lost in the usual simplicity of his expression.

It gave her pause since she'd never seen anything but kindness in Arnie. "Could I have a little time to think about your proposal, Arnie?"

He ducked his head and nodded. "I'll d-do anything for you, Caroline."

At least someone would. She gave him a smile before letting herself into the house. Once the door closed behind her, she sagged against it, and a sob welled up and drowned her smile.

The sob unleashed a flood of anxiety so strong it rose into her throat and choked her. She squeezed her eyes shut and tried to calm herself before she lost the ability to breathe.

"Oh, Father," she whispered, "why did you have to leave us?"

If only her father hadn't gone out that day in the storm. If only she'd been born a boy. If only she had more time to make plans . . .

Helplessness washed over her, making her want to slide to the floor and curl up into a ball.

At the voices of the others in the kitchen, she swiped at the wetness on her cheeks and straightened her shoulders. She had to stay strong for everyone else. They depended on her. They wouldn't be able to survive without her.

"*God is good.*" Her father's gentle voice seemed to whisper the words in the dark recesses of her mind. *"All the time."*

If her father could believe it, even with all he'd suffered, then she could too. Couldn't she?

❦

Caroline paced in front of the boathouse and glanced again at the darkening sky. Now that summer was over, the nights were growing cooler and longer. Darkness was settling earlier each evening.

It was past time to light the lantern.

She halted and attempted to peek through the boathouse door, open only inches, but it was too dark and crowded inside for her to see anything clearly.

Where was Ryan, and why wasn't he coming out to light the lantern?

She'd considered going up and lighting it herself, but she hadn't wanted to overstep her bounds. She wasn't the keeper anymore. He was.

She couldn't chance angering him, not now, not when she needed to stay in his good graces so that they could continue living in the house temporarily.

"Mr. Chambers," she said into the crack. "Are you awake?"

The only sounds were the low chirps of the crickets beginning their nightly chorus and the rattling of the wind among the long marsh grass. She looked up at the dark tower windows and nibbled her lower lip. She couldn't wait much longer.

Had something happened to the man?

"Mr. Chambers," she said louder, giving the door a shove. It creaked open. The mustiness of damp wood and the staleness of lake water greeted her. She raised her lantern over the interior of the shed.

Squeezed between crates and buoys, Ryan lay on a tattered army bedroll, his shirt bunched up for his pillow. He was on his back, one arm thrown across his eyes, with his injured hand resting gingerly next to him, draped over a wooden cross made out of driftwood.

She moved the lantern closer, casting light over his unmoving frame. The sleeve of his undershirt had risen up to his elbow, showing a dozen slashes and scars scattered across his arm above the puckered skin of what was left of his hand.

Her breath caught, and her own arm pinched with phantom pain at the thought of what he'd experienced. She couldn't even begin to imagine the torture he'd suffered with his injury. From the stories she'd heard, she knew Ryan was relatively unscathed compared to many of the men coming home from the war.

Even so, she had to swallow and look away from his arm to quell the churning in her stomach.

"Mr. Chambers," she said softly, focusing on his face instead of his arm.

He didn't budge.

She pushed at his bare foot with her boot. He gave a soft moan but didn't awaken. "You need to get up. It's time to light the lantern." She glanced around the tiny shack. Should she whack him with an oar? Maybe that would wake him.

Her attention landed upon his leather satchel lying on the pallet next to his injured hand. The flap was open, revealing a dark bottle.

She crouched, picked it up, and sniffed. At the pungent scent of whiskey, her nose wrinkled. She sloshed the bottle, guessing from the feel that it was more than half gone.

Her heart plummeted with a growing sadness she couldn't explain. She returned the bottle to the satchel, and in the process her fingers grazed a smaller vial. Too curious to resist the temptation to pry, she slid it out and examined it.

The bottle had no label. But it rattled as if about half full of pills. She slid a glance toward Ryan's sleeping face covered with his arm. Then she popped the cork off the vial, tipped it, and let several pills spill into her palm.

Opium pills.

Ryan gave another moan and removed his arm from his eyes, his hand automatically going to the cross at his side and clutching it, as if he were in the habit of holding it. But his eyes remained closed. And she could only surmise that he'd lost consciousness from the combination of whiskey and pain pills.

He would obviously not be waking up any time soon.

She stared at his unshaven face, at the blond strands of hair that fell across his forehead. On the one hand, she had the urge to smooth the hair back. From the brief encounter she'd had with him, she guessed he was suffering from more than just physical wounds, that his pains went much deeper.

But on the other hand, she had the overwhelming urge to slap his cheek and give him a rude awakening. It was his sacred duty to light the lantern each night. If he couldn't manage to pick himself up off the ground and do his job, then he shouldn't have agreed to take it.

She dropped the vial of pills, not bothering to put it back in his satchel, not caring if they spilled all over his bedroll. She pushed down the anger that had been building inside her all day.

It wasn't fair. She'd done a nearly flawless job lighting the lantern. She'd taken care of it with the tenderness of a mother with her babe. Everyone for miles around could attest to her unswerving duty these past months. And here was this new-comer, this intruder, who couldn't get himself up the tower steps to light the lantern the first night on the job.

She wanted to scream at the unfairness of the situation.

Somehow he was supposed to be better than her, more suited to the work, simply because he was a man?

She spun away from him, strode out into the fading evening, and slammed the shed door shut with a force that caused several shingles to fall.

"He's worthless!" she cried, her chest aching with frustra-tion. "Absolutely worthless. And he probably doesn't know a thing about how to work a light either."

She crossed the grassy yard to the tower. Her ire swelled with each step, until she was stomping like a two-year-old having a temper tantrum. But she didn't care.

Ryan Chambers didn't deserve the keeper position at Windmill Point Lighthouse. And she most certainly hadn't deserved to be fired from the job, only to be replaced by someone as inept as him.

"It's not fair!" she cried again before yanking open the passageway door.

She stepped inside, but then halted at the base of the staircase that led up the tower. Maybe she should just go back into the house and let Ryan take responsibility for his job. If he didn't want to make a point of lighting the lantern, then that was his problem. Not hers. Maybe then Mr. Finick would hear about Ryan's irresponsibility and decide to let her stay after all.

With one foot on the bottom step, Caroline stared up at the underside of the winding metal stairway.

A battle raged in her heart for only a few seconds before the anger dissipated like a storm after it had unleashed its fury.

She felt strangely tired and old. With a sigh she forced one foot up after the other, the cast-iron steps pinging with each slap of her boots.

If Mr. Finick fired Ryan, he wouldn't let her stay. He'd only find another man to take the job. The truth was, her time at the lighthouse was through. And she needed to accept that, no matter how hard it was.

The other truth was that she couldn't leave the lantern unlit—not as long as she had breath and the ability to climb the stairs. She would go up and keep the light burning, no matter what. Sea captains and sailing vessels depended upon the Windmill Point Light for their safety. And she'd never willingly put them in danger. Not even to spite the man who'd taken her job away from her.

She loved the light too much to ever neglect it.

She halted halfway up and pressed her hand against the cool brick wall. For a moment she imagined that she could feel its pulse, the tower's lifeblood pumping through the walls, beckoning her to remain strong and steady.

Her legs trembled, but she nodded and then continued up the stairs. She needed to stay strong.

Chapter 7

*R*yan's mouth stunk, like a rat had climbed inside and built a nest there. His throat was parched, and his head pounded. He stumbled across the grass toward the tower. "Idiot," he berated himself. "You idiot."

The faint light of dawn was showing pink on the eastern side of the lake. And he'd shirked his duties by hours.

When he'd awoken from his medicated stupor, his heart had squeezed with panic. First he'd realized someone had rummaged through his satchel and taken out his pills. The clinking of pills against the glass indicated they were still there. He'd been relieved, but only for a moment, until he'd remembered where he was and why. The panic had returned like a cavalry stampeding toward the front line.

He'd forgotten to light the lantern last night.

"How could you be such an idiot?" He cursed himself again and paused at the causeway door to glance up to the lantern room. The flashing beam prevented him from seeing anything inside the room. He knew right away who had been responsible for lighting it, even though it was now his job.

He hesitated at the doorway. Should he knock? It wasn't his home yet. And after last night's neglect of his duty, he wasn't sure it should ever be.

A fresh burst of remorse pushed him forward through the door. He forced himself into the tower and up the stairs, each step jarring him and sending shards of pain through his head. When he reached the ladder that led the last distance up, he paused and pressed his hand against his temple to fight off dizziness. How would he be able to climb the stairs each day on multiple occasions without causing himself intense pain?

His heart sank at the thought, but he forced himself forward. One-handed, he started up the ladder and hesitantly poked his head through the hatch. The lantern room was empty.

He released the breath he hadn't realized he was holding and finished ascending. He didn't know much about lighthouses, but he knew enough to understand that the light at the center of the room was a small sixth-order lens, the smallest light designed for lighthouses. He'd expected a larger lens for a station located in such a strategic position, one that handled the heavy commerce of boats traveling around the horseshoe of Michigan from Chicago to Detroit and on to Buffalo.

He could tell that Caroline was an immaculate keeper. The floor was swept, the windows were spotless, and the brass base polished until it shone. Even the oil can sitting on the floor near the light had been buffed to a coppery glow.

The half door that led to the gallery swung open, and he took a quick step back, bumping into the round metal wall. Caroline stooped to enter through the low door. Once inside, she straightened and flipped her loose hair over her shoulders before she caught sight of him.

She gave a start, and her eyes rounded. "Mr. Chambers." The surprise was then replaced with a look of censure.

"Aye. It's me." He squirmed and wished he'd thought to run a comb through his hair or soap down his face. He could only imagine how he must appear. "I'm sure I look like a dead man who's risen from the grave."

She didn't respond except to purse her lips together.

"I probably smell like one too." He wasn't sure why he was attempting humor. In fact, he was certain he'd lost his sense of humor when he'd lost over half his company that bloody day at Gettysburg.

She held a long nautical spyglass in her hands and had obviously been out on the gallery scanning the lake, keeping watch on the ships that relied upon the light for their safety. Her cheeks were pink from the coolness of dawn, her hair mussed from the wind. She was entirely too pretty.

He couldn't resist sliding a hand through his hair, although he knew it was a feeble attempt to make himself presentable. He was as disheveled on the outside as he was within. He hadn't cared before, hadn't given his appearance a second thought for months.

But under this woman's scrutiny, he couldn't keep from fidgeting. Had she been the one to come into the boathouse and rifle through his satchel? If so, she would have seen the awful truth about the kind of man he'd become.

"I overslept," he offered. "I guess the ride out here from Detroit wore me out."

Her eyes only narrowed at his weak excuse.

Aye, he had no excuse. He should have woken up in time to light the lantern. "It won't happen again."

"I hope not." Then she shrugged almost as if she didn't believe him.

"Thank you for lighting it for me."

"I didn't do it for *you*. I did it for them." She nodded curtly toward the lake.

The condemnation in her tone added to the guilt already weighing upon him. He couldn't keep from thinking about the oath he'd taken when he'd accepted the appointment to Windmill Point Lighthouse. He'd promised to carry out the assigned duties with energy and enthusiasm, and to serve loyally and honorably. So far he'd failed on all accounts. Caroline had every right to scold him, even though she was obviously refraining from doing so.

"Since you're here now, I'll leave you to your work." She bent to retrieve the oil can and then stepped toward the hatch.

He glanced at the lantern, to its gears, weights, and wick. How was he supposed to turn it off? And when?

She brushed past him and lowered herself through the narrow hatch in the floor.

"Wait," he said, unable to stop the panic from creeping into his voice.

She paused on the top rung and refused to look at him.

He couldn't very well admit he had no idea what he was supposed to do, could he? She was already angry enough that he'd taken away her job. She'd hate him if she realized Mr. Finick had replaced her with an idiot. Sure, his sister, Emma, had shown him how to turn off the Presque Isle Light. But he'd never done it himself.

"What?" she asked, finally lifting her eyes. The sadness in their depths socked his stomach.

He wanted to tell her he was sorry. But he already had, and saying the words again wouldn't make the situation any better.

There wasn't anything that could make the situation better . . .

except maybe if he left. But he couldn't leave. Not yet. Based on the salary Mr. Finick had quoted, Ryan figured he needed to work about a year to save up enough. And even then, he'd probably not have all that he owed.

"I need this job," he said, the deathly white face of the nameless boy rising up to taunt him.

Caroline's eyes radiated with accusation. "You're not the only one who needs a job, Mr. Chambers." And with that she disappeared through the hatch.

He stared after her, fighting the urge to retreat, to give in, to let her have the post. He didn't really want it. All he wanted to do was go back to the shed, quench his thirst, and return to a world where he didn't have to think or feel anything.

Shame heaped onto the guilt and made his knees weak. What kind of man had he become? He muttered a low curse at himself. He was exactly the kind of man he'd sworn he would never become. He'd always told himself he'd never end up a no-good drunk like his dad. He'd always told himself he wouldn't hang on to the pains of the past and let them control him like his father had.

Yet here he was, a wretched excuse for a man.

Anguish smoldered inside him. "Oh, God, why didn't you take me? Why didn't you let a better man than me live?"

He'd asked himself a thousand times why God had spared him when so many of his comrades had died. He hadn't deserved to make it through the war when there were men with wives and children waiting for them back home, better men who were far more deserving of life.

"I can't do it," he said aloud with a bitter tone. "I've already injured one family. I can't bring heartache to another." He would leave. He'd go down and tell Caroline she could have her job back.

He took a wavering step toward the ladder, but the faint light spreading over the horizon stopped him with its beauty. Slowly he moved to the east window, rested his forehead against the cold glass, and stared into the distance. The swirls of pink and orange broke through the darkness and cast a warm glow upon the still waters of the lake.

He stood motionless and stared at the beauty of light in the darkness. The peace of the sunrise cracked through the storm clouds in his soul. *Turn to me*, a gentle voice seemed to whisper. *I'm all you need.*

He swallowed the pain that rose up in his chest, taunting him, telling him that he didn't deserve God's love and grace. Instead he let the gentle beam of light inside, and he whispered back the words pressing for release from the depths of his being. "I need you."

Maybe it wasn't much of a prayer, but it was a start.

Caroline stooped over her cluster of basil plants and clipped several of the stems. The peppery aroma tingled her nose and added to the delectable scents of the horsemint and thyme she'd already cut.

Pruning her garden always brought her such delight. But today, under the growing cloudiness of the afternoon sky, she found no joy in the task. In fact, on numerous occasions she'd considered simply abandoning the garden, leaving it to fend for itself. Just as she'd abandoned Ryan earlier that morning in the tower and made him fend for himself.

She gave a sideways glance toward the boathouse, where he'd disappeared again after somehow managing to turn off the light. She'd had to restrain herself all day from going back up to the lantern room and making sure he'd done it right and that he'd cleaned up after himself.

Instead she'd forced herself to get some much-needed sleep before getting up to care for Sarah, to change and wash her, reposition her, and try to make her as comfortable as possible.

Through the open window of Sarah's bedroom she could hear Tessa's dramatized voice as she read to Sarah from one of the books she'd borrowed from Grosse Pointe's schoolteacher. Even though Tessa had stopped attending the school several years ago, she still often pestered old Mr. Lund for books or sonnets or plays.

Caroline often had to pry the books from Tessa's fingers and admonish her to do her work, but she never had the heart to stop her when she was reading to Sarah. Tessa relayed the stories with so much liveliness and expression that Sarah could listen for hours.

Caroline supposed the stories refreshed Sarah's soul the same way the flower gardens outside her window refreshed the girl's sights. For all the times Caroline conflicted with Tessa, she knew they were both only attempting to make Sarah's life happy in their own ways.

"One more chapter" came Sarah's sweet voice through the window. "Please, Tessa."

"All right," Tessa replied. "Only one more, though, or Caroline will skin me like a raccoon and string me up for sitting around all afternoon and leaving her with the work."

Caroline stifled a sigh and sat back on her heels, the soft moss at the edge of the garden cushioning her knees.

For once, she'd neglected the work needing to be done too. She'd told herself she would walk into town with the boys that morning when they went to school, that she'd spend some time asking around for work and seeking a new place to live. But when the boys had tramped off across the marsh, she'd hung behind, making an excuse that she was too tired.

She'd planned to start packing their belongings, but the empty crates for storage were in the boathouse and she hadn't wanted to face Ryan again. At least that was what she'd told herself.

Caroline paused and looked around, scanning the back of the house, her fading flower garden, the fenced-in vegetable plot, and the gnarled apple tree drooping under the weight of its fruit. A swell of sorrow threatened to crush her chest.

She wasn't ready to leave Windmill Point. She loved the beauty of the isolated marsh and living along the lake. She didn't want to make her home someplace where she couldn't wake up to the lapping of waves, the muddy-grassy scent of the water, and the endless blue of the lake.

She loved the peacefulness and the quiet. She loved the wild creatures that made the lake their home. She even loved the mysterious history of the area. Some claimed Windmill Point was an Indian graveyard and old battlefield where the Fox tribe had fought and been slaughtered by early French settlers.

Through the tall reeds among the distant woods to the north, she caught sight of a red flannel coat. Within seconds an old man burst out of the woods. He wore a coonskin hat, its striped tail flopping down his back, alongside his long gray hair that was pulled back in a queue. His gun was propped against his shoulder, and his black eyes glared at her across the distance.

It was Monsieur Poupard, their neighbor.

Caroline stood, fisted her hands on her hips, and stared back, refusing to let the old French trapper intimidate her. "You'll be very glad to see us go too, won't you?" she said.

Every once in a while she glimpsed him in the woods, hunting. Usually, though, the hermit kept to himself in his log house near the ruins of the old windmill.

He'd likely come over because he'd heard the news about her replacement. She had no doubt he was rejoicing that they were leaving. He'd rejoice to be rid of the twins, since they bothered him to no end, always encroaching on his land, or fishing on his section of the lake, or making too much noise near his house.

The only time he came over was to complain about the boys in his thick French accent.

She was surprised when he waved at her with a jerk of his arm. When she didn't move, he waved again, this time more forcefully.

"Make haste," he called, his leathery face scrunched in a scowl.

"What do you need?" she asked.

"The twins," he said.

She didn't have the time to listen to him grumble about Harold and Hugh. They'd be out of his way soon enough. Couldn't he tolerate them a few more days?

"I'm sorry they're bothering you again, monsieur. I'll be sure to talk to them about it." She'd told them to come straight home after school and not to get into any trouble. They'd clearly disobeyed.

"*Non*, non, non." The Frenchman's scowl deepened, and he sliced the air with his hand to cut her off. "The boys. They are in trouble. You must come at once."

Trouble was nothing new for the twins. They were always getting dirty, ripping their trousers or scraping their knees in one of their many escapades. But there was something urgent in Monsieur Poupard's voice that caused an eerie stillness to descend over her, as if she were swimming underwater where there was no sound.

"The abandoned well by the ruins." Monsieur Poupard cocked his head to the north. "This is where they are. One of them has fallen inside."

Fallen into the old well?

Caroline shuddered, and the outside world came rushing back to her senses with the force of a roaring gale. She picked up her skirt, bunching the material into her shaking hands, and darted toward him.

"You must get rope," Monsieur Poupard shouted.

She nodded and veered toward the boathouse. As she ran, her heart pattered in time to her feet. She didn't bother to knock at the half-open door. She barged inside and almost tripped over Ryan's feet.

He was lying on his bedroll, his head resting against a life jacket. In the dim light she could see his eyes were closed and there was a whiskey bottle near his hand next to the driftwood cross.

Had he been drinking again?

She shook her head in disgust, quickly stepping around him and reaching for the rope hanging on the back wall.

"Is it time to light the lantern already?"

At the sound of his groggy voice, she jumped. "No," she snapped. "It's not nearly time."

He sat up slowly and wiped his hand across his eyes. "What's wrong?"

"It's not your concern."

He watched her uncoil the rope from the hook and loop it over her shoulder. "Is someone drowning? Are you heading out on a rescue mission?" His voice lost the sleepiness and instead took on an edge.

"I said it's not your concern." Her muscles were tight, urging her to get to the boys as fast as she could. Without a second glance at Ryan, she started out of the shed. His grip on her arm stopped her. She pivoted, astonished to see him on his feet.

His expression was alert, his eyes serious. "It is my concern now," he said in a low voice. For an instant she could see the man he used to be—conscientious, hardworking, determined.

But at the sourness of alcohol on his breath, she yanked back from him and pulled free of his grip. "I don't have time to waste dealing with you right now," she said. "My brothers are in trouble, and I'm going to rescue them."

At her declaration, he released her. The determination in his expression wavered.

She spun away, her chest tightening at the thought of what awaited her at the old well. She didn't have another second to waste. Especially arguing with a half-inebriated man.

As she raced across the yard, she shouted instructions to Tessa through the open window. A few seconds later, the front door banged open and Tessa called after her as she rushed toward the marsh. Caroline didn't stop to answer but began pushing her way through the woods.

When she broke through the clearing by the ruins of the old windmill, her lungs burned with the need for more air. Her legs almost collapsed beneath her. Ignoring the pain, she sprinted the rest of the way to the crumbling brick structure of the windmill.

She gave a wheezing cry and fell to her knees at the sight of Harold leaning over the top ledge of the well. His arms were stretched down, and he was shouting instructions over his shoulder to Monsieur Poupard, who had a tentative hold on his legs.

"No, Harry!" she called.

At the sight of her, Harry wiggled out of his precarious perch and planted his feet on solid ground. His face was dirty and streaked with tears. "Hugh is down there!" he shouted. "And he can't keep afloat much longer."

Tessa staggered past her, her breath coming in gasps from running. She didn't stop until she reached Harry. "What happened?" Tessa demanded, gripping the boy's shoulders.

"Are you all right?" came a voice behind Caroline.

She turned and was surprised to see Ryan. His brown eyes regarded her with concern, and he grasped her arm and steadied her.

"Don't worry about me," she said hoarsely.

"Hugh's under the water!" Tessa screamed. "He's drowning!"

Ryan sprang forward. Caroline stumbled after him, begging her weak legs to carry her to her brother. *Oh, God*, she silently pleaded. *Not Hugh too . . .*

She'd had to stand back and helplessly watch her father drown. She couldn't do it again. She couldn't watch Hugh die without attempting to save him.

Ryan kicked off his boots and shed his shirt at the same time, then hopped onto the edge of the well with a nimbleness that spoke of his strength despite his injuries.

"Hugh!" he yelled into the darkness. "Hang on! I'm coming down." Without waiting for a response, Ryan slid over the edge and jumped. There was a splash, followed by several long seconds of silence.

Caroline lifted the rope from her shoulder and peered down into the deep well. Through the shadows she could make out the tops of two heads.

"I've got the boy!" Ryan shouted up. "He's swallowed a lot of water, but he's alive. Throw me the rope."

As her eyes adjusted to the dark interior, she could see Ryan's upturned face and shoulders. His muscles were stretched taut in his effort to keep himself afloat while holding on to Hugh.

"I'll tie the rope around him, and then you pull him up." Ryan's voice exuded a confidence that gave her a boost of energy.

She lowered the rope until she heard it hit the water. Within seconds he had the rope looped around Hugh's chest and under his arms. The weight pulled the rope so that it burned against Caroline's hands. Thankfully, Monsieur Poupard had already taken hold of the rope behind her, aiding her hold of Hugh.

"All set!" Ryan called. "Pull him up."

Tessa and Harry grabbed the rope too. With the four of them heaving, they pulled Hugh's limp body to the surface. At the sight of him, a dismayed cry slipped from Tessa's lips, and she flung herself toward the boy.

She lifted him the last bit of distance into her arms and carried him away from the well. Caroline followed and knelt next to Tessa. The young girl had turned Hugh on his side and was pounding his back.

Seconds later, Hugh began coughing up mouthfuls of water. His eyes fluttered open and made a connection first with Tessa, then with his brother, Harry. Finally he looked at Caroline. "I'm sorry," he whispered through trembling blue lips.

A wave of relief crashed over Caroline, and her body sagged. She cupped his freckled cheek and smiled. "You're safe. That's all that matters."

"I didn't know the water was so deep," he said. His hair was plastered to his forehead.

Caroline choked back a rebuke. Now wasn't the time to scold him. She would save that for later.

"I thought I could get out." The innocence in Hugh's eyes unleashed guilt within Caroline, for she should have filled the well with rocks earlier that summer when the boys had first stumbled upon it. She'd known it posed danger. But then she'd gotten so caught up with her keeper duties that she hadn't given the well another thought.

And to think of what had almost happened . . . She fought back tears. She'd almost lost Hugh.

The twins had been adventurous even before their father had died. But over the summer they'd steadily gotten into more trouble. Maybe she hadn't been paying them enough attention. Maybe she'd been too busy with her job to give them the supervision and training they required.

What if Mr. Finick was right? As a woman, perhaps she needed to focus on her home and family. Perhaps she'd placed too much attention on her work and not enough on caring for her siblings. Maybe losing her job as keeper was best for all of them. She could marry Arnie and then be able to spend her days taking better care of the twins and Sarah.

"How is he?" Ryan asked, kneeling next to her. His breathing was labored, and water dripped from his hair and clothes and puddled on the ground around him.

In her worry over Hugh, she'd completely forgotten about Ryan still at the bottom of the well. She glanced toward Monsieur Poupard, who was dragging the rope out of the well. The opposite end was wrapped in a tight knot around one of the supporting beams that rose to the dilapidated roof of the well. The old Frenchman had tied the rope and then thrown it back down to Ryan, who had apparently pulled himself up hand over hand.

She could only imagine the pain the effort had cost Ryan. She was tempted to look at his hand and his arm, but instead she focused on his face.

Every line was drawn taut, and his eyes radiated agony. But then he looked down at Hugh tenderly. "How are you, son?"

Hugh lifted a hand, and Ryan grasped it within his good one. "Thank you," Hugh whispered. "You saved my life."

"Aye. You're welcome," Ryan said. "That was a dangerous thing you did."

Hugh lowered his eyes at the same time that Harry let his head drop.

"A boy needs to have fun," Ryan went on. "I won't argue with you about that. But foolish and fun are two different things altogether." His blond hair hung over one of his eyes and curled up at the back of his neck.

She'd wanted to loathe this man or at the very least blame him for her current troubles. But how could she? He might be scarred and suffering, but he seemed to be a good man underneath it all.

As if sensing her scrutiny, he shifted his attention to her. The brown of his eyes was warm but firm. "How about if I bring the boys out here tomorrow and put them to work filling the well?"

His words contained no anger, only a logical tone that spoke of his desire to help prevent further mishaps while also giving the boys some needed discipline.

"That's a good idea," she said past a swell of gratefulness that clogged her throat.

"What do you say, boys?" Ryan glanced from one to the other. His expression was still kind but filled with the admonition the boys needed.

The twins both nodded and looked at Ryan with new respect.

Yes, deep inside Ryan Chambers was a good man—a man worthy of respect, someone they could even come to like. Maybe it would take some time for him to heal, to be able to live fully again. And she'd be long gone by the time that happened.

But one thing was certain, she couldn't fight him, couldn't even be angry at him any longer. She'd simply resign herself to the fact that, for better or worse, he was taking over the lighthouse.

Chapter 8

Caroline flapped Sarah's rug again, even though she'd already loosened all the dust from it on the third or fourth shake. In the morning sunshine, the dust particles glinted in the air and floated lazily away. They all seemed to make their way down the gently sloping span of yard toward the rocky beach and draw her attention to Ryan, where he kneeled next to the water's edge.

The sunlight kissed his bent head and turned his hair into a fetching shade of golden brown. And the bright reflection off the water showed a face, hands, and arms scrubbed clean of the dust and grime that had coated them previously.

Donned in his undershirt, he was bent over and scrubbing his shirt. Using only one hand and a bar of soap, his efforts were valiant but feeble. The longer she watched, the more she was tempted to go to him, grab the shirt, and clean it herself. But somehow she knew that such an offer would humiliate him. He probably hadn't done much of anything since his injury, including taking care of himself. Maybe one of the first steps in his healing process was to begin taking an interest in his grooming and to do some of the difficult tasks for himself, to prove to himself he was still alive.

After all, he'd only lost a few fingers, not his life.

Nevertheless, she wanted to do something for him. At the very least she needed to thank him for saving Hugh's life yesterday. But she hadn't had the chance since he'd ridden off and hadn't returned until much later. From his wobbly walk, she guessed he'd spent the remainder of daylight hours at the Roadside Inn. So when evening fell, she'd ascended the tower stairs by herself and taken care of the light alone just like she usually did.

She'd expected him to come barging through the hatch, disheveled and dazed at dawn like he had yesterday. But when the sun had risen and she'd extinguished the lantern, he still hadn't staggered out of the boathouse. So she'd turned off the light and completed the morning chores in his stead.

For the hundredth time, she'd been furious at the unfairness of the situation. Inwardly she'd railed at Mr. Finick for replacing her simply because she was a woman and for giving her job to someone who didn't care about the light as much as she did.

But she couldn't muster any anger toward Ryan. Not after yesterday. Not after seeing the real him.

She let the rug droop against her calico skirt and stared at his bent back, at the strength that radiated from him even as he wrung at his shirt with just one hand.

There was a decent man buried somewhere beneath his layers of heartache, she was sure of it. The same way she'd noticed there was a handsome man beneath all the grime.

"You've sure been out here long enough," Tessa said, stepping out the door behind her.

Caroline focused quickly on the rug and gave it another

shake. Her cheeks tingled—but only from the chill of the morning air.

"I thought you were going to town." Tessa joined her on the grass, her apron smudged and her hands dusted with flour. She carried a cup of coffee in one hand and a plate piled with egg and porridge leftovers from breakfast in the other.

"I *am* going to town," Caroline said. "I wanted to make sure Sarah's room was clean first." Even though she tried to look at Tessa, she couldn't help but glance back at Ryan.

Tessa gave an unladylike snort. "I think you just like being out here watching the show."

"I don't know what you're talking about."

Tessa nodded toward the shoreline. "Mr. Chambers giving himself a bath."

"He's not bathing."

"And how would you know that if you're not watching him?"

Caroline's cheeks tingled again. She forced herself to pivot so that she wasn't facing Ryan.

Tessa's lips crooked into one of her disarming grins. "You're blushing."

"No, I'm not."

Tessa's grin only inched higher, and she turned to stare boldly at Ryan. "I admit he's a much nicer man than I thought he'd be. And he's also better looking. *Much* better looking."

"Tessa!" Caroline peeked over her shoulder to see if Ryan had heard her sister's declaration.

He gave them a sideways glance but otherwise appeared preoccupied with his soggy shirt.

"Put it this way," Tessa continued. "I won't mind taking him his breakfast." The young girl sashayed her hips and winked at Caroline before lifting the cup and plate.

Caroline swiped the plate from Tessa before she could take another step. "I'll take it to him."

"What if I want to take it?"

"Young, unmarried girls don't take plates of food to strange men."

The girl's eyes narrowed, and her smile disappeared. "I'm eighteen now. I'm practically an adult."

Caroline wanted to roll her eyes but resisted the urge. After just turning eighteen, Tessa acted as if she were twenty-six and thought she knew everything. Without Father's admonition, she'd steadily become more resistant to Caroline's leadership. In fact, Caroline found herself fighting with her sister over the littlest of things.

It was true that, for some time now, Tessa had been forced to bear a large load of responsibility, beginning when their father's rheumatism had worsened and Caroline had taken over the light. The care of the twins and Sarah had fallen onto the girl's shoulders and she'd handled it well. But just because she'd managed the load didn't mean Caroline wanted her flouncing down the beach and making eyes at a man they'd only just met.

"I'm sorry. I shouldn't have brought up your age," Caroline said, reaching for the coffee mug. "Still, I'll take him the food."

Tessa's pretty dark eyes flashed. "I'm old enough to have a beau if I want one." She straightened and pushed back her shoulders, which only served to emphasize her womanly curves, much fuller and more rounded than Caroline's.

Lately, Tessa had been a little too encouraging with the few men she met at church or in town. She'd smiled at them too brightly, too invitingly. And Caroline hadn't liked the reaction of the men. They hadn't been able to pick their chins up off the ground and stop their drooling. Tessa was still innocent and unaware of the effect she had upon men. But sooner or later, if Caroline didn't protect her sister, she was bound to get into trouble.

"But you've only just turned eighteen." Caroline kept her voice low and controlled. "You're still very young."

"I suppose you want me to end up an old maid like you."

This time Caroline couldn't keep from rolling her eyes. Tessa's line of reasoning was irrational. At twenty, Caroline didn't consider herself an old maid. And just because she wanted Tessa to be careful didn't mean she wanted Tessa to wait forever. Yet Caroline knew from past experience that it was pointless to argue with Tessa when she was in one of her belligerent moods.

"I don't want you to go down there and flirt with the new keeper, Tessa. He doesn't need to be bothered by such silliness. And that's all I'm going to say about it."

"It's not silliness to talk with a man," Tessa shot back. "Most girls my age are getting themselves beaus now that the boys are coming home from the war."

Caroline pinned her with a sharp look. "You don't need a beau. Especially not now, not when our lives are in upheaval."

"So I suppose it's perfectly okay for a 'young, unmarried girl' like you to take breakfast to a stranger?"

"At least I don't giggle and flutter my eyelashes at every man I meet." With an admonishing last look, Caroline started toward Ryan. Tessa's dark gaze bore into her back, until the slamming of the front door told her that Tessa had gone back inside.

Caroline's footsteps squeaked in the dew on the grass, and as she neared Ryan, her insides creaked with strange jitters. She supposed all the talk of courtship and beaus had made her self-conscious now.

At the sight of her, Ryan stood and stuffed his injured hand into his pocket. In the bright morning sunshine, his eyes were clear, the haze that came from the medication gone. The brown in them was as warm and kind as it had been yesterday when he was talking with the twins after the incident at the well.

But this time he didn't smile. He simply stood and watched her, the backdrop of the lake and the sunshine causing him to glow. There was a quality about him, a vulnerability that made her want to be sensitive and patient with him. He didn't need her censure. He probably got much more than he needed from himself already. What he needed instead was someone to encourage him and believe in him.

Maybe she wouldn't be with him for more than a few days, but while they were together, she could show him a little more kindness, couldn't she?

She held the plate out to him. "Tessa saved you a little breakfast. And some coffee."

His eyes lit with hunger at the sight of the food. "Please tell her I appreciate it."

While he ate ravenously, she picked up his discarded shirt. "This would come cleaner on the washboard with a bar of lye."

"Probably," he said between mouthfuls.

"Tomorrow's washing day. If you bring your clothes over to the house, I'll scrub them with the others."

He swallowed a big bite and then stopped eating. He looked at her with a seriousness that made her pause. "Thanks for the offer, but I'm leaving tomorrow."

"Leaving? What do you mean?" But even as her question tumbled out, the resignation in his face gave her the answer. He was quitting his job as keeper.

"After your brothers are home from school, I'll take them over to the well and we'll fill it together. But then first thing tomorrow, I'm riding out."

Her heart gave an uncertain thump. Wasn't this what she'd wanted? For him to leave so that she could have her job back?

Ryan studied the tower rising into the blue sky behind her. "I'm not fit to take care of the light."

She agreed with him, but he didn't need her rubbing the fact in his face.

"Besides," he added, "you need the job. And I can't take it away from you."

"You didn't take it away," she said. "Mr. Finick did." If Ryan left, Mr. Finick would only send another man to replace him. And she doubted another man would be as kind and understanding as Ryan had been.

"Maybe if I talk to him, he'll let you stay," Ryan suggested, setting aside his plate and retrieving his coffee mug from the rock where he'd placed it.

"Mr. Finick wants me out of here. He's wanted me out ever since my father died, maybe even before that. He won't be happy until he has a man back in the keeper position."

Ryan took a long sip of the coffee, staring at the calm lake and the water lapping in a gentle, soothing rhythm against the shore. "So my leaving won't do you any good?"

"Not in the least. One way or another, I'm done here." It was the truth, and the sooner she accepted it, the sooner she'd be able to make plans for her family. "I'm heading into town this morning to try to find a place for us to stay."

If she couldn't figure out something, she'd have to accept Arnie Simmons's proposal. And that wouldn't be the worst that could befall her. At least Arnie was a sweet, kind man.

Ryan stared into the distance. The muscles in his jaw rippled, and his eyes narrowed. "What if you didn't have to be done?"

"I've already tried to convince Mr. Finick, but I don't have any say in the matter."

"Maybe I do, though." His expression was hard. "Since I'm the keeper now, I'll tell Mr. Finick that I'm letting you stay on . . . as my assistant."

She shook her head at the impossibility of such a suggestion. "Mr. Finick would never allow it."

"I'll tell him I need your training and help." He cocked his head toward his injured arm. "Which is the truth."

A tiny ray of hope speared through the confusion and disappointment that had fallen since the inspector's visit. Ryan *did* need help.

"You can continue to live in the house with your family, and I'll stay in the boathouse." A glow began to light his face and smooth away the hard lines.

"With the colder nights coming on, you won't make it in the boathouse much longer."

He shrugged. "We'll figure something out."

Everything within Caroline urged her to agree to his solution. It would solve her problem of where to go, at least for the short term. But she couldn't imagine Mr. Finick would ever agree to such a plan permanently. He seemed determined to drive her away one way or another.

"We'll split the wages," Ryan offered.

Mr. Finick wouldn't agree to that arrangement either. But she peered out over the water, the glassiness momentarily blinding her. Maybe Ryan's offer would only put off the inevitable, but it could buy her the needed time to find work as well as a suitable place for Sarah.

"I've already hurt enough people in my life," he said softly. "I don't want to add you and your family to the list."

She met his eyes, an expression of pure sincerity. "I guess we can give your idea a try then."

He stuffed his other hand into his pocket and rocked on his heels, the tension rolling away and a smile tugging at his lips. "Good."

"Thank you." In spite of the temporariness of the plan, she was still grateful to him for his sensitivity and kindness.

He nodded and said, "Your beau will be disappointed."

"I don't have a beau."

"Could have fooled me." His tone was teasing. "Arnie Simmons sure has it bad for you."

"Arnie's just a friend."

"It's obvious he doesn't think of himself as *just* a friend."

"I've never encouraged him in anything beyond friendship. I've only shown him the courtesy and kindness that others neglect to give him."

"But he's still a man." Ryan grinned. "And a man would have to be blind not to notice how pretty and sweet you are."

Ryan thought she was pretty. Even though his words were spoken lightly, they made something warm flutter to life in the pit of her stomach, something she'd never felt before but that she liked.

"I guess you're just going to break his heart," Ryan teased.

She wished she knew how to banter with a man. But the fact was, even if there had been suitors available, she wasn't sure she could have flirted. She wasn't like Tessa. Making eyes and joking didn't come naturally to her.

Even so, Caroline couldn't resist returning Ryan's smile. "Arnie was only trying to help me. I don't think he really wants to marry me."

"Oh, he wants to marry you," Ryan insisted, his eyes dancing with a light that sent another flutter through her middle, this one warmer than the last.

She wasn't sure how to respond. There was something honest and clear in his eyes, something that beckoned her to banter with him. And there was also a frank appreciation of her as a woman—something she hadn't experienced before either.

His gaze held hers, bold and unswerving, until she squirmed and looked away toward the rocky beach. The warmth inside spread in a pleasurable trail to her limbs.

She needed to go. Needed to keep her dignity. Before she made a fool of herself and ended up acting silly like Tessa. She spun to leave, but then stopped. "You'll join us for meals in the house, won't you, Mr. Chambers?"

"Nay. I can't."

Her lips stalled around her sentence.

Seeing her surprise, he fought back a smile. "I won't join you unless you promise to call me Ryan instead of Mr. Chambers."

"I can't." It was her turn to try to hold back her smile. "I'll only use your given name if you bring your dirty laundry up to the house tomorrow and allow me to wash it. Ryan."

He laughed, giving her a smile wide enough to reveal the full power of his attractiveness. The humor and laughter in his eyes transformed his face into one of the handsomest she'd ever seen, and her breath caught in her throat.

"Do I stink that bad?" he asked too innocently.

She flipped her hair over her shoulders and started back to the house. "Perhaps on the morrow I'll draw water so that you can take a bath. I'm not sure which needs the scrubbing more, you or your clothes."

His low chuckle followed her.

And it wasn't until she was inside the house, her back pressed against the closed door, and her knees trembling, that she realized she'd done it. She'd flirted.

For the first time in her life, she'd flirted. And she couldn't deny that she'd rather liked doing it.

⁓

"You will absolutely not lose your keeper job simply because you wear skirts and have the ability to bear children." Esther Deluth's voice boomed over the town square, making Caroline want to jump into one of the large barrel flowerpots that dotted the corners and burrow under the dirt.

Esther stood at the base of a ladder, staring up at a banner that read, *Help build the library. Help build a better tomorrow.* One of the assistants from her husband's office wobbled at the top of the ladder.

Esther had one hand on her plump abdomen and the other shielding her eyes. "It's hanging down on the left," Esther called to the man, who was sweating profusely under the Indian summer sunshine of midday.

The man moved the sign higher.

"I won't stand for this." Esther turned to face Caroline. "This is absolutely the most ridiculous thing I've ever heard of."

"I'm sorry, Mrs. Deluth," the assistant replied, raising the banner again, apparently not realizing that Esther wasn't speaking to him but had shifted her attention to other issues.

Without another glance at the man on the ladder, Esther bustled forward, taking hold of Caroline's arm and steering her toward a basket filled with pamphlets and signs. "This is 1865, not the Dark Ages. Men like Mr. Finick need to realize that women are quite capable of doing more than acting as bed partners to their husbands."

Caroline stumbled at the bluntness of Esther's statement and chanced a look around to make sure no one else had heard her friend. There were several other women standing nearby and chatting, their young children playing together on the grass of the square. They weren't paying any attention to Esther. Neither was the group of men seated in front of the general store, many of their wagons parked in front, empty but for a scattering of grains that hadn't made it to the mill.

At midday Grosse Pointe wasn't anything like the busy metropolis of Detroit, which lay six miles to the south. But for a small town it had more than its share of activity, especially with Esther Deluth living here. Her father had recently been elected to the Michigan State Senate, and her husband was the town mayor. And Esther was never without one political cause or another, particularly women's suffrage.

Caroline increased her stride to keep up with her friend. "So what do you think I should do?" she asked, knowing Esther would have advice for her. She always had, ever since they'd first met after Caroline had moved to Windmill Point as a young girl of twelve.

Though Esther had gotten married last year and was now expecting her first baby, Caroline still counted Esther as her closest friend.

"What should you do?" Esther's voice rose with incredulousness. "What should you do? I can't believe you're even asking me that." She stopped in front of the basket of flyers, picked it up, and looped it under one arm.

Next to her, Esther stood a head shorter and was stocky. Caroline wouldn't have known Esther was six months pregnant from looking at her abdomen. The baby blended in well with Esther's well-endowed form.

After all of Esther's declarations when they'd been growing up about how she didn't want to get married and have babies, that she wanted to have a career instead, Caroline thought it was rather ironic her friend was married and expecting before Caroline had even given marriage a second thought.

She hadn't been opposed to it the same way Esther had. In fact, she'd always dreamed of finding a godly man like her father and working alongside him. She wanted someone she could love and take care of, someone who would feel the same way about her. And of course she wanted babies too.

But during the past several years, she'd had little time to think about marriage. Since her father's death, she'd decided she couldn't leave her siblings. She'd never abandon them for a man. And she couldn't ever ask a man to shoulder the responsibility of caring for her family.

She hadn't expected that any man would ever want to take on such a heavy load, which was one of the reasons she knew she had to seriously consider Arnie Simmons's offer of marriage. Even if he acted somewhat like a child, he was nearing thirty, had a steady job, and could provide her a home. What more did she need at this point?

"Esther, please." Caroline latched on to her friend's arm to keep her from charging to wherever she was going next with her basket of flyers. "Please tell me what you think I should do."

Esther finally came to an abrupt halt and turned her flashing eyes upon Caroline. "Okay. I'll tell you what you're going to do. You're going to stay out at the light. That's what."

"But Mr. Finick won't let me—"

"He's discriminating against you based upon your gender,

and we won't stand for it. We just fought a war to end slavery against our black brothers and sisters. Now it's time to fight the war to end oppression against women."

Caroline gave an exasperated sigh. She was used to Esther's political tirades, but that wasn't what she needed now. "How can we stop him, though? The Lighthouse Board has given him the power to hire and fire."

"We'll find a way." Esther patted her arm firmly. "I'll talk with my husband, and we'll think of something."

"But I need to have a backup plan," Caroline insisted. "I can't afford to be homeless and without a job, not with Sarah's condition."

"You said yourself that the new keeper is willing to let you stay on. And if that doesn't work, you know you can always stay with Paul and me."

Caroline glanced at Esther's bungalow across from the courthouse. With a fresh coat of white paint, it was pretty from the outside, but Caroline had been inside often enough to know it was tiny, having only two bedrooms. With the baby on the way, Caroline knew she couldn't impose on her friend, at least for very long.

"I need to find another job, Esther."

Esther pursed her lips and glanced around Main Street to the smattering of little shops and businesses—the smithy, the tailor, the butcher, and others. They were all largely family-owned and operated. They wouldn't need help from a young woman like Caroline. And even if they did, she doubted they'd be able to pay her what she'd need to support her siblings.

As if drawing the same conclusion, Esther patted her arm again. "We'll think of something. But in the meantime, you dig in your feet and stay at the light. It's your home and your job. And no one has any right to take it away from you because you're a woman."

Caroline nodded and pushed down the growing frustration. She'd come to town hoping Esther would offer her a viable solution. But Esther was apparently just as helpless as she was.

Was her only solution to travel down to Detroit and hope she could find a job in one of the factories there?

She loathed the idea of having to move her family into the squalor of the rentals. It certainly wouldn't be a healthy environment for Sarah or a proper place to raise the twins. She could only imagine the trouble they'd get themselves into running loose in the slums reserved for factory workers.

Esther handed Caroline a stack of flyers from the basket. "Now, you can help me distribute these flyers to raise support for a new library."

Caroline sighed and took the papers.

"Don't worry, Caroline," Esther said over her shoulder as she started toward the men gathered in front of the general store.

Telling her not to worry was like telling a rain cloud not to release any rain.

"And remember to come back to town on Saturday for my protest rally against cockfighting," Esther called. "If four other states can outlaw such barbarism, then we can outlaw it here in Michigan."

Caroline only nodded. She hadn't told Esther about Arnie's proposal. She knew Esther would scold her for considering it. Esther detested Mr. Simmons and made no secret over how much she opposed not only the cockfighting but also the sale of liquor at his establishment.

Though Caroline didn't approve of Mr. Simmons's activities either, she'd been trying to convince herself that Arnie was different. He wouldn't hurt a soul. He was one of the kindest men she knew. In light of her current situation, he was still her best option.

Even so, she couldn't make herself ride out to the inn and accept his proposal . . . not quite yet.

Chapter 9

*R*yan scraped the razor down a fraction and flinched as the blade nicked his skin again. He pulled back and was tempted to toss the steel down into the grass and trample it in frustration.

He peered into the broken triangle of glass, which was all that remained of his shaving-kit mirror. He'd shaved less than half his cheek, and it was so shredded he looked as if he'd been showered with shrapnel.

The slap of a door closing told him one of the women had stepped outside the house.

He hunkered closer to the small mirror leaning against the outer sill of the boathouse window and pretended to be busy. He wished he hadn't decided to act upon the unusual urge to shave. He'd gotten by without shaving for many months. Why had he felt the need to start again today?

He gripped the razor with his good hand and smoothed the shaving soap with the other. Now that he'd started, he would have to finish. He certainly couldn't walk around with half of his face shaved smooth and the other half hairy. Although he wasn't sure which was worse, the half shave or a cut-up face that resembled Frankenstein's monster.

"We missed you at dinner last night" came a voice from behind him.

He angled the piece of mirror so that he caught a glimpse of Caroline's reflection. Her hair was tied into the usual knot she wore at the back of her head. For a fleeting second he remembered the way it had flowed down her shoulders and back the first day he'd met her, when she'd been full of fire and horror at finding him in her bed.

The memory brought a swift smile to his lips.

"Did you find the plate that Tessa left for you?"

"Aye," he answered. "Many thanks for the delicious food." When he'd awoken from his medicated sleep that morning, he'd found the food waiting for him outside the boathouse door. It was cold and covered with ants, but once he'd picked off the insects, he'd enjoyed every bite.

After all, he'd grown up in Ireland during the potato famine. His mother had died of starvation, giving up her portions of food to save him and his sister. Even though those days were a distant memory, he'd never forgotten the hunger spasms, the weakness, and the frantic need for food.

The war hadn't been nearly as bad. He'd even been grateful for the pieces of hardtack that were full of weevils and maggots. Aye, he'd had a constant ache in his stomach day in and day out during some of their toughest campaigns. But no matter how hungry they'd been, they shouldn't have stolen from the civilians.

The admonition burned through him as it had a hundred times since the war. Of course, at the time, he and the others in his regiment had justified their pillaging by saying they were taking from their enemies. The Southerners were the reason for their hunger in the first place. If only they hadn't started the war, then he and his buddies wouldn't have been so hungry and so far from their homes.

Maybe they'd been able to make excuses for taking the food, but Ryan knew there was no justification for what they'd done that fateful night.

He blinked hard and started to sink beneath a crashing wave of despair.

"The boys told me you got the well filled about halfway." Caroline's voice pulled him back to the surface.

Ryan nodded and dragged in a breath. "They're hard workers." In the several hours he'd shoveled dirt and rocks into the well with the twins, they hadn't once complained. They'd worked steadily and followed his instructions without question. "They're good boys," he added. "They just need a firm hand once in a while."

He'd dreaded spending time alone with them, expecting memories of the dead boy to taunt him. But surprisingly he'd found himself enjoying the twins' presence and listening to their conversation.

While he'd spared his injured hand the brunt of the shoveling and lifting, he'd come back to the lighthouse with so much pain in his arm that he'd been unable to do anything but collapse onto his bedroll and swallow a couple of pills.

He was ashamed that he'd been incapacitated through dinner. Even worse, he hated that he'd failed once again to attend to the lighthouse. He'd resolved then to stop being so useless and make some effort to do his keeper duties.

Maybe that was why he'd wanted to shave—to give himself a fresh start.

But it was a feeble attempt, and he'd only managed to mangle his face. Was that the way it would be with everything he tried to do?

Her footsteps on the gravelly path crunched closer, until she stood next to him and he caught the whiff of something sweet, like flowers. The fresh scent wafted around her. She picked up the half bar of shaving soap he'd left near the broken piece of mirror.

She wiped off the lather he'd made and ran her finger over the coarse grains of the soap. She glanced to his cheeks and then to the blade he gripped with ever-whitening fingers.

He tensed as he waited for her to say something about his useless arm, his failed shaving attempt, and how inept he was at everything. He deserved it.

"Your soap's no good," she said matter-of-factly. "It isn't lathering well."

They both knew the soap wasn't the problem, but he appreciated that she wasn't making him feel more inadequate than he already did.

"I have a bar of my father's soap inside that you can use," she offered. "In fact, I used to shave my father's beard, and I'm quite accomplished at it. Or at least I used to be."

Was she offering to give him a shave? He wasn't sure whether to be mortified or flattered.

They made eye contact but only for a second or two. Her summery blue eyes reflected only shyness and not the pity he'd grown accustomed to.

"I'd be obliged," he said. "Maybe you can save me from skinning myself alive."

He tried to form his lips into a smile but only managed a twitch. But she'd already spun away from him and was walking toward the keeper's cottage.

"I have a few minutes now," she called over her shoulder, "while I wait for my laundry water to boil."

He watched her retreat, her movements graceful even though each step was firm. Caroline Taylor was a strong woman. He could see it in the stiffness of her back and in the way she held her shoulders. She'd weathered his coming and losing her job with much more decorum than he would have.

Even after all the frustration and uncertainty his coming had caused her, she was kind to him—kinder than anyone had been in a long time, maybe even since the last time he'd visited his sister at Presque Isle before he'd enlisted.

He watched Caroline until she disappeared into the house. His heart welled with gratefulness. She was being considerate toward him, though she had no reason to.

❧

The steam from the kettle rose in the air, and the heat from the wood-burning stove radiated throughout the kitchen. Even with the window open, letting in the cool fall breeze, the room felt hot and humid.

The back of Caroline's dress stuck between her shoulder blades, and a loose piece of hair was plastered against her neck. But she swirled the brush in circular motions vigorously anyway, working it around the shaving soap to create a thick lather.

She'd laid out her father's shaving supplies on the worktable near the window—the tin and the soap made from goat's milk, the four-inch stainless steel blade, like new still, and the badger-bristle shaving brush. She'd even found a bottle of the lotion he applied after a fresh shave, but she wasn't sure she had the nerve to uncork it. One whiff of the spicy, woodsy scent would only send her into a lapse of melancholy.

It was better not to think too much about losing her father and the repercussions that were now coming as a result.

At a creak of a floorboard in the other room, she knew it was Ryan entering the house and crossing the front room. His footsteps were hesitant, and when he reached the doorway of the kitchen he stopped, his brow raised, showing the uncertainty in his eyes.

She nodded toward the chair she'd placed directly under the window so that she could have the maximum amount of light to aid her efforts. "Have a seat. I promise I won't cut you."

"You can't cut me any worse than I've already done myself," he said wryly.

"True." She offered him a small smile of encouragement.

He plodded to the chair and lowered himself, leaning back and stretching his long legs in front of him. He kept his injured hand in his pocket as usual.

His presence in the kitchen seemed to make the heat rise a degree or two. He wasn't an overly large man, but his masculinity seemed to fill the space around the large center table and attune her to the knowledge that he was a handsome man, and she a naive young woman, just as naive as Tessa.

Except for her father, she'd never touched another man before. What had made her believe she could touch Ryan with such familiarity?

A tremor of nervous anticipation rippled through her. She reached for a hot towel she'd hung above the steaming pot, and then she forced herself to approach him.

When she stood above him and he looked up at her with his brown eyes so full of trust and gratefulness, she tried to ignore the whispers of warning about being too friendly. Maybe if she tried to picture her father sitting in the chair instead of Ryan?

She laid the warm, moist towel over his face, covering all but his eyes, which followed her every move with bright interest.

"Tell me about your family" came his muffled voice from behind the towel. "Where are you from? How long have you been light keeping?"

She pressed the linen firmly against his skin, cleaning it and blotting away the blood from his earlier attempts. While answering his questions distracted her a bit as she prepared for his shave, her stomach still did strange flips every time she briefly touched him.

After she removed the towel, he answered her questions freely in return about his past. She learned that at ten he'd emigrated from Ireland with his older sister and father in order to flee from the famine. Once they arrived, he'd never lived in any place for very long but had spent most of his years before the war fishing in northern Michigan and then in the Detroit area.

"So you're a man of the sea," she said as she scooped the lather onto the end of the brush and then transferred it into her cupped palm.

"Aye. It's been in my blood since I was a lad, fishing with my dad back in Ireland."

She wanted to ask if he'd ever return to fishing, but at the sadness in his tone she held back her question. Instead she rubbed her hands together to mix the cream and create an even richer lather, and she turned the direction of the conversation to something safer. "With your seafaring background, you'll make a good keeper."

She supposed that was one of the reasons Mr. Finick had hired Ryan, even though he obviously didn't know much about lighthouses.

"Do you think so?" Ryan asked, his voice hopeful.

"I'll show you everything you need to know," she assured him. If she had to move out of the lighthouse, then at least she could make sure she left it in capable hands. "I promise."

"You're an angel," he said softly, and the intensity of his gaze burned into her.

The creamy texture of the soap finally felt full enough for application. She bent over his face and raised a hand, but then hesitated. Before she lost courage, she slipped her fingers over his scruffy skin, smoothing the soap in gentle waves across his cheek.

He stiffened and closed his eyes.

She halted. "Am I hurting you?"

"Not at all," he said, his voice somewhat strained.

After another moment's hesitation, she continued lathering his face. His Adam's apple rose up and down, and his fingers splayed across his thigh tightly.

"Are you sure I'm not hurting you?" she asked.

His lips curved into a grin, and his eyes flashed open to meet hers. "Rest assured, Caroline, the last thing you're doing is hurting me."

There was something in his eyes that sent a wave of heat pulsing through her middle and up into her face. She quickly averted her eyes and hoped she wasn't blushing as much on the outside as she was within. And she prayed that Tessa would stay in Sarah's room awhile longer. She didn't want her sister seeing her flustered and flushed as she shaved Ryan's face.

Besides, she didn't want to give Tessa the impression that she'd overstepped the bounds of propriety. Certainly there was nothing improper about her helping Ryan by giving him a shave. But she didn't want Tessa thinking she could take such liberties.

Willing her fingers not to shake, Caroline began the careful process of sliding the razor down Ryan's cheek, inch by inch. The scraping of the blade against bristle was the only sound save the pounding of her heart.

When she finished the first half, she released a long, slow breath and realized that he did the same. Her touch was obviously having an effect upon him too, although she couldn't be sure what sort of effect.

If it wasn't pain, was it pleasure? The thought only made her insides heat all the more.

She worked carefully around his lips, trying not to touch them with each upward stroke. When the pad of her thumb accidently brushed against his upper lip, he hissed in a quick breath.

"I'm sorry," she whispered, but she found she couldn't tear her attention away from his strong mouth; she was mesmerized by both the firmness and the infinite softness of his lip.

She'd never kissed a man before. In fact, she'd never really given it much thought, other than that it was something she'd maybe do one day with her husband.

But now, hovering over Ryan, with her face just inches from his, she couldn't stop from thinking about kissing. What would that first touch of lips be like? How would it feel to share such intimacy?

As if sensing her thoughts, his eyes shifted to her mouth. They hardly knew each other. They were still almost strangers. And yet something seemed to spark between them.

Though she knew he wouldn't dare kiss her at that moment, the desire to do so had etched a sudden intensity into the lines of his face.

"What's going on here?" Tessa's sharp voice made Caroline jump back.

Her entire body was filled with mortification. Ryan too bolted to a straight-backed position.

Tessa stood with one hand on her hip, the other hand clutching a volume of *Romeo and Juliet*. She'd loosened her long ebony hair from its simple plait and now wore it in loose abandon, likely as a result of playacting for Sarah. She scowled at Caroline. "I see now why you don't want me delivering meals to Mr. Chambers."

"I'm merely giving him a shave," Caroline replied. But her statement sounded weak, even to herself. "Since I'd shaven Father, I thought I could do the same for Ryan."

"Oh, so it's *Ryan* now? You're using his given name?" Tessa's dark eyes flashed. "Admit it, Caroline. You want to keep this man's affections for yourself."

Caroline took a quick step away from Ryan. The hot steam from the bubbling pot on the stove was stifling. "That's absolutely not true. I have no aspirations for his affection. None in the least." Why would she when they would soon be leaving? Not to mention the fact that he was clearly in the habit of imbibing too freely with alcohol and his pain pills. He was in no condition for any sort of relationship.

Tessa's attention darted between them, her face filled with accusation.

"I was only trying to be nice—"

"Caroline?" A new voice came from the other side of the kitchen.

Arnie Simmons stood in the doorframe, his boyish face crumpled with hurt, his big eyes widened with surprise. He too was glancing between Ryan and Caroline, as if trying to make sense of the intimacy of the situation.

"I was only shaving Mr. Chambers," she rushed to explain.

But from the way the red bloomed in his ears, she guessed he'd seen the flash of intimacy that had transpired between her and Ryan.

"Aye," Ryan chimed in. "I was having a terrible time at it on my own. All the cuts are from my bumbled efforts earlier."

Arnie glanced at Ryan, who wore spots of lather around the edges of his mostly shaven face. Even amidst the tension of the moment, Caroline couldn't keep from noticing what fine features Ryan had now that the whiskers were gone. He cleaned up well. And would probably be downright irresistible with a haircut.

"It's a good thing Caroline offered to help," Ryan continued, "or I might have sliced off my face entirely."

Tessa gave a suspicious *harrumph*, and yet some of the fight faded from her face.

"I c-came . . . by," Arnie said, his cheeks turning as red as his ears, "to check . . . on you."

"That was very kind of you, Arnie." Caroline forced herself to look away from Ryan. She reached for the nearby towel and wiped off the soap that coated her fingers. "We're managing just fine."

Arnie shifted his enormous feet and stared down at them. "My d-dad let me bring the horse and w-wagon out."

"How nice." Caroline picked up the razor and dipped it in the basin of water she'd placed on the sideboard near Ryan's chair.

"I can h-help you . . . start moving y-your things." Arnie's stuttering sounded choppier than usual.

Caroline paused in her cleaning off the razor, turned and smiled at the man. "You always amaze me with your thoughtfulness, Arnie."

At her words of praise he lifted his head, and his eyes lit up.

"But I'm glad to report that I won't need to move out this week."

"This week?" Ryan echoed. "How about never?"

Caroline shook her head at Ryan, but spoke to Arnie. "Mr. Chambers has agreed to let me stay on as an assistant keeper for a little while so that I can train him."

"Not a little while, Caroline," Ryan insisted, sitting forward. "I want you to stay. Indefinitely."

Arnie's eyes widened, and his mouth opened into a rounded O, as if he wanted to say something but couldn't find the words.

"We can't stay," Tessa said, stomping her foot. "Especially indefinitely."

Over the past summer, since their father had died, Tessa had made no pretense about her growing dislike of living at the lighthouse. But this was no time for belligerence, not when their situation was already precarious.

"I'm not pushing you out," Ryan said. "In fact, I welcome the help."

"You'll manage fine by yourself," Tessa said quickly. "It's time for us to move on. To do something different with our lives."

"But you have nowhere to go," Ryan added. "And this is your home."

"We'll make a home somewhere new and exciting."

"We're staying here for now," Caroline interrupted her sister and at the same time, out of the corner of her eye, she noticed Arnie's shoulders sag.

"But, Caroline—" Tessa started.

"We'll have to move on eventually," Caroline said in her firm tone, the tone she used whenever she had to be the parent. "I doubt Mr. Finick would agree to letting me stay on here, even as assistant keeper."

Ryan sat back in his chair with a frown, while Tessa's features relaxed into a smile.

Arnie shuffled forward several steps, his childlike eyes fixed on Caroline's face. "I can take care of y-you, Caroline."

Caroline swallowed the rapid refusal that arose. She couldn't turn down Arnie's kind offer. Not yet. "I'm still considering your marriage proposal, Arnie. It's a very good option for me."

At her words she could feel Ryan's attention snap back to her. She didn't dare look at him. She didn't want to see his mocking or disapproval. It was her choice what she did with her life and whom she married.

"I'll help you m-move your things," Arnie said eagerly.

"No," she said a little too sharply. For an instant she thought she saw hurt, maybe even anger, flash in his eyes. But he ducked his head.

"I'm sorry, Arnie," she said gently. "I need more time to think things through, to decide what's going to be best for my family in the long term."

"You won't . . . won't regret m-marrying me," he said. "I'll m-make sure of it."

She didn't quite know how to respond, especially with Ryan and Tessa watching her with curiosity or disapproval, she couldn't be sure.

At the same time, she didn't want to hurt Arnie's feelings. "I know you'll be a good husband," she said. "I have no doubt about that."

He toed a loose strand of the braided rug that lay centered on the floor and wiped his sleeve across his dribbling nose.

"But . . ." she continued. Was she stringing him along? Was it selfish to consider marrying him when she held no affection for him? "I'm not sure that I'm the best choice for you. Perhaps you'll find someone better—"

"You're the only one f-for me, Caroline," he blurted, his words coming out loud in his effort to speak them.

Caroline's insides squirmed at the awkwardness of the situation.

"Please . . . say you'll m-marry me."

Ryan gave an exasperated sigh and stood, almost knocking his chair over in the process. "She's not going to marry you. She doesn't need to, because she's going to stay here and do the light keeping, just like she always has."

Arnie cringed and took a quick step back, lifting his arms to shield his head.

Did he think Ryan was going to throw something at him or hit him? She was sure the defensive stance was one he assumed often around his brute of a father.

She crossed around the table and held out a hand to Arnie, unable to keep the pity at bay. "I can't promise I'll marry you. But I promise I'll think about it."

Behind her, Ryan groaned.

Arnie lowered his arms slowly. His hopeful eyes met hers.

"In the meantime," she said, "I'm going to stay here at the lighthouse, since no one is pushing me out the door just yet."

"How much longer w-will you stay?"

She hadn't really thought about it. "I suppose until circumstances force me out." Maybe she'd stay until Mr. Finick came back. Maybe she was clinging to the very slight chance that he'd let her stay as an assistant. Or maybe she'd stay until she'd had the chance to find another job and a good place to live.

Whatever the case, she wasn't planning to leave until she absolutely had to.

Even though she didn't speak the words, Arnie seemed to read them in her eyes. She caught sight of the disappointment clouding his expression before he turned to go.

At a cry from down the hallway, all thoughts of marriage and the future fled. She bolted forward, and her heart sped with a burst of panic as it did every time Sarah cried out. Tessa flew ahead of her and into Sarah's sickroom. Caroline followed close behind.

At the sight of Sarah in a heap on the floor, Tessa rushed over to draw the girl into her arms.

"Sarah!" Caroline said. "What happened?"

The young girl's face was deathly pale. The blue veins in her temple seemed to pound through her translucent skin. The pallor made her dark hair all the blacker and her green eyes even brighter.

"I'm all right," Sarah whispered. "I just wanted to hear what everyone was saying and got too close to the edge of the bed."

Crooning words of comfort, Tessa helped Sarah back to her bed, positioning her on her side. Sarah bit back small cries of discomfort and pretended to smile. But the girl's brave efforts didn't fool Caroline. She knew Sarah lived in a constant state of pain that was made worse every time she moved.

Caroline fought back images of Sarah when she was little, of how she'd been an energetic girl who danced and ran and climbed trees. Now all her sister could manage was scooting a few inches in bed.

Caroline wished there was more she could do for Sarah, to make her life more bearable, more pleasant, or more interesting. She couldn't imagine being cooped up day after day in the same room, breathing the same stale air, and never being able to do anything, and she loathed that she couldn't make life better for Sarah.

With firm steps, Caroline crossed the room to the bedside table, to the small vial of Dover's powder, all that was left of the pain medicine. "Should I give her some?" she quietly asked Tessa.

Tessa shook her head as she smoothed Sarah's unruly hair off her face and back against the pillow. "I'll massage her first and see if that helps."

In the doorway, Ryan cleared his throat.

Sarah's eyes popped open and locked on their guest.

Ryan, his face still nicked and edged with traces of shaving soap, stepped into the room. "You must be Sarah."

Sarah nodded. "You're the one everyone's talking about."

"We're not *all* talking about him," Caroline rebuked softly.

"Yes, you are," Sarah said with more strength than she'd showed recently. "You and Tessa can't stop ogling."

Tessa gave Caroline a sideways look. "I said *Caroline* can't stop ogling."

"I've seen you ogling too," Sarah replied with a giggle.

Before Caroline could correct Sarah, Ryan chimed in. "At least now you get to see for yourself that I'm not worth the ogling."

Sarah peered past Tessa, taking in Ryan's appearance.

"I can see that you, on the other hand," Ryan continued smoothly, "are the prettiest one in this house."

At his words of praise, Sarah smiled, a dazzling, unforced smile. And when he grinned back, a slight hue of pink formed in her cheeks. He came into the room then and lowered himself onto the chair next to Sarah's bed as though he planned to stay awhile. Sarah's eyes took on a dreamy quality.

"So, tell me," he said, "what exactly do your sisters say about me?"

Sarah giggled again.

Caroline exchanged a glance with Tessa above the girl's head. Whatever discord Ryan might cause between them, she could tell from the look in Tessa's eyes that they both could agree Ryan would be a good diversion for Sarah.

That was really all that mattered.

Chapter 10

The breeze coming in the half-open door of the tower was cold. Caroline gazed out the window facing east toward the brightening sky. As the days of September ticked away, the sun grew lazier in making its appearance, and Caroline was having to keep the light on longer every morning.

She didn't mind lingering in the tower. Even though she was tired from the sleepless night, the first light of dawn always seemed to bring a fresh reminder of God's presence. She might have darkness in her life, and her current predicament might be confusing and hard, but God was still bright and unchanging behind the clouds. As her father had always said, God was good all the time, no matter what bad things came into their lives.

Right now, with the uncertainty and difficult choices that lay before her, she needed that fresh reminder more than ever.

At the slap of footsteps against the metal tower stairs, Caroline pushed away from the window. Now that she had to stay in the tower later, she guessed Tessa had sent one of the twins up to deliver her breakfast and coffee before they set off for

125

school. Even if she and Tessa had their areas of disagreement, Tessa never wavered in her thoughtfulness.

When Ryan's head poked through the hatch, Caroline's ready smile of thanks faded.

"May I come up?" His eyes pleaded with her and were as warm as heated molasses.

She hesitated. He hadn't come up to the tower again since that first morning. She'd been relieved to have the tower duties to herself. She wasn't ready to relinquish them. But she knew she had to prepare him to take over at some point. She cared too much about the light and the vessels it protected to let an inexperienced keeper take the helm without sufficient training.

"I'm not stopping you," she said, reaching for the rag she'd discarded earlier. She swiped at an invisible blotch on the window, the rag squeaking against the glass.

"I meant to come up last evening," he admitted from his spot on the ladder rung, "but I wasn't in the right frame of mind."

She wanted to tell him that if he didn't combine whiskey with pain pills, he'd likely have a better chance of staying alert. Instead she rubbed on the glass harder.

Out of the corner of her eye, she watched him ascend until he was standing awkwardly and staring around the room.

"Listen, Caroline," he said in an almost anguished voice. "I hate myself for not being able to follow through with the work. You have to believe me when I say I want to, that I'm trying to make myself a better man. But sometimes I think I'm hopeless and that I'll never be able to do anything right."

His confession tore at her, along with the droop of his shoulders, the lump of his hand stuffed into his pocket, the unseen scars on his arm. She knew all of that only mirrored the wounds deep inside him. He was a hurting man inside and out, and she could do nothing less than show him the compassion he so desperately needed.

"You're not hopeless," she said gently. "You're here now, aren't you? Would you like me to show you how to turn off the lantern properly?"

"Aye. I'd be eternally grateful." His Irish brogue sounded thicker in the mornings, for some reason.

She found that she rather liked it. In fact, she was finding that she liked all too many things about him. Her thoughts flashed to yesterday's shave, to the softness of his skin and the firmness of his lips. Even though she'd told herself she wouldn't think about the shave again, she glanced at his cheek and then his upper lip.

He'd cleaned up nicely, and it was difficult not to admire his smooth face. His tousled hair flopped back and forth across his forehead.

"I didn't have the chance to thank you for the shave," he said, patting his cheek, apparently well aware of her perusal.

"You're welcome." She spun toward the lantern, her insides rolling in strange waves. "I was happy to help." As soon as the words left her mouth, she ducked her head. What was she saying? She practically admitted that she'd enjoyed the experience.

He didn't say anything in response. But his footsteps clanked closer, until the heat of his presence was behind her. Her stomach gave another lurch, and she waited, hardly daring to breathe. She almost believed he'd slip his arms around her and pull her back against him.

Why was she thinking such thoughts now? Especially with a man whose very presence had turned her comfortable life upside down?

"So what do I need to do first?" he asked, his voice low.

The lantern room was small. The lens stood on its pedestal in the middle. There was enough space to walk comfortably around it. But with two adult-sized bodies angled at the lantern, closeness was inevitable.

At least that was what she told herself.

She opened the little door at the back of the lens, its brass hinges creaking faintly. She reached in and pointed to a knob. "First, you have to turn the wick down slowly so that you don't cool off the chimney too suddenly."

He stretched past her, brushing against her arm as he grasped the wick. Though she was tempted to lean into him, she stepped aside to give him better access.

Once the flame was low, he turned to face her, his body altogether so near that her thoughts became jumbled.

"What next?" he asked.

She had to swallow hard before she could speak. "Now that it's low, you can blow across the top of the chimney to extinguish it. Be careful not to blow down inside, but just across the top. Like this." She demonstrated by giving a gentle puff.

A smile crooked his lips. "I don't think I can extinguish it with your expertise, but I'll try."

With one breath the flame went out, and the lantern turned black. It would have plunged the lantern room into darkness, except that over the years she'd learned to have her kerosene lantern lit ahead of time so that she could finish the remainder of the tasks with the aid of more than just the natural light of dawn.

"How'd I do?" he asked, his eyes glimmering with playfulness.

"You're catching on fast. But only because you have such an expert teacher." She was surprised by her attempt at banter and had to turn away to hide her smile.

Was she flirting again? What was wrong with her?

She busied herself with removing the chimney and explaining how to wrap it in flannel until it was entirely cooled. She showed him how to wipe the ash from the wick and then how to clean the whole length of the air spaces in the burner with a long goose feather.

She demonstrated the rest of the duties she performed each morning to keep the light in the condition that was laid out in the *Instructions for Light-Keepers*. Of course, even though she followed every regulation, her efforts were never good enough for Mr. Finick.

She found that she could talk with Ryan easily, just as she had when she'd shaven him. As they worked, he asked her plenty of questions about the light, proving himself to be an eager learner, and she was all too happy to share her knowledge about the lens, equipment, and navigation on the lake. The sun had risen above the tree line by the time she showed him the supply room at the bottom of the tower stairway.

"Tomorrow morning I'll let you go through the whole process by yourself while I watch," she offered as she closed the closet door.

The enthusiasm in Ryan's expression fell away. "If I make it up to the tower in time." His eyes took on the weariness and sadness she'd seen there too often.

"How many opium pills are you taking at a time?"

"Two."

"That's a powerful dose." There had been plenty of times when she would have sold everything they owned for even a quarter of an opium pill to give Sarah, especially during those long nights when her sister's muscles had begun to constrict and cause her excruciating pain. She would have done anything to ease the dear girl's suffering, even taking it upon herself.

"You must be in a lot of pain to need two pills," she said.

His face was shadowed. The light from the hand lantern she held at her side didn't reach high enough, and she was tempted to lift it to allow herself a closer examination of his face and his injuries. But as before, she held herself back.

She wouldn't pry. She'd wait for him to share.

He didn't say anything for a long moment. Finally he opened his mouth to speak, closed it. Then opened it again. "The doctor who worked on my arm couldn't get the piece of shrapnel out without digging in and destroying muscles and possibly bone."

He stopped, his eyes round with the agony of the nightmare he was reliving.

She wanted to put a hand up and tell him he didn't need to say anything else, that she understood.

But he swallowed and continued, "When the doctor told me he needed to cut off my arm from the elbow down, I begged him not to. At the time, I thought I'd rather live with the pain than lose my arm. Especially since half my hand had already been blown off."

She could picture him on the operating table, already suffering from his injuries, likely half delirious with pain. She'd heard horror stories about the conditions of the medical tents, the blood and flies, the buckets of sawed-off limbs, the stench of decay.

"I didn't want to lose any more of myself." His voice tapered to a whisper. "But I don't think it worked very well."

She couldn't help but think he was referring to his soul, that maybe he'd saved his body but had ended up being so miserable that he drank and medicated himself into a stupor most of the time.

"I make very soothing birchbark tea that eases Sarah's pain," she said. "I also have some feverfew in my garden. Sometimes chewing a fresh leaf or two can lessen the aching."

"Do you think they'd work on me?"

"Most of the time lately all I've had for Sarah are the natural remedies I make from my flowers and herbs. They don't work any miracles, but they take the edge off her suffering."

He studied her face. Sunlight had begun to creep through one of the windows cut into the tower wall halfway up and was making the stairwell glow.

"I can't promise the herbal medicines will help you," she said, "but it's worth a try. Then perhaps you'll gradually be able to cut back on your pain pills."

He nodded, but not too convincingly.

She didn't have to be an expert to know that the opium pills caused a powerful craving for more, that even if he wanted to cut back, his body would resist, especially since he'd been taking them for a while. She'd heard that the Union Army surgeons regularly prescribed opiates to injured soldiers in spite of the drug's highly dependent quality. It provided temporary relief, but at what price? How many soldiers had returned home unable to survive without the drug?

Whatever the case, she'd do what she could to help him in the short time she had left at the lighthouse. And she'd start by cutting him the feverfew to chew.

She led him outside and started around the house. She'd pruned most of the perennials that grew in front of the house and missed them already.

"I take it the beautiful garden behind the house is yours?" he asked while following her.

She nodded. "I always let the back garden bloom as long as

possible for Sarah." She breathed in the crisp moisture coming off the lake and drew her shawl about her shoulders. "I've even planted varieties that would bloom at different times of the year, so that Sarah would have a continuous array of color to greet her every time she looks out her window."

"You take good care of everyone, Caroline." The admiration in his tone was like a much-needed pat on the back.

She worked hard day after day to take care of her family, and most of the time no one noticed. Of course, she wasn't doing it for the recognition or the praise. She did it because it was the right thing, and because it was her duty as the oldest to step into her parents' shoes—first her mother's and now her father's—and provide for her brothers and sisters.

"But the question is," Ryan said, tugging on her arm and gently pulling her to a stop, "who takes care of you?"

"I don't need anyone to take care of me. I've done just fine since Father died."

"I'm not saying you're unable to take care of yourself. It's obvious you're a strong woman." He stood taller than her, but not by much. The sunlight touched his hatless head, glinting through his hair, turning it the color of sun-bleached sand. "You're very capable, yet you bear so much by yourself. You're always worrying about everyone else's needs and putting them before your own. Maybe you need to take care of yourself too."

She started to shake her head in protest, but at the tenderness in his expression, a gentle hand seemed to reach around her heart and squeeze. "I'm doing fine," she said, but her tone was unconvincing even to her own ears.

"I suppose that's why you're considering marrying Arnie. Because you love him and know you'll have a life of happiness by his side."

A ready retort died upon her lips.

His fingers on her arm became more firm, and his expression turned grave. "Admit it, the only reason you're thinking about marrying him is because once more you're looking out for your siblings. You see it as a way to take care of them, regardless of the sacrifice you'll have to make."

He was absolutely right. Even so, she didn't want to admit it. "I won't have to sacrifice anything. Arnie's a very nice man. He'll make a good husband."

Ryan's brow shot up. "He's got the mind of a child. If you marry him, you'll end up having one more person to take care of."

She wouldn't agree with him. She couldn't. "I know he'll treat me with the utmost respect and kindness."

"Like a child treats his mother."

"He's a man. And he'll treat me as such—"

He cut off her words by tugging her with the same strength he'd used when he rescued Hugh from the well. She stumbled against his chest in mortification and had to tilt her head back to keep her face from brushing his.

Before she could protest, he swooped forward and brought his mouth down against hers.

The move was so unexpected she drew in a sharp breath, which was cut off by the pressure of his lips. The firmness was more than she imagined when she'd shaved him, a strange mixture of strength and softness. The touch sent a rushing current through her, flooding her with warmth.

His lips lifted a mere fraction, and she expected that he'd end the kiss, back away, and put a proper distance between them. Instead he only angled his mouth so that he took more of her and captured her fully.

She could do nothing less than respond, letting his lips guide hers, pressing against him, tasting of his warmth and fullness until she was heady with the heat of the kiss.

As abruptly as he started, he broke away from her, leaving her lips bare and craving more.

"That's what it's like to be with a man." He took a step away. His chest heaved and his breathing came hard, as if he'd just swam a great distance. "Arnie will never kiss you like that."

She didn't know how to respond. She could only stand there trembling from the power of his kiss, her lips swollen and now cold from the morning air that had taken away the warmth of his touch.

He dragged in a ragged breath and stared at her through the hair that hung down his forehead. His brown eyes regarded her in a way that sent more hot waves lapping against her insides.

She had to lower her eyes or burn up altogether. She focused on the toes of her boots and her hem dampened by the dew on the long grass.

"Don't settle for Arnie. You shouldn't have to marry someone like him just so you can take care of your family."

She continued looking down at the water-stained leather of her boots. "Maybe over time I'll learn to love him."

Ryan muttered a groan.

Before he could protest, she hurried on. "Love and passion"—she flushed as the words left her lips—"aren't nearly as important as duty and loyalty to my family."

"That's what I mean." His voice was exasperated. "You're taking care of everyone else and not considering yourself."

"It's called sacrifice," she said, striding forward and brushing past him. "Maybe that's not something you care about, but I do."

"Of course I care about it." He trailed after her.

She rounded the corner of the keeper's dwelling, her body attune to his overpowering presence behind her. For a moment she couldn't see anything except his face and the desire that had rippled across his taut features when he'd pulled back from their kiss. Then her sight cleared, and she stopped with a gasp and glanced around at the utter destruction that met her.

Every single one of her precious plants had been ripped from the ground, roots and all. Zinnias and marigolds, impatiens and geraniums, even her parsley and thyme. They'd been snapped, shredded, and trampled so that all that was left of her beautiful garden were piles of debris. Every remaining greenery and even those that had faded had been viciously uprooted and sliced. Nothing salvageable remained.

A cry slipped from her lips. Overwhelmed, she dropped to her knees.

"What in the name of all that's holy," Ryan muttered. He was at her side in an instant, kneeling next to her, concern crinkling his brow.

"My garden," she whispered, reaching for the bulb of one of her rare lily plants. It was mashed into a dangling pulp.

Ryan slipped his arm around her waist, solidly supporting her and keeping her from crumpling altogether. Somehow even amidst the mindless destruction that sprawled before her, his simple act of comfort stopped the hysteria that was cutting off her airway.

She sagged against him and allowed his weight to support her.

"It looks like a tornado came through," he said solemnly.

She reached for another plant, or what was left of the shredded roots. She brushed the damp soil away to reveal the white interior that had obviously seen the sharp slice of a knife blade. "This was no accident."

"Who could have done it?" Ryan asked, his expression mirroring disbelief. "And why would anyone want to?"

She stared at the years of loving labor ruined in one fell swoop. Ryan's question echoed in her mind. *Who would have done such a thing?*

She looked up to Sarah's window and was relieved to see the curtain still pulled. Her sister hadn't witnessed the devastation.

"Caroline." Ryan turned her so that she faced him. His brows came together, and worry darkened his eyes. "We need to find out who did this."

She nodded but couldn't speak past the grief clogging her throat.

"Do you think the twins did it? As a practical joke?"

She shook her head. Harry and Hugh were mischievous, but they'd never destroy her garden so thoughtlessly. Would they? What if they'd come out in the early morning before breakfast and thought to play a game of sorts?

"No," she whispered. "They couldn't have done this." At least she wanted to believe Harry and Hugh weren't becoming so wild and undisciplined that they'd resorted to violence. But the guilty voice at the back of her mind whispered again that they'd been deprived of the supervision they needed since before her father died.

Ryan's grip on her upper arm tightened. "What about enemies? Have you made any enemies?"

She wanted to blurt out that of course she didn't have enemies, but at the thought of Mr. Finick, she blanched. Had he heard that she was staying on as an assistant? Had he sent someone out to the light to threaten her into leaving?

Her attention shifted to the north woods, to the direction of the old windmill and where Jacques Poupard lived. Had the old Frenchman finally gotten tired of the twins' antics? Had he decided to repay them for all the trouble the boys had been to him?

She didn't want to believe Monsieur Poupard would resort to such destruction, especially since he'd been the one to alert her when Hugh had nearly drowned in the well. He might be grumpy, but he wasn't mean-spirited.

"Think about who might want to do this to you," Ryan added.

What about Mr. Simmons? He'd never liked Father. Maybe he'd heard she was staying. But what harm was her presence at the light doing him? Last night his supply boat had unloaded goods under the cover of darkness along a smooth stretch of beach just south of the lighthouse—most likely illegal goods. Part of her wanted to alert the authorities. But she didn't want to stir up any unnecessary strife with Mr. Simmons, not now with her job so tentative.

She looked Ryan in the eyes and saw the worry there. "I don't know."

Even if she had unknown enemies, she had no idea why any of them would want to ruin her garden. It made no sense.

A breeze rippled under her shawl, sending a chill over her skin. She tugged the knitted wrap closer to her shoulders. But the chill penetrated under her flesh all the way to her heart.

All she could do was sit in helpless despair and stare at the ravaged garden while her soul wept.

Chapter 11

Ryan swallowed the last bitter mouthful of the rum Simmons had generously poured him. He plunked the glass down on the bar and then pushed back.

"You're not going yet, are you?" Behind the bar, Simmons paused in wiping a beer glass. The giant's bald head glowed in the dim lighting of the tavern.

Ryan nodded, guilt pouring in his gut and sloshing there like sour whiskey. He hadn't planned on staying at all. In fact, he hadn't really wanted to come here in the first place.

But his empty flask had taunted him mercilessly until his thirst had driven him from the boathouse. He'd saddled his horse, telling himself he was only going for a ride to distract himself. But his horse had ended up at the Roadside Inn, and once there, Ryan hadn't been able to resist going inside.

Simmons had gladly filled up his flask, then poured him a glass without even asking. Soon one drink had turned into two.

"You need another shot before you go," Simmons said, lifting the decanter and tipping it toward Ryan's abandoned glass.

"Nay," Ryan protested.

Even though the warm rum was moving through his veins and dulling his aches, it wasn't taking away the guilt. It only seemed to magnify it, until his head was pounding, not with pain but from the need to get away from the tavern.

Ryan pulled the last of his coins from his pocket and dropped them onto the bar with a rattle.

Simmons waved the money away just as he had during the last couple of visits. "Drinks are on me, Chambers."

Ryan pushed the coins back toward Simmons. "I'll not be indebted—"

With a guffaw, Simmons cut him off. "You're my friend. And as I told you before, I'm always kind to my friends."

Ryan didn't quite understand how he was Simmons's friend. But he wasn't about to question the man's sincerity.

"Take it," Simmons said again in his smooth voice that belied the tattoos covering his arms from his wrists to the rolled-up sleeves that hugged his bulging biceps. "It's my way of saying thanks for being such a good keeper."

"Then thank you," Ryan said, ducking his head to hide the shame he felt. He wasn't a good keeper. Aye, he'd made it up to the tower again that morning, and this time Caroline had let him complete the duties of extinguishing the light while she only looked on and offered him a few tips now and then. But that didn't make him a good keeper, not when Caroline was still handling the majority of the work while he drank the days and nights away.

He started to back away from the bar. The inn was more crowded than the last time he'd been here. The tables were full, and the laughter and smoke swirled around him, jeering at him and reminding him that he didn't belong in such a place. He never had.

His shame only rose higher, searing his chest, until he knew he couldn't remain silent. Simmons had turned away to pour a drink for another customer, but Ryan addressed him anyway. "If anyone deserves praise for being a good keeper, it ought to go to Caroline Taylor."

Through a crescendo of raucous laughter, Ryan couldn't be sure if Simmons had heard him. For a long moment the giant didn't acknowledge Ryan's comment but merely corked the flask and placed it back among the collection of bottles on the shelf.

Simmons finally shot Ryan a look, his eyes hard. "The only place for that headstrong girl is in my son's bed."

Ryan glanced to the broom standing abandoned in the corner. He hadn't seen Arnie since he'd arrived, and he'd been somewhat relieved. He knew if he saw the young man, he'd have to tell him to stop pestering Caroline to marry him.

"I agree with Finick one hundred percent," Simmons said, leaning over the bar toward Ryan. "Let men do men's work. And keep the women in the home."

Ryan scrambled to find a response, but all his thoughts swam together in a murky puddle. He'd always held the belief that women shouldn't do men's work, that as a man it was his duty to take care of and protect women and children. But Caroline was as good at light keeping as his brother-in-law, Patrick Garraty. If she enjoyed it and wanted to do it, why should anyone deny her the opportunity simply because of her gender?

The tavern door opened, letting in a stream of sunlight that made Ryan blink. Along with the sunlight came a chorus of shouts.

At the ruckus outside, Simmons banged a fist against the bar, causing the glasses to clink together. He uttered several oaths under his breath, then with quick, thudding steps rounded the bar and elbowed his way through the tavern toward the door.

Ryan pulled the brim of his hat lower and started after Simmons, careful to avoid any jostling against his injured arm. He wanted to get back to the lighthouse before Caroline noticed he'd left. But he doubted that would happen now, and he dreaded facing her questions about where he'd been.

Not that she'd ask. He'd learned that she wasn't one to pry.

Even so, with each passing day he realized he coveted her respect, and he hoped she wouldn't be able to smell the cigar smoke on his clothes or the rum on his breath when he returned.

She'd been in a state of mourning since she'd come upon her ruined garden yesterday. Afterward, he'd spent the morning helping her clear away the rubbish and burn the slashings. Every time he'd glimpsed her stricken, pale face, his resolve to find the perpetrator had grown.

Of course, the pain in his arm from all the activity had sent him to the boathouse even earlier than usual to his pills and whiskey. He hadn't had the chance to question the twins yet. Caroline said they claimed innocence, but Ryan wanted the opportunity to look them in the eyes and find out for himself.

As Ryan pushed his way out the tavern door, he almost bumped into Simmons, who'd parked his bulky frame only a step from the door. He was shouting curses at a group of people who'd assembled on the dirt road in front of the hitching posts.

They held signs on sticks, pumped them in the air, and called out, "Stop cruelty to animals! Outlaw cockfighting!"

"Get out of here. Now!" Simmons shouted, raising a fist.

"Call off the cockfight for tonight and we'll leave," yelled a plump-looking woman in the front of the group. She was shorter than the others in the gathering, which Ryan noticed was mostly made up of women.

"Go home, woman!" Simmons shouted. "Before I ride out and find your husband and tell him you're disturbing the peace again."

"You know he'd be out here protesting with me if he were home," the woman called back. She stepped forward away from the others, the obvious leader of the group.

It was then that he caught sight of Caroline's face. She'd been tucked out of sight at the back of the group. She slouched her shoulders, lowered her head, and kept her sign lower than anyone else.

Ryan tipped his hat up. What was she doing among the rabble-rousers?

She glanced up under the brim of her bonnet. Her beautiful blue eyes connected with his. At the sight of him, she straightened and her eyes widened.

Guilt came roaring back, and he took a quick step back, wanting to disappear inside the tavern. But he knew it wouldn't do any good now. She'd seen him, and there was no use pretending otherwise. If she hadn't known before, now she'd know exactly just how low he'd sunk.

He waited for the disappointment to register in her eyes, but at another shout from Simmons, she lowered her head again.

Was she afraid of the man? Of what he'd do to her if he saw her there in the crowd of protestors?

Blue veins bulged in the back of Simmons's neck above his shirt collar. Ryan had the feeling the giant wasn't the kind of man anyone wanted for an enemy.

Simmons yelled a string of profanities. "If you don't get out of here, I'll be sending you home with my fists! I don't care if you are a bunch of women, I won't be afraid to give you the discipline your husbands are neglecting."

At that, Ryan started past Simmons. He wouldn't stand back and let Caroline get punched around. He slipped around the hitching posts and pushed aside the gathering until he stood in front of her. She didn't look up at him but instead stared down at her boots.

Then the protests faded as a dozen pairs of eyes burned into him, including those of Simmons.

"I'll take you home now, Caroline," he offered.

"Is that the lightkeeper girl?" Simmons called.

Ryan held out the crook of his arm, and he was relieved when she didn't hesitate to hook her hand into the fold and allow him to lead her toward his horse.

"That's right." Simmons's voice followed them. "Get her on out of here. Unless of course she's here to marry Arnie."

"Let's go," Ryan said under his breath. "You're not marrying Arnie."

"You can't go now, Caroline," said the round woman leading the protest. "We're just getting started."

Caroline glanced apologetically over her shoulder. "I'm sorry, Esther. I need to go."

Esther pursed her lips together as if she wished to say more, but thankfully she'd didn't object further.

He assisted Caroline up onto his horse, helping her get comfortable sitting sideways before hoisting himself behind her. His good arm strained under the effort, yet the moment he was situated he forgot about everything but her soft body in front of him.

He had to lean into her to grab the reins. She turned rigid momentarily, but once he straightened again, he could feel her relax.

The crowd had resumed their protests, Esther the loudest of all, drowning out Simmons's curses. Ryan urged the horse into a trot down Big Marsh Road, which led out to Windmill Point. After several minutes the shouts faded, replaced by the crunching sound of hooves pushing through the dry leaves that had already begun to fall.

He glanced at the profile of Caroline's cheek and neck, the smooth stretch of skin teased by strands of hair that had come loose from her bonnet. He wished he could read her emotions and know what she was thinking. He wanted her to speak her piece and get the lecture over. Instead they rode in silence.

Finally after several moments, he cleared his throat. "I'm sorry, Caroline." He wasn't exactly sure what he was apologizing for—maybe for drinking or for being at the tavern or for any other of his innumerable sins.

"You don't need to apologize to me," she said gently, turning slightly so that he could see more of her face. Her expression was sad but resigned.

Had he put the sadness there? The thought sent a shard into his heart. The last thing he wanted to do was add to her despondency. "I shouldn't have gone to the tavern."

She didn't deny it, but her fingers closed around his on the reins. And when she squeezed, the pressure went deep and soaked into him. He drew a deep breath, and it was like getting a fresh gasp of air for the first time in years. A sense of purpose surged through him, something he thought he'd never feel again.

His throat clogged with emotion, and he was overwhelmed with gratefulness for this woman sitting in front of him. She was unlike anyone he'd ever met. She hadn't condemned or judged him. Instead she seemed to understand what he was going through, even though he hadn't shared the awful truth with her.

He turned his palm over and threaded his fingers through hers.

Her gaze flitted down to the intimate hold. When she didn't protest, he laced his fingers tighter, sliding their hands together. Then at the jostle of the horse, her body sagged against his chest as if she'd finally given up the effort to hold herself away from him. He tilted his head, breathing in the flowery scent that he'd recognized belonged to her.

The smoothness of her neck stretched before him. Another tiny bend forward and his lips would touch the soft skin that beckoned him.

He thought of the kiss they'd shared yesterday morning, of the eager way she'd responded. He hadn't intended to kiss her. And ever since, he'd felt uneasy about taking advantage of her that way. He could have made his point without being so brash.

But now he couldn't stop from wanting to twist her around in the saddle and kiss her again.

He swallowed hard. He couldn't. He respected her too much to use her for his own pleasures.

"I'm sorry for kissing you yesterday," he whispered.

"You are?" She tilted her head, giving him full access to her neck.

He looked away from the temptation and had to swallow his desire again. "I shouldn't have kissed you without your permission. Will you forgive me?"

She hesitated. "There's no need to forgive you, Ryan," she finally said. "It didn't offend me."

He breathed out his relief, and a smile spread across his lips. "Since it didn't offend you," he said against her ear, "then maybe I'll kiss you again sometime." Her soft gasp made his smile creep higher. "But next time I'll ask you first."

She chewed her lower lip and stared at their hands intertwined together and resting against her leg.

They were passing through the last grove of cedars and willows. A marsh was all that separated them from the lighthouse. In the distance he could see the twins beyond the tower near the water's edge. Tessa's dark head was bent close to theirs, and they were examining something.

He slowed the horse, not ready for his time with Caroline to come to an end, to be interrupted by the busyness of others needing her attention.

Was it possible that a woman could ever care for him? He hadn't believed anyone could. Not when he was maimed and only half the man he used to be. Not with all the ghosts that still haunted him.

Caroline turned in the saddle and offered him a smile that at the very least offered friendship. It sent warmth into his bruised and battered soul. He smiled in return, surprised at the strange sense of happiness that covered him like a healing balm.

A few women had been sweet on him before the war. One had even sent him a couple of letters after he'd joined the army. But he soon gave up all thoughts of being in a relationship. He hadn't figured there was any use holding out hope, not when death stalked his regiment day and night.

"Caroline!" called one of the boys. He'd risen to his tiptoes and was waving at her with both arms. "Come quick!"

There was an urgency in the boy's tone that made Ryan tense at the same time Caroline sat forward.

"Something's wrong," she said.

He could sense it too.

When Tessa straightened and he caught sight of the revulsion on her face, his gut knotted. He kicked the horse into a trot, closing the distance to the beach.

When he reined the horse next to her siblings, Caroline was already sliding off. "Is everyone all right?" she asked breathlessly. "Sarah?"

Tessa touched Caroline's arm in a reassuring gesture. "Sarah's fine."

The pinched muscles in Caroline's neck relaxed. "Then what's wrong?"

Ryan slid off the horse and stood next to her.

The twins were barefoot, their trousers damp up to the knees with sand coating their hands and cheeks. Though it still wasn't easy to be around them because of the memories they invoked of the boy that haunted Ryan's dreams, he'd been able to endure their presence more each day.

Harry, especially, seemed to want to be with him whenever they were home. There had been times when he'd caught the boys peeking in the boathouse window at him while he was in one of his stupors. He'd been embarrassed that they'd seen him that way and had wanted to distance himself from them all the more.

He didn't want to set a bad example for them. In fact, he ought to be showing them how to handle pain and disappointment like a man, instead of like the weak coward he'd become. But he wasn't sure he remembered how to be strong anymore.

Tessa gave a visible shudder and then hugged her arms across her chest. "The boys found something nailed to a log when they got home from school."

"Nailed to a log?" Caroline's eyes swept over the rocky shore, the leaves floating on the water, and the rising smoke of a distant passing steamer. "What was it?"

Tessa stepped aside at the same time as the boys, and there on the ground, nailed to a piece of driftwood, was a goldeneye duck. Its wings were outstretched with nails embedded through each one. Even more gruesome was the nail that punctured the duck's head through one of its bright golden eyes.

At the bloody sight, Caroline gasped and jumped back.

Ryan reached for her arm to keep her from falling.

"Who did this?" She scanned the house, the tower, and then the woods beyond as if she expected someone or something to appear.

"We think it drifted here," Harry said, looking up at Ryan with blue eyes so much like Caroline's. "We waded out and looked for more evidence, but we didn't find anything."

Ryan studied the duck. The blood oozing from the wounds was too fresh for the log to have drifted a long distance. Whoever had done this lived nearby. But why would anyone kill a duck by nailing it to a log?

Caroline shuddered against him. He steered her toward Tessa. "You ladies go on up to the house. The boys and I will take care of burning it."

Tessa grasped Caroline's hands, and then huddling together the two began walking toward the cottage.

Caroline stopped and looked back at him. "Who would do this, Ryan? What kind of person could hurt something so cruelly? It's such a waste."

Ryan nodded. He had a dozen answers for her. He'd seen cruelty beyond measure during the war. And unthinkable waste. As much as he wanted to deny it, he'd even been a part of some of it. Yet all he could say was, "I don't know."

And all he could do was pray that whoever was behind the tortured duck wasn't the person who'd been responsible for destroying Caroline's garden.

Chapter 12

Ryan leaned against the stern of the old canoe. He unplugged the cork from his whiskey bottle, the pop and the swish whetting his parched tongue.

At a scuffle against the side of the boathouse, he looked to the cracked window in the back wall. Two pairs of eyes peered through grimy glass, watching his every move. Seeing that they'd been spotted, the twins quickly disappeared from sight.

Ryan put the cork back into the bottle and stuffed it into its hiding spot behind a tackle box. He straightened and ran his fingers through his overlong hair, wanting to ignore the guilt that barraged him like gunfire. But somehow that morning, he couldn't keep it at bay.

Ever since yesterday and the ride home from the tavern with Caroline, the shame over having the whiskey had grown heavier with each passing hour. Of course, Caroline hadn't said anything about it. She hadn't asked why he'd gone to the tavern. She hadn't admonished him to stop drinking. She hadn't even looked at him with disapproval, although he'd certainly deserved it.

Instead she'd welcomed him with a warm smile that morning

when he ascended the tower to turn off the light. Aye, she'd been subdued, obviously still shaken from the sight of the duck nailed to the log. However, she'd only been encouraging as he completed the keeper tasks, instructing him on how to manage the logbook. Through all the conversations they'd had that morning, she never once issued him a single rebuke.

Tessa had passed him a plate of breakfast and cup of coffee on his way down the tower as she'd begun to do each morning. He'd retreated to the boathouse to eat. And drink, as had become his habit.

Except that most mornings the twins weren't there watching him. They were away at school.

He expelled a long sigh and glanced out the half-open door. Why were they home? He calculated the passing of days and realized it was Saturday, that they likely didn't have school today. That meant he'd been at the lighthouse almost a full week, which was the longest he'd been anywhere since the end of the war.

The ping of an ax against wood told him that Caroline had set the boys to chopping wood. He listened for a long moment, and the sound soothed his muscles and reminded him of the summer he'd chopped cordwood at Burnham's Landing in Presque Isle, the time he and his sister had been stranded after their steamboat had been robbed and set afire by pirates.

He'd chopped more wood that summer than any one man likely did in his entire life. But it had been wholesome hard work, and he looked back on his time at Burnham's Landing with fondness.

Could he still swing an ax?

He flexed his injured arm and waited for the usual piercing pain. It came, and he had to grit his teeth. Even if he put his good arm behind the weight of swinging the ax, the movement was sure to jar his injury.

Maybe if he used the feverfew leaves Caroline had given him, he'd be able to dull the pain. He'd been surprised that she managed to find anything useful among the wreck of her garden. But she set aside a number of plants and salvaged what she could.

He rummaged around for the leaves, and his fingers brushed against the driftwood cross next to his bedroll. His sister, Emma, had given him the cross when he'd stayed at the Presque Isle Lighthouse. The letter that went with the cross was folded up and tucked safely away in his satchel. He hadn't read the letter in years, but he'd never forgotten the beautiful tale of love and loss that it contained.

Emma had meant for the cross to bring him hope, as it had to her and as it had to the original owner. He'd carried it with him during the war in his bag. It had gone everywhere with him. And even though he cherished the gift, he'd long since decided he was past hope.

He chewed several of the bitter feverfew leaves and then stepped out of the boathouse into a cloudy fall morning. At his approach, Harold and Hugh stopped swinging their axes and hung their heads, obviously waiting for his admonition regarding their spying on him.

He stopped several feet away and stood before them without speaking, letting them squirm. They were in need of some censure. Although he could see that Caroline and Tessa did all they could to care for the boys, there was nothing like the presence of a man to keep young ones in line.

Harry finally peeked up at him. The wide-eyed innocence wrenched Ryan and pulled him into the past. A pale face flashed before him. Lifeless eyes stared up at him, accusing him of standing by and doing nothing.

Ryan blinked and tried to block out the memory. He couldn't do anything to bring that other boy back to life. And he could never repay the remaining family for the loss of their son. But he could pay them for the destruction of their home and all that his regiment had stolen. He'd determined to save up enough to cover the damages. When he'd done so, he'd return and give it to the family and tell them he was sorry for his part in that fateful night.

Nay, he couldn't bring their boy back to life. Yet perhaps he could have a hand in shaping Harry's and Hugh's lives for the good. Perhaps he could influence them to be wise and steady and level-headed. Investing in them would be one more way he could atone for his past mistakes.

He reached for a log and propped it upright. "You're doing a fine job, lads," he said, positioning the wood. "Now, if you bring the blade down in the middle, right about here"—he pointed to the log's center ring—"you'll have a much easier and cleaner cut."

The boys both raised their heads and drew closer. The respect and interest on their faces sent renewed energy pumping into his limbs. He reached for Harry's ax, and the boy relinquished it without a word. He simply stood back and watched.

Ryan was about to stuff his injured hand deeper into his pocket, then decided against it and forced himself to grip the ax handle with both hands. He tried to ignore the boys' stares fixed on his mangled hand, even though everything within him screamed to stuff it back into his pocket.

He focused instead on the grain of the wood beneath his grip. It felt right, like a welcome home. He studied the rings of the log, and then he lifted his arms and swung.

The axhead hit the target and the wood fell away in a clean split. The impact sent pain radiating up his injured arm, but surprisingly it wasn't the torture he'd expected.

He propped up one of the halves, steadied it, and brought the ax down again. This time the pleasure of the clean slice drowned out the pain ricocheting in his body. When he glanced up to see admiration shining in the twins' eyes, he forgot about his injury altogether.

Caroline stared out the window at the fading afternoon.

Ryan brought the ax down effortlessly, his muscles rippling across his sweat-drenched shirt.

The splashing of water behind her drew her attention back to the kitchen, to the large tub where Hugh was finishing his bath.

"Guess me and Harry won't need to chop any more wood this fall," Hugh said as he soaped his arms. "Mr. Chambers has chopped enough to last us through the winter, hasn't he?"

"Looks that way," Caroline said, unable to remind Hugh that it didn't matter how much wood they had, because they probably wouldn't be here that winter to use it.

Ryan had been chopping all day. Or at least that was what the boys had claimed when she awoke to the sight of him wielding the ax. He'd taken several breaks since she started watching him, and she could see that he was growing slower, obviously tired.

Nevertheless, a thrill had wound through her at the thought that he'd found something he could do, something to occupy his time and take his mind off his pain. Perhaps the hard work and the purpose it gave him was the medicine he needed.

She just hoped he hadn't overdone it, that he wouldn't cause his injury more agony as a result of the activity. Maybe it would help if he soaked in a tub of heated water, and if she gave him some of her birchbark tea? She could even make him a hot onion poultice to press onto his arm. . . .

"Harry," she called to the boy on the couch, who sat pulling his socks on over still-wet feet. "Run out and tell Mr. Chambers I'll have a hot bath waiting for him."

Harry jumped up and started for the door.

"Shoes first, please."

Her command halted him at the door. His shoulders slumped as he shuffled back to his discarded shoes lying nearby.

While she heated more water, made the tea, and cleaned up the puddles left from the twins, her thoughts strayed to the ride home from the Roadside Inn the previous afternoon, to the way Ryan had held her hand. It had been much more than a friendly grasp. His fingers had intertwined with hers . . . intimately. His breath had been so warm and near her neck. And his solid chest had pressed into her back.

She drew in a breath and fanned her face with the edge of her apron. The crispy scent of the roasted chicken Tessa was baking for dinner mingled with the sweet cinnamon of the apple pie cooling on the table. Even with the tantalizing aromas around her, Caroline had no appetite. She couldn't think of eating, not when she was so full of thoughts of Ryan. The kiss he'd given her a couple of days ago had been enough to make her forget about food. But now, after holding her hand and telling her that maybe he'd kiss her again sometime, her belly was tied into knots all too often.

Had she really told him she hadn't been offended that he'd kissed her? She smiled. She couldn't believe she'd been so bold.

"Caroline?" His voice startled her.

He filled the doorframe, his hair plastered to his forehead, with streaks of dust making his face look more rugged. He cocked his head and regarded her with curiosity.

She busied herself by picking up a damp towel and draping it over the back of the chair, praying he hadn't been able to read her thoughts. She shouldn't have been thinking of him so intimately. He needed her help and friendship right now, nothing more. "The water for your bath is almost ready. And there's a mug of birchbark tea for you in the warmer."

"Thank you." He stepped into the room hesitantly.

"I'll make sure everyone stays out of the kitchen so that you can have some privacy." Her insides flamed at the idea that in a few moments he'd shed his clothes and be completely bare . . . in her house. "I think they're all busy in Sarah's room," she said hurriedly, hoping to cover her embarrassment. "Tessa likes to involve the boys in performing plays for her."

The happy chatter coming from down the hall brought a smile to her face. In all the hardships over the past months, at least they still had each other. So long as she kept them all together, they'd be fine.

With a rag she lifted the bubbling pot from the stove and poured hot water into the tepid bathwater that remained in the tub. The steam swooshed up and dampened her face.

Ryan looked eagerly at the steaming water. "It's been a while since I've had a hot bath."

"Well, best get in before it loses the heat." She couldn't resist one more peek at his broad chest outlined beneath his shirt.

He snapped a suspender off his shoulder, and the motion sent her scurrying to leave the kitchen, to closet herself in Sarah's room until he was done.

"Caroline, wait," his soft call chased her.

She paused and pressed a hand against the thudding in her chest.

"I was wrong to go to the tavern."

"You already admitted that on the way home."

His face was lined with earnestness. "I need to stop . . ."

She waited for him to finish, but when he didn't say anything more, she nodded. "You will."

Her simple statement seemed to lift his shoulders back up. "My dad drank himself to death," he continued, slipping off his other suspender. "He let the guilt and shame of his past drive him to the bottle instead of to his knees."

She pondered his revelation for a moment, searching for a way to respond. Finally she said, "My father always said that our enemy, the devil, is doing his best to get us to look to everything and everyone else to save us from our pains and sorrows. The devil doesn't want us to take those pains to the Lord, because he knows that when we cry out to God with our need, He'll rescue us from the pit."

Ryan's head cocked, and his brow crinkled.

She hadn't meant to preach to him. She was the last one who ought to be preaching, considering how often she let her worries control her. "Take your time with the bath," she said, spinning around. "The hot soaking will do you good."

"Should I call you when I need my back scrubbed?"

His voice was so serious, it stopped her. She couldn't resist turning and looking at him. He was in the process of tugging off his socks. She was too shocked by his request to speak. The mere thought of being in the same room with him bathing was scandalous. She was already asking for local gossip by living on the same premises with an unmarried man. But scrub his back?

He tossed her a grin and then winked.

She steadied herself, forcing calmness on her outside that belied what was happening on the inside. "Oh, sure. And maybe after I'm done scrubbing your back, I can do your feet too."

He burst into laughter.

She spun to hide a grin and the embarrassment that likely infused her face.

Her humor faded at the stark reality of the situation. What was she doing flirting with him? He was a sick man, a man who needed to face his inner demons before he'd ever be whole enough or ready enough for anything beyond friendship.

Even so, the pleasure in his laughter embraced her. And she knew she wanted to hear it again. Very soon.

Chapter 13

Caroline raised the chimney holder close to the surface of the burner. While the evening provided some light still, she didn't need it. She'd lit the lantern often enough that she could do it in the dark if need be.

"Caroline?" came Ryan's voice from the hatch.

Surprised, she craned her neck to watch him ascend.

After his bath, she'd invited him to join them for dinner. She'd only eaten a couple of bites before pushing back from the table. With Ryan sitting across from her, his damp hair combed neatly and his brown eyes melting her with every glance, she hadn't been able to manage much.

She'd used the excuse that she needed to light the lantern, which was true. But more than that, she couldn't stop looking at Ryan, and she was sure she would embarrass herself if she stayed any longer.

Of course, Tessa's face had lit up when Ryan joined them, and she'd smiled and flirted with him. But Caroline hadn't the heart to admonish her sister. How could she rebuke Tessa for something she herself was doing?

And who could blame them? They'd had so little contact with young men during the war, and now that one was practically living on their doorstep—especially one as appealing as Ryan—it was hard to resist the pull to banter with him.

At least that was what she'd told herself after another incident of joking with him before dinner when they'd all sat in Sarah's room and watched the twins do a mock sword fight. Surely a little friendly teasing wouldn't hurt anyone.

"Since I'm awake for once," Ryan said, climbing into the room, "I thought I better take advantage of the opportunity to watch how you light the lantern."

"You can't miss out on Tessa's chicken dinner."

"You weren't eating it," he said, his tone hinting at playfulness, "so I figured something must be wrong with it."

She smiled at him and then turned her attention back to the lantern. "The chicken was one of the losers of last night's cockfight."

Ryan's brow shot up. He wore a clean shirt, one of her father's. He'd gladly taken the offer to put on something besides his sweaty shirt. And now in the heavy flannel of black and gray, his eyes were darker and more enticing than before.

"Most Saturdays, Arnie brings us one of the mutilated chickens that died in the fighting."

"I didn't see him around today." Ryan stepped nearer so that she caught a whiff of his clean, soapy scent.

"He's like that sometimes," she said. "He's here one minute and gone the next. I rarely see him coming or going." Especially when he delivered his gifts. She'd supposed he wanted to do the giving anonymously.

"I'm surprised you take the chickens. I thought you'd oppose eating them. As a statement of protest." Ryan's voice was tinged with humor.

"I am opposed to the cockfighting," she said, rising in defense of herself and the demonstration Esther had staged on Friday afternoon before the usual weekend cockfights. "It's cruel to allow animals to hack each other apart until one of them dies."

"I agree," Ryan said. "But some people consider it a sport. It's been going on for thousands of years. I don't think there's much you or anyone else can do to stop Simmons from having his cockfighting."

"Slavery had been going on for thousands of years too, and we just stopped that, didn't we? At least here in our country?"

In the fading light of the tower, his eyes reflected admiration for her response.

"There are a lot of people who would like to see cockfighting made illegal," she continued. "Mr. Simmons has received enough protests from groups in Detroit that he's had to resort to bringing in his supplies across Lake St. Clair from Canada."

Together, she and Ryan peered out at the lake. In some spots to the south, the opposite shore—the Canadian side of the lake—was visible on clear days.

Caroline didn't consider herself the protesting type of person, not like Esther. She was especially uncomfortable whenever Esther had one of her rallies at the inn. She didn't want Mr. Simmons to get angry at her and to start making threats like he'd done to her father.

Maybe Esther could afford to be daring since her husband and father's status as politicians protected her. But Caroline had her family to think about. And she dreaded what Mr. Simmons was capable of doing if he became angry enough with her. Even so, she couldn't resist Esther's passion for her causes. Her dear friend always had a way of pulling her in.

Ryan had drawn closer, and she could see the weariness in

his eyes. Even with the hot bath and birchbark tea, she had a feeling unbearable pain would soon catch up to him.

"I think I may have overdone it today," he said with a weak smile.

"Do you think so?" she teased.

His smile inched higher. "I guess I was relieved I could finally do something without failing." He stood an arm's length away, his hand stuffed in his pocket like usual.

His vulnerability squeezed her heart. "I know eventually you'll do many things without failing."

He didn't respond, but his eyes softened and seemed to reach out and caress her.

Her stomach fluttered to life. She half expected him to follow up with a real caress, but he didn't move. Why did she always act like a love-starved old maid whenever she was around Ryan? She didn't want him to think she was desperate for a man's attention.

She pivoted to face the lantern. "We better get to work before it grows any darker."

As she explained the steps for lighting the lantern, she was acutely aware of his nearness. Even after dusk had fallen and the beam was rotating with its pattern of six flashes per minute, her body was attuned to his every move. It wasn't until he wearily descended a short while later that she was finally able to breathe normally.

⌘

The next morning, when Ryan didn't arrive to help her turn off the lantern, she tried not to be disappointed. Even with his good intentions, she had no doubt he was addicted to the pain medicine. And even if he hadn't needed it last night—which she was sure he did after the day of splitting wood—his body still craved it.

After she came home from church with the twins, she hoped he would be awake. But a peek into the boathouse showed that he was still sprawled out on his bedroll.

He awoke in the late afternoon and came sheepishly up to the house, clearly embarrassed at having slept for so long. She welcomed him with a smile and invited him in to sit with Sarah and watch the play that Tessa and the twins were performing for their sister again.

She wasn't surprised that evening when he accompanied her up into the tower and watched her light the lantern. His expression was warm and his attention undivided, making her self-conscious.

He stayed longer than the previous evening, but eventually he left, the hungry craving and pain in his eyes telling her that he was headed back to his pills.

"Patience," she whispered to herself the following day as she creaked open the wooden plank door to the root cellar. Cool mustiness greeted her, along with the earthiness of the onions and potatoes she'd stored there.

"Healing takes time," she whispered into the darkness of the small cellar her father had dug out of a hill on the opposite side of the garden. The shade of the poplar and the thickness of the soil had made it an ideal spot for a cellar, even if it was a chore to trudge to it in the wintertime.

She hoisted a basket of apples into the black interior and then crunched back through the fallen leaves to retrieve the second basket she'd left beneath the lone apple tree that sat a distance from the house.

"He's made progress," she reminded herself as she picked

up the remaining basket. She propped it on her hip and started back across the long grass, breathing in the tanginess of the apples that had already fermented on the ground.

She wasn't sure why she was going to the trouble of collecting apples when she ought to have walked into town instead of Tessa and continued her search for work and lodging. But with each day they stayed, she was finding it more difficult to plan for the future. It was all too easy to pretend that Mr. Finick hadn't ordered her to leave and to just continue on as she had before.

The cloudy sky overhead threatened rain, and as a few fat drops fell she picked up her pace.

Besides, Ryan needed her. Didn't he? He wasn't capable yet of taking over the keeper duties. In fact, she wasn't sure that he'd be ready for a while.

A flash of red in the woods beyond halted her footsteps. She stared through the golden foliage with a shiver creeping up her spine, the memory of the duck nailed to the log all too fresh. The wind rustled through the grass and the dry leaves. The call of a distant goose echoed faintly.

Perhaps she'd only imagined the red. Or maybe it was only Monsieur Poupard out hunting, she told herself. He often wore a red flannel coat when roaming about the woods. Still, as she crossed the span to the cellar, her nerves prickled with the thought that someone was watching her.

As she entered the cellar, she lowered the basket and released a breath. She was letting her imagination get the best of her. She couldn't let her worry turn wild.

"This is quite the cellar." At the voice from within the dirt hole, Caroline jumped.

It took her a moment to realize the voice belonged to Ryan and that while she'd been away, he'd crawled inside the cellar.

"Where would you like me to put the apples?" he asked.

She pushed her load of apples ahead of her and followed behind it. Through the darkness she could make out Ryan's crouched frame.

"You scared me." Her voice was muted by the dirt walls. "I didn't expect you to be in here."

"Now I know where to go whenever I'm hungry. No wonder you were hiding this cellar from me."

Ducking low, she sat back on her heels and smiled at his easy way of relating. He was a lighthearted man when he was sober and not consumed with memories of his past.

"Of course, I wasn't about to reveal our treasure house," she countered, "not when it holds my secret stash of sweet potatoes."

The hillside cellar was hardly big enough for the two of them, along with the baskets of apples and other vegetables she'd stored. But instead of feeling crowded, a comfortable coziness settled over her.

Outside, more raindrops pattered the ground while the wind rattled the cellar door, threatening to close it.

She reached inside the basket of apples and found one that was smooth to the touch. "Here." She held it out to him. "You might as well enjoy an apple while it's still fresh. In a couple months they'll be soft and shriveled."

He took it, his fingers brushing against hers, not immediately moving away. In the dim light coming in from the open door, she could see that his expression was grateful. "You're much kinder to me than I deserve," he said, so softly that she almost didn't hear him.

"Anyone else would do the same thing," she replied, knowing he was referring to much more than just the apple.

"I don't think so. You brim with a compassion most people don't have. I can see now why Arnie likes you as much as he does."

Even as a cool gust swept into the cramped space, warmth swirled around her.

Ryan sat back, and the dark shadows hid his face. At the juicy crunch of his bite into the apple, she smiled. "You're rather likable too, you know."

"Am I now?" His Irish brogue rolled off his tongue. "And just how likable am I to the young lady?"

She busied herself with finding another smooth apple, hoping to hide the embarrassment of admitting she liked him.

"I suppose it's my charm and good looks that have won you over? Aye?" he teased.

"No. It's more the sweat from chopping wood that did it."

He chuckled, the low rumbling making her smile widen. He took another bite of the apple, and her fingers finally found a small one for herself.

"Since I've cut enough wood to last ten winters, I ought to move on to something else," he said. "I was thinking I could start making repairs to the tower and then give it a fresh coat of paint."

"The tower is in sore need of repairs and a painting," she agreed. "I'd hoped to do it myself this fall to protect the stone before another winter wears it away, but I just haven't had the time."

"If you show me what to do, I'll start today."

"I'd love to." She quickly bit into her apple to cover her eagerness.

At the slam of the door closing behind her, she nearly dropped her apple. Complete darkness descended, except for a thin crack between the floor and the bottom of the door.

"The wind must be picking up," she said. "Maybe we'll have to wait on tower repairs until later." She didn't like the idea of anyone being up on a ladder with the wind gusting.

A scraping against the outside plank of the door made her shudder. Every time they had rain and wind, her memory opened up with the heartbreaking image of her father clinging tenaciously to the boat, the wind and the waves lashing against him, weakening his hold and pulling him under.

Her chest tightened. The air in the cellar felt damp and stifling. She pushed at the door, needing to get back into the light and to fill her lungs with a fresh breath.

The door didn't budge.

She shoved harder. Still it didn't move.

"The door's stuck," she said.

Ryan crawled forward, and she scooted out of his way.

He pushed and banged against the door, at first lightly, then with more force. But it did nothing but rattle. Almost as if the lock were back in place . . .

She started at the sudden realization of their predicament.

They were locked in the cellar.

Chapter 14

"Aye. It's locked," Ryan said, shoving against the door again. "Could the wind have done this?"

She gulped. "I don't know."

Maybe the wind had pushed the door closed and the impact knocked the lock in place. It was possible, she tried to tell herself. Or had someone slipped the lock back in place without realizing she and Ryan were inside? Maybe Tessa had returned from town, noticed the cellar was open, and shut it without thinking.

"Tessa!" Caroline pressed her face close to the crack at the bottom of the door. "Tessa, I'm in here! Open up!"

She strained to listen through the thick plank and heard nothing but the whistling of the wind and the tapping of raindrops.

It was too early for Tessa to be back. Her sister had planned to stay in town until the boys were done with school and then walk home with them. Nevertheless, Caroline had to believe their getting locked inside the cellar was because of either the wind or one of her siblings. The other option was too frightening to consider.

"Tessa!" she called louder. "Anyone! Please open the door."

There was nothing, no answer. She sat back on her heels and let out a sigh. What about the flash of red she'd spotted in the woods? Had someone been watching her after all? And waiting for her to return to the cellar to trap her here?

She hadn't wanted to believe anyone was trying to hurt her, that what had happened in the garden was a mistake, and that the duck was also a fluke. But she couldn't keep from thinking again that perhaps someone was threatening her. But who, and why?

Through the darkness she could faintly see Ryan examining the hinges as if searching for a way to unscrew the door or take it apart. But it was a solid plank intended to keep wild animals out, especially raccoons. If the door could keep critters out, then it could certainly keep them trapped within.

Ryan banged it again and rammed his good shoulder into it, then sat back with a barely contained groan.

"You won't be able to break it open," she said. "Not with the lock in place."

He leaned close to the ground and put his face against the bottom crack.

"Can you see anyone?" she asked.

He sat back up. "I can't see anything but grass and dirt."

"I guess we'll just have to wait for Tessa and the boys to get home."

"How long do you think that will be?"

"If they don't stop anywhere, I'd say we have at least another hour before they return from town."

"An hour's not bad," he said, crawling back to his spot, almost touching her as he went. "Might as well make ourselves comfortable." Crates scraped and jostled in his effort to move them. "There's a space here for us to sit comfortably. It's tight, but I think we'll both fit."

She hesitated. She knew she shouldn't encourage him in any way, not even by sitting next to him.

"I promise I won't bite."

Biting wasn't what she was worried about. She was more concerned about her reaction to being in such close proximity to him. But she couldn't very well admit that.

But if they had to wait an hour, they might as well relax. There was no reason to worry. As soon as Tessa and the boys came home, she and Ryan would shout and bang on the door and attract their attention. They'd be free in no time.

She drew in a shaky breath.

"Are you okay?" Ryan asked.

She crawled toward his voice, bumping his outstretched legs. "I'll be fine in a minute." At least she hoped she would.

As she settled into the narrow spot next to him, he shifted and attempted to scoot his body over and give her more room. Yet no matter how she tried to hold herself away from him, her shoulder and arm wedged against his.

She sat rigidly, conscious of the warmth of his arm, the rhythm of his breathing, and his soapy scent.

The thought that he'd cleaned himself up when he awoke that afternoon reminded her of the progress he'd made since first arriving to the lighthouse over a week ago when he'd been a filthy mess and hadn't seemed to care about anyone or anything.

But even with the strength of his presence at her side, she couldn't keep her thoughts from skittering in a dozen different directions. What if someone was out there trying to scare her? Or worse, harm her? What if they hurt her family next?

Her fingers brushed against the smooth dirt floor and bumped against something slimy. She drew back. Something feathery seemed to creep along her neck. She swatted her skin only to find nothing.

Panic surged in her chest. Her breath caught, and her whole body tightened. She didn't want to worry, but there were times that she couldn't seem to control the panic, when it rose up and threatened to swallow her alive.

Ryan's shoulder pressed against hers in a strangely comforting way. "Did I tell you about the time I got shot in the arm by pirates?"

She couldn't squeeze out an answer past the tightness of her throat.

"It was the summer I was chopping wood up at Burnham's Landing near the Presque Isle Lighthouse."

He relayed the story to her in the same dramatic way that Tessa often used. After he finished regaling her with one tale, he launched into more exciting adventures on the Great Lakes he'd had during his fishing days.

She noticed that all his stories and everything he related took place before the war. But she didn't mind, because as she listened to him, her body began to relax and her pulse resumed its normal pace, until she all but forgot her panic and what was happening.

She didn't blame him for steering the conversation away from the war. She could only guess that the memories of all he'd experienced were too fresh and horrible to put into words. Even so, she wondered if sharing them would bring about further healing. Or if conjuring up the images would only bring more pain.

"Now it's your turn," he said, shifting his position, likely as stiff as she was from sitting on the hard ground for so long. "I want to hear some of your adventures from your childhood and light-keeping days."

"My life is rather boring compared to yours," she said.

"As a lightkeeper? Surely you've had your share of danger."

She knew what he was doing. She could sense it in his tone. He was trying to take her mind off the situation, which filled her with gratefulness for his consideration.

"I'm doing better," she said softly. "Thank you for helping distract me."

"I was just passing the time."

"I admit I don't handle worry very well. And I'm not proud of it."

He was quiet for a moment. Then he said gently, "No one's perfect. Least of all me."

"I guess it's a good thing that God doesn't require perfection."

Ryan was silent.

"My father always used to tell me that God is good. We can't do anything on our own to be righteous. But that when we turn to Him, He'll fill us with His goodness."

If only she could remember to turn to Him when she most needed it, like now.

A gust of wind rattled the door, and she sat forward. "Maybe I better keep a lookout for Tessa's return." She couldn't be sure how much time had passed, but she certainly didn't want to miss Tessa and the boys coming home.

She peeked through the crack, hoping for a glimpse of someone, but could see nothing except the rain splattering the grass. For a while they took turns pounding against the door and calling out to Tessa and the twins.

When her hands became sore and her voice raw from yelling, she sank to the ground and leaned her head against the door. Ryan knelt down beside her.

"They should be home by now," Caroline said.

"Maybe the wind and the rain are drowning out the noise we're making," Ryan offered.

Over the last several minutes the wind had picked up, and the rain was coming down harder. He could be right. No one would be able to hear their muffled voices over the clamor.

Or maybe something had happened to Tessa and the boys. Caroline shuddered at the unbidden thought. What if they hadn't come home at all? Maybe whoever was responsible for locking them in the cellar had trapped the others too.

Anxiety clamped its viselike grip around her chest. Maybe Sarah was even now all alone in the house with no one to move her or feed her or change her. She would get bedsores, and they would become infected from lying in her own filth.

"You're worrying again," Ryan said. "I can tell from the change in your breathing."

"I don't want to worry." She closed her eyes against the darkness and the fear. "But I can't seem to stop."

"I've grown to hate platitudes, so I won't tell you anything trite—like everything's going to be okay." His voice was low and assuring. "But I want you to know that you don't have to go through this alone. Whatever happens I'll be here, and we can get through it together."

His fingers made contact with her arm and then slid down to her hand.

She clutched him with a desperation that was almost embarrassing. She was glad for the darkness that hid her face and her eagerness for his comfort.

"Thank you, Ryan," she whispered. "I'm glad you're locked up too." If someone had trapped her inside, had they meant to trap Ryan too?

"Glad I'm locked up?" His voice rose in surprise.

"I didn't mean it like that." Mortified, she started to pull away from him. "Of course I wish you didn't have to suffer in here with me."

He laughed softly as his fingers intertwined with hers, linking their hands together, preventing her from pulling away. "I'm just teasing. I know what you meant. You meant that if you had to be trapped in a cellar with someone, you couldn't imagine anyone better to be with than me."

"Maybe."

"Well, let me tell you something," he said, lowering his voice. "If I had to be trapped with someone, I couldn't ask for anyone better than you too."

Warmth traveled up her arm and made a trail to her heart.

"And for your information," he continued, "I wouldn't exactly use *suffering* as the word to describe my time with you. It's more like heavenly pleasure, even if we're together in a hole in the ground."

"You're too flattering," she said.

"It's not flattery. It's the honest truth."

Once again she was glad for the darkness, so he couldn't see the effect he was having on her.

"Let's get comfortable, shall we?" he said, tugging her back to the interior wall. "Once the rain and wind die down, we'll do more shouting for help. Until then, let's try not to think about it."

Unsure whether she could stop her worrying, she settled next to Ryan again, surprised when he didn't relinquish his hold on her hand.

"Besides, they'll realize we're missing soon enough," he said. "And then they'll come searching for us."

She hoped so, but a hundred possibilities lingered in the back of her mind and none of them involved happy endings.

⁓

Pain slammed through Ryan's head with the force of a cannonball. His throat was parched beyond endurance. Even though Caroline had opened a jug of apple cider, it hadn't quenched his thirst.

Night had finally fallen, and after pounding on the door several more times, they hadn't been able to get anyone's attention and help. Caroline had worried herself to exhaustion over who would light the lantern if she couldn't get free to do it.

She'd finally collapsed next to him, her voice shaking with the tears she was trying to hold back. He wished he could find a way to rip the cellar door from its hinges, but everything he'd tried had failed. They were stuck. With the rain and wind still drowning out their cries for help, he'd resigned himself to spending the night here.

He was glad, though, that he was trapped with her, that he'd trailed her to the open cellar and had been here when they got locked inside. He loathed the idea that she might have had to spend the night in the dark cellar all alone.

If he'd slept an hour longer that afternoon, he wouldn't have known she was trapped in the cellar. Like everyone else, he wouldn't have heard her shouts. He would have searched the woods and town, yet he probably wouldn't have thought to look in this cellar. He tried to ignore the nagging voice inside that told him he shouldn't have been sleeping at all.

Even so, as the blackness and coldness had slithered under the crack in the door and crept toward them, his head had begun to fog and pound simultaneously. The realization began to sink in that he wouldn't be able to take his pain medicine or drink his whiskey and that he was in for a long night.

She shivered. He was tempted to pull her onto his lap and wrap both of his arms around her and shield her like a blanket. But he had the feeling if he did that, she'd scramble to the other side of the cellar.

Aye, she'd let him hold her hand from time to time throughout the evening. But from her shyness each time he'd done so, he knew he needed to refrain from pulling her onto his lap. Instead he slipped his uninjured arm behind her back and positioned her in the crook of his arm, drawing her body against his. "To keep you warm," he explained.

It took several moments before her body settled in and relaxed against his. Her body was thin and graceful and fit perfectly next to him. She was warm and soft, and he couldn't resist leaning his face into her hair. She had it tied into her usual knot at the back of her head, but it had loosened and the silkiness beckoned him.

Strands tickled his nose and jaw, and he had the sudden urge to unpin the knot and let her hair cascade down around her shoulders. Sucking in a final breath of her, he tilted his head back and rested it against the dirt wall, putting a safe distance between his wayward thoughts and the beautiful woman in his arms.

The top of her head brushed against his chin, taunting him with the need to press a kiss there. But he held himself in place.

He had the feeling it was going to be a long night in more ways than one.

Another blast of pain ripped through his head. He gritted his teeth to keep from crying out at the intensity of it. He held himself rigid until the ache dissipated.

"Are you all right?" she asked.

Though he couldn't see her face in the darkness, he could tell she'd leaned back and was trying to view him more clearly. He didn't want to admit his pain to her . . . not yet.

"I'm okay," he replied, praying that his suffering wouldn't get much worse as the night wore on.

"I'm here for you too, you know."

Her words told him that she probably knew more about how he felt than she was letting on.

He nodded, and for a long moment they sat silently listening to the wind howl through the cracks of the door.

"Sitting in this cellar brings back memories," he said.

"Of the war?"

"Nay. Of my childhood in Ireland."

Dark memories rose up from the graveyard of bygone days. He'd been young and thankfully didn't remember much of that torturous time of starvation, but there were certain events that came back to haunt him, no matter how hard he tried to forget.

Caroline didn't probe, one of the many things he appreciated about her. She waited patiently for him to speak and never pushed him if he didn't. While he was tempted to bury the memory of the time he and his sister had hidden in a cellar, he forced the words out.

"We were starving," he began, "and so whenever we came across a cellar, we searched it for anything edible. Dad always went in ahead of us to make sure it was safe."

It had been a rainy night, similar to the one they were experiencing now. He and Emma had shivered in the cold outside, drenched and weary, waiting for their dad's call for them to come in behind him. Ryan had prayed they'd be able to find shelter and warmth for a few hours. And he'd hoped for a few greens or roots that had been overlooked by other scavengers.

"As Emma and I waited," he continued, swallowing the bitterness that came every time he thought of that dark night, "I heard protests and then pained cries. I thought maybe someone was hurting Dad, so I stuck my head inside the cellar, even though Dad had told us to wait for him outside."

He dragged in a sharp breath. "There was a family inside. A couple of boys and their mam."

Caroline touched his arm. Her fingers spread over his tense muscles.

"The mam was almost dead," he whispered. "And the boys were close to death too. But they'd started a small fire and were roasting a red squirrel."

He swallowed again, and Caroline rubbed his arm, the touch giving him strength to finish. "Dad took the squirrel. And when the oldest boy protested, he hit him. The blow wasn't very hard, but because the boy was so weak, I have no doubt it killed him."

Ryan had wanted to call out and stop his father, but he'd stood back and done nothing. He should have protested. He should have demanded that his dad return the squirrel. But instead he'd turned a blind eye and devoured the tiny bit of greasy meat, too hungry to care about anything else.

He hung his head, the weight of his sins crushing him, pain reverberating through his head straight to his heart.

"I should have done something," he whispered harshly, hating himself for his weakness.

"You were just a child," Caroline said, running her hand down his arm again. "You were starving. You didn't know."

"But I did know!" His voice rose in anger. "I could have yelled at my comrades. I could have gotten off my horse. I could have warned the boy."

His mind flashed with the pale face of the boy sprawled on the ground, the blood trickling from the gash in his skull. The lifeless eyes stared up at him, accusing him as they always did.

"I should have done something to stop them from ransacking the house."

"Your comrades? The house?"

Sharp knives lanced his temples, blinding him with pain. A moan slipped out. Somehow his mind had jumped from his childhood sins to the present haunting ones.

Caroline's hand rose to his cheek, her fingers cool against his skin. "You don't have to say any more."

He shook his head. He had to tell her the truth about the weak excuse for a man he really was. She wouldn't be so kind to him once she knew. But at least she'd understand why he despised himself.

"The spring was hard that year," he said. "Food supplies trickled into our camp slower than a winter thaw. So our officers formed groups to go out and commandeer food from the locals. I didn't want to go. But I decided maybe I could encourage my group to forage in the unplanted farm fields. I knew how to do it. I'd done it often enough in Ireland."

The pounding in his head grew louder with each passing moment, yet he pressed on. "The first farm we came to, several of the men dismounted, but instead of going to the barn or the fields, they went straight to the house and made the family come out."

The starless night had been illuminated by a half-moon. Though it hadn't been much light, it'd been enough for him to see the way his buddies had started roughing up the young woman who had answered the door in her nightgown.

"I shouted at them to get the food so that we could be on our way. When they entered the house, I expected them to return in a few minutes with food, but for some reason they'd decide to ransack the place. They smashed in windows, broke furniture, and ripped apart bedding."

The darkness of the cellar seeped into Ryan. For a moment he was back at that house, seeing the look of fear and shock in the faces of that poor, fatherless family standing in the scant moonlight as their home was destroyed before their eyes.

"A young boy of about ten stepped forward." Ryan had to squeeze the words out. "He waved his ancient hunting rifle and yelled at my buddies to stop. I could see his anger, could taste his hatred. And I didn't blame him. He edged forward until he was blocking the door. I wanted to call out to him to stay out of the way, to stick by his mam . . ."

Caroline's hand cupped his cheek.

He'd known what was about to happen. His gut had warned him.

"One of the soldiers came forward to confiscate the gun. The boy yelled at him to stop, to go away, to leave them all alone."

Ryan could see the mother lurch forward, only to be held back by one of her daughters. The mother had seen the disaster coming too. And she'd glanced his way, her frantic eyes pleading with him to stop the maddening scene unfolding before them.

His voice dropped to almost a whisper. "But I didn't do anything. Not even when I heard the boy click the hammer in place."

Caroline didn't say anything, but neither did she move away from him in horror as he'd expected.

"He didn't have the chance to aim. He took a bullet in the head and was dead the second he hit the ground."

One of his comrades had fired the deadly blow. Even if the

shot had been to protect one of their own, Ryan knew it had
been a needless death, especially because he could have jumped
down and done something, anything to put a stop to the raid.
Instead he'd turned away again, unable to watch as the mother
had rushed to the dead boy's side. Her anguished sobs filled
the night air.

An apology had stuck in Ryan's throat and it had lodged
there ever since. He knew it would stick there until he returned
to that farm in Virginia and paid them back for all the damage. The payment would never be enough to compensate for
the loss of their son. But he had to do something, no matter
how small.

"That's why I need the keeper job. So I can go back to that
farm and pay for the damage."

Caroline's fingers on his cheek were motionless. Was she
too disappointed in him to respond? He exhaled a frustrated
sigh.

She quickly reached around with her other hand so that she
was kneeling next to him and cupping both of his cheeks. "You'll
earn it," she whispered. "And you'll repay them."

"But don't you see? I stood back and did nothing. Both
times." His heart wrenched almost as painfully as his head at
the knowledge that he should have done more. He could have
been braver. But because he wasn't, he was no better than an
accomplice to murder.

"You didn't mean for anything to happen," she said firmly.
"You didn't want it to."

"I could have done something," he insisted. His chest and
eyes stung, and his throat ached from the pressure of so many
unshed tears.

He could feel her rise higher, her hands splayed against his cheeks. "Maybe you could have done something, but maybe it wouldn't have made any difference. You can't blame yourself anymore."

Her admonishment was like a cool dipper of water on the hot battlefield. He'd shouldered his guilt for so long that he was weary of hanging on to it. And telling someone else seemed to lift the burden, even if only slightly.

"So now you see what kind of man I really am," he said. "I'm surprised that you don't despise me."

"I see that you're an honorable man." She was close enough that the warmth of her breath tickled his face. "A man of integrity and compassion."

He was tempted to reach both of his arms around her and pull her down against him. She was so near, so vibrant, so comforting. She was everything he needed. And although she knew his deepest secrets and scars, she hadn't reviled him. She'd accepted him anyway.

He didn't deserve her kindness. "You're too nice to me, Caroline," he said, starting to lean away, knowing he wasn't worthy of her.

But she didn't let go of his cheeks. Instead her breath came nearer, hovering above his mouth.

The pain in his head dulled to a distant ache, and his muscles tensed. He wanted to kiss her, but he'd promised her that he wouldn't without asking her first. And how could he ask her now?

Before he could think of a solution, her lips dipped in and brushed his, tentatively. The touch was achingly soft and only fanned the frenzied fire racing through him. He held himself back, letting her take the initiative.

The fact that she wanted anything to do with him after his

confession amazed him. But that she wanted to kiss him? It was like a shot of healing tonic coursing through his veins.

She'd barely touched his lips before she retreated a fraction and her breath came in a gasp, as if she'd surprised even herself with her boldness.

He didn't move. He willed himself to be patient. To wait for her to kiss him again, this time more thoroughly.

For a long agonizing moment she lingered just out of reach, her breath coming in soft bursts against his mouth, taunting him, tempting him to close the distance. Then finally she moved in again, touched her lips to his but with more force.

The pressure was all the permission he needed to respond. He tilted his head so that he could meld their mouths, taking her completely, without reservation.

She met his passion with a strength of her own, responding to him with lips parted and eager.

He didn't want the kiss to end. He wanted to wrap his arms around her and pull her down on top of him. It would be so easy to tug her body against his. They were alone in the dark, and he could go on kissing her all night . . . if he let himself.

But warning bells clanged at the back of his mind, the admonition to stop now. That kissing her here alone was just asking for trouble. Already he risked sullying her reputation once everyone discovered they'd spent the night together in the cellar. If he hoped to salvage her character and modesty, he would need to do so with a clean conscience.

With a groan he dragged his mouth away from hers.

"I'm so sorry." Her breath came in heavy gasps, and she let go of his cheeks. "Did I hurt you?"

His body cried out with the need to capture her and press his lips to hers again. Instead he took a wavering breath and told her, "I'm definitely facing a long night." Very long if that kiss was any indication of the passion that was possible between them.

"What can I do to make you more comfortable?" She slid backward, taking the sweet temptation of her lips away from him. Which was in both of their best interests.

Still, he could sense her embarrassment, and he didn't want her thinking he hadn't liked the kiss, because that would have been the furthest thing from the truth. "If you kissed me again, I'd be very comfortable. In fact, I'd be back in heaven," he said softly. "But I'm only a man, and I'm not sure that I'd have the strength to pull away from you again tonight."

"Oh" came her surprised response.

"I may have made some pretty awful mistakes in my life," he added, "but at least I've remained honorable in how I've treated women."

As hard as it might be, he was determined to do the right thing by Caroline too. For he was more attracted to her than any woman he'd ever met before. And although the pull to share intimacies with her was strong, he had to resist.

He would resist or die trying.

Chapter 15

The rain and the wind continued through the night. And with each passing hour, Ryan grew more miserable. Though he didn't say anything, Caroline could see he was in great pain. He gripped his head and writhed in agony, his body shook with chills, and his muscles contracted with spasms that only seemed to aggravate his wounded arm.

She knew he was suffering the ill effects of not having his opium pills and that in the long run he'd be better off without the medicine. Even so, she was desperate for something she could give him—tea, a salve, anything—that would ease his suffering. But she could do nothing but run a soothing hand over his forehead, cradle him after the spasms, and whisper urgent prayers that God would help him survive the night.

At one point he finally fell into a restless sleep. She was grateful that he could have a reprieve from his agony, even if for a short time. When he awoke, the faint light under the door told them morning had come. Caroline resumed her banging on the door and shouting for help. Yet the rain and wind continued in a steady patter that stifled her efforts.

She prayed Tessa would make a trip out to the cellar, but as the hours passed without anyone coming, the worry began to creep deeper into Caroline's chest so that she could hardly breathe. She couldn't keep from thinking that maybe no one would come to rescue them, that they would die here once their supply of food and apple cider ran out.

Ryan's chills and shaking finally diminished, and he grew lethargic, hardly stirring when she offered him sips of cider throughout the day. When the evening faded once again, she could only close her eyes and fight back the worry clawing at her insides. Another night without knowing how her family was faring. And another night that the lantern would remain unlit.

If only she'd insisted that Tessa learn to operate the light. She'd tried to teach her sister once, but Tessa had never liked going up into the tower and had protested so profusely against learning anything about the light that Caroline decided the issue wasn't worth the fight.

Oh, God, I need you, her heart cried as she attempted to drag a breath into her air-deprived lungs. *I need you. I need you. I need you.*

It was the only prayer she could utter.

But it was the only prayer that mattered.

After a moment, her chest loosened, the muscles in her back relaxed, and her eyelids fluttered down. The last thought she had before falling into an exhausted sleep was that somehow God was with her, that He'd lifted her burden and given her His peace in its place.

Caroline jolted awake and sat forward, only to find Ryan's head in her lap and his arm thrown across her legs. Light streamed in from the crack under the door, illuminating his face enough for her to see that he was sleeping and that his features had finally smoothed. The crevices of pain were gone. The taut muscles had loosened. He seemed to be resting almost normally.

She reached out a hand and boldly combed back his hair from his forehead. After the past day of nursing him, the gesture seemed natural to her.

He stirred and exhaled a long breath.

She shifted to get more comfortable and in the process let her hand delve deeper into his hair. She couldn't deny how much she loved its silkiness and the way it cascaded through her fingers.

She brought her other hand to his face and pressed it against his cheek, letting the stubble graze her. She also couldn't deny how much she relished the strength of his jaw and the bristle beneath her fingers.

He moved again, and this time twisted so that her hand slipped to his mouth. In the same movement he wrapped his hand around hers, preventing her from moving it from his lips.

She tensed with the embarrassment of having been so free in touching him. "You're awake," she said, extricating her fingers from his hair and attempting to move her other hand away from his face.

But he didn't relinquish his grip, and instead his lips pressed against the soft center of her palm. The gentleness and warmth of the kiss made her close her eyes, and she had to bite her lip to keep in a sharp breath of pleasure.

"How are you feeling?" she asked.

His only response was to press his lips again, this time grazing against the rapid pounding of the vein in her wrist that surely gave away her desire for him.

She couldn't keep herself from thinking about the kiss she

gave him the first night of their being trapped together. How had she dared it? Yes, he'd just bared his soul to her. He'd been distressed, broken and honest.

But she'd been brazen to kiss him like she did, acting like a common hussy. What would he think of her now?

"Stop worrying, Caroline," he whispered, positioning her fingers against his cheek again. "Whatever you're thinking, it's not true."

"How do you know?"

Before he could respond, the door rattled.

She gasped, and he shot off the ground.

"Hello!" she called while crawling forward, renewed desperation giving her a burst of strength.

The plank door rattled again, this time with more force.

Within seconds the door opened, and brilliant light poured over them, blinding them. Cold air rushed in to replace the warmth their bodies had created inside the cellar.

She blinked hard and scrambled through the doorway into wet grass and damp leaves. She bent over it and gulped a breath of the fresh scent of earth.

An oversized pair of scuffed shoes stood only inches away. Kneeling in the grass, the wetness soaking through her skirt, she looked up to find Arnie Simmons standing above her, his eyes wide with concern.

"Caroline." His voice was wobbly. "Are y-you . . . okay?"

She wanted to hug him. She'd never been happier to see anyone in her life. But before she could get her words of gratitude out, Ryan was crawling out next to her, and Arnie's brows rose into his receding hairline.

"Wow, the sun's bright," Ryan said. His face was pale, and he shielded his eyes with his uninjured hand.

"He was with you?" Arnie's large ears flamed a bright shade of red.

"We've been trapped inside since Monday," she explained, glancing first to the position of the sun and then to the tower that glistened like a diamond in the morning light. It was still fairly early. What was Arnie doing out at the lighthouse at this time of day?

"Where is everyone else?" she asked, sitting up straighter and stretching her cramped limbs. "Are my brothers and sisters safe?"

Arnie glared at Ryan. Something dark, almost dangerous flashed in Arnie's eyes before disappearing. "Everyone's here." Arnie turned back to her. "Search p-parties met here at . . . at f-first light."

"Search parties?" Finally she stood and then scanned the area. Here and there, groups of people walked together, calling out, searching the forest, the marsh, even walking along the lakeshore.

"We've b-been looking for y-you," Arnie explained.

Out in the marsh she caught sight of Esther's bulky frame, along with several other women from town. She spotted Tessa and the boys near the forest edge. A group of men milled along the shore, including Esther's husband, the mayor. Even Monsieur Poupard was combing the woods.

Ryan straightened next to her. He swayed, his knees almost buckling beneath him.

She reached for him, linking her arm through his and steadying him. In the bright yellows, greens, and reds of the fall morning, his face was ashen, the dark circles under his eyes testifying to the torture he'd undergone the past two days without his medication.

Arnie took a step back, his attention darting between them with hurt and confusion chasing away his concern.

"It's not what you think, Arnie," she rushed to explain. "Nothing happened between Ryan and me. He's been so sick."

A shout in the distance told her the group had noticed her and Ryan standing with Arnie.

Dismay took away her joy at finally getting set free. If Arnie thought the worst had happened between her and Ryan, she could only imagine what everyone else would think.

For a short time, everyone was so glad to see her and intent upon hugging her that they hardly seemed to notice Ryan at all.

Tessa hugged her the tightest of all and then stood back and wiped the tears from her cheeks. "I can't believe you were here in the cellar all along."

"At first we thought maybe you went to Detroit to look for a new job," Harry said, holding her hand.

"But then Tessa realized you hadn't taken anything with you," Hugh added, gripping her other hand.

Caroline bent and placed another kiss on each of their heads, grateful they were all right.

Esther stood next to her husband and rested her hands on her swollen abdomen. "I knew you wouldn't leave the kids without telling them where you were going. That's just not like you."

Caroline smiled at all the faces surrounding her, overwhelmed by the support of the townspeople. "Esther's right. I wouldn't have left without telling you where I was going."

"So of course when I heard you were gone," Esther said, "I organized a search party. It was too late in the day yesterday to do anything—and too stormy. But we decided to meet out here at first light and begin searching the area."

"Thank you." Caroline reached for Esther's hand and

squeezed it. "And thank you to Arnie for deciding to check the cellar."

She turned then to Arnie, who was standing awkwardly near the door of the cellar. He'd been so faithful to her, probably the first to arrive that morning ready to search. Throwing caution aside, she reached for the young man and threw her arms around him in a hug.

He immediately held himself as straight as a boat paddle.

Sensing his embarrassment and catching a faint hint of onion on his breath, she released her hold and smiled at him instead.

His face lit up, and he smiled back shyly.

No one else appreciated him. The least she could do was express her gratitude for his kindness.

"Aye, thank you, Arnie, for finding us," Ryan said, leaning back against the mound that formed the cellar. His legs and hands trembled from time to time, and from the way he shielded his eyes from the sun, she could tell the bright light was making his head ache all over again.

"It's a miracle Arnie checked the cellar," Ryan added. "Most people wouldn't think to look in a place that locked from the outside."

"Good point," Esther said, turning to Ryan and taking in his wrinkled and dirty garments. "Someone had to have been waiting and watching for the opportunity to lock Caroline in the cellar. That kind of thing wouldn't happen by chance."

Caroline stifled a shudder, not wanting to think about the fact that somehow she'd gained an enemy.

"It would appear that someone has purposefully set out to harm you," Esther declared, which started a murmur among the rest of the group gathered around them.

"Or maybe someone is trying scare her," Ryan said.

Esther's full form contrasted her husband's lanky body, made even taller by his top hat. The pair reminded Caroline of the newspaper pictures she'd seen of the late President Lincoln and his first lady.

Monsieur Poupard on the fringes of the group wasn't paying any attention to what they were saying. Instead he was frowning at the area that had once housed her beautiful garden, now completely barren except for a few stray stems she'd yet to pull.

At the rattle of a wagon and the sharp crack of a whip, everyone's attention shifted to the path that wound through the marsh and the approaching wagon.

Two men sat on the wagon's front bench. The one driving was a hulk of a man, his arms bulging, his torso double the size of the man sitting next to him. It could be none other than Mr. Simmons. No one else was as big.

Arnie took an involuntary step backward, bumping into the cellar door, worry flashing through his eyes.

As they drew closer, Caroline's heart sank, and she wanted to slink back next to Arnie and cower with him out of sight.

The man sitting next to Mr. Simmons was Mr. Finick, the lighthouse inspector, the last person on earth she wanted to see, especially at that moment. Mr. Simmons finally brought his team to an abrupt halt behind their gathering. Beneath his bowler hat, his dark eyes were sharp like those of a bird of prey searching out its next meal.

Mr. Finick sat with his lips pursed tightly enough to turn them blue. He cautiously descended, careful not to brush his light-gray pinstriped suit against the dusty wagon. At the same time, Mr. Simmons jumped down in one lunge that nearly tipped the wagon off its wheels.

"Looks like you found the missing keeper," Mr. Simmons bellowed.

"Locked in the cellar." Esther leveled a glare at him as if she placed the blame squarely at his feet for all that had happened.

Caroline studied Mr. Simmons's face, his outwardly composed facade, knowing that calm could dissipate as fast as a sunny spring day only to be overshadowed with storm clouds. Had Mr. Simmons been the one to start causing her trouble? He'd seen her at the rally outside his inn last week. Maybe he'd thought to teach her a lesson.

"Your son saved our lives," Ryan said, pushing away from the hill and making an effort to stand on his feet without swaying. "If not for him, we'd still be locked in there."

"Arnie would tear apart heaven and earth for that girl," Mr. Simmons replied. "Too bad she's stringing him along instead of marrying him like a decent woman."

Mr. Finick clucked under his breath, flipped open his record-keeping book, and scribbled something there. His long black mustache twitched with all the disapproval that likely coursed through his wiry body upon learning that she and Ryan had spent the past couple of days locked up together.

"Mr. Chambers was sick most of the time," she hurried to add.

"I was nearly dead from pain," Ryan confirmed.

She didn't dare look at him for fear of revealing the intimate moments that had passed between them in spite of his sickness.

"Nevertheless, Miss Taylor," Mr. Finick said, "your behavior is unacceptable, and you've quite possibly sullied Mr. Chambers's reputation as well."

"She didn't sully my reputation in any way," Ryan protested. "I'm only sorry if I've caused anyone to question her character in the least. I can attest that she's completely innocent."

"If you'd left when I instructed you," Mr. Finick snapped at her, "none of this would have happened."

Before she could respond, Ryan once again stepped in to defend her. "I told her she could stay as my assistant."

Mr. Finick flashed Ryan a look of irritation. "You don't have the power to make those kinds of decisions."

"But I need her help—"

"I'll determine if you need help," he said. "And if you really do need help, it won't be from this woman."

"And what does being a woman have to do with it?" Esther stepped forward, letting go of her husband, who watched her with pride beaming from his thin face.

"Women aren't allowed to be keepers."

"There are plenty of women who've been allowed to be keepers in other states," Esther insisted in her usual clipped manner. "And even if there weren't, it's time to put aside such antiquated rules and embrace a new way of thinking about women and their abilities."

Mr. Finick narrowed his eyes upon Esther. "And exactly who are you? And what business do you have interfering with my job?"

Esther reached for her husband's arm, slipped hers through it, and tipped up her chin. "My husband is the mayor of Grosse Pointe, and my father is a Michigan senator."

"Well, that has nothing to do with the Lighthouse Board, now, does it?" Mr. Finick's lips again pressed together. "And since I don't meddle in town or in state policy, I would ask you to refrain from meddling in lighthouse issues that you know nothing about."

This was the moment Caroline had been dreading, the day when Mr. Finick came back and ordered her to leave once and for all. The truth was, as sweet as Esther and Ryan had been about defending her right to stay at the lighthouse, Mr. Finick was the final authority in the matter. There was nothing they could do to change his mind.

Mr. Simmons stood back, crossed his arms over his chest, and grinned, clearly happy to see Esther put in her place.

But Esther's eyes sparked. "Everyone here can vouch for the excellent job that Caroline has done as keeper." She glanced around at the others who'd joined the search party, her expression urging the townspeople to agree with her.

To Caroline's relief, they didn't need Esther's urging. They were already nodding and murmuring their assent.

"She's managed this lighthouse as well as any man—if not better," Esther said. "And all of us think she deserves to stay on as head keeper."

Mr. Finick picked an invisible dust mite from his coat sleeve. "Miss Taylor has been dismissed from her position. She cannot stay as head keeper or assistant. I absolutely forbid it—"

"I've asked my father to take the matter before the Senate."

"She needs to leave Windmill Point today."

"She's staying until we get word back from my father."

"She leaves. Today."

"She's staying."

Esther and Mr. Finick locked eyes in a glare that rivaled a duel to the death.

Caroline's chest squeezed, as though the two were pressing against her and flattening her between them.

Ryan moved to stand beside her. "Listen. I'm not capable of running this lighthouse by myself." With his pale face, sunken eyes, and unsteady legs, he certainly looked as if he were about to fall over and die.

"Then I'll have to begin to look for a replacement for you," Mr. Finick said, jotting something in his book.

"Or you can let Miss Taylor stay as my assistant and continue to help me. If not for her, the light would have remained unlit many more nights than the past two."

Even though he didn't touch her, his presence next to her was solid and strong and comforting. She wanted to reach for his hand, to thank him for his support. But she didn't dare to even look at him for fear of revealing the growing bond she felt between them.

"Even if I were to allow Miss Taylor to stay—which I'm not—the living situation here is completely unsuitable for an unmarried man and unmarried woman."

"I'm living in the boathouse," Ryan said quickly. "She can continue to live in the house."

"That's unacceptable."

"After making my home in a tent for the past four years, the boathouse is paradise."

Ryan's comment garnered some laughter from the crowd, but only a frown from Mr. Finick.

"She just needs to marry Arnie," Mr. Simmons said. "Then all these problems will be solved."

Arnie had been pushed to the back of the gathering, but even there his face bloomed crimson.

"She's not marrying Arnie," Esther spoke up again, her intense expression admonishing Caroline to stay strong. "And she's not leaving the lighthouse. Not until we hear back on the Senate ruling."

Mr. Finick turned to Esther's husband. "You ought to take your wife home where she belongs."

The mayor only smiled down at his wife. "She belongs out

200

here, championing for the rights of the people and causes she believes in."

The seriousness in Esther's countenance softened. She returned her husband's smile with love and gratefulness radiating from her face.

Caroline watched her friend, unable to stop longing from snagging her. Would she ever find a man who could believe in her the same way? She was tempted to look at Ryan to see if he'd noticed the couple's sweetness with each other. But she knew it shouldn't matter what Ryan thought. No matter what had transpired between them in the cellar, no matter that he was started on the road to healing, he still had a long ways to go. She had to respect that and give him the space and time to become whole again.

Esther rubbed a hand over her belly as if to say that she could be a mother and still continue with her calling. "Mr. Finick, none of us in Grosse Pointe will let you remove Caroline from the lighthouse simply because she's a woman. If she must leave, then you must have much greater cause than her gender."

Mr. Finick's grip on his notebook turned his knuckles white. In the morning sunshine, the darkness that flashed in his eyes made Caroline shudder. The man didn't say anything but instead climbed back aboard the wagon. He perched on the edge of the seat, straightening his trouser legs and smoothing out the wrinkles.

Finally he looked down at Esther. "You know as well as I do that the Senate has no authority in lighthouse business, and that you're only spouting nonsense."

The gravity in his words sent another chill through Caroline, especially when Esther didn't respond.

"I'll be back," he continued. "And next time I come, I'll be bringing the sheriff along with official papers expelling Miss Taylor. If she refuses to leave, I'll have her physically removed and thrown in jail."

Mr. Simmons rounded the wagon with a meaningful glance at Arnie. "Don't worry, she'll be gone by then."

"Mr. Chambers, see to it that you have no further incidents," Mr. Finick warned. "Or war veteran or not, you'll leave me no choice but to fire you."

Caroline wondered why Mr. Finick was with Mr. Simmons so early in the morning. Had he ridden out from Detroit last night? She knew he favored cockfights and attended them from time to time. Or maybe he'd arrived late in Grosse Pointe yesterday and thought to ride out to the lighthouse early for one of his surprise inspections?

Whatever the case, he'd made it clear that her days at the lighthouse were indeed coming to an end. Even as he scribbled furiously in his notebook, she guessed he was writing down every sordid detail as further proof of her inadequacy.

At last the crowd began to disperse. Hugh and Harry were already playing, throwing fuzzy black caterpillars at each other, and Tessa was scolding them. Esther started to mingle and thank people for coming.

Ryan expelled an exasperated sigh. Caroline echoed him, yet she made a point of not turning to look at him, though she wanted to do nothing more than exactly that.

"Chambers," Mr. Simmons called, "I've got a little something for you." The big man dug through the wagon bed and then lifted out a brown bottle.

At the sight of the liquor, Caroline wanted to grab Ryan's arm and stop him from going to Mr. Simmons. But instead she spun away and crossed toward Esther, knowing she couldn't interfere. Ryan had to fight his own battles. If she stepped in and tried to control his life, she wouldn't be helping him.

Out of the corner of her eye, she watched him make his way toward Mr. Simmons. He conversed with the man for several moments, then shook his head.

Mr. Simmons pushed the bottle at Ryan, but he kept both hands tucked in his pockets.

The tension in her chest loosened, replaced by a swell of relief. He was doing it. He was resisting.

But for how long?

Mr. Simmons's grin faded, and he smacked the bottle harder into Ryan's chest. Ryan stumbled backward, his face set with determination.

For a long moment, Mr. Simmons glowered at Ryan. The anger in his eyes was cold and brittle. A chill skittered across Caroline's skin.

What would happen if Ryan made an enemy of Mr. Simmons?

"We'll win this, Caroline," Esther said, drawing Caroline's attention. Esther reached for her hands, squeezed them, and gave her a look that exuded more confidence than Caroline felt.

"I don't know—"

"I do know," Esther replied firmly. "You'll stay here. And in doing so you'll be standing up for the liberties of women everywhere."

Caroline nodded. "Yes, of course."

She agreed with Esther. It wasn't right for Mr. Finick to discriminate against her because she was a woman. But deep inside, she wasn't sure if the battle was worth it. She didn't want to make an enemy of Mr. Finick any more than she already had.

Chapter 16

Caroline smoothed Sarah's ebony hair off her face, which was as white and delicate as a single wood nymph flower.

"Monsieur Poupard would never lock you in the cellar," Sarah whispered in her raspy voice while she peered out the window overlooking the backyard.

"I'm sure you're right, but still . . ." Perched on the edge of Sarah's bed, Caroline had a perfect view of the sprawling back garden that was now completely barren . . . except for the presence of Monsieur Poupard, who was kneeling in the dirt.

With the falling of dusk, Caroline had been about to ascend the tower when Sarah's call had stopped her. Her sister had pointed outside to the bent form of the man digging furtively in their garden. Caroline had spun angrily toward the door, ready to confront the old French trapper. After all, she'd seen a spot of red cloak in the woods the day someone had locked her in the cellar. He'd obviously been nearby.

But Sarah's weak grip on her sleeve had stopped her. "He's planting something," the girl insisted. The darkness of Sarah's room concealed them, and they could watch Monsieur Poupard without his realizing it.

Caroline knew that Monsieur Poupard wasn't capable of imprisoning her in the cellar. But it was so much easier to try to pin the blame on him than to have an unknown culprit on the loose waiting to strike again.

Sarah peered more intently at the crate the old man had brought with him.

"I have to go out there and talk to him." Caroline started to rise, but Sarah's cold fingers stopped her once again. If he wasn't to blame, perhaps he'd seen the real offender.

"Wait, Caroline," she said. "It looks like he's planting bulbs."

Caroline broke away from Sarah and stepped closer to the window. She squinted through the growing darkness to the small item he cradled in his hand.

It looked like a stringy onion.

Caroline's breath caught. Sarah was right. He was planting bulbs.

He scooped dirt out of the ground with gnarled fingers, gently laid the item inside the hole, then covered it with soil. He patted it firmly before reaching into the crate he'd brought and lifting out another.

As if sensing her eyes on him, he paused and looked around. When he glanced at the bedroom window, she ducked away.

"So what do you think?" Sarah asked.

"I don't know." Why was he planting bulbs, and in secret?

"He seems like a nice man," Sarah said. Against the mound of pillows, she was cushioned like a rare jewel.

"How do you know if he's nice or not?" Caroline asked.

"I see him every once in a while passing by. He always stops and waves at me."

Caroline turned to face Sarah. "He waves at you?"

"One time, when the window was open, he spoke to me."

Caroline glared at the bent back of Monsieur Poupard. What was he up to? Why would he make conversation with a sick little girl?

"It was only for a minute," Sarah said quickly. "He's always been kind to me."

Caroline peeked at the man again, but he'd straightened as much as his hunched shoulders would allow. He picked up the crate and began to limp around the garden, the wings of his red cloak trailing in the wind behind him.

A soft knock on the doorframe drew Caroline's attention back into the room, to the sight of Ryan standing in the doorway. He glanced first at Sarah, then his eyes settled upon her, warmly, almost shyly.

"Do you mind if I come in?" he asked.

"Of course not," Caroline said, waving him in.

Sarah smiled, and her expression took on a glimmer of adoration. "Ryan," the young girl said breathlessly, sounding so much like Tessa that Caroline had to stifle a smile.

Apparently Ryan had cast his charm over Sarah too. At thirteen she was probably old enough to recognize just how handsome Ryan was, even if she didn't realize her own reaction to him.

"Hi there, beautiful." Ryan gave Sarah a return smile.

A flush of faint color spread into Sarah's cheeks. The sight sent a pang into Caroline's heart. Though they'd tried every medicine they could find and had gleaned the opinions of several doctors, there wasn't much hope for Sarah living to adulthood. In fact, there wasn't much hope of her surviving the year if she continued to deteriorate as quickly as she had been.

Sarah would never get to experience falling in love, getting married, and having babies. And that reality wrenched Caroline every time she thought about it.

"How are you feeling today?" Ryan asked Sarah as he crossed the room to her bedside.

"I'm just glad the two of you are safe," she whispered.

Ryan reached for her limp hand and lifted it with his good one. "We're perfectly safe." His voice held a confidence that Caroline didn't feel.

The truth was, she didn't feel safe at all. All day after they'd been freed from the cellar she hadn't been able to stop thinking about who might have locked her in and why.

Whoever had done it was still out there. She couldn't keep from constantly looking over her shoulder and thinking someone was watching her and waiting to strike again.

She glanced out the window. There was no sight of Monsieur Poupard in the shadows of night. She gave a start at how quickly darkness was falling and moved across the room toward the door. She wouldn't let the tower go unlit another minute longer than necessary, not after the past two nights of utter blackness. She hadn't heard of any accidents, but she wouldn't take any more chances.

"Wait, Caroline," Ryan said, releasing Sarah's hand and reaching into his pocket. He tugged something out.

Even in the dimness of the room, she could distinguish a small, dark bottle.

"I want you to have this," he said, extending the vial toward her. Something inside clinked against the glass.

"Your pain pills?" she asked.

He nodded. And for the first time since he'd entered the room, she noticed the haggardness in his face, the dark circles under his eyes. Hadn't he taken any medicine all day? After everyone had left, he'd gone back to the boathouse. She assumed he'd taken his pain pills to put himself out of his misery.

He shook the bottle in indication that she should take it from him. "I've decided I'm not going to take them anymore."

"You're not?"

"No. Not after my body just went through the nightmare of ridding itself of the drug. Now that it's mostly out of me, I might as well keep it out."

"That's probably a good idea."

He stretched the pills toward her, his eyes begging her to take them before he changed his mind.

She reached for the bottle and took it from him.

"Use the medicine for Sarah," he said, stuffing his hand into his pocket so that both hands were hidden away. "If you give her a pill now and then when her pain is especially bad, she probably won't develop a craving like I did."

Caroline wanted to rush to him and throw her arms around him in a big hug. But Sarah was glancing back and forth between them, her eyes wide and much too perceptive.

Instead, Caroline offered Ryan a smile, hoping he could read her encouragement. He was doing the right thing. Getting rid of the pills was another step toward healing. But it still wasn't easy.

"We'd better get the lamp lit now," he said.

She nodded in satisfaction. Not only had he turned down Mr. Simmons's offer of liquor and given up his pain pills, but he was taking the initiative to climb the tower steps and work, even though he was clearly still suffering.

She led the way to the lantern room, and together they worked quickly and efficiently to light the lantern. She stood back after the beam flashed over the lake and crossed her arms. "You did well," she said, breathing in the familiar scents of kerosene and smoke, relieved that tonight the passing ships would once again be safe. "I don't think you'll need my help much longer."

He was bent over and inspecting the gears. "Maybe I won't *need* it, but I want it."

"You heard Mr. Finick. He won't let me stay. In fact, maybe he's behind all of the so-called accidents. Maybe it's his way of driving me away."

Ryan straightened. "We can't let him scare you off, Caroline. You deserve to be here. Much more than me."

She sighed. The whole issue of whether to stay or leave had been weighing on her all day. As much as she wanted to be strong like Esther had admonished her, and as much as she wanted to fight for her rights, she also knew that Mr. Finick wouldn't be swayed. Not only did he believe women shouldn't be doing men's work, but he was a stickler for the rules. And if the rules said a woman wasn't allowed to be keeper, then he would consider it his sacred duty to make sure a man was running Windmill Point.

"At least stay until Esther hears back from her father," Ryan pleaded.

She found herself sinking into the lush brown of his eyes, unable to resist the pull to lose herself in them. While her heart advised her to use caution, that neither one of them was in a position to have a relationship, she still hadn't been able to stop thinking about their intimate conversations in the cellar. And of course she hadn't been able to stop thinking about the kiss she'd initiated. They hadn't talked about it, but it was there between them nonetheless.

He straightened, wiped his greasy hands on a rag, then rounded the room toward her. His footsteps clanked against the iron floor, causing her pulse to thud in anticipation of his nearness.

When he was less than a foot away, he stopped. The power of his presence radiated between them, tempting her to lean in, to fall into his arms and close the distance that separated them. He lifted tentative fingers, hovered above her cheek, and lightly grazed her jawline.

Her breath snagged in her chest. She started to turn her head into his touch, but then he dropped his hand, stuffed it back into his pocket, and released a pent-up breath that was warm and only reminded her of the way it felt against her mouth when they'd kissed.

"I'd love to stay up here with you all night," he whispered hoarsely, taking a step away from her, "but I don't trust myself when I'm around you."

There was something raw and powerful between them. It was like nothing she'd ever experienced before, like nothing she'd ever imagined between a man and a woman. She couldn't deny that she liked it.

"I don't think we should be alone together," he said, "at least not for long."

His comment and the insinuation behind it made her look down at her boots in a mixture of embarrassment and desire, neither of which she wanted him to see.

"I thought maybe we could come up with shifts," he continued, his voice strained. "Maybe we could each work half the night?"

She nodded. Other keepers and their assistants often had shifts for watching the light so that one person didn't have all the responsibility. "I'll take the early shift," she said. "Why don't you sleep first?" She didn't have to mention that he would benefit from the extra sleep, since his body was still ravaged from the lack of the opium pills.

At her proclamation, he pressed his fingers against his temple and let his guard down, revealing the mask of pain he'd been hiding. "Thank you. I'll sleep for a few hours and then relieve you."

"There's no rush," she said. "In fact, why don't you rest in the keeper's room. I won't have use for the bed . . ."

Should she make such an offer? Was it proper? What would the townspeople think if they learned Ryan was now sleeping in the house? Especially after he'd told them he would stay in the boathouse?

She opened her mouth to tell him to forget her suggestion, that it was a bad idea, but the longing that filled his eyes stopped her words. He'd admitted to everyone that he'd lived in a tent for years. She could only imagine how much he wanted to sleep in a real bed.

It wouldn't matter if he took comfort on the bed for a few short hours. It might even relieve his injury of some pain if he didn't have to sleep on the hard ground. It would only be for one night.

Besides, Tessa slept with Sarah to help when she awoke with pain. All Caroline needed to do was run down and inform her sister of the arrangement and tell her to lock Sarah's door. Tessa would understand.

"Yes, go on. Take the bed," she said before she convinced herself it was a bad idea. "It will do you good."

He smiled, and the pleasure in his face swept away her doubts.

Chapter 17

*G*iggles from the kitchen awoke Caroline from a restless sleep. She rolled over and buried her face into the pillow. Too late she realized her mistake. She breathed in Ryan's scent, the clean, sudsy smell of his soap and shaving lotion combined.

Her toes curled, and for a long forbidden moment she imagined that the pillow was him, that he was lying in bed with her, his arms around her.

Heat spilled into her middle.

"Caroline Taylor," she chided herself, pushing the pillow away and sitting up amidst a tangle of sheets and quilt.

Somehow Ryan's short rest in the bed one night had turned into two, and then three. At his words of pleasure at the luxury of sleeping in a real bed, she'd pushed aside the nagging doubts that told her he shouldn't be sleeping in the house, even for a minute. She'd told herself no one else needed to know, that it wasn't anything to worry about, that her overanxious mind was only making more of it than need be.

Besides, she'd prided herself on her self-control. She'd resisted daydreaming about him and had tried to think of him as just a friend. She couldn't stop now, especially with how hard Ryan was working to keep appropriate boundaries between them.

But the heat inside her belly only charged into her blood at the remembrance of all the times his gaze had strayed to her when he thought she wasn't looking. Or the times they'd inadvertently brushed in passing. Or the moments when their eyes met, no matter how hard she'd tried to refrain, leaving her breathless with longing.

At another giggle from the kitchen, she sat up and swung her feet out of bed. In the unheated room, the floorboards felt icy against her toes. With the coming of October the first hard frost had finally come too, bringing them one step closer to winter.

And one step closer to having to leave . . .

She sighed and stood.

With each passing day, Ryan was growing stronger and more knowledgeable about the light. Though his war injury still caused him pain, and his mangled hand inhibited what he could do, she was confident that he was well on his way to recovering from the horrors of his past.

He wouldn't need her much longer.

She donned her everyday skirt and blouse, slipped on her stockings and shoes, and ran a comb through her long hair.

From the other room, Tessa's voice rose in delight and was followed by Ryan's low rumble. Caroline frowned, the comb midway through a tangle. A hot shard needled her. Not jealousy, she told herself. Only concern.

Tessa had been altogether too flirty lately with Ryan. Caroline hadn't wanted to say anything to her sister, consumed as she was with her own guilt of flirting so shamelessly at times with Ryan. But maybe it was time to rebuke Tessa again.

She made her way down the hallway, following the yeasty aroma of freshly baked bread. At her first step into the kitchen, she froze.

Ryan sat by the window with a towel across his shoulders. And Tessa stood over him, one hand in his hair, the other holding a pair of scissors. Her face glowed, and her eyes radiated excitement. Was she giving Ryan a haircut?

Sharpness pricked Caroline's chest again, and it only grew sharper when Tessa ran her fingers through his strands like a comb. She was chattering, and Ryan was grinning, obviously enjoying himself.

From the feathery hair clippings scattered on the floor, she could see Tessa had been at work for a while. Four loaves of bread perfectly browned were cooling on the table. An abandoned bowl of apple cores and peelings sat next to a pie that was filled with sliced apples but still missing the top crust.

"Tessa!" The word came out sharply.

Her sister jumped away from Ryan, her face flashing with guilt.

But Ryan didn't move. His grin only widened at the sight of Caroline. "Good morning, lazybones. It's about time you got up."

Caroline was too mortified at Tessa's behavior to smile back. Instead she scowled at her sister. "What do you think you're doing?"

The guilt fluttered rapidly from the girl's face, replaced by sullenness. "You're not the only one who gets to help Ryan."

"It's Mr. Chambers to you."

"If you can call him Ryan, then I can too."

"No, you may not. And you may certainly not cut his hair."

Tessa's arms at her sides turned rigid, and her face flushed. Ryan's gaze swung back and forth between them.

Caroline tried to rein in her growing frustration toward Tessa. She needed to pull her sister aside and have this conversation privately, and not embarrass her in front of Ryan.

"Since I used to give Father his haircuts, I thought I could do the same for Ryan." Tessa's dark eyes challenged her, her tone defiant. It was all too reminiscent of Caroline's own defense the day she'd given Ryan a shave.

Caroline's rebuke died inside her. How could she reprimand Tessa for cutting Ryan's hair when she'd shaved Ryan's beard? She certainly hadn't set a good example for her impressionable sister—not with the shaving or with the flirting.

She would need to try harder not to flirt with Ryan and work at being a better role model for Tessa. Until then, what right did Caroline have to admonish her? She'd only be a hypocrite if she did.

Caroline gave a long sigh. "I thought you were supposed to be watching Hugh and Harry." She'd assigned Tessa that duty on Saturdays while she caught up on her sleep.

"They're out fishing," Tessa replied. "They're fine."

Ryan stirred in the chair and tugged the towel from where it was wedged in his collar. "I think we're done anyway, don't you, Tessa?"

Her sister angled her head and studied him. Caroline did likewise. Gone were the scraggly, overlong locks. Instead, his sandy hair fell in trim, attractive waves. With several days' worth of whiskers on his cheeks and chin, he still had a rugged appearance about him. But he'd shed the lost and haunted look that he'd carried. His face was no longer so thin either. The home-cooked meals were beginning to add to his strength.

A bright light shone from his eyes that reached across the room and touched her, filling her with warmth. His eyes lingered upon her unbound hair still hanging in disarray over her shoulders.

Seeing the direction of Ryan's attention, Tessa glowered at Caroline. "Oh, I see why you don't want me to cut Ryan's hair. You want his attention all for yourself."

"That's not true," Caroline retorted, but the guilt washed back through her. Did she want his attention?

Even though Tessa was pouting, her features were unmistakably pretty and her curves all too noticeable. As much as Caroline wanted Tessa to stay a girl, she was turning into a woman. Surely Ryan had noticed. How could he *not*?

"Tessa, please," Caroline pleaded, "let's not argue anymore. Let me finish cleaning up in here, and you go check on the boys."

Tessa narrowed her eyes. "Admit it. You want me out of the way so that you can be alone with Ryan."

"Tessa!" Caroline pulled herself to her full height and glared at her sister. It was the kind of glare she hoped proclaimed that she was in charge and that she'd had enough.

Tessa huffed, dropped the scissors onto the table, and stalked from the room.

After the front door banged shut, Caroline let her shoulders slump.

"Sorry for causing problems," Ryan said, tipping back on his chair. "I wouldn't have agreed to her offer if I'd known it would bother you."

"It's not your fault," she said, crossing to the broom, mortified that Ryan had just witnessed her interaction with Tessa. She busied herself by sweeping the hair clippings into a pile, hoping to hide her embarrassment.

"Tessa's just growing up too fast," she said, the inadequacy of her situation falling upon her. Tessa needed both a mother's and father's wisdom to guide her during these years of transitioning from a girl to a woman. Instead all she had was an older sister who scolded her whenever she misbehaved.

Caroline had been doing her best to take good care of her brothers and sisters, but it never seemed to be enough.

"You're doing a good job, Caroline," Ryan said.

She paused in her sweeping. How did he always know what she needed to hear? "I wish she had Mother."

"She's got you. You're working tirelessly in training her to be a godly young woman."

"And she hates me."

"Nay, she's stretching her wings. Pushing against the limits a little. Getting ready to fly. She may not recognize the blessing you've been to her right now, but someday she will."

Caroline leaned on the broom handle. "I'm worried that she'll do something completely reckless just to spite me."

"She's a good girl." Ryan sat forward, the front of his chair clunking against the floor. "She'll turn out all right. Just like you have." He grinned, his eyes taunting her.

She smiled back, unable to resist the bait. "I'm just 'all right'?"

"You're more than all right," he whispered.

Her stomach fluttered. "What about wonderful? Incredible?"

His grin stretched wider. "I'll only admit how wonderful you are if you admit that you want my attention all for yourself."

She started to sweep again, furiously but blindly. He was altogether too close to the truth, yet she couldn't admit it to him.

He gave a soft chuckle as if he'd guessed the truth, though she hadn't confessed anything. Then he rose. She thought he'd be on his way out of the house, but instead his footsteps brought him closer until his fingers closed around her arm.

At his touch, she sucked in a breath. Her body stilled so that all she could hear was the rapid beating of her heart.

He leaned in, and she could feel his breath against her hair. "So is it true that you wanted to be alone with me?"

She wanted to sway against him, to feel the hardness of his chest and the strength of his arms. Maybe Tessa was right with all of her accusations. Maybe she was simply a jealous big sister who wanted Ryan all to herself.

A scream from outside jarred Caroline. She sprang away from Ryan at the same time he did.

"Caroline! Caroline!" Tessa's shouts were filled with a panic that pummeled into Caroline.

She raced through the house and out the door. Ryan ran close behind her, and when she reached the front lawn of the house, he was beside her.

Tessa stood on the rocky shore, screaming and pointing to the lake. "Harry and Hugh! Their boat is sinking."

At the sight that met Caroline, her airways closed up and her knees buckled. Ryan caught her before she collapsed.

At least a hundred feet from the shore, Harry and Hugh were scooping water out of the rowboat, which was quickly sinking. They were already knee-deep in water, with the boat growing heavier by the second and nearing the level of the lake.

All Caroline could think about was the image of her father clinging to the bottom of the cutter, clutching the boat with one hand and the doctor with the other, the heavy, dark waves crashing against him and dragging him under.

Against her, Ryan's body tightened. He lowered her to the ground. "Stay here," he said. Then he kicked off his boots and shed his shirt and trousers so that he was down to his under-clothes.

He cupped his hands and called to the boys, "Keep bailing! I'm coming!"

Caroline cried out but could barely get out a wheeze. She struggled to her feet. She had to go out there too. She wouldn't sit back and let her brothers and Ryan drown before her eyes. She'd had to watch her father die, and she wouldn't do that again.

Ryan sprinted into the water. Once he was in up to his waist, he dove and began to swim against the waves toward the boys.

Caroline stumbled to the shore after him. She bent to unlace her boots, but her fingers twisted in the strings. She yanked at them harder and only made a knot. A frustrated cry slipped from her lips.

Tears streamed down Caroline's cheeks as she called to the boys over and over to hang on, to scoop faster. But soon the lake water began to pour into the boat faster than they could bail it out. The boat dipped lower until the edge disappeared underwater altogether, and fear filled the boys' faces.

The panic in Caroline's chest was paralyzing. She couldn't breathe, couldn't move, couldn't even speak. Once again she could only watch in horror, her soul screaming but her voice silent.

Ryan shouted at them as he approached, and once they saw him swimming steadily toward them, they fixed their attention upon him and began to follow his instructions. They climbed out of the sinking vessel and started to swim toward Ryan. Fortunately, Father had made sure his children learned how to swim at an early age. Even so, Caroline knew the big lake was no match for two young boys. A current or a strong wave could pull under even the strongest of swimmers.

She released another wheeze when the boys finally made it

to Ryan. They were gasping and spitting out water, but they'd managed to stay afloat. They clung to Ryan as though he were a lifeline.

Caroline shuddered, and when Tessa sidled next to her, Caroline slipped an arm around her sister. No matter their differences, she loved Tessa, and they needed each other at that moment.

With the weight of the two boys holding on to him, Ryan sank underwater, his head disappearing for several long seconds. When he popped back up, she began to shake. She didn't want Ryan to die either. In fact, the very thought of life without him filled her with an aching hollowness. Tessa's steady strength at her side was the only thing that kept her on her feet.

They watched wordlessly as Ryan began the swim back to shore, one twin on either side gripping his shoulders and paddling alongside him. When they finally reached shallow water, Tessa let go of her and rushed into the water to meet them. Sobbing, Tessa grabbed Harry, relieving Ryan of one burden.

At the sight of Harry shivering violently, Caroline plunged in. The bitter cold of the water chilled her to the bone and seemed to wake her from her stupor. She floundered toward Hugh, lifting him off Ryan and dragging him the rest of the way back to shore.

She sank to the rocky ground next to Harry and Tessa, pulling them both into her arms, letting her tears mingle with theirs.

Panting, Ryan crawled out of the water. He sank into a heap, his face pinched in agony, his injured arm cradled against his side.

For a long moment, Tessa's sobbing, Harry's and Hugh's sniffling, and Ryan's labored breathing filled the air. A distant call of a migrating goose and the lap of waves couldn't bring peace to Caroline's soul today.

With teeth chattering, Harry wiped his sleeve across his dripping nose. "I'm freezing."

Caroline turned toward Ryan, wanting to thank him, needing to know he was okay. He lifted his head wearily. "Take the boys inside," he said. "Get them dry and warm before they catch a chill."

She nodded and stood to her feet with Hugh. She reached a hand toward Ryan. "Come inside too. You need to get warm."

"Take care of the boys first," he rasped, letting his head drop, almost as if the pain was too much for him to bear.

She hesitated, but when Hugh shuddered again, she nodded and rushed him toward the house.

Ryan leaned against the boathouse and wrapped the wool blanket around his torso. Even though he'd warmed long ago, his entire body still trembled at what had almost happened earlier in the day.

Hugh and Harry had almost drowned.

If Tessa hadn't gone outside when she did . . .

He whispered another prayer of thanks that God had seen fit to give him the strength to make it back to shore. There had been a time or two he'd wanted to cry out from the bite of the piece of shrapnel in his arm. It had been so agonizing, he'd had to fight not to black out. But somehow, by the grace of God, he'd made it in spite of the pain.

Maybe God was trying to tell him that he could do more than he believed he was capable of doing. Maybe he'd assumed that with his injury he'd never be able to shoulder real work again, that he'd be useless and half a man the rest of his life.

But like with so many other things, he was realizing he'd been mistaken, that perhaps he could do more than he'd ever thought possible.

He glanced through the grimy boathouse window to the place where his leather satchel sat with the rest of his belongings. He'd refused to take more whiskey from Simmons. He'd given up his pain pills. All he had left was one little tin flask in his satchel. There was no sense in getting rid of it. Such a tiny thing would be easy to resist. In fact, keeping it would force him to grow all the stronger in his resistance.

The door of the keeper's cottage squeaked open. In the gray light of the afternoon, Caroline came striding toward him, a steaming mug in her hand.

His pulse quickened at the sight of her. Maybe he hadn't had enough faith in himself. But Caroline had never doubted him. Not once. She'd believed in him all along.

She stopped several feet away and held out the mug.

He took it and wrapped his good hand around it, letting the warmth seep into his skin.

"How are you?" she asked.

Somehow he knew she was asking about his arm, that she'd known the incredible effort it had taken to rescue the boys. "I'm in some pain," he admitted.

She nodded at the mug. "Maybe the birchbark tea will help a little."

He took a sip of the bitter brew.

"Thank you for saving their lives." Her lower lip trembled.

"How are they?" The hot liquid made a trail down his throat to his stomach.

"We gave them both hot baths, fed them warm milk, and snuggled them under piles of quilts. And now Tessa's reading to them."

"Then they're not too shaken up?"

"I think they'll be just fine. They're sturdy little men."

"Good." He breathed out the pent-up anxiety that had settled in his chest since they'd disappeared inside the house.

"Tessa feels guilty about not watching them closer."

He nodded gravely. "She can't be too hard on herself. Boys are boys, and regardless of what anyone does to protect them, they're bound to make some mischief."

"They said the water came in through a small hole in the side of the boat." Wisps of hair floated around her face, which was still pale.

"They didn't notice the hole before they set out?"

"Apparently it was plugged up. The plug pushed out once they were in deeper water and started fishing."

His mind scrambled to make sense of Caroline's words. Had someone tampered with the boat? Cut a hole and then plugged it in anticipation of the boat's sinking?

"Do you think someone intentionally cut a hole through the hull?" Her voice was raspy with the effort to speak, her lips still shaking.

He wanted to reassure her that no one would do such a thing, but he couldn't lie to her. "We won't know for sure what really happened unless we get a good look at the boat." But the boat was down at the bottom of the lake. They'd likely never see it again.

"What if the same person who did the other things did this . . . ?" But Caroline couldn't finish the thought.

The fear and worry in her beautiful blue eyes made him long to pull her into his arms, to wrap himself around her and promise her that he'd take care of everything, that she'd never have to worry again. But he couldn't make such an extravagant promise, even though he wished he could. "We'll have to keep a better watch out for anyone snooping around the place."

Maybe he'd stay up the next couple of nights and keep a lookout for anyone or anything suspicious. He was having a hard time sleeping in the bed anyway. Every time he lay down, thoughts of Caroline tormented him and only stirred his yearning for her. And of course his slumber was tortured by other, less pleasant, thoughts too.

Sometimes he couldn't help wondering if he'd been too hasty in giving up his pain pills. There were still too many times when he wanted to escape, to sleep without any nightmares of the war and of the slain boy.

Aye, telling Caroline that night in the cellar had been freeing. But he knew he wouldn't be truly free until he returned to the family and paid them the debt he owed, and asked their forgiveness for his standing by and doing nothing.

Caroline stared out over the lake, the waves ebbing with a steady rhythm, the gray water reflecting the low, dark clouds. "I think it would be safest for us to leave. It's becoming too dangerous here."

"Nay, you can't leave. Not yet."

"Someone is clearly trying to force me out," she said, glancing to the woodpile, then to the well, as if someone were lurking nearby and waiting to spring out at her.

"We don't know for sure—"

"Ryan, look at everything that's happened. They can't all be a coincidence."

"Do you have any idea who the culprit is?"

"It could be any number of people. Mr. Simmons, Mr. Finick, perhaps someone Mr. Finick hired, maybe a complete stranger."

Ryan shook his head. Mr. Simmons had shared his dislike

for Caroline's father, and his desire for Caroline to be out of the lighthouse. Still, Ryan couldn't picture Simmons sneaking around the lighthouse. "I doubt Simmons is doing this. He seems more like the kind of man to pick a real fight, not resort to these underhanded tactics."

"He knows I'm like my father, that I won't ever turn off the light for him during one of his smuggling attempts. So maybe he shut me in the cellar so that the light would stay dark. Then he wouldn't have the worry of getting caught bringing in his supplies."

Ryan wasn't surprised to learn that Simmons was smuggling, but his muscles flexed at the thought of the man doing such a terrible thing in order to carry out his plans.

"Has he asked you to turn off the light yet for him?" she asked, hugging her arms across her chest.

"Nay," he began, but then he thought back to the conversations he'd had with Simmons whenever he visited the Roadside Inn, the free whiskey Simmons had given him. Was the tavern owner plunging him into debt so that he'd have no option but to repay the friendship by turning off the light during the smuggling operations? "You don't think Simmons and Finick are working together, do you?"

Caroline raised an eyebrow. "I highly doubt it."

"But it makes sense." Ryan straightened, and the wool blanket fell away from his shoulders. "The day I arrived, Simmons said Finick hired me, saying I was the sort of man they'd be able to work with."

His gut roiled at the implications. As an injured drunk with a craving for opium pills, he'd likely be considered a good candidate to aid Simmons in his smuggling. Simmons wouldn't have to ask him to turn off the light. He would miss lighting it on his own . . . if not for Caroline.

Ryan hung his head.

Caroline didn't speak for a few moments, and he could see that she was coming to the same conclusion as him. Finally she spoke. "I don't think Mr. Finick would be involved in the smuggling. Allowing the lantern to remain unlit goes against everything he stands for."

"Aye, but sometimes money has a way of persuading even the staunchest of men."

"You think Mr. Simmons is bribing Mr. Finick to put a light-keeper here who will aid the smuggling?"

"Maybe not *aid*," Ryan said, "but at least not oppose it."

"And because I'm still here, the light has remained lit."

The whole explanation stung his pride, although he knew it shouldn't. He'd done this to himself with his foolhardy drinking. But no longer. He was changing.

"From now on, it will remain lit," he promised.

She turned her big eyes upon him, sweeping him off his feet in one little movement. "But apparently they want me gone. And as long as I'm here, I'll be putting my family in danger."

He didn't like the thought that she was in danger either. He didn't want to think about what the perpetrator might do the next time he attacked and who would get hurt as a result. But still . . .

"I don't want you to leave," he whispered. "Please . . ."

He knew it was selfish, yet he didn't want to lose her. She'd become a rock in his life, and he didn't know how he'd go on without her near him.

"Please stay." He didn't care that he was practically begging her. "I promise we'll stand strong and fight this battle together. I'll go out today and confront Simmons. I'll tell him to leave you alone. I'll make sure he knows that even if you're not here, I'll be lighting the lantern every night."

For a long moment she didn't say anything. When at last she gave a nod and said, "Okay," he let out his breath, relieved he wouldn't have to lose her. Not yet anyway.

❦

Ryan let the tavern door slam behind him. Standing at a nearby table, Arnie spun so quickly that he dropped a mug. It crashed against the wood-plank floor, the shards of brown glass skittering in all directions.

"Where's your father?" Ryan demanded.

Arnie didn't speak. Instead his fingers tightened around a knife he'd cleared from the table. Although the instrument was blunt and covered with grainy butter, Arnie had twisted it until it was pointing straight at Ryan.

"Chambers," Simmons called from a side door that Ryan presumed led into the man's office. In the dim lighting, Ryan could make out a large oak desk, along with ledgers. "What can I do for you, my friend?" Simmons's smile turned up knowingly. "I figured you wouldn't be able to stay away for too long." His sleeves were rolled up, showing off his muscles and tattoos.

Ryan tried to ignore the bar and the bottles lining the shelves on the wall. Nevertheless, a sudden and powerful thirst parched his throat and made his tongue dry with desire.

A drink wouldn't hurt anyone, would it? What if he sat down at the bar and had just one mug of beer while discussing matters with Simmons?

As if sensing the direction of his thoughts, Simmons started toward the bar. "Come on. I'll get you a shot of whiskey."

Ryan glanced around the nearly deserted room, with only a few men seated at a far table. No one would have to know.

Arnie bent down and began picking up the broken glass as if giving him permission too.

Ryan's mind shouted at him to back out the door now while he still had the chance. But he dragged in a lungful of the tanginess of beer that lingered in the air, and the craving for it hooked into him and seemed to pull him forward against his will.

A crash of glass stopped him short, and his attention shifted to Arnie kneeling on the floor and sucking his finger with the pieces of glass strewn around him again.

At the commotion, Simmons spun and glared at Arnie. "Why don't you ever watch what you're doing?"

Arnie lowered his head and said nothing as he went on cleaning up the mess he'd made.

Ryan struggled to remember why he'd come to the tavern in the first place.

Simmons started toward his son, his bald head wrinkling with the intensity of his frown. He wound a bar towel tighter with each step he took.

"Stay away from Caroline Taylor," Ryan blurted.

Arnie's head snapped up at the mention of Caroline's name.

"Stop harassing her or you'll have to answer to me," Ryan added.

Simmons halted, and his frown faded into first surprise, then anger. "I don't know what you're talking about, Chambers. And I certainly don't appreciate you coming in here and leveling accusations at me. That isn't the way friends treat one another."

"Then you're telling me you know nothing about the hole in the boat or the mutilated duck or the ruined garden?"

"You're spouting nonsense." Simmons's voice rose with his mounting irritation.

Ryan studied the tavern owner's face, the hard set of his jaw and the furrowed brow. Something told him the man wasn't putting on an act, that he really had no knowledge of the recent harassment. His earlier observation was correct. Simmons was too forthright. If he wanted Caroline out of the lighthouse, he'd ride out and tell her so face-to-face.

"Is Finick behind the harassment?" Ryan asked.

"I don't worry myself with Finick's methods," Simmons said. "So long as he gets the right man in the lighthouse, I don't care how he goes about it."

"And am I the right man?" Ryan pressed.

Simmons narrowed his eyes. "So long as Caroline is there, I doubt you'll be much help. But once she's finally gone, then I'm sure you'll be just right for the job."

The tavern owner's words cut deep. Ryan had thought he was getting better. But a nagging at the back of Ryan's mind told him that perhaps he hadn't changed enough yet, that maybe he wasn't as strong as he needed to be.

"I'm not the man you think I am," Ryan said.

Simmons laughed and started again toward Arnie, who'd picked up most of the broken glass off the floor and set the pieces on the table.

"I'm planning to do a good job with the lighthouse," Ryan stated more firmly. "I'm committed to making sure the light is always on."

But Simmons was already upon Arnie, grabbing him by one of his large ears. "I'm docking the broken mug from your pay."

"Y-yes, s-sir," Arnie managed to get out.

Then Simmons snapped the towel like a whip against Arnie's back. The young man cried out at the contact and then hunched into a ball, covering his head with his arms.

"Leave him alone!" Ryan demanded. "The broken mug was an accident."

Simmons shoved his son into the table, causing the pieces of glass to topple to the floor again. He marched toward Ryan, his eyes blazing with a fury Ryan hadn't seen there before. He'd heard rumors about the man's hot temper and guessed he was about to see it for himself. He steeled his body for the first punch.

But Simmons stopped a foot away and nodded to the door. "You best get on out of here before I decide to teach you a lesson you won't soon forget."

Ryan hesitated before turning and making his way to the door. Although he was tempted to teach Simmons a lesson of his own, one that involved treating his son with more respect, Ryan had the feeling he'd only end up causing more trouble. He'd gotten the answers he came seeking. For now, he needed to return to the lighthouse and make sure Caroline and her family were safe.

He still wasn't any closer to discovering the culprit, yet he was reasonably sure it wasn't Simmons. Or at least he hoped it wasn't.

Chapter 18

*L*ook!" Harry called as they neared the lighthouse yard. "I think that's our boat!"

Walking next to Ryan, Caroline's gaze followed Harry's pointed finger to the beach south of the lighthouse. Sure enough, there on the water's edge, flipped upside down, was a rowboat. With each lap of the waves, the boat wedged farther up onto the rocks.

For a moment, she could picture her father rowing away, raising his hand in good-bye to her. She'd always waited on the shore until he waved, and then she lifted onto her toes, stretched her arm, and waved back. Somehow the memory didn't sting anymore but filled her with a bittersweet warmth.

Harry and Hugh were already racing toward the hulk before Caroline could say anything.

Ryan stopped and smiled at her, and there wasn't a trace of the usual pain etching his face. He appeared relaxed, happy. She was getting a glimpse of the whole, strong man he'd once been.

The fall sunshine poured down on them. Though the temperature was cool, the sun warmed her face, and the day seemed

233

bright with endless possibilities. Especially because Ryan had gone to church with her and the boys for the first time. And also because it had been a week since the near-drowning incident and nothing more had happened.

Ryan had insisted that Mr. Simmons wasn't behind the distressing events of late at the lighthouse. But Caroline couldn't keep from noticing that nothing else had happened since Ryan had ridden to the Roadside Inn last week. Perhaps it was because Mr. Simmons knew he was under suspicion. Or perhaps it was because Ryan had been standing watch at night, his rifle at his side. He'd patrolled the perimeter and had even put Hugh and Harry on guard while he slept.

Had Ryan's presence scared away the perpetrator, or had she simply worried for nothing?

Maybe she'd made a bigger deal out of everything that had happened than was warranted. Maybe the near-drowning had just been an accident after all. The rowboat had been old, one they'd bought from a retired fisherman after the lighthouse-issued boat had sunk when Father died. Perhaps the old boat had finally sprung a leak.

Caroline sighed, inhaling the crisp air laden with the scent of damp leaves and wet grass.

"Have I told you yet today how pretty you look?" Ryan asked, then reached for her hand and laced his fingers through hers.

"Yes. You've told me." She couldn't—didn't want to—resist the gentle pressure of his fingers surrounding hers.

His eyes swept over her again, taking in her best Sunday-meeting dress. It was a pale blue color that her father had said matched her eyes. The dress accented her slender waist and had a modest neckline that still revealed more skin than her everyday blouses.

Ryan's gaze shifted to her face, to her cheeks and mouth, before settling on her eyes. "You're beautiful," he whispered.

His tenderness sent the usual pleasure to her belly. Over the past week, they'd had very few opportunities to be alone. At times Ryan seemed to go out of his way to make sure they had a chaperone whenever they were together for any length of time.

But she wasn't sure how much longer they could go on this way. There was something altogether too strong between them, and instead of it diminishing from their being apart, it only seemed to grow. Surely she didn't need to have any concerns about her involvement with Ryan. He was healing. He wasn't drinking anymore.

He didn't let go of her hand but instead tugged her forward, his happiness contagious. His touch burned into her and made her middle do several flips, but she resolved to be as carefree as him, at least for the rest of the day. If he could simply enjoy being together without worrying about their attraction and where it was leading, then couldn't she?

"Let's race," he said with a grin. Without waiting for her protest, he pulled her along with him until they were both breathless and laughing. By the time they reached Harry and Hugh, she felt fully alive, the air cool on her flushed cheeks. Her heart swelled with the joy of being with Ryan and holding his hand. Since it was the Sabbath, the day spread before her with nothing to do but spend it with him. And she couldn't imagine anything better.

The boys had discarded their shoes and socks, rolled up their trousers, and were wading in the frigid water, attempting to flip the boat over. Ryan quickly shed his shoes and joined them.

She stood back and watched, savoring the beauty of the day,

the bright blue of the water, and the vivid reds and oranges that still remained on the maples.

"Are you afraid of getting your feet cold?" Ryan teased her as he splashed in the lake.

"I'm just the smart one," she said, then gave an easy smile. "I'm staying warm and dry and letting you boys do the dirty work."

She wasn't surprised anymore by how effortless it felt to banter with him. Even if she was flirting at times, he'd become a true friend. Not only could she tease him and enjoy his company, but she could talk to him about anything, and he'd not only listen but understand.

She'd never experienced such a relationship with any girl friend, not even with Esther. It was strange but not unpleasant to have such an open and easy friendship with Ryan. She supposed that made her attraction to him all the stronger.

With Ryan's strength at the stern and the twins' at the bow, they managed to carry the boat up onto the shore. Once they had it a safe distance from the water, they turned it over onto its hull.

For a moment, Caroline couldn't make sense of the sight that met her. And then she screeched and shrank back. For nailed to the thwart was a mallard duck, its wings outstretched and its glossy-green head twisted at an odd angle, blood oozing from the eye that had been punctured with a nail.

Hugh and Harry both made exclamations at once, their questions and cries of dismay filling the pristine day. Ryan stepped closer to examine the duck.

Caroline cupped a hand over her mouth. Her body had frozen, but her mind sped forward with all the horror of the past month, each incidence coming back to echo the reality that someone was behind everything. That nothing had been an accident.

"What do you think it means?" Harry stepped into the boat next to Ryan.

"Is someone trying to send us a message?" Hugh asked, joining his brother.

Caroline couldn't make her lungs work to answer her brothers. She knew what it meant. The message was growing louder. Someone wanted her gone from the lighthouse. And now she knew with certainty that whoever was doing this wasn't going to stop tormenting her until she left.

Ryan straightened. His handsome face was creased with an angry frown. He scanned the distant woods beyond the marsh as if studying every tree, every blade of grass. He glanced beyond her to the boathouse, then the cottage and tower. His eyes narrowed, and he stiffened.

Caroline whirled around to see a plume of smoke rising from the passageway that connected the tower and the house. Her lungs constricted into tight balls. It couldn't be what she thought it was, could it? Yet rising smoke usually meant one thing . . .

"Fire!" Ryan shouted, leaping out of the boat.

Hearing the word *fire*, Hugh and Harry hopped out of the boat after him.

Wisps of smoke curled out of cracks in the window frame and rose into the air like long, dark fingers clawing the blue sky.

"Sarah, Tessa . . ." Caroline tried to shout their names, but they came out a croak.

Ryan had already started running toward the house, but at the names, his stride lengthened into a sprint, regardless of the fact that his boots were lying among the rocks near the rowboat.

"Caroline," he shouted over his shoulder, "start filling buckets of water as fast as you can. Hugh and Harry, you help too."

The boys didn't need to be told twice. They raced after Ryan, stopping at the boathouse to retrieve buckets while Ryan dashed to the front door of the cottage and disappeared inside.

Caroline tried to make her feet work, to run as fast as she could, but she tripped and stumbled all the way to the boathouse, where Hugh thrust a bucket already brimming with lake water into her hands.

She wanted to follow Ryan inside, to make sure that Sarah and Tessa were safely removed from the house. But panting for each breath, she forced her feet to veer toward the passageway, to the flames that were beginning to glow on the other side of the window. She had to trust that Ryan would rescue her sisters. And she had to do everything she could to save the lighthouse.

Let them lose the cottage. Let everything they owned burn up into oblivion. But she couldn't allow the fire to consume the tower, the beacon of hope for all the many ships that depended on it night after night.

When she reached the passageway door, she touched the knob only to jerk away at the searing heat. She dropped her bucket and picked up two large decorative stones she'd placed in her flower bed. Without a second thought, she heaved them against the window.

The glass shattered with sparks and flames shooting out the jagged holes left by the stones. She pulled back at the blast of heat and fumes. Harry was already next to her and tossing his bucket of water through the opening. As the water hit the flames, black smoke rose with a sizzle.

She picked up her bucket and threw the water at the flames. The smoke momentarily blinded her, and when she blinked past

238

the acridness, her heart plummeted. The two pails of water had hardly made a difference against the hungry fire.

Panic pushed her to action so that all she could think about was dousing the flames before they reached the tower. She raced to the water next to Hugh and Harry and rushed back with them to throw water again into the open window.

Out of the corner of her eye, she saw with relief that Ryan was carrying Sarah out of the house cradled in his arms and that Tessa followed close behind, dragging a bundle of possessions with her.

"We need help putting out the fire!" Harry called, running up the grassy knoll from the lake, his pail of water bouncing against his leg and sloshing over the rim.

Soon Tessa joined them, and they formed a bucket brigade from the lake to the house. They passed the water as fast as they could one after another, until the muscles in Caroline's arms grew weak from the heavy loads and her lungs ached for fresh air.

Ryan made several more trips into the house, carrying buckets of water, until finally he joined them outside. He kicked at the passageway door, and it crashed open. Caroline passed buckets to him, and he emptied them faster than she could supply. They worked hard for endless minutes, putting out the remaining half-dozen small fires.

Finally, after many more buckets, every flicker and glow of orange had disappeared. Instead, thick smoke filled the little room, escaping through the broken window and through a hole the flames had made in the ceiling.

Caroline collapsed on the grass and gasped for air. Through watery eyes she caught a glimpse of the interior, the blackened walls, the table, her logbooks, and everything else charred and half burned.

Ryan stepped out of the doorway. He was wearing her father's old boots, which he must have slid on when he'd gone in to rescue Sarah and Tessa. His shirt and trousers were seared in spots from sparks. His face was black with soot, making the whites of his eyes even whiter. His attention flitted to each person where they rested on the grass as if assessing their condition before finally coming to rest on her.

"Are you all right?" he asked.

She didn't have the energy to do much more than nod. She could only stare straight ahead, wheezing and trying to catch her breath.

Ryan's brow furrowed and he came over and knelt beside her.

"I'll be okay in a minute," she said past the tightness in her throat.

He laid his hand on her back. "Everything's going to be fine." His tone was gentle and soothing. He started to knead the tight muscles in her neck.

After a while she could feel her body begin to loosen from the viselike grip of panic.

"Everyone's safe," he assured her. "And we saved the house and tower."

His fingers on her neck were firm and warm. Slowly they squeezed the worry out of her system. Her hair hung in disarray, having come free from the knot she'd worn at the base of her neck earlier to church. His hand now moved from her neck to the loose hair. He tenderly brushed the strands, caressing them down her back, and then looked at her with wrinkled brows.

"I'm doing better," she said, but her words came out weak and shaky.

He wiped a finger across her cheek, which she had no doubt was covered with soot. It took her a moment to realize that one hand was still on her back—his good hand—and that he was touching her face with his injured one. She was surprised he had the hand out of his pocket. He did most things one-handed, keeping his scarred hand out of sight.

As if realizing what he'd done, embarrassment flickered in his eyes and he dropped the hand, ready to stuff it back in his pocket. Before he could do so, she grasped his hand and lifted his two remaining fingers back to her face. Without hesitating, she pressed them against her cheek.

His eyes widened.

She leaned into his palm, hoping he could see the truth in her eyes, the truth that his battle wounds didn't frighten her or cause her to think less of him. She admired him for his bravery and his willingness to go on with life after all the suffering he'd gone through.

His muscles turned hard beneath her touch.

She was tempted to slide his hand over to her lips and kiss his injury to show him that his mangled flesh didn't repulse her. But with her brothers and sisters sitting only a short distance behind her, likely watching her interaction with Ryan, she refrained.

Instead, she smiled at him, hoping he could read her thoughts and that he wouldn't mistake them for pity. But before he could react, Monsieur Poupard rounded the house at a limping run. His weathered face was red, and he was breathless, his chest heaving as if he'd run the entire distance from his tiny log cabin by the old windmill to the lighthouse.

Ryan stood and stuffed his hands quickly into his pockets.

Monsieur Poupard staggered to a stop at the sight of them all resting in the grass in front of the lighthouse. "I saw smoke," he managed, looking to the blackened passageway and then back to the children.

"Aye, we had a fire," Ryan said.

The old Frenchman turned toward Sarah, who lay motionless, curled up on a blanket where Ryan had deposited her. Her lips were blue, almost the same color as the lake, and her face was even paler in the bright sunshine of the afternoon. Though too weak to move, she smiled at Monsieur Poupard.

At her attention, the man seemed to melt. The wrinkles in his scowling face smoothed, his eyes lit, and his mouth curved into a gentle return smile.

Caroline could only stare in amazement at the transformation.

"The little sick girl is safe?" he asked.

"Aye," Ryan replied. "Thank the Lord. We're all fine."

"I hurried here as fast as I could." Monsieur Poupard wiped his brow with the edge of his red cloak.

"We were able to contain the fire to the passageway," Ryan said, nodding at the still-smoking roof. "I doused the inner door and wall with water to slow down the spread of the flames into the keeper's cottage."

Gratefulness welled up in Caroline. Ryan's quick thinking had saved the house.

Monsieur Poupard hobbled toward the door and peered inside. "How did the fire start?"

"One of the lanterns looked like it had been knocked over," Ryan answered.

"But it wasn't lit," Tessa said from where she was sprawled in the grass. "I never leave the lanterns burning during the daytime. Caroline has always warned me that it wastes oil."

"Maybe there was still a small flicker of flame?" Ryan suggested.

Or maybe someone purposefully started the fire. Caroline

didn't speak the words aloud. She didn't want to scare her siblings any more than they already were.

"You have to believe me." Tessa rose, and her lovely features were stricken. Her long hair had come loose too, but somehow it still looked beautiful and even fluttered in glorious dark waves. "I didn't leave the lantern burning. It wasn't my fault."

"Nay," Ryan said. "I'm not blaming you, lass. Not in the least. It was probably just an accident. That's all."

An accident? Just like all the other bad things that had happened recently? A shiver crept up Caroline's back. Deep inside she knew the fire wasn't an accident. Just like her getting trapped in the cellar wasn't an accident. Or the ruined garden, or the boys nearly drowning, or the duck nailed to the rowboat . . .

She had to face the truth once and for all. Someone wanted her to leave, and they would keep on threatening her and her family until she complied.

Hugh and Harry had risen from the grass and joined Ryan and Monsieur Poupard at the door of the passageway, looking inside and trying to determine the cause of the fire.

But Caroline couldn't make herself get up, not even to check on Sarah. She could only stare at the scorched house, tears blinding her at the awfulness of all that had happened lately, especially how close her siblings had come to losing their lives. First Hugh and Harry in the boat, and now Sarah and Tessa in the house.

What if she and Ryan and the boys had lingered in town longer after church? Or what if Ryan hadn't turned around and noticed the smoke?

Caroline shuddered.

Her family could have been killed both times. They still could be killed or harmed if she didn't do something to stop this madness.

She had to put an end to it. Today. Now. Before anything else happened. Blinking back her tears, she glanced around the lighthouse grounds, the barren flower beds, the yellowing grass, the rocky shore, the various-sized buckets now lying abandoned. She tried to view everything coldly, through distant eyes. She willed her heart to let go of this place she'd come to love.

Her family's safety was more important than anything else.

As hard as leaving Windmill Point Lighthouse would be, and as much as she'd wanted to put it off, she couldn't any longer. It was time to say good-bye to the lighthouse. She couldn't risk another day here. Not another minute.

She sat up, straightened her shoulders. Suddenly she knew where she needed to go and what she had to do. She didn't dare look at Ryan or the others. Instead, she swallowed the inner protest that rose all too swiftly, stood to her feet, and walked to the lake to clean herself up.

They would stop her if they knew where she was going. She felt certain of it.

Her best course of action was to sneak away when everyone was busy, when no one was looking. Then she'd rush to get the deed done as quickly as possible before anyone could step in and talk her out of it.

Chapter 19

Ryan spread another blanket on the grass, hoping the fresh air would lessen the smoky scent that permeated each fiber. While he'd contained the fire to the passageway, smoke had seeped into the house and filled every crevice and corner.

"Last one," Hugh said as he tossed down a quilt.

Everyone had worked tirelessly for the past hour, including Monsieur Poupard, in trying to clear out the house. They'd focused primarily on Sarah's room, since the chill of day had caused her to start wheezing. When they finally settled her back in her bed, they started opening up the rest of the house and fanning out the smoke.

Tessa and Caroline had been busy boiling herbs that would supposedly lessen the effects of the smoke, and they'd also been hanging rugs and linens on the clothesline.

Ryan straightened, ignoring the burning that rippled through his arm. He'd gotten better at pretending the pain didn't exist, and at times could almost believe he no longer had a piece of shrapnel buried in his arm. It certainly didn't bother him the way it first had, and he supposed the strengthening of his muscles and constant use had built up his endurance.

He flexed his arm and looked down at the place where his fingers had once been, at the puckered red skin that existed in their place. He'd forgotten about his mangled hand and had touched Caroline's face with his ugly stump. Humiliated at the thought, he tucked his hand in his pocket.

Caroline hadn't minded the contact, but had pressed his hand back against her cheek, as if telling him that his deformity didn't matter to her. Could that really be true? Doubts warred within him, working to cloud the truth. The truth that she'd accepted him with all of his glaring problems, that she'd been kind and helpful when she had no reason to be, and that she'd never passed judgment even when he'd deserved it.

His chest swelled with gratefulness—and something more. He searched the yard, needing a glimpse of her.

"Are you looking for Caroline again?" Hugh asked, peering up at him, his freckled face still streaked with soot and his brown hair flying away in all directions.

"You're always looking at her," Harry said. He had a broom in his hands and was beating one of the rugs that hung from the clothesline.

Was it that obvious that he longed for Caroline?

Both boys stopped their work and watched him, waiting for an explanation for why he stared at their sister so much.

He thought about making up some excuse, but he had a feeling the boys would see right through him. He reached over and ruffled Hugh's hair and then grinned at Harry. "Aye. Guilty as charged. I can't keep my eyes off her, can I?"

"Do you like her?" Hugh asked, stuffing one hand in his pocket.

Ryan studied the boy. Was Hugh imitating him? With his hand in his pocket, the way his feet were spread, and even the way he cocked his head, all reminded Ryan of himself. Without their father to influence them, were the boys looking to him and following his example?

He bit back a glib answer about how he felt about Caroline and chose his words more carefully. "Your sister is a very fine woman. One of the finest I've ever met."

Harry stepped around the rug, his face and hair just as messy as his brother's. "Are you gonna marry her?"

Marry Caroline? Ryan had a sudden flash of earlier that day when they'd walked back to the lighthouse after church, the way she'd smiled at him, as if offering him the whole world in that smile.

Aye, he wanted to wake up to her encouraging smile every morning and let it be the last thing he saw every night. But he wasn't ready to get married, was he? He still had a debt to pay, and he couldn't settle down or support a family until he'd made good on his vow.

"Caroline would sure make a good wife," Hugh said, his eyes expectant, hopeful.

"Aye, she would," Ryan agreed. "She'll make some man a good wife. But I'm not certain that man is me—"

"She left a little while ago," Harry said, cutting him off, nodding in the direction of the dirt road that ran through the marsh.

"Left?"

"I think she was sneaking off," Harry said. "She walked away like she didn't want anyone to see her."

"How long has she been gone?"

Harry shrugged. "A while."

A strange stillness fell over Ryan. He stared at the road. He couldn't imagine why Caroline would sneak away without telling anyone where she was going or why.

Aye, she'd been upset after the fire. But after she calmed down, he thought she'd be all right. Sure, her face had remained pale and pinched, and she'd spoken very little. He'd just assumed she was still shaken up a bit and that was all.

Then an awful thought clamored within him. What if she'd decided to move out of the lighthouse? What if today's incident with the duck and the fire had pushed her too far?

His body tensed with the need to go after her, to soothe her and assure her that everything would be okay. But would it be okay? Or was he simply fooling himself and her too? Maybe by living at the lighthouse, she was truly putting herself and her family in grave danger.

If she'd come to that conclusion, then she probably acted on the need to protect them. She was too loyal and too devoted to them to do otherwise. A thousand possibilities flashed through his mind, none of them pleasant.

"Do you have any idea where she was going?" Even as he asked the question, another horrible thought flooded him. Had she gone to Arnie Simmons?

Raw fear jolted his body into action. He started toward his horse that was tied on a long rope under a nearby tree.

"Where are you going?" the boys called, following after him.

Tessa stepped out of the house, letting the door bang shut behind her.

"I have to go after Caroline," he replied.

"Where did she go?" Tessa had bunched her long skirt in her hand and began running behind him.

"I think she went to the Roadside Inn to marry Arnie."

"What? She can't do that," Tessa cried.

"Don't worry, I won't let her." Ryan reached the horse and fumbled at the knot, his fingers unable to work. The need to stop Caroline had his nerves on edge.

Tessa and the boys stood behind him and watched, their faces solemn and filled with concern.

"If she marries Arnie, then we'll be stuck here at Grosse Pointe," Tessa said.

"If she marries Arnie, she'll be in for a life of misery," Ryan added. But he knew that alone wouldn't stop Caroline. She'd sacrifice her life and future for her family, even if that meant marrying someone she didn't love. And he wouldn't let her do that; he had to reach her before she went through with the deed.

What if she and Arnie were on their way to the pastor's house even now?

Ryan used his injured fingers, not caring that the others were watching. Caroline was more important than his hand, his dignity, and everything else.

"What if she refuses to come back?" Tessa asked.

With a last jerk, he freed the horse. He hoisted himself into the saddle and urged the mare forward. "I'll bring her back." He nodded at the boys and then shifted his horse so he was looking down at Tessa. "The keeper job belongs to Caroline. It's never been mine. I should be the one leaving, not her."

Tessa peered up at him, shielding her eyes from the sun. "If you leave, where will you go?"

He dug his heels into the horse's flanks. "I'll go West. I hear there's plenty of work out there."

"West?" Her face lit up. "I've always wanted to go West."

He gave the horse another kick, and the beast bolted forward. He honestly didn't know what he'd do. All he knew was that ever since he'd arrived here, bad things had started happening to Caroline and her family. Maybe the threats were a warning to *him* and not her. If he pretended to leave for the West for a few days but secretly stayed nearby to keep an eye on her, perhaps he could discover what was really going on.

"Take me with you!" Tessa's call followed him. "Please! We could get married. I'd make you a good wife."

With a flick of the reins, he pushed his horse into a gallop. The pounding of hooves drowned out Tessa's voice. Under any other circumstances, he would have stopped and gently informed her that they could never get married. Even if she was a lovely young lady, he had no feelings of attraction for her. He viewed her as a sister, not as a possible bride.

Aye, he'd noticed her flirting, but he hadn't made much of it. But perhaps he needed to make sure he wasn't encouraging her affection. She was obviously reading more into their relationship than was there.

With his head bent low, he tore down the dirt road, his pulse pounding in a wild and reckless rhythm that matched the horse's. He urged the horse faster. How could Caroline even consider marrying Arnie?

For an instant, betrayal sliced into Ryan's heart. Didn't she care about him? He thought she'd enjoyed being with him, talking and laughing together. And he thought he'd seen attraction in her eyes. What about the kisses they'd shared? Hadn't they affected her the same way they had him?

As he rode, the chilled breeze cut through his shirt and slapped his cheeks as if to remind him that he was losing Caroline. If she married Arnie, he couldn't have her. His gut flamed in protest.

The truth was he wanted her. Aye. He'd never wanted a woman as much as he wanted Caroline Taylor.

Simmons's Roadside Inn loomed ahead, the peak of the slate

roof rising above the trees, and the whitewashed boards showing through the branches.

Galloping around the last bend in the road, his heart skittered to a stop at the sight of Caroline in her pretty blue Sunday dress. Even though it was covered with soot, it was still a bright spot among the browning landscape. She was walking with firm, steady steps, apparently resolved in her mission.

At the sound of his horse's hooves, she glanced over her shoulder.

"Caroline!" he shouted. He quickly closed the distance between them, reined in his horse beside her, and slid down off the saddle. His chest heaved from the strain of the ride. "Please . . . don't marry him."

Her beautiful blue eyes drooped like wilted flowers amidst the paleness of her face. "I have to."

"Nay, you don't."

"It's my best option, Ryan."

"I'll leave the lighthouse. I'll find a new job."

"That won't solve the problem." Her voice sounded so anguished, it tore at him. "Don't you see? The danger is all because of me. Because I haven't left the light yet."

"But none of this happened before I came. I'll leave and then things here can go back to the way they were before."

Her grip on her shawl was tight enough to turn her knuckles white. "Whether you're here or not, I'm clearly not wanted. And I can't put my family in danger any longer."

The determination in her eyes was palpable and sent alarm racing like cold water through his blood.

"My best option is to marry Arnie," she repeated, then turned away from him, lowered her head and walked forward, albeit more slowly than before. "Please don't try to stop me, Ryan."

"Nay!" He stalked after her, frustration pummeling him. He reached her in two easy strides, grabbed her arm, and forced her to stop and face him. "Nay, I'll not sit back and do nothing while you throw your life away."

Her eyes flashed, and she tried to yank out of his grasp.

"And marrying Arnie is *not* your best option." He held her tight and glared at her. "Your best option is marrying me."

At his words she froze.

He froze too, hardly daring to breathe. Had he just proposed marriage to her?

Her eyes widened in disbelief.

What was he thinking? Hadn't he just told the twins he wasn't ready to get married?

As if hearing his doubts, she started to shake her head.

"Aye," he said, sliding his hand into hers before she could pull away. Why not marry her? "If we get married, then you won't have to leave, and you won't have to move Sarah."

His words stopped her protest.

"The boys and Tessa would be taken care of. And you'd have everything you need."

"But we'd still be in danger," she said but less adamantly. "The person or people trying to drive us away might continue to hurt us."

"If someone is trying to drive you away, they wouldn't have a reason to do so—not after we're married." If Simmons wasn't behind the attacks, his next best guess was Finick. And if he married Caroline, Finick would have no choice but to leave them alone. That was his hope anyway. "You'd have every right to live at the lighthouse as my wife."

His wife . . . He'd been working hard to keep proper boundaries between himself and Caroline, but if he married her, he wouldn't have to worry about being alone with her anymore. He could touch her whenever he wanted. And kiss her . . . He couldn't stop his gaze from dropping to her lips.

As if sensing his desire, her lashes fell and she nibbled her lower lip, telling him she was probably thinking the same thing he was.

"No one would be able to make you leave the light." His voice came out husky. "Not if you're my wife."

"True," she said softly. "There are plenty of keepers' wives who serve as assistants."

"It's the perfect solution." He wondered why he hadn't thought of it earlier. He supposed part of him knew that Caroline wouldn't have considered it before. And he likely wouldn't have considered it either. But now she was willing to do anything to keep her family safe—even marry Arnie. And now he was desperate to keep her from doing so. The option seemed so much more viable.

"I may not be a much better choice than Arnie," he said, "but if you think you can put up with me . . ."

She smiled. Her eyes lit up and sparkled.

Before he could come up with any more excuses why he shouldn't marry her, he lowered himself to one knee. He placed his hand around hers and looked up into her face with as much earnestness as he could muster. "Caroline Taylor, will you do me the honor of becoming my wife?"

"Oh, Ryan," she said breathlessly. Her eyes shouted her acquiescence. He could see that she wanted to agree. Surely she couldn't deny her desire for him. He'd seen it, felt it.

"Please?" he whispered, not caring that he was practically begging her. He wasn't sure why he was so desperate for her to agree to his proposal, but his muscles tightened with anticipation.

She studied his face. The light in her eyes wavered. In that moment of hesitation, all the insecurities of the past months crept back.

"Would you mind if I take the night to think about it?" she asked gently.

Was she hoping that if she had the whole night, she might be able to come up with a kind way to turn him down?

He shook off the morbid thought, forced a grin, and rose to his feet. He didn't let go of her hand. He couldn't break the connection yet. "Of course I'll let you think about it tonight." He tried to make his voice playful. "But you have to promise me that you won't go running off again, especially to marry Arnie."

"I promise."

"Will you give me your answer in the morning?" he asked. The sooner they got married, the sooner they'd be able to send the message that they weren't leaving, that the scare tactics hadn't worked. And it was past time to involve the sheriff. They needed to find out who was responsible for the threats once and for all.

"I'll tell you first thing," she said.

"Good. I'll be waiting." Then something inside him coiled tight. He didn't want to think about the fact that she might say no. Now that he'd asked her, he realized he couldn't imagine life without her.

In the few short weeks he'd known her, she'd brought more healing to his life than months of medicine and treatments had. She'd become the soothing balm he needed. And now he didn't want to lose her. He was too afraid of the kind of man he might become again if he didn't have her by his side.

"Ready to go back home?" he asked.

At the snap of a nearby branch, Caroline started, fear flashing across her face.

"You're safe," Ryan assured her, twining his fingers through hers and tugging her close to his side. "I'll make sure of it."

Even as he said the words, he peered in the direction of the sound. He didn't see anyone, but that didn't stop the skin at the base of his neck from prickling. Instinct told him someone had been watching them.

"Let's go," he said, reaching for his horse.

When Caroline nodded at him, he breathed out his relief and whispered a silent prayer that by this time tomorrow night, he'd be a married man.

Chapter 20

By the time Caroline arrived back at the lighthouse, a strange calm had settled over her. Not even the sight of the blackened door of the passageway or the broken window or the charred siding could call forth the usual anxiety.

She wasn't exactly sure why her panic had evaporated, the panic that had almost driven her to Arnie, to almost accept his offer of marriage. It wasn't because Ryan had dropped to one knee and formally proposed to her. It couldn't be. There were still too many uncertainties and no guarantees that her family would be safe, even if she married Ryan.

She shrugged out of her shawl and tossed it over the back of the wing chair in the living room. She took a deep breath of the smoke-laden air, surprised that her nerves hadn't pinched her airways as they had earlier.

"Caroline?" Tessa's voice sounded from the kitchen. When she stepped into the doorway, her brow was creased with worry. She held the bottle of opium pills in one hand and a pestle and mortar in the other.

Caroline had no doubt that Sarah was in a great deal of pain after having been moved out of the house and that Tessa was grinding the pain medicine to ease the girl's discomfort. If such a short distance could disturb Sarah, Caroline didn't want to think about what a longer move would do.

Tessa inspected Caroline's ring finger. "You didn't marry him, did you?"

"Not yet." Ryan opened the door and stepped into the sitting room behind Caroline.

Her body thrummed to life at the sound of his voice and the hint of humor in it. She didn't dare turn around and look at him. She was afraid she'd fling herself into his arms and tell him yes, that she'd marry him—tonight. Especially if she saw the hurt in his eyes that he was trying to hide.

She hated that her hesitancy had brought him some pain, but she had to sort through her confusion before she gave him her answer. His proposal had happened so abruptly that she couldn't think, couldn't react or begin to make sense of what it meant.

He moved behind her, not quite touching her but close enough that she could feel his breath by her neck. "But our wedding will be soon, won't it?" And with that, he brushed a soft kiss against her cheek.

The merest touch ignited a flame in her belly. She had to hold herself rigid to keep from melting backward into him. She had the urge to run with him all the way to town and get married. Right then. Without waiting a second longer. But the rational part of her warned her that she couldn't marry him simply because she wanted to kiss him again, that a marriage needed to be built on much more than physical attraction.

"I don't understand," Tessa said. "I thought Caroline was running off to marry Arnie."

"She was," Ryan replied. "But I asked her to marry me instead."

Tessa's face drained of all color. "You can't marry Caroline."

"Why not? Then you can all stay here. You won't have to leave."

"But I want to leave!" Tessa cried. "And I told you that I want you to take me with you when you go."

Caroline shook her head, trying to make sense of what Tessa was saying. "You can't go with Ryan—"

"I'm old enough!" Tessa shot back. She took several steps forward, her dark eyes filled with determination. "I'm a woman now. I can make my own decisions."

"You can't just run off with Ryan or any other man—"

"I can do whatever I please." Tessa stamped her foot, her supple body shaking with a frustration Caroline didn't understand. "I'm perfectly capable of taking care of a man and my own house. I've been managing this house for years while you've been busy with the light."

The resentment that laced Tessa's declaration stopped Caroline's response. Had Tessa been unhappy all these years? Maybe Caroline had been wrong to assume that Tessa had been willing to take over so much responsibility.

Ryan cleared his throat. "Listen. I don't want to get into the middle of this, and the last thing I want to do is hurt you, Tessa."

Tessa lifted her chin, the slightly stubborn gesture frustrating Caroline all the more. The girl removed the cork on the vial of opium pills. Even that small sound and movement reeked with defiance. Tessa tipped the bottle and let a pill slide out into the mortar.

The motion drew Ryan's attention. At the sight of the medicine, hunger flashed across his expression. Though his body was free of the addicting pills, he obviously still struggled with craving them.

Tessa quickly recorked the vial and slipped it into her apron pocket.

Ryan took a breath and continued, "I'm not planning to leave the light."

"You said Caroline deserved the keeper job," Tessa insisted. "You said you'd leave so that she could have it. And you promised you'd take me with."

"I didn't promise you that," he said firmly.

Tessa pressed her pretty lips together into a pout. "I asked, and you didn't tell me no."

Ryan shook his head. "If Caroline agrees to marry me, then I'm staying. If she doesn't marry me, I'll gladly relinquish the lighthouse to her. I'll even ride into Detroit first thing tomorrow and make sure the Lighthouse Board knows exactly how qualified Caroline is for the job. And I'll tell them we suspect Finick is trying to drive you out."

He turned to Caroline and looked directly into her eyes. "One way or another, we'll get to the bottom of all that's happened."

Caroline gazed toward the rising sun, a faint outline of pink and orange behind a haze of clouds. She'd expected Ryan to relieve her hours ago, as had become his custom. He'd come up during the wee hours of the morning to take over extinguishing the light.

Their arrangement had allowed her to get more sleep and have more time during the day to do other things she'd been neglecting since her father's death.

She exhaled and savored the sense of calm that had stayed

with her all night. In fact, she hadn't worried during Ryan's absence either. She'd decided that he probably wanted to give her the opportunity to think about the marriage decision without pressuring her.

She'd been grateful for his sensitivity, since she hadn't been able to think about anything else all night long.

It had taken her some time, but she'd finally sorted out some of the reasons why she'd hesitated to accept his proposal. For one, she wasn't sure that he was completely ready for such a responsibility. It had only been a few weeks since he'd been drinking and medicating himself into a stupor. Was he healed enough to move forward with life?

She'd also realized that she longed to hear him say he wanted to marry her because he loved her and not just to rescue her from all her problems. But the truth was, there hadn't been any love between her and Arnie, and that hadn't stopped her from rushing off to marry him. Why did love have to be a part of the agreement with Ryan?

After struggling through that question during the dark hours of the night, she'd come to the conclusion that love didn't matter. Even if Ryan didn't love her, even if he was only marrying her to do the noble thing and save her from danger, they could still have a good life together. Perhaps they'd eventually fall in love. It was known to happen in marriages of convenience on occasion.

Besides, if she was completely honest with herself, she had to admit, she was already falling in love with him. At least that's what she thought was happening. Since she'd never been in love before, never even had a beau, she didn't quite know what all her feelings meant.

But she did know she admired Ryan, especially for his kindness and tenderness. She appreciated his sensitivity, his sweetness. And he was braver and more daring than he gave himself credit for. He never feared charging into dangerous situations. He was always willing to risk his own safety for the sake of others. And he never asked for anything in return.

Not only that, but he knew her. He could see inside to her fears. He accepted her despite her weaknesses, and somehow had a way of making her feel stronger. With him at her side, she felt as though she could bear the problems better.

The truth was, she couldn't ask for a better husband than Ryan Chambers. She didn't want any other man but him. She wanted to spend her life by his side. Together they could face whatever came their way.

She pushed away from the rounded window and her view of the eastern horizon, her heart light and bubbling with excitement.

Yes, she loved him.

Even if he hadn't said the words to her, even if he didn't love her yet, even if he wasn't completely healed, she'd still marry him. She'd give herself fully to him and pray that eventually he'd do the same.

With a lightness to her steps, she rushed down the spiraling stairway. She couldn't wait to see him and tell him the news of her decision. She could imagine his grin and the teasing spark in his warm, brown eyes.

She exited the doorway at the bottom of the tower to avoid the damaged passageway. As she made her way around the outside of the house, the silence and stillness of the house nagged her. Reaching the sitting room window, she peered inside. The room was dark without a trace of the usual activity for early morning.

She glanced to the roof, to the stovepipe, and wondered why no smoke was rising from it into the open air. If she didn't know better, she'd almost believe Tessa hadn't started the stove yet. But that couldn't be true because she was always up early to wake the boys, cook them breakfast, and send them off to school.

A sliver of unease pinched Caroline as she opened the front door and stepped inside the dark house.

Where was everyone?

She quietly closed the door behind her and tiptoed across the center rug, noting that nothing seemed out of place. The crocheted afghan was folded neatly across the rocker. Tessa's books were stacked on the low bookshelf. The boys' boots were lined up on the rug next to the door.

Caroline paused. The boys' coats were still hanging on pegs above their boots. Shouldn't they be on their way to school by now?

With growing alarm, Caroline walked into the kitchen. The same stillness greeted her there. The chairs were pushed into the table, which was bare except for a bowl of apples that graced the center along with two candles on either side.

The stove was cold. There were no scents of breakfast, only the lingering smell of smoke from yesterday's fire.

Picking up her pace, she continued through the kitchen and down the hallway. The bedroom doors were still closed. Dread filled her as Caroline opened Sarah's door. Faint light was beginning to peek in through the edges of the curtain, illuminating Sarah's form on one half of the bed.

At the sight of her approach, Sarah smiled, although weakly.

"Where's Tessa?" Caroline asked.

"I don't know," Sarah whispered. "She didn't sleep with me last night. I'm worried."

Where was Tessa? The dread increased tenfold. What if Tessa had become the next victim in the string of cruelties inflicted on her family? What if she'd been kidnapped . . . or worse?

A scuffling on the boards overhead told her the twins were still home and just getting out of bed. They were late, but at least they were safe. She hurried out of Sarah's room and went across the hall. Her hand hovered above the doorknob. Although she didn't want to disturb Ryan, the urgency racing through her veins demanded that she wake him and enlist his help in finding Tessa.

Maybe Tessa had decided to ride off. Maybe she'd finally had enough of living at the lighthouse. Whatever the case, Caroline wouldn't put it past Tessa to think she was grown up enough to make it on her own now.

Caroline stifled a frustrated sigh and turned the knob. The door opened soundlessly. She peeked into the room, which was cloaked in darkness.

"Ryan," she whispered loudly.

The shifting of covers and a soft moan came from the bed.

"Ryan," she said again. "Wake up."

A groggy "Hmm" was his only response, and it was all too reminiscent of the way his voice sounded when he'd been taking his pain pills.

Halfway in the room she stopped, and a new dread flooded her. Had Ryan taken a couple of pills? She'd seen the longing in his eyes when he'd spotted them yesterday in Tessa's hand. Maybe he'd been in such extraordinary pain after fighting the fire that he was unable to resist the temptation to take one or two of the pills.

That would explain why he hadn't come up to the light for his shift. The dread swiftly changed to anger and hurt. How could he? After all the progress he'd made recently.

She stalked across the room, not caring if she made noise now. She reached for the thick curtains and yanked them wide open. While she knew she shouldn't expect Ryan to be perfect so soon after he'd come off the pills, the disappointment pierced her sharply anyway.

The bright morning light streamed into the room, and for a brief moment she was reminded of the first time she'd met Ryan, when he'd accidentally crawled into bed with her and she'd hit him with her pillow.

She was tempted to snatch up a pillow and give him the smack he deserved for being so foolish. Instead she dragged in a deep breath and turned.

At the sight that met her, a gasp slipped from her lips, and she jumped back as if she'd been slammed in the chest.

There in the bed, under a mound of covers, were the outlines of two bodies—Ryan's and Tessa's. Tessa lay on one side of the bed, Ryan on the other.

Caroline could only stare in horror.

Neither of them moved, but their closed eyes scrunched in protest against the bright light that was disturbing their apparent tryst. The light also revealed a tall, dark bottle on the bedside table that was almost empty.

It was the whiskey she kept in her medicinal cabinet, the whiskey she used only in emergencies as a pain-killer.

Fresh anger erupted inside. So it wasn't enough to fall into temptation with his pain-killer. He'd gone and helped himself to her whiskey too?

She could just imagine the scene last night. Under the influence of his pain-killer, he'd overindulged. Tessa had probably been there talking with him in the dark hours of the night. With the way she'd been enamored with Ryan, she'd likely flirted with him. And being the beautiful and enticing girl that she was, obviously Ryan had lacked the strength to resist her.

Caroline had no doubt one thing had led to another, so that the two had ended up drunk and in bed together. What other explanation could there be?

With a strangled cry, Caroline strode over to the bed, grabbed the covers, and ripped them away from the slumbering bodies. Without their covers, the frigid air in the room slapped them instantly. Tessa began shivering, and Ryan draped his arm over her in a protective measure.

The sight ripped at Caroline's heart. Even in his drunken, opium-induced state, Ryan was a kind and sensitive man. He cared about others more than he cared about himself.

Tears pricked her eyes. If he cared about *her* as he'd led her to believe, why then had he allowed himself to get carried away with Tessa?

The girl gave another shudder and then a soft groan before she lifted a hand to cover her eyes.

"Caroline?" came a whisper from the doorway.

With mussed hair and wide eyes, the twins stood side by side staring at the bed, at Ryan lying next to Tessa.

"What are Ryan and Tessa doing?" Harry asked.

"Did they get married?" Hugh looked confused.

Both embarrassment and horror washed over Caroline. It was one thing for her to witness this indiscretion, but another altogether for the twins' innocent minds to try to make sense of.

She was about to rush to them, to shield the boys from seeing any more than they already had, when a sound coming from the living room stopped her in her tracks. Footsteps clomped across the wood floor and entered the kitchen.

"Miss Taylor?" a clipped voice called.

Mr. Finick.

"Go!" Caroline whispered to the boys, moving frantically to shoo them out of the room. She couldn't let Mr. Finick catch a glimpse of Ryan and Tessa in bed together. She just couldn't.

But she was too late. Mr. Finick, wearing an immaculate cream-colored suit and a bowler hat, appeared in the hallway behind the boys. He took in the scene in one rapid sweep. And his brow furrowed with immediate fury. "What on earth is going on here?"

His sharp question cut through the room and seemed to penetrate Ryan's hazy sleep. He yawned loudly.

"Mr. Chambers, this is totally unacceptable." Mr. Finick's voice rose a notch. "As if it's not enough to have to witness the destruction from a fire, but now I must see this too? Fornication right here at the lighthouse in broad daylight goes against every rule set in place by the Lighthouse Board."

Ryan stretched, lifting his arm away from Tessa for a moment before lowering it again. At the fresh touch of her body against his, his eyes flew open and he froze. He glanced at his arm draped over her, and then he jerked it off as if Tessa were scalding hot.

Confusion, followed by panic, rippled across his features before he scrambled away from Tessa. He rolled to the edge of the bed but in the process caught sight of them all standing by the doorway. He struggled to focus, first on Harry and Hugh, then on Caroline, and finally on Mr. Finick, who'd pulled out his record book and was now furiously scribbling something inside.

"What's going on?" Ryan asked, his voice slurred, his eyes clouded over.

"That's what I'd like you to explain to me, Mr. Chambers." Mr. Finick's pencil made a sharp scratching noise as it moved across the paper. "Why don't you tell me how it is you're in bed fornicating instead of being up and performing your duties as lightkeeper?"

"Fornicating?" Ryan pushed up from the bed, and the mattress squeaked in condemnation. He glanced again at Tessa, who was still shivering and reaching for the pile of covers at her feet.

Once again, Ryan started as if he hadn't expected to see the girl there. And this time he sat up completely and scrambled off the bed. Instead of making it to his feet, he dropped in a tangled heap on the floor, apparently still weak and disoriented from the effects of so much liquor and opium.

Caroline almost couldn't bear to watch. She knew she needed to remove Hugh and Harry from the room at once, yet she couldn't get her feet working. She wanted to blink and make the ugly scene disappear. But the frigidness of the unheated room had seeped into her skin, sending chills all the way to her core. There would be no ignoring what had happened here, no brushing away the incident with excuses. No way to hide what had obviously taken place. Instead, she would have to take charge and salvage what she could of her pride, along with Tessa's reputation.

Worst of all, she would have to ignore the incredible, oozing pain that ravaged her body, the pain of betrayal.

She steeled her shoulders and ushered Hugh and Harry from the room with orders to light the stove and get water heating. Then she hurried back to Tessa. The girl had finally opened her eyes and was sitting up in bed, tousled and dazed. Caroline had to bite back an anguished cry at the image of Ryan touching Tessa. The only woman Ryan should have been touching was her.

Caroline wrenched at the blankets and wrapped them tightly around Tessa, then quickly led her out of the room amidst Mr. Finick chastising Ryan with a barrage of threats. Even though Ryan's eyes followed them, she couldn't make herself look at him. She didn't know how she'd ever be able to face him again.

Chapter 21

Ryan sat at the kitchen table with his elbows on his knees and his head bent.

"Of course, I'll have to write up the citation and present your case before the Board." Finick sat across the table from him, his notebook spread in front of him.

Ryan had donned his clothes, but he shivered against the chill of the room, the stove still not at full strength. His mind felt the same way—sluggish. A vague uneasiness nagged him about the fact that Finick was at the lighthouse so early, that he was probably working with Simmons to get Caroline to leave. But he couldn't make sense of his jumbled thoughts, not when he was trying to sort out how he'd ended up in bed with Tessa.

Last night, after Caroline had gone up to the tower, he remembered sitting in the kitchen near the stove, greasing several traps he'd planned to set in the swamp and woods in the areas Poupard had told him were good for trapping muskrats. Tessa was cleaning up after dinner and had given him his usual mug of birchbark tea to help ease the pain in his arm after the long day. The boys were playing a game of checkers at the table.

There was nothing out of the ordinary about the evening, except that Tessa had been petulant about his marriage proposal to Caroline. She'd stomped around banging lids and answering his questions with one- or two-word quips.

He hadn't tried to console her, figuring she'd eventually get used to the idea that he was going to marry Caroline. He was preoccupied with the fact that the woman he loved was up in the tower, thinking about his proposal. He remembered feeling more and more insecure as the evening passed, especially after Hugh and Harry had come up to him before bed and given him hugs.

The boys had never hugged him before. And he was a little taken aback to think they'd soon be his charges. After he married Caroline, he would become like a big brother to them, perhaps even a father figure. But who was he to take on such a role? In fact, who was he to think that he was worthy of a fine woman like Caroline Taylor?

All he'd done in the past year flooded back to his mind. He'd stood by and let his comrades kill a boy without doing a thing to stop them. He'd stolen food from innocent people. He'd become a drunk just like his father. And then he'd shown up in Caroline's life and caused her all kinds of trouble.

With a stifled moan, Ryan's shoulders sank lower as the accusations of the previous night returned to taunt him with even greater force . . . along with the memory of the drinks he'd had.

When Tessa had pulled out a whiskey bottle and plunked it down on the table, he'd shaken his head no. He'd been tired already, almost groggy, the same way he used to feel when taking the pain pills. He was about to get up and go to bed when she poured two glasses and shoved one in front of him. The amber liquid had looked so soothing, so comforting. He told himself he'd have only one drink.

How was it that the one drink turned into two, then three, and only the Lord knew how many more after that.

He pressed his fingers into his temples and tried to rub away the pulsing pain. How was it that he had so little self-control? Even if Tessa had been drinking right along with him, pouring him a fresh glass every time his had emptied, that was no excuse.

And how was it that he ended up in bed with Tessa? And what in the name of all that was holy had he done with her?

Guilt raged through him. When he'd finally pushed away from his drinking binge last night, he was left dizzy and unsteady, buckling every time he stood. Tessa had come to his aid. He'd needed her help getting to the bedroom and onto the bed. He thought she'd simply assisted him out of his shoes and shirt. He hadn't realized she'd slipped into bed next to him.

Swishing skirts and slapping footsteps entered the kitchen. He raised his head and, at the sight of Caroline, sat up in his chair. She was alone. Thankfully, Tessa was nowhere to be seen, probably still feeling ill from the whiskey. "Caroline," he began, "I'm so sorry."

Without even a glance his way, she walked past him to the cast-iron stove. She opened the oven door, tossed in a piece of kindling, and slammed it shut.

Finick glowered at her. "Miss Taylor, this morning's occurrence is just one of the many reasons why you were asked to leave the lighthouse." His voice was biting and had the sound of one gloating. Ryan wanted to boot the man out of the house.

"This has nothing to do with her staying," Ryan cut in.

"It has everything to do with her!" Finick's chair scraped loudly across the floor as he pushed away from the table. "She's distracted you from doing your job. I'm guessing that's how the fire started yesterday, because you were too busy to pay attention—"

"Maybe you started the fire to drive her out," Ryan countered. "Maybe you've been behind all of the recent trouble around here."

"How dare you accuse me of starting the fire!" Finick said.

The horror in Finick's eyes seemed too genuine for Ryan to implicate him. While the man ranted for a full minute, Ryan suspected that the inspector might have been working with Simmons to get an incompetent keeper like himself at Windmill Point, but he doubted the man would purposefully set fire to the lighthouse. However, if Simmons and Finick weren't responsible, then who was? Ryan clutched his head, unable to think past the throbbing.

"If you want to maintain your job here at the lighthouse," Finick went on, "I expect that you'll resolve the scandal you've created by marrying the young woman you've compromised."

Marry Tessa?

The suggestion rocked Ryan and nearly knocked him off his chair.

At the stove, Caroline's back appeared to turn to stone, and her hands stilled at the coffee grounds she'd been scooping. Was she as shocked by Finick's admonition as he was?

"We cannot have word of your dalliance spreading," Mr. Finick warned. "It would set the wrong example for other single lightkeepers."

Ryan scrambled to come up with an excuse, to find some reason why he couldn't marry Tessa. They hadn't done anything besides share a bed. Even if he'd blacked out, he would surely remember if they'd done more than sleeping.

Yet his gut told him that he could do nothing less than wed

Tessa to preserve her reputation. It was the right thing to do in the situation. He hoped he hadn't actually touched her, but the fact that he'd spent the night with her in the same bed was devastating enough.

"So if you want to stay on as keeper," Finick said again, "you'll marry that young woman. Today."

What about Caroline? What about marrying her? His heart cried out in protest at the thought of having to give up his plans to be with her. Maybe he'd first offered to marry her as a way of keeping her from leaving the lighthouse and marrying another, but once he'd proposed he'd quickly realized just how much he wanted to be with her. All the memories of the times they'd shared together over the past month came rushing back, reminding him of how much she'd supported and cared for him.

He couldn't relinquish her. He wouldn't.

Caroline didn't turn, though he stared at her and willed her to tell him what to do to save their relationship.

What if she'd decided to reject his marriage proposal anyway this morning? She'd been hesitant yesterday. After his behavior last night, she had every right to say no.

At the opening and closing of the front door, Ryan dropped his head again, his misery escalating with each passing second. He couldn't let one more person witness his indiscretion with Tessa.

He knew that, no matter what, he had to protect Tessa. He couldn't let anyone else find out what had happened. He needed to save her the shame and embarrassment. The only way to do that was to marry her at once.

"Aye. I'll marry Tessa," he said, not caring that his voice was flat. "Today."

"Marry Tessa?" stammered a surprised voice. Arnie Simmons

shuffled into the kitchen. His eyes darted between Caroline and Ryan, a hopefulness in his expression that Ryan had the sudden urge to punch away.

Did Arnie think that if he was out of the way, he'd have a better chance winning over Caroline?

"Why are you here, Arnie?" Ryan demanded, turning his pent-up wrath upon the young man. Maybe it was Arnie who'd somehow managed to drag him into bed with Tessa. Maybe he'd knocked them both unconscious and put them in bed together.

As ludicrous as the thought was, Ryan couldn't contain his suspicion of the man. Arnie Simmons might appear innocent and naive, but he'd seen a dangerous flash in the man's eyes one too many times. And he knew Arnie was more like his father than anyone recognized.

"I d-drove Mr. Finick over f-from the . . . the inn," Arnie said. He looked at Caroline, who was still facing the stove, before turning his focus back on Ryan. And there, as dark as the muck on the bottom of the lake, was Arnie's anger. He was an expert at hiding it when Caroline wasn't looking.

Arnie stared at Ryan without blinking. "Mr. Finick h-heard about the f-fire and . . . and arrived late last night s-so he could visit the light t-today."

And catch me in bed with Tessa? Ryan wanted to shout. Instead he stared right back, hoping the man would reveal the truth, praying that indeed Arnie had done something to force him into bed with Tessa.

But Arnie looked down at his shoes before Ryan could probe deeply enough. Once again guilt rammed into Ryan. He shook his head in disgust with himself. He was trying to pass the blame on to someone else for all that had happened. It would be so much easier than taking responsibility for what he'd done and acknowledging the fact that he was still a weak man.

"I'll need to stay and witness the wedding," Finick said, rising from his chair and slapping his notebook closed.

Caroline resumed measuring the coffee. "Does this mean Tessa and the children are free to stay at the light?"

"So long as she's married," Finick replied, "she's legally allowed to remain."

"And the children?" Caroline asked, banging the lid closed on the coffee canister.

"They'll stay too," Ryan said, leveling a glare at Finick. Maybe he'd failed Caroline, but that didn't mean he couldn't take care of her family. "I'll raise them and provide for them like they were my own."

Finick pursed his lips but thankfully didn't protest.

"Where w-will you go, Caroline?" Arnie asked.

"She can stay here too," Ryan said before she could reply.

"No. I insist that she leave," Finick said, his mustache twitching. "If she's not gone by this afternoon, I'll return with the sheriff."

Ryan didn't understand how the sheriff could have any grounds to force Caroline out once he was married to Tessa. She'd be family. But Finick's tone boded no arguing, and Ryan knew he wasn't in the right frame of mind to oppose him and risk losing his position at the light, which he couldn't afford to lose now that he had Tessa and her siblings to care for.

"Don't worry," Caroline said. "Once Ryan and Tessa are married, I'll leave." There was a resigned sadness to her voice that sliced Ryan's heart.

He wanted to jump up, walk over to her, and drag her into his arms to reassure her that everything would be all right. But that was far from the truth. The world was falling down around them, and it was all his fault.

"You c-could marry me," Arnie said shyly.

At the suggestion, Caroline finally spun around. Pain etched her eyes and rippled across her face. "I can't marry you, Arnie."

Arnie's boyish features showed determination. "P-please, Caroline . . . I p-promise I'll make you h-happy."

Caroline pressed her lips together and shook her head. "I can't marry you, Arnie, not now or any time in the future. I'm only sorry it's taken me so long to figure out what I need, and that I let you have hope when there is none."

What did Caroline need? Ryan sat back in his chair and stared at her.

"I . . . I will m-make you happy," Arnie insisted again, his ears turning red.

"I need more than happiness, though," she said. "I need love."

Ryan wanted her to look him in the eyes. He'd never even come close to feeling love for another woman before Caroline. But with her, he could almost believe that the powerful attraction between them was indeed love.

Instead of looking at him, she turned in the opposite direction, peering out the window in the direction of the backyard.

Arnie's hands balled into fists.

"I'm sorry, Arnie," she said softly. "I realize now that when I get married, I want it to be for love or not at all."

Ryan stared at her back, at the strength that emanated from her. Was she admitting that she'd fallen in love with him? Or was she telling him that she would have turned down his proposal because she didn't love him?

He swallowed the possibility past the bitter remnants of whiskey that stung his throat. Even if she'd once loved him, he doubted she'd be able to anymore, not after what had happened. Regardless, it didn't matter if he cared about her. Duty called him to marry Tessa.

And nothing or nobody would sway him from doing the honorable thing.

⁓

Ryan glanced over his shoulder to the cottage and the lighthouse in the distance. The lake spread out beyond it, choppy and gray in the growing breeze of the morning.

A thick stand of poplars protected him from the chill in the air, yet he was cold to the bone anyway. He knelt next to where he'd laid his trap, marking the area with a piece of red cloth, so that the boys and Monsieur Poupard would know to steer clear of the spot.

He brushed some leaves around the metal jaw to conceal it. If Monsieur Poupard could make a living from trapping muskrat, then surely he could bring in a few extra dollars from the trade. He'd need the additional cash if he hoped to provide for Tessa and the boys and still save enough money to pay his debt to the grieving family he'd hurt during the war.

The shriek of a gull called Ryan's attention to the cottage again. He expected Tessa to come out any minute. After Mr. Finick and Arnie had left, he told Caroline he'd wait outside as Tessa got ready to ride into town to visit the pastor.

If he was going to marry her, he figured he might as well do it first thing in the day . . . before he talked himself out of it.

Hugh and Harry had long since left for school, but not before watching him with curious and troubled eyes. He suspected they were disappointed in him after finding him drunk and in bed with their sister outside the bounds of marriage.

But they probably didn't know how to give voice to their feelings.

And they were right to be disappointed. He'd let everyone down, including Caroline, and even himself . . .

He should have been stronger. He shouldn't have considered drinking anything at all. If he hadn't allowed himself a drink, he might have been engaged to Caroline this morning instead of her sister.

The thought that he'd taken advantage of Tessa, even if she'd been a willing partner, made him sick to his stomach. He straightened and let his hand slide into the satchel he'd hung over his shoulder. His fingers found a tin flask there, the one he'd carried with him all through the war.

With a quick glance in the direction of the cottage, he took another swig, letting the liquid burn his throat. *Last sip*, he told himself again, just like he had a dozen other times over the past hour as he waited for Tessa. He twisted the cap back into place and stuffed the flask back in his satchel, then wiped a hand across his mouth. Part of him wanted to wipe away the evidence, while another part of him didn't care.

Maybe it would be easier to endure the day if he numbed his pain, if he became oblivious to what he was doing. Even though Tessa was a nice girl, she wasn't the one he wanted. And he would need all the help he could get to make it through the wedding.

At least those were the excuses he was giving himself every time he took a drink.

He stepped away from the trap, his feet crunching through the dry leaves and twigs. Something sharp poked into his back.

"What in the name of all that's holy," he muttered, starting to spin to see what he'd bumped into. A branch maybe?

But the second he turned, the sharpness punctured his flesh. "Don't y-you m-move," a voice stuttered.

Before Ryan could think of what to do, one of his arms was wrenched behind his back, quickly followed by the other. The tightness of a rope wrapping around his wrists finally jarred him out of his numbness.

He jerked hard to pull himself free, but the point in his back dug deeper and paralyzed him with agonizing pain.

"I s-said not t-to move." The voice could belong to only one person.

"Arnie." Ryan let his shoulders relax. "What are you doing?"

"You're c-coming with m-me."

"You don't need to tie me up. All you have to do is ask politely and I'll come with you." He tried to give the young man a grin over his shoulder, but the sullen eyes staring back at him took all the humor out of the situation. In fact, there was something deadly in Arnie's expression that sent a warning through Ryan's clouded mind.

Arnie yanked on the knot binding his wrists together. The pressure chafed his skin, and the pain rippling through his injured arm nearly made him pass out.

"What's going on, Arnie?" Ryan asked.

Arnie tugged on the rope, dragging him farther into the woods, leaving him no choice but to stumble backward. Either that or have his arms dislocated from his body.

Ryan couldn't make sense of why Arnie was tying him up at knife point. Was Arnie jealous?

"Listen," Ryan said, trying to keep up with Arnie, which wasn't easy to do while being dragged backward. "I know you're upset about Caroline's refusal to marry you, but that doesn't have anything to do with me."

Arnie didn't reply, except to continue to haul him into the thick woods, away from the lighthouse.

"Come on, Arnie," Ryan pleaded, digging in his feet despite the pain in his arms and shoulders. "Let me go!"

Arnie stopped abruptly, and before Ryan could react, the young man pressed the knife against his throat. The blade scraped his skin like a razor, making him wince. Ryan knew that the alcohol in his system had dulled his ability to react, that if he'd had his senses and strength at full capacity, he probably would have broken free of Arnie by now. In fact, he probably would have heard Arnie sneaking up on him in the first place.

As it was, he was in no condition to fight off Arnie.

"If . . . if you c-cooperate," Arnie said, "then m-maybe I'll let y-you live."

The wind rattled the dry leaves overhead. Through the leafless spots, he caught sight of the gray-blue sky. It reminded him of Caroline's eyes, especially their smokiness when she was troubled.

Could he overpower Arnie? He tensed and tried to make himself think of how.

As if sensing his thoughts, Arnie drew back the knife and then rammed the butt of the knife against Ryan's injured arm.

Ryan couldn't hold back a cry, and his knees began to buckle. Arnie pressed the blade against his throat again, and the cutting pain forced Ryan to stay on his feet.

"If y-you don't c-cooperate," Arnie said in a harsh whisper, "I'll cut you up and t-turn you into f-fish bait."

Chapter 22

Caroline stepped back and studied Tessa, who stood in the middle of the kitchen. In contrast with their mother's beige wedding dress, Tessa's skin and hair looked even darker and more radiant.

"You look beautiful," Caroline said, realizing just how much Tessa took after their mother.

After plying her sister with several cups of coffee, Tessa was still groggy and grumpy. But she'd managed to rouse herself enough to don the wedding gown. At first Tessa had protested, saying she would wear her Sunday best, but Caroline had insisted.

"So you're not angry with me?" Tessa asked, tucking a last loose strand of hair into a messy knot.

Caroline suppressed a weary sigh. How could she be angry? Not when it was partially her fault that Tessa was in the current predicament. If only she'd rebuked Tessa for flirting. If only she'd set a better example herself. If only she hadn't invited Ryan to sleep in the house. If only she'd exercised more caution.

If only she'd accepted Ryan's offer of marriage last night . . .

Maybe then he wouldn't have felt insecure and hurt. Maybe then he wouldn't have needed to drink. Maybe then he wouldn't have turned to Tessa for comfort.

She shook her head, ignoring the regret she felt when considering how close she'd come to getting engaged to Ryan. She had to put it out of her mind once and for all. Ryan was marrying Tessa. There was no other choice.

"What's the use in my being angry?" Caroline answered, unable to keep her voice from breaking. "He was only offering to marry me because he wanted to help me out, not because he loved me." At least that was what she'd been telling herself. Whether or not she fully believed it was another matter altogether.

Guilt passed over Tessa's face, and she lowered her chin.

Caroline hadn't asked her what had taken place. She supposed part of her was afraid to hear the truth. She didn't want to think that Ryan had desired Tessa the same way he had her. Surely it was all a terrible mistake, the result of the drinking. A mistake he wouldn't have made if he'd been sober.

Nevertheless, she couldn't stop thinking about the two of them in bed together.

"I know you like him," Tessa said, picking at the lacy hem of her sleeve. "But I like him too. He's handsome, and funny, and sweet—"

"He'll make a good husband," Caroline said past the ache in her throat. She spun away from Tessa, tears pricking her eyes, tears she didn't want her sister to see.

What was done was done. There was nothing she could do to change anything now. The only thing she could do was endure the rest of the day. Then she'd leave. She'd go to Esther's and stay with her friend, at least until she could pick up the pieces of her broken heart.

"Finish up quickly," Caroline called over her shoulder. "I'll meet you outside."

Earlier, Ryan had put on his Sunday best and had hovered around the kitchen, his shoulders slumped, his demeanor imploring her to look at him.

But she'd refused to glance at him, even briefly. She hadn't wanted to see the apology that was sure to be in his eyes.

Finally he'd shuffled outside with his traps, and though she hadn't wanted to think about him, she watched him head off slowly, almost dejectedly, toward the woods. She didn't want to be happy that he was upset, but part of her was glad that at least he was a little despondent about the whole predicament.

Caroline grabbed a basket from near the door and went across the yard toward the cellar. Finally alone, a sudden sob caught in her throat.

"Stop it this instant," she chided herself. "He's not worth the tears. Not when he can jump into bed with any pretty face he meets. I'm just glad I found out what he's really like before committing to him."

But another sob pushed for release. She wasn't fooling herself with her tirade against him. No matter his faults and weaknesses, she'd allowed herself to fall in love with him. And the truth was he *was* worth the tears. Deep down, past his wounds, he was a good man.

As she stopped in front of the cellar, her mind filled with images of their time together locked inside, of sitting shoulder to shoulder in the dark, cramped space, of bearing their secrets to each other. Even though he'd been sick and she'd been worried, they helped each other through the difficult time.

Wasn't that part of the blessing of having a partner, so that they could help bear each other's burdens?

A gust of wind pushed against her, swirled her skirt, and crept underneath, sending chills up her body. Leaves blew against the wooden-plank door and rattled the lock.

The skin on the back of her neck pricked, as if someone were watching her. She glanced around, taking in the tower, the keeper's cottage, the boathouse, and the lake beyond. She scanned the marsh with its long grass turning golden, and finally she studied the woods where Ryan had gone.

No one was there, not even Ryan. Yet as her fingers closed around the cold iron of the lock, her pulse quickened unsteadily. She considered waiting to retrieve the vegetables she needed for a stew. What if someone was out there waiting to lock her in again?

"You're just being silly," she whispered to herself. She was allowing worry to control her again, and it was about time she stopped.

With trembling fingers she fumbled at the lock, slipped the lever, and opened the door wide. At last, she forced herself to step inside, setting the basket against the door to prop it open.

Inside, she swiftly gathered what she needed, tossed the vegetables in the basket, and then scrambled backward.

Halfway out, she bumped into a man's shoes and legs. She gave a start and yelped.

The man didn't budge, and she had to let go of the basket to squeeze past him, crawling across his scuffed, overlarge shoes.

She looked up and released a breath of relief at the sight of Arnie towering above her. "Arnie! You startled me."

He didn't say anything. Nor did he move. Instead he glanced about the yard, almost nervously.

She stood and untangled her skirt, brushing off the dirt and bits of leaves. "I didn't expect to see you again this morning."

His nose was red and dripping, and he lifted his arm to wipe it with his sleeve. "I n-need you to c-come with me. N-now." His hand clamped around her wrist.

She froze, staring down at his grip, then up at his face—at the shifting of his eyes and the hard set of his jaw. Her insides twisted with worry. "What's wrong? Has something happened to Ryan?"

He hesitated, glanced at the woods, and then nodded. "He . . . he needs your h-help."

All thoughts of keeping Ryan at arm's length fled. If he was in trouble, she had to go to him. "Where is he?" She started forward, but Arnie's tight hold on her wrist stopped her.

"I'll t-take you t-to him," Arnie said. There was a sharpness to his voice that worried her even more.

"I'll go tell Tessa." Once again she tried to break free, but his grip proved too firm.

"There's no time f-for that," Arnie said. "We h-have to go now."

The urgency in his tone propelled Caroline into action, and she didn't resist when he pulled her toward the woods.

"Is he hurt?" she asked breathlessly, trying to keep up with his fast pace.

Again he nodded. "There's b-blood."

Her heart plummeted, and she stumbled. But his grip on her arm kept her from falling. He led her through the thick woods, over fallen logs and under low branches, until they reached the clearing by the old windmill. Beyond it was the old well that Hugh had fallen into and that Ryan and the boys had subsequently filled with dirt and rocks.

The crumbling ruins of the windmill stood only a short distance from the shore. Just to the north rose a tiny spiral of smoke. Monsieur Poupard's log cabin.

Caroline's breathing was ragged, her chest pinched by the time Arnie finally stopped. She bent over, trying to catch her breath, and was surprised when Arnie didn't relinquish his hold on her wrist. If anything, his clasp seemed to tighten.

"This w-way," he said, jerking her toward the bricks that still formed a circular wall of what had once been the base of the windmill.

"What happened to him, Arnie?" she asked through her huffing. "Why is he here?"

Arnie didn't answer but instead narrowed his eyes on the open doorway.

She followed, confusion mingling with her worry. Each step closer to the ruins, her dread mounted. What would she find inside?

Arnie stepped over a pile of bricks and stones in front of the door and then ducked into the windmill. The broken, jagged walls were all that remained. The roof and the windmill itself were long gone. With the exception of one shadowed corner, the daylight flooded the interior.

It took her a moment to distinguish Ryan. He was sitting against the wall, legs outstretched with his hands behind his back.

"Ryan!" she cried. In the dimness of the corner she couldn't see anything wrong with him, didn't spot the blood Arnie had mentioned.

At her voice, he sat forward. "Caroline," he croaked. "Run!"

Run? Why? She started toward Ryan, but Arnie yanked her back with enough force that she careened into him and caught a whiff of fish and onions on his breath.

"Arnie," she said, struggling to tug her arm free and put some distance between them. "Would you please let go now? I need to help Ryan."

"Get out of here, Caroline!" Ryan called again.

"Arnie," she said louder, "let me go to him. Isn't that why you brought me here? To help him?"

For once, Arnie didn't blush, didn't shuffle his feet or act in any way embarrassed. Instead his jaw tightened, and his eyes flashed with a wildness that took Caroline by surprise.

"The b-best way to h-help Ryan is to m-marry me."

She gentled her tone as though talking to one of the twins. "Arnie, do you remember what I explained to you earlier? I can't marry you."

"You c-can if you decide t-to." His fingers dug into her arm. A vicious look came over his face, reminding her of Mr. Simmons when he'd lashed out at her father.

Fear tingled up her spine. She'd never been afraid around Arnie before. He was always so kind and soft-spoken with her. What had happened to the young man she once knew?

"Let her go, Arnie," Ryan demanded, wriggling his arms. "Do with me what you want, but let Caroline go unharmed."

Was Ryan tied up?

She looked more closely and saw that a rope was wound around his feet in a tight knot. Although she couldn't see his hands behind his back, she guessed he was attempting to get loose, but unsuccessfully.

She made a move toward him, to unbind him, but once again Arnie stopped her. Pain shot into her shoulder and down her arm, and she couldn't prevent a half scream, half gasp from slipping out.

Ryan thrashed. "Don't hurt her! Kill me, set me on fire! But let her go."

Before she could think past the burning in her shoulder, Arnie twisted both arms behind her back and wound a rope around her wrists several times before knotting it. He pulled her backward and looped the rope around an iron post sticking up from the ground.

She was too shocked to react.

"You c-can save Ryan's life," Arnie said, "b-but only if y-you marry me."

Ryan shook his head. "Don't do it, Caroline."

Arnie shoved her aside at the same time he unsheathed a long hunting knife. He strode across the ruins toward Ryan.

"No," Caroline squeaked, filling with panic. She wanted to believe that Arnie wouldn't really hurt Ryan, that something strange had gotten into him and that he'd be back to his usual sweet self in a minute.

But when he reached Ryan, he raised the knife up and brought the hilt down onto Ryan's injured arm with such force that Ryan cried out, writhing in agony.

Arnie lifted the weapon again, the blunt end poised to thrust into Ryan once more. Ryan braced himself for the blow.

"No!" she screamed.

But her protest did no good. Arnie swung the knife, driving the butt end against Ryan's arm with all his weight.

Again Ryan cried out, the anguished sound echoing among the ruins like a wounded animal.

A sob rose in Caroline's chest, and tears sprang to her eyes. "Please, Arnie. Please! Don't hurt Ryan anymore."

Arnie swung around and twisted the knife so that the blade pointed upward. The tip was smeared with blood.

Was that Ryan's blood? Her stomach swirled with fear. Then everything made sense. Arnie had hurt Ryan. Arnie had tied him up. And Arnie had brought him out here as his prisoner.

But why?

"If you don't m-marry me," Arnie said as if sensing her question, "I'll k-kill him!"

Ryan now lay twitching on the dirt floor, gasping for air.

Caroline hesitated. She'd decided not to marry Arnie. She had no reason to do so now, not with Ryan marrying Tessa and agreeing to take care of everyone.

At her reluctance, Arnie turned and aimed a sharp kick into Ryan's side. Then another.

"Stop!" She strained against the rope binding her hands.

Arnie acted as though he hadn't heard her. He lashed out with another kick, this one directed at Ryan's head.

Ryan grunted, but hardly moved.

"I'll marry you!" she screamed. "Just stop!"

Arnie took a step away from Ryan. Even in the coolness of the fall day, his face was flushed, and sweat had formed on his balding hairline. His eyes held that same wildness as before, and for a moment she wondered if he was crazy. She'd always known he was a simple man, but she'd never imagined that a monster lurked beneath his bashful exterior.

If she hoped to save Ryan, she would need to stay level-headed and try to placate Arnie.

"I changed my mind. I'll marry you." She forced calmness to her voice that belied the churning inside. She had to save Ryan, even if it meant her marrying a monster.

Arnie cocked his head, his eyes still narrowed.

"I didn't realize you were so intent upon marrying me, Arnie. I thought you made the offer out of compassion, to provide an alternative to my predicament at the lighthouse. I didn't know you wanted to marry me regardless."

Arnie wiped his sleeve across his forehead, seeming to wipe away some of the tightness in his face.

She hurried on. "Now that I know how you really feel, I'll go back with you and we can get married."

Arnie stared at her as if testing the truth of her words. "T-today?"

"Yes, of course, today." She made herself smile at him.

After a brief moment of hesitation, he gave her one of his shy smiles. "Are you s-sure?"

"I'm positive."

His smile widened, and the crazed look in his eyes dimmed a bit.

She drew a shaky breath. "Now, why don't you untie Ryan and let him go. He needs to get back to Tessa. She's in her wedding dress, waiting for him to take her into town to get married."

The hard lines returned to Arnie's face, and he turned to Ryan, who lay unmoving on the floor.

A dark wet spot seeped through the back of Ryan's coat. Was it blood?

She wanted to rush over to him and tend to his wound. Instead she forced herself to look away and pretend to ignore Ryan. She had to draw Arnie's attention away from hurting him any further.

"Let's go, Arnie," she coaxed. "We can go get married right now."

Arnie nudged Ryan with the tip of his big shoe. "We'll g-go, but I'm leaving him t-tied up."

She didn't know how she could walk away and leave Ryan bleeding and wounded. She had a strong feeling, though, that if she protested, Arnie would likely inflict more pain on him.

Arnie toed Ryan one last time before turning and joining her. He unhooked the rope from the post but wrapped it around his hand. He led the way toward the door, stepping over the fallen bricks and stone. She stumbled along, her wrists chafing against his pull that tugged her arms at an awkward angle.

She cast one final glance over her shoulder to where Ryan lay. She willed him to wake up and look at her, so he could see the message in her eyes—that she would come back for him after the wedding. Or somehow she'd get word to Tessa to go to him.

One way or another she'd rescue him.

Chapter 23

Ryan moaned. Fire seared his arm. He was in the middle of a battlefield, facedown in the trampled dirt. He knew he was alive only because of the grit coating his teeth, the dust lining his nostrils.

He lifted his head and found himself staring at a dismembered arm almost touching his face. The dirt-encrusted fingers were rigid and spread wide, as if reaching out to him and begging for help.

For an instant, he wondered if he'd died and this was hell.

He dropped his face back to the ground. The screams of the wounded penetrated the ringing in his ears caused by the blasting of cannons.

A white-hot burning sensation shot down his arm and ended at his hand. He wiggled his fingers, only to feel more fire licking at his skin. Strangely half his hand was numb. He could feel nothing in several of his fingers.

He tried lifting his hands, but something bound his arms behind his back. He yanked, then cried out as pain once again sliced like a knife into his arm.

His mind raced back to what had happened. He'd been sneaking along the edge of the clearing, low to the ground, crossing to the woods with his regiment. His comrades had been on either side of him, breathing hard, the stench of sweat and fear swirling about them.

Then the gunfire and cannon blasts hit them without warning, decimating them before they'd had the chance to return fire.

He shook his head, trying to clear his mind of the fog. This time Caroline's face flashed before him, her blue eyes wide with shock and worry. She'd tried to rush to his side, but she hadn't been able to come to him.

He'd wanted to warn her to stay away, that it was too dangerous, but he'd fallen back into a state of oblivion where everything was black.

"Caroline," he murmured, his tongue swollen and sticking to the roof of his parched mouth. "Stay off the battlefield."

He pried open his eyes. A brick wall and silence greeted him. Where was he?

He pushed against the dirt, broken pieces of brick cutting into him. He lifted his head enough to see crumbling walls surrounding him.

Everything came crashing back: Arnie dragging him through the woods, tossing him into the windmill ruins, and binding him so that he couldn't move. The young man had been strong and ruthless. And Ryan hadn't been able to fight back. He'd simply lain there, half conscious, not really caring if he died.

After a while, Arnie had returned with Caroline, had bound her too, and then had proceeded to beat him in front of her.

Being the sweet, caring young woman that she was, Caroline had caved to Arnie's demand that she marry him. She was always sacrificing for others. She didn't take the time to think about what she needed or how the decision would impact her.

Arnie had known she wouldn't be able to withstand watching the beating, that she'd have too much compassion, that she'd want to put an end to his suffering, even though he'd deserved it.

Aye, he'd deserved every punch and kick for being so stupid and turning back to his drink. He'd been a fool to believe that he could just have one glass of whiskey or one sip. The craving inside him was still too strong.

He knew now that if he wanted to truly stop drinking, he would have to stay far away from the temptation. Turning to drink was the cowardly way to deal with his problems. He'd been afraid last night, afraid that Caroline wouldn't want him, afraid that he wasn't good enough for her, afraid that he wouldn't be able to be the kind of man she or her siblings needed. And he'd let his fears push him to swallowing the whiskey.

He didn't want to think that maybe he'd even unconsciously sabotaged his relationship with Caroline, giving her an easy way to say no to his proposal.

Even so, he hadn't meant for everything to get so far out of control. He hadn't meant to fail so utterly. He slumped back into the dirt.

Not only had he failed himself, but worst of all, he'd failed Caroline. If he'd been fully alert and at his strongest, he could have protected her. He could have figured out a way to help free her from Arnie.

He released a long, frustrated groan. There was no telling what Arnie might do to her. The man was dangerous. And he couldn't let Caroline marry a man like that, especially not to save him.

Ryan jerked against the ropes binding his hands and feet,

but they burned his flesh and dug into his skin. He had to free himself so that he could rescue her. He strained once more, but all he managed to do was rub his flesh raw. The pain ricocheting up and down his injured arm was almost as intense as the day he'd gotten the wound. His body throbbed, and his head pounded. Bile churned, the nausea rising up. He was going to be sick.

After several heaves, he moaned and lay listless, the stench oozing next to his face.

He closed his eyes, not bothering to move. He thought he'd been in hell on the battlefield, but the thought of Caroline marrying Arnie was worse. And there was nothing he could do to stop her.

<hr />

Arnie shoved her into an empty chicken coop and then locked the door. She tried to protest past the gag over her mouth, but her muted cries only burned her throat.

"I'll be b-back . . . just as s-soon as I get the p-preacher," he said, then turned and stalked off.

She was trapped again. She'd thought during the walk back to the inn that his anger had dissipated, for his expression had grown kind again. He hadn't rushed her as he had when leading her to the old windmill. They'd walked along amiably enough, or at least she'd tried to give the appearance of friendliness.

She didn't want him to know how he'd reviled her. But with each step away from Ryan, she hadn't been able to stop shivering as she thought about how brutal Arnie had been. And with each step the thought of marrying him grew more repulsive.

Nevertheless, she'd kept up her charade of civility, praying that when they arrived at the inn, he'd free her hands and remove the gag. She'd hoped perhaps she could reason with him and make him understand that they needed to release Ryan.

But Arnie was determined to marry her before doing anything else. He probably thought Ryan would try to prevent the marriage if he was set free.

Ryan had tried to warn her to run. He'd known the danger she was in. But at the time, she was too confused to heed him. And now it was too late. Even if Ryan managed to free himself, he wouldn't know to look for her in this chicken coop. No one would think to look for her here.

The darkness closed around her. The only light slanted in through a few cracks in the walls. The air was stale and reeked of chicken droppings and the metallic scent of blood.

She crouched into a ball with her hands still bound behind her. She shifted, her knee squishing against something slimy. She shuddered to think of what remained in the coop. Body parts of one of the cocks killed in the weekend's fights?

"Arnie! Anyone! Let me out!" she cried. But the gag in her mouth choked the words back, making her cough. Her breath caught in her chest, and all she could think about was that she was going to die here. In the dark. Alone.

And if she died, then no one would know where Ryan was. No one would come to his rescue. He'd die too. What would become of her family then? Who would take care of them?

Tessa had no skills for earning an income. Mr. Finick would force her out of the lighthouse, and the Lord only knew what kind of work the girl would find then. Sarah would die. The twins would have to scrounge on the streets.

In a burst of panic, Caroline banged her shoulder repeatedly against the side of the coop. She had to find a way out. A hollow echo was all her pounding elicited. Finally she stopped, dropped her head to her knees and gasped for air.

Darkness hovered all around her, ready to claim her. She felt dizzy and weak. All she could do was huddle in a shivering mass.

Chapter 24

Ryan wasn't sure if minutes or hours had passed as he fell in and out of consciousness.

At the crack of a gunshot, he stirred. His eyes flickered open, and he found himself staring at the faded brick wall of the old windmill.

A gunshot meant someone was out hunting.

A jolt of energy propelled him up. He could hardly move without causing unbearable pain in his arm, but he somehow managed to rise into a sitting position. The knife abrasion in his back stung, and blood had plastered his shirt to his back. Yet he could tell it was only a surface wound; a few stitches should take care of it.

He strained to hear more gunshots. Instead, only the eerie silence of the overcast day met him.

"Help!" he shouted, hoping his voice would rise over the crumbling wall. If anyone was out in the woods, they would have a difficult time hearing his call for help. Still, he had to try.

"Help me!" he cried with all the strength he could muster. "I'm here in the old windmill."

More silence.

"Help! Please help!" For several minutes he kept up his calling, until his voice turned hoarse. Finally he slumped back and listened for any sign he'd been heard.

The only sound was the faint whining of the wind. He expelled a sigh of exhaustion.

Where was Caroline now? Was she already married? Not only did he abhor the idea of her marrying Arnie, he felt the same about her marrying anyone else . . . except for him.

A new kind of pain speared his chest. "Oh, God," he breathed, leaning his head back and staring up at the clouds that blanketed the sky. Now that the effects of the alcohol were wearing thin, the reality of the situation hit him with full force.

He'd fallen in love with Caroline.

Aye. He loved her more than any other woman he'd ever known. He loved her enough to die for her. The realization brought an ache to his throat.

That was why he'd been so desperate yesterday after the fire to stop her from running to Arnie. And that was partly why he felt so miserable now. He still wanted to marry her, even though he didn't deserve her, even though he was pledged to marry Tessa.

"Oh, God, what have I gotten myself into?" he said through bruised lips.

He'd thrown away the opportunity to marry Caroline, to have her love, and now he would spend his life trying not to think about her. If he allowed himself to desire her in even the slightest way, it wouldn't be fair to Tessa. He had to try to care for Tessa. He had to give their relationship his best effort. But it was going to be one of the hardest things he'd ever done.

"I'm tired of being a weak man, God," he whispered. "I don't want to live this way anymore."

He didn't want to rely on medicine or alcohol or even another person for strength. Doing so only weakened him, just like it had weakened his dad.

But what could he do? How could he be strong? He just didn't have it within himself.

"I need you, God," he admitted.

The strains of an old hymn played in the dusty corners of his mind. *"I need thee, oh, I need thee. Every hour I need thee . . ."*

He hummed the tune and searched for the words to one of the stanzas. *"I need thee every hour, stay thou nearby. Temptations lose their power when thou art nigh."*

Temptations lose their power . . .

"Yes. I need you, God," he said again, digesting the truth. He'd been turning to everything else to cope with his pain, to the things that could never heal him or give him strength. Maybe for a time they could ease his inner demons, but ultimately if he hoped to heal, he needed to start turning to God, every hour. And once he did, God would fill him with strength. He'd be able to turn his back on the temptations.

"I need thee, oh, I need thee. Every hour I need thee . . ." The chorus played in his mind until it became his prayer. He couldn't think of much else to say, but somehow in the process of making the song his inner cry, he sensed a moving of grace flowing over the depths of his sin.

He closed his eyes as tears of gratefulness pressed for release. During the war, the agony of all he'd experienced had driven him from his true source of strength. But since he'd arrived at the lighthouse, God had been gently drawing him back to himself.

Another gunshot sounded in the distance, this time echoing

louder. Maybe the hunter was drawing closer. He sat forward with a start that sent a burning ripple up and down his arm.

"Help!" he shouted. "Somebody, please help!"

He made as much ruckus as he could for several minutes, but to no avail. No one came running to his rescue.

He would have to accept that he was stuck, at least until after Caroline married Arnie. After that, perhaps Arnie would come back and let him go. And if Arnie didn't, he knew Caroline would find a way to help him. She wouldn't neglect him if she could help it, especially not when Tessa and the boys needed him now more than ever.

He leaned back and closed his eyes again, letting his heart return to the prayer of earlier.

"What is the meaning of all this shouting?" an ornery voice said from the doorway.

At the sight of Monsieur Poupard's red flannel coat and coonskin hat, Ryan pushed himself up straighter. "Here! I'm over here!"

"I see you," the old man said, limping forward. "I'm neither blind nor deaf. Yet."

The Frenchman dropped a lifeless turkey by the door and propped his rifle against the wall, all while muttering under his breath in French.

"What is going on?" Poupard asked, unsheathing the hunting knife belted under his coat. "Why are you sitting out here in the windmill tied up? Did those wild twins do this to you?"

"Nay." Ryan twisted to give Poupard access to his wrists. "Arnie did it in order to trap Caroline into marrying him."

"Arnie Simmons?" The Frenchman used the knife to cut the rope and free Ryan's hands. The muskiness of tobacco and woodsmoke hung in the air around the old trapper. Even though the man came across as abrasive, Ryan had noticed a softer side to him, especially after the fire when he'd treated Sarah with tenderness, covering her with extra blankets, giving her sips of water when everyone else was too busy, and finally carrying her back to her sickbed and laying her there as gently as a porcelain doll.

He wouldn't have guessed Poupard to have such a gentle side, just as he hadn't expected Arnie to have such a cruel side.

"Believe it or not," Ryan said, "Arnie Simmons has a monster living inside him."

"I believe it," Poupard said.

Ryan flexed his numb hands and moved his injured arm gingerly. "I suppose every son has a little of his dad in him." That was what he'd learned about himself. He hadn't wanted to struggle with drinking the same way his dad had. For years he'd prided himself on being a better and stronger man. But now he'd learned the truth, the truth that he was just as sinful.

Poupard bent over Ryan's feet, wedged in the knife and began sawing at the rope. "That boy has a twisted side to him. A couple weeks ago I saw him driving nails through a duck."

Ryan sat back as if the old man had just thrown a cold bucket of water in his face.

"The poor bird was squawking in pain. But that boy tortured it anyway."

Ryan's chest turned to ice. "That means Arnie's the one behind all the mishaps at the lighthouse."

"Mishaps?"

"The hole in the boat, the fire, the destruction of Caroline's garden." Maybe he'd even been the one to lock Caroline in the cellar. How else would he have known to look there?

Poupard paused in his sawing. The gravity in his expression

sent chills into Ryan's limbs. "I would not doubt he's responsible for those things."

"But why would he try to hurt Caroline if he cares about her and wants to marry her?"

"Perhaps he thought he could scare her away from the lighthouse and into his arms."

Ryan nodded. "Aye. Unless his father or Mr. Finick put him up to the task of driving Caroline away from the light."

The Frenchman finished cutting the rope. "Mr. Simmons wouldn't have asked his son to scare anyone for him. He takes too much pleasure in scaring folks himself."

"You're probably right. Arnie is desperate for Caroline to marry him. Maybe he thought that by creating danger at the lighthouse, she'd want to leave so she could protect her family. And by rescuing her from the cellar, he thought she'd admire him for being the hero and fall more easily into his arms."

The Frenchman grunted his agreement.

Ryan scrambled to his feet, almost falling in his attempt to make his legs work. He stumbled toward the door. He had to save Caroline from Arnie, now more than ever.

"Here. Take my rifle," Poupard called after him. "You may need it."

Ryan grabbed the weapon and said over his shoulder, "Tell Tessa to stay with Sarah until I get back. And go find the sheriff and ask him to meet me at the inn."

He didn't wait for an acknowledgment from Poupard but instead forced himself to move faster.

～～～

She was going to die.

Her soul cried out from the darkness creeping into her

consciousness. *God, you're good. You're good all the time. Even in the bad times.*

Her father's prayer sifted through her mind, the prayer he'd shouted during the brightest sunshine and whispered during the fiercest storms. He'd never wavered in his faith, had clung to the promise of God's goodness as if it were the buoy keeping him afloat.

Caroline's cheek pressed against her knee, her tears dampening her skirt. Her hair stuck to her face and neck in the cramped heat of the cage. She'd lost all feeling in her arms and legs except for a painful numbness. Dizzying blackness threatened to pull her under completely.

She'd always given in to her worry, had always let it control her.

"Cast your cares on Him, honey," her father had always told her.

But had she ever really followed his instruction? Had she ever cast her cares on the Lord?

She pictured the twins casting their fishing lines, tossing the bait as deep and as far as they possibly could. Was that what it was like to cast her cares? Did she need to mentally throw them as far away from herself as she could and let God swallow them up?

God, I cast my cares on you, she silently prayed. *I'm tired of hanging on to all my concerns and worries. I want to give them to you to hold. I cast my cares on you. . . .*

The prayer echoed quietly in her heart until it touched her lungs. She drew in a life-giving breath past the gag. As sour and stale as that breath was, she somehow knew His presence was with her.

She couldn't be sure that Ryan would be safe. She couldn't

be sure her sisters and brothers would be safe either. But she had to keep casting her worries on God.

The door on the coop rattled, rousing her from her drowsiness.

"Caroline?" came Arnie's voice as the door opened.

Relief swept over with the fresh air and the light.

"I've g-got the preacher," he said, his fingers wrapping around her bound arms. "It's t-time to get m-married." He dragged her out of the cage, wrenching her arms painfully in the process. He yanked her to her feet impatiently, and she couldn't keep from crying out.

When she was finally standing, she swayed, the darkness still hovering and threatening to overwhelm her.

Arnie's eager smile faded, and his eyes flickered with anger. "Aren't y-you excited?"

Excited? She almost laughed, except the rag in her mouth stopped it. How could Arnie possibly think she'd be excited after he'd kidnapped and beaten Ryan and then bound and gagged her, forcing her into a filthy chicken coop?

Arnie had changed into clean trousers and a fresh shirt. He wore the black bowler hat he donned when he went visiting. It was obvious he was taking the marriage ceremony seriously and that he expected her to do the same.

A chill rippled up her back and warned her that she couldn't stop placating him. Not yet. She tried to smile and hoped it reached her eyes. "Of course I'm excited," she said into the rag.

At her mumbling, he reached over and removed the gag. She sucked in a shuddering breath while he used his knife to cut the rope binding her hands.

When she was finally free, her first thought was to bolt, to get away from Arnie as fast as she could. She glanced toward the back of the inn where the door stood wide open. Arnie must have rushed out and forgotten to close it.

Then she examined the road and the woods beyond, searching for an escape route or for anyone she could run to and plead for help. But even as the thought of fleeing came, she saw right away that she wouldn't get far and would only anger Arnie all the more.

As if sensing her thoughts, his fingers snaked around her upper arm and turned into a chain. "Be h-happy, Caroline." His voice was hard. "If you're n-not happy, then . . . then I w-won't be happy."

He crossed the cockpit, leaving her little choice but to stumble to keep up with him. Her legs were weak from the cramped coop and lack of oxygen. And whenever she tripped over her feet, he'd yank her up with a bruising strength.

She wanted to protest, but instead she gritted her teeth. She'd have to resign herself to marrying him, though her dread of doing so had grown into a mountain.

He led her through the inn's back door into a small storage room. She had to step around beer barrels and stacks of crates containing an assortment of bottles. At the sight of a long, red cloak hanging from a peg near the door, she gave a start. Was it Arnie's or Mr. Simmons's?

As he tugged her into the large kitchen, the smell of boiled chicken filled the room, along with the tantalizing scent of several potpies steaming on the sideboard.

An old woman was stirring a bubbling kettle on the cast-iron stove. The woman paused and glanced at Caroline with a blank expression, but then quickly focused again on her task. She turned her back as if to send the message that she was too busy to pay attention to anything but her work.

A young girl was sitting on a stool in the corner, paring po-tatoes. The floor around her was covered with slimy peels and plucked chicken feathers. Wariness filled the girl's dirty face, and her sullen eyes followed them across the kitchen.

Caroline's hope sank. She'd thought perhaps she could elicit help from someone inside the inn, but her chances of doing that were looking bleak.

Once in the hallway that led to the front, Arnie stopped. His fingers dug deeper into her arm, making her flinch.

"You m-must cooperate," he said, his foul breath too near her cheek, "or I'll p-punish the children."

Her insides quaked. It had been bad enough for Arnie to hurt Ryan. But she couldn't bear the thought that he'd do anything to harm her siblings. *I cast my cares on you, God,* she cried silently. She couldn't drag her worries back or she'd sink under the weight of them.

"Don't worry, Arnie," she said in a strangely calm tone. "I'll cooperate."

And she knew then she had no choice. She had to do whatever he asked. She wouldn't be able to plot an escape. She wouldn't be able to plead to the pastor or anyone else for help.

She was stuck marrying Arnie.

As if sensing her resignation, Arnie continued into the dimly lit tavern. Through the haze of cigar smoke she could see sev-eral men sitting at tables. They paused in their conversation to stare at her.

She could only imagine how she looked, her hair askew, her face and clothes dirty from her time in the smelly coop. Would they question what had happened to her? She could only pray they would sense something wasn't right and step in to defend her.

She saw Mr. Finick sipping from a beer glass. His lips crooked into a smile at the sight of her with Arnie. Had it been only hours ago that he was out at the lighthouse, witnessing Ryan and Tessa in bed together? It seemed like weeks had passed.

Reverend Blackwell stood near the door. He was talking with Mr. Simmons, who had a towel in his big hands that he was twisting and then snapping. She was surprised the reverend had stepped into the tavern. Esther had recruited him early in her campaign against cockfighting, and it was no secret that he preached the benefits of temperance.

Arnie wound through the tables, his grip on her arm unwavering.

When he stopped in front of his father and the preacher, she gulped in a breath trying to still her trembling.

Mr. Simmons flicked the towel at Arnie. It snapped against his chest with a sharp crack. "I never thought I'd see the day when my boy would get married," Mr. Simmons said with a grin. "But wouldn't you know, here he is with his bride-to-be."

Reverend Blackwell glanced at Caroline. At the sight of her disheveled appearance, his eyes widened and filled with questions, questions she wanted to answer.

But Arnie's fingers squeezed her arm, reminding her of his threat. She smiled, praying the reverend could read the despair in her eyes.

"I figure any woman who wants Arnie must be pretty desperate," Mr. Simmons continued in his smooth voice, followed by a laugh.

Arnie's hand flexed, and his eyes narrowed. But the angry look was gone before Mr. Simmons finished laughing. Instead, Arnie shuffled and stared at his shoes.

"So, Caroline," Reverend Blackwell said, "was Arnie speaking the truth when he told me you're agreeable to the union?"

Now was her chance to shout her protest, to put an end to this charade. Yet at Arnie's slight shift next to her, she knew his threat to hurt her siblings wasn't empty. After seeing what he'd done to Ryan, she couldn't take any more chances. "Yes, Arnie is correct. I've agreed to marry him."

Reverend Blackwell stared at her intently for a moment. Did he doubt her? She prayed he would.

"Arnie might be able to perform for the wedding," Mr. Simmons said with a widening grin, "but I don't think he has what it takes to perform later—if you know what I mean." He laughed again, as did several of the patrons nearby.

Mortification poured into Caroline, and she wanted to slink under the nearest table and hide. She hadn't really considered what being married to Arnie would be like. She'd simply thought to survive. But Mr. Simmons's lewd comment only served to repulse her even more.

Arnie's ears turned bright red, and he kept his gaze fixed on his shoes. Were his eyes filled with the deadly anger again? Maybe staring at his feet was his way of hiding his true feelings, keeping him from lashing out at his father. Caroline could only imagine all the teasing Arnie had endured over his life from his father. Perhaps he'd once tried to defend himself, only to find the retribution severe.

And now, after years of holding in the resentment, had it grown into a raging storm capable of destroying anyone who got in its path, namely her and her family?

The reverend cleared his throat. "Caroline, if you're truly in agreement to the union . . ." He waited for her reply, giving her another chance to escape.

"I'm in agreement," she repeated.

"Then I'd prefer we have the ceremony outside—"

"No," Simmons said, clamping his arm across the reverend's shoulders. "Don't tell me you're going to make an issue of my establishment on my son's wedding day."

"Not an issue. Just a preference."

"If my son wants to get married in his home, then I say you'd better marry him right here. Now." Mr. Simmons drew the reverend away from the door to the middle of the room, shoving aside tables and chairs as he went, until he'd cleared a spot in the tavern.

"There you go, Reverend." He let go of the man, stood back, and crossed his arms over his broad chest, as if daring the preacher to defy him.

"Caroline, what would you prefer?" Reverend Blackwell said. "This is your wedding day too."

With Mr. Simmons glaring at her, she knew she had no choice but to agree to the current arrangement. She'd witnessed Mr. Simmons's temper and flying fists against her father. His anger was as lethal as Arnie's.

"I don't wish to stir up any strife, Reverend." Caroline forced her tone to remain even. "If Arnie wants to get married here in the tavern, then I'm willing."

Again the reverend leveled an intense look at her. He knew she'd participated in Esther's protests against Mr. Simmons, and now he had to know something was wrong for her to agree to the demands so quickly.

If only he would grab her and run away . . .

But she knew that would do no good. Arnie would find her and then hurt her family.

Her pulse clattered to a halt. Had Arnie been the one all along trying to hurt her family? She gave herself a mental shake. He wouldn't have set the fire. He wouldn't have cut a leak in the boat. How could he?

She slid a sideways look at him, at his childlike face that had always appeared so simple and kind. She forced down the fear that rose in her throat, threatening to cut off her breathing. She couldn't believe he was the one who'd brought her and her family so much distress over the past weeks.

But with his threat against her siblings, how could she ignore the connection? Especially with the red cloak hanging by the kitchen door as evidence? She'd believed the spots of red she'd seen in the woods now and then had belonged to Monsieur Poupard. But perhaps Arnie had been there all along, slinking around and spying on her.

Reverend Blackwell stood stiffly for a long moment, staring at her, as if waiting for her permission to proceed.

"Let's get on with the nuptials," Mr. Simmons growled. "I don't have all day, and neither does Arnie. Some people have real work to do."

Mr. Simmons shoved the reverend forward so that he stood directly before her and Arnie. He hesitated an instant before slowly opening his Bible.

Arnie's grip on her arm didn't slacken, and a deep despair settled over her. She couldn't listen as the reverend began reading about how marriage was a covenant and holy estate and that it was not to be entered unadvisedly. She tried to tell herself that love didn't matter, that she was doing what was best for her family. And that was all that mattered.

Reverend Blackwell's voice seemed to grow softer and slower the longer he read, and when he finally came to her vow, she wanted to turn away and ignore him.

"Caroline, wilt thou have this man to be thy wedded husband, to live together after God's holy ordinance in the holy estate of matrimony? Wilt thou obey him and serve him, love, honor, and keep him, in sickness and in health? And forsaking all others, keep thee only unto him so long as you both shall live?"

She started to speak, but the words caught and she couldn't squeeze them out.

Arnie's fingernails dug through her sleeve into her flesh.

The reverend stared at her, his eyes beseeching her to say no.

"I—" she began.

The front door of the tavern flew open and hit the wall with a crash that shook the windows.

"Stop!"

Chapter 25

"Stop!" Ryan shouted again. "Don't marry him!"

After running the entire distance from the old windmill to the tavern, his chest was heaving, his sides aching. He swiped his sleeve across his forehead, clearing away the sweat, and at the same time he leveled Poupard's rifle at Arnie.

"Ryan!" Caroline cried, both anguish and relief in her voice.

Through the smoky haze of the room, he didn't want to take his aim off Arnie, but he chanced a quick glance at her. Seeing the scratches on her cheek, the dirt smeared on her face and neck, a fierce anger swelled in his gut.

He let out a roar of frustration and stepped forward. "I should kill you!" he yelled at Arnie.

Before Ryan could make another move, Arnie seized Caroline and dragged her in front of him, pinning her and using her as a shield.

"Let her go, you big coward." The heat of frustration fanned hotter. All he could think about was killing Arnie. He wanted to blast a hole through the man's black heart so that he could never again hurt Caroline or her family.

317

"Now, hold on, boy," Simmons said, standing near Arnie. "What makes you think you can barge in here and stop this wedding?"

"He's coercing her into the marriage."

Simmons puffed out his chest, and his thick arms flexed. "There's no coercing going on here. We all heard the girl say she wanted to marry Arnie."

Ryan's mind scrambled to come up with a plan, a way to take out Arnie and Simmons without harming Caroline. Though Arnie was stronger than he'd expected, he had no doubt that he could get the upper hand now that he was alert. But he wasn't sure he could take on Simmons at the same time.

Maybe he'd have to shoot Simmons first.

The reverend had closed his Bible, wariness creasing his forehead. Could he count on the reverend to help him if he lunged for Arnie? Or would he only put Caroline in more danger?

"Caroline isn't marrying Arnie because she wants to," Ryan said, eyeing the bar where Finick sat with his beer and watching with an eagerness that only fueled the rage in Ryan's belly. "She's agreeing to marry Arnie only because she wants to save me. Arnie threatened to kill me if she didn't marry him."

Arnie yanked Caroline backward so that she gasped and fell against him. His arms slipped around her body in a possessive hold, one that was too intimate.

Her wide eyes flooded with panic and called out to Ryan for help.

His hold on the rifle tightened, although he knew he couldn't take a shot at Arnie, not while Caroline was anywhere nearby. He'd have to figure out a way to get Arnie to loosen his hold.

"Why don't you stand up and face me like a man?" Ryan

called, hoping to bait Arnie. "Instead of sneaking around like a coward."

"Arnie doesn't sneak around," Simmons bellowed.

"Aye. You've raised a coward." Ryan spat the words. "Instead of squaring off with me to my face, he's been sneaking over to the lighthouse and trying to scare Caroline into marrying him."

"Not my son—"

"Aye," Ryan insisted. "He's the one causing all the trouble. He locked us in the cellar, almost drowned the twins, and started the fire yesterday."

Arnie's ears had turned red again, and he stared over Caroline's shoulder defiantly, confirming Ryan's suspicions.

Caroline's face didn't register any surprise at the revelation, only resignation, as if she'd already guessed Arnie's role in all the problems that had occurred at the lighthouse.

Finick set his glass down with a clunk and slid off his stool. "Setting fire to a lighthouse is a federal offense."

Ryan was tempted to point out to Finick that he was a hypocrite, that aiding illegal smuggling was a federal offense too. But now was not the time to confront the inspector with his own misdeeds. Not when Caroline's life was at stake.

"Is this all true, son?" Simmons glared at Arnie. "Have you been sneaking around and causing trouble?"

Arnie shook his head. "I'm not a c-coward. She was t-taking too long in her decision to . . . to m-marry me."

Simmons cursed under his breath. "Then she's not here willingly after all?"

"You w-want to marry me," Arnie said in a childlike voice, clutching Caroline and looking at her with desperation in his eyes. "Don't y-you, Caroline?"

"No, Arnie. I was only agreeing to marry you because you threatened to hurt Ryan and my family if I didn't."

Hurt flashed into his expression, followed rapidly by anger.

Trepidation surged through Ryan, and he jolted forward with an urgency to save Caroline, but he was too late. Arnie's long fingers closed around Caroline's neck with a quickness that allowed only the barest of gasps from her, before his grip cut off her airway.

"Let Caroline go, Arnie," Ryan said.

But Arnie's grip tightened on her neck. Ryan then realized that he was determined to kill Caroline rather than let her go.

Her eyes bulged in fear. She lifted a hand in an attempt to pry away his fingers, but his hold was too firm.

Ryan started toward the two with steady steps.

Caroline's eyes turned wild with the need for a breath, and she clawed at Arnie's hands, growing more desperate with each passing second.

Simmons began shouting at Arnie, berating him for being a coward. And Finick was going on about how much trouble Arnie was in for starting the fire, how he would need to have him arrested. The reverend was beseeching Arnie to release Caroline at once. But their voices couldn't penetrate the alarm screaming in Ryan's head.

He wanted to rush at Arnie and tackle him, but he was afraid the man would snap Caroline's neck and kill her instantly if he did.

Caroline's eyes started to roll back. She was losing consciousness.

Oh, God, help me! He had no choice. He had to attack the monster before he strangled Caroline.

"Caroline!" he shouted and then leaped for her.

Before he could reach her, something smashed into Arnie's head.

The jolt forced him to loosen his grip. It was all Ryan needed. He grabbed Arnie's arm, twisted it away from Caroline, and yanked her free.

She wheezed for a breath and nearly crumpled at his feet.

Arnie pounced after her, but another slam across his head sent him reeling backward in pain.

Ryan scooped Caroline into his arms and lifted her against his chest as though she weighed no more than an infant. At the same time he saw Simmons beat Arnie over the head again with a broom handle.

"No son of mine is a coward!" Simmons shouted, his face ruddy and etched with fury.

Arnie lifted his arms over his head and cowered into a ball. He did it so quickly and naturally that Ryan couldn't help wondering how many times he'd crouched into such a position during his life to protect himself from his father's rage.

Ryan didn't give the two more than a passing glance before spinning around and striding across the tavern with Caroline in his arms. He kicked open the door and burst outside.

Caroline's face was pale, and she gasped for air, still wheezing. He walked a good distance away from the tavern before kneeling and setting her on his lap.

Her eyes still showed her panic, and she clutched her throat. Beneath her fingers, bruises were already forming on her skin where Arnie had choked her.

Ryan brushed his hand across Caroline's cheek, trying to calm her. "Shhh," he whispered. "Everything will be okay now."

She nodded, but she struggled still to breathe normally.

He gently smoothed her hair back, then leaned forward

and placed a kiss on her forehead. "I've got you now," he murmured, trailing kisses to her temple. "No one will hurt you again."

She let out a shuddering breath, and her body melted against him.

He pulled back and looked her in the eyes. The franticness had dissipated, replaced by gratefulness.

"I was afraid I wouldn't see you again," she croaked. "How did you get free?"

"Monsieur Poupard heard my call for help."

"Thank you for coming for me."

"I was so afraid," he whispered, his heart pounding with the thought of how close he'd come to losing her.

"Are you hurt?" she asked, searching his face.

He probably looked a mess from the beating Arnie had given him earlier. His arm still ached badly, but the relief at rescuing Caroline drowned out everything else.

"I'm fine. Now that I have you." He ran his fingers along her jawline to her chin and then to her lips. Her color was beginning to return, and she appeared to be breathing more evenly.

"I'm sorry, Caroline," he said hoarsely. "If I hadn't been drinking again, none of this would have happened."

"You don't know that."

"Aye. I would have had my wits about me. I wouldn't have ended up in bed with Tessa. Arnie wouldn't have captured me. I would have been able to fight him off. You wouldn't have gotten hurt."

"You can't expect yourself to be perfect, Ryan. You're still healing."

"Apparently I need a lot more healing than I thought."

"You'll get there." Her voice contained all the confidence in him that he'd grown to love. Aye, he loved her through and through, especially for always believing in him.

He pressed another kiss to her forehead. "Ah, Caroline," he whispered against her soft skin. "You're a beautiful woman, both inside and out."

At her swift intake, his attention dropped to her lips. The warmth of her breath beckoned him, and the sweet fullness tantalized him to draw more comfort from her. He shifted so that his lips hovered above hers.

He hesitated only a moment before leaning in. He pressed hard, all of the fear and desperation driving him, urging him to lay claim to her.

She slipped her arms over his shoulders and around his neck and clutched him, her hold tightening with her own desperation. Her lips melted into his, gently at first, but gradually growing more demanding, her breath hot and passionate.

"Ahem" came a voice above them.

Caroline broke their kiss with a gasp. They pulled away from each other to the sight of Reverend Blackwell standing above them, watching them.

"Reverend Blackwell," she said, mortification spilling across her features. She moved to extricate herself from Ryan's hold, sliding onto the dirt road with a thump.

Ryan was loath to let her go. His body ached to draw her close again. But she scrambled away from him and tangled in her skirt in her attempt to rise and make herself presentable.

He jumped up and offered her a hand, but she looked away and rose on her own, busying herself with brushing and straightening her skirt. She was clearly embarrassed, and guilt prodded him to try to put her at ease.

"I'm sorry, Reverend," he said, clearing his throat. "I was so relieved Caroline was safe that I got a little carried away."

The reverend's lips twitched with the beginning of a smile. "I was hesitant to carry out the marriage ceremony between Caroline and Arnie. Now I know why."

Caroline wiped at a stain on her skirt, her cheeks flushed.

"Besides the fact that Arnie is mad," the reverend continued, "she can't marry him when she's obviously in love with someone else."

In love? Ryan's gaze snapped back to her, and he willed her to look into his eyes so that he could see the truth there for himself. Did Caroline love him after all?

"We should all be thankful to God that Ryan intervened when he did." The reverend held out the rifle Ryan had left behind in his haste to get Caroline out of the tavern.

"Aye, Reverend. I'm mighty thankful." Ryan took the rifle, but his attention didn't budge from Caroline. He loved her. Was it possible that she felt the same way?

"I guess this means I should prepare myself for a real wedding?" the reverend said, a hint of teasing in his voice. "When should we set the date?"

Caroline's expression froze, stricken, almost as if the reverend had knocked the wind from her. She glanced briefly at Ryan, yet it was long enough for him to read one word there: *Tessa*.

His chest caved under the weight of the name. He was engaged to Tessa. In fact, if Arnie hadn't kidnapped him and dragged him to the windmill ruins, he'd likely already be married to the girl.

His mind raced for an excuse, for something that would release him from marrying Tessa. He didn't want her, didn't love her, and couldn't imagine spending the rest of his life by her side. Not when he was desperately in love with Caroline.

"So what do you say, young man?" The reverend's smile blossomed brightly. "You might as well do the right thing for Caroline and marry her, since it's quite clear you care deeply for her too."

Ryan glanced at the sky, trying to guess the position of the sun behind the clouds. It was already afternoon. He couldn't go through with marrying Tessa today, not after all that had happened.

But he'd have to do it first thing tomorrow.

He gulped down the lump lodged in his throat. Aye, he'd be seeing the reverend soon for a wedding. But it wouldn't be to marry Caroline.

A shout from the road leading to town drew their attention. It was Poupard, riding his horse much faster than any old man should, his long gray hair having come loose from its leather binding. Galloping behind him was the sheriff.

Ryan raised a hand in greeting, relieved that the law would finally prevail. He'd personally make sure the sheriff took Arnie away and locked him up for a long time . . . if Simmons hadn't already killed the boy with his beating. Maybe he couldn't have Caroline for himself, but the least he could do was make sure she was safe from now on.

Once he talked with the sheriff, he knew there would be nothing left to do but go back home to the lighthouse and to Tessa.

Ryan shifted away from the reverend and his probing eyes that were still awaiting an answer to his question. The truth was, he wasn't free to marry Caroline and never would be. He'd made poor choices, and now it would cost him the one thing he wanted more than anything else.

Caroline.

He may have saved her life, but he'd thrown away his chance of having her.

Chapter 26

"There," Caroline said, pressing the bandage to Ryan's back. "That ought to hold the skin together and prevent infection."

He was hunched on the stool she'd had the twins carry down from the tower. The lantern on the sideboard illuminated the remnants of the clean linen she'd used to cover the knife wound Arnie had given him.

Numerous scars covered his broad back, shocking her when she first saw them. One more wouldn't mar him much. Even so, she'd doctored him with as much care and gentleness as she could. The bruises Arnie had left on her neck paled in comparison with the anguish Ryan had suffered during the war.

"Hopefully it will heal quickly," she said, letting her fingers linger on the bandage against his cool skin.

He looked at her over his shoulder with tortured eyes, the longing in them causing heat to spread through her middle, just as it had every time their eyes met since that kiss he'd given her outside the tavern.

She shouldn't have kissed him back. She tried to tell herself that she'd merely been relieved, that she'd been weak and vulnerable and hadn't really felt anything.

But it was all a lie. She knew it as well as he did. The kiss had been full of all the passion and desire that simmered between them. And now it had boiled over, searing and taunting them about what could never happen again.

The twins had already come and gone, having begged Ryan to retell his role in rescuing Caroline several times. She could hear their animated voices coming from down the hallway and suspected they were in with Sarah, relaying the story to her with boyish embellishment.

Tessa sat quietly in a chair across the table. She hadn't spoken much since they'd returned. She'd already changed out of the wedding gown into her everyday attire. And she'd prepared a pot of soup that was cooking on the back burner, although Caroline doubted anyone but the twins had an appetite.

Ryan hadn't looked at Tessa since he walked through the door. And now, hunched over with his elbows on his knees, he stared at the floor again.

Caroline could sense the agony in his every muscle and movement. And she knew it wasn't from his physical pain. He desired her. Maybe even loved her.

No, he still hadn't said the words. But he'd come for her, had charged into the tavern to rescue her. His expression had been deadly. He'd wanted to kill Arnie for hurting her. And when he'd finally wrapped his arms around her, she'd felt his love. She knew that he cared for her deeply—just as the reverend had said.

It thrilled her to know that Ryan cared for her instead of Tessa. She couldn't keep from gloating over it, just a little. It was her only consolation in the completely hopeless situation.

For just a little while, she didn't care if Tessa knew that Ryan didn't want to marry her, that he wanted her instead. It served Tessa right for stealing Ryan away from her. And for just a little while she wanted to ignore the fact that Ryan had gotten drunk again. She wanted to pretend that it didn't mean anything, that it was just one tiny mistake and wouldn't happen again.

Ryan hung his head lower, the misery weighing heavily upon him.

She couldn't stop herself from grazing a finger across the bare skin of his back just above the bandage.

He tightened, gave a soft groan, and then bolted off the stool, knocking it over in his haste. He grabbed his bloodstained shirt from the back of the kitchen chair and turned away from her as he tugged it on.

Tessa stared at Ryan's bare chest boldly. And Caroline couldn't prevent the jealousy that pinched her heart. "Turn your eyes away, Tessa," she said crossly. "You're not married yet, even if you'd like to think you are."

Tessa had the grace to look embarrassed.

"I'm heading up to the light," Ryan said behind the flannel shirt sliding over his face.

Caroline glanced out the window, surprised to see the lengthening shadows of early evening. "I'll go up," she offered.

He combed his fingers through his hair and shook his head. "I need to go tonight, Caroline." His tone told her that he wouldn't be swayed, and his eyes told her that he needed to be alone, that he needed time to think.

"I think I should take over the keeper duties from now on anyway." He rubbed a hand across his eyes. "Don't you think?"

She wanted to protest. The thought of not ascending the tower and doing her job was as discouraging as the thought of not marrying Ryan. But she knew she had to stick to her original plan and leave the lighthouse after Ryan and Tessa were married. If being together now was difficult, what would it be like on a daily basis?

"Yes, you should take over now," she conceded.

Tessa straightened, her black eyes darting between them. "Why does Ryan need to take over? That doesn't make any sense if we're leaving."

Caroline picked up the leftover linen scraps and began folding them. "I'm leaving. Not you. The plan is for you and the boys to stay here with Ryan."

Panic flitted across Tessa's features, and she pushed out of her chair. "The plan is for Ryan and I to leave this place. Just as soon as we get married."

Ryan paused in strapping his suspender back over his shoulder and quirked his brow. "We can't leave everyone—"

"But you told me you were going West!" Tessa glared at Ryan. "You said you were leaving and giving the lighthouse back to Caroline, that the keeper job belongs to her."

"Aye, it does belong to her," Ryan said, blowing out a breath. "The Lighthouse Board couldn't find a better keeper to run this light."

"Then let her have the job. And we'll go," Tessa said.

Caroline searched her sister's face. She wanted to understand Tessa's strong desire to move away, to live somewhere else besides the lighthouse, but she just couldn't make sense of it—not when her own heart was breaking at the thought of being forced away from the one place she wanted to be.

"I can't leave the lighthouse now," he said wearily, his shoulders slumped. "I'll have a family to support. Sarah and the twins will need someone to take care of them."

"Caroline can do it," Tessa suggested.

"Mr. Finick will be back tomorrow to make sure we're married. And if we leave Caroline here to fend for herself, I have no doubt he'll send for the sheriff and have her kicked off the grounds."

Caroline nodded. She wasn't sure if Mr. Finick would be back tomorrow to check up on whether Ryan married Tessa. He would likely be busy dealing with Arnie. She prayed he wouldn't let Mr. Simmons sway him out of prosecuting Arnie for setting fire to the lighthouse. Mr. Simmons could be quite persuasive when he wanted to be.

Whatever the case, Mr. Finick would come back to the lighthouse at some point. When he did, he'd make sure Ryan and Tessa were married. And he'd make sure she was gone.

"It's best for you and Ryan to stay," Caroline said. "Ryan will take care of all of you, and we won't have to worry anymore about where we'll go or what we'll do."

Tessa's eyes flashed. "Don't tell me what's best for me! You've always tried to run my life. And now that I'm getting married, I don't want you telling me what to do ever again."

Tessa's words echoed in the sudden silence of the house. Even the boys in Sarah's room had grown quiet.

"If you stopped thinking like a selfish child," Caroline said, "maybe I wouldn't have to tell you what to do."

"You're just jealous," Tessa shot back. "You're jealous that I get Ryan and you don't."

"How I feel about Ryan has nothing to do with it. He has a good job here at the light; he'll be able to provide for you. And he's willing to let Sarah and the boys stay here. What more could we ask for?"

"It's a good job for you, but Ryan doesn't love this place like you do. I can tell."

Ryan's mouth was partly open as if he'd tried to speak but was unable to get any words out.

"It doesn't matter how he feels about it. It's a job. And that's all that counts at this point."

"What matters is that Ryan and I are happy together."

"What matters is that you think about others for a change." Caroline knew she wasn't being fair in her accusations. Tessa tirelessly cared for Sarah and the twins. She did more than most girls her age to help run the house. Even so, she was being entirely too selfish.

Ryan used the pause in their conversation to speak up. "Listen. The situation isn't ideal for any of us. But now we have to make the best of what's happened." Tessa opened her mouth to reply, but Ryan continued before she could interrupt. "Tessa, whether you like it or not, we're making our home here." His expression then turned grave. "I hope that if we work hard enough, we'll be able to be happy together anywhere."

Another shard of jealousy poked at Caroline, and she had to busy herself again with the linen scraps in order to hide a wave of hurt.

Tessa crossed to him, wrapped her arms around his waist, and laid her head against his chest.

Ryan stood awkwardly without returning the embrace. After a few seconds, he patted her back.

"Please . . ." Tessa tilted her head and peered up at him with her most beguiling smile, her eyes enticing. "Please won't you take me away from here? Someplace where we can be together, just you and me, where we can start our life together without all the worries of the lighthouse?"

Above Tessa's head, Ryan's gaze collided with Caroline's. For an instant the pain and regret in his eyes mingled together so tangibly that it made her own heart ache with such intensity, tears pricked the backs of her eyes.

She had to look away. She couldn't let him see how much it hurt her to see him with Tessa.

"We're staying here," he said, his voice taking on a sudden edge. "This will be our home. Please resign yourself to the fact."

With that, he extricated himself from Tessa's embrace and stepped back. Her lips drooped into a pout, but she didn't say anything else.

He didn't speak again either. He grabbed his coat from off a chair and left the room, leaving Caroline and Tessa alone in silence.

For a long while, neither of them moved.

Finally, Tessa shoved a chair back under the table with a clatter. "I hope you're happy," she hissed.

"Why would I be happy?" Caroline's heart was breaking.

"You got Ryan to stay here, that's why. And now you'll work your best to woo him away from me."

Caroline's anger boiled over. "Stop it, Tessa! Just stop it. You know Ryan and I cared about each other. You know he wanted to marry me. But you decided to take him for yourself regardless. And now you have to continue to make things completely unbearable."

Remorse flashed in Tessa's eyes for a brief instant. But she shook her head and glowered back. "If he wanted you so much, then why did he fall into bed so easily with me?"

Caroline had already asked herself that question and had no answer.

"You know I'm telling the truth," Tessa added, lifting her chin.

Once again, Caroline couldn't keep from wondering what

had gone wrong with her relationship with the girl. What had she done to make Tessa dislike her so much? Sadness settled over Caroline. She'd tried to raise Tessa the way her mother would have wanted, yet somewhere along the way she'd failed her sister.

"Well, I'm moving out tomorrow," Caroline said. "So I won't be here to interfere in your relationship with Ryan. Believe it or not, I want you both to be happy . . ."

She was embarrassed when her voice cracked, and she spun away from Tessa before she saw the tears that hovered too near the surface.

Tessa didn't speak for a long moment. Finally, Caroline heard Tessa's footsteps softly cross the room and fade down the hallway.

Once she was alone, a sob rose up before she could stop it. It burst out, but she quickly pressed a hand to her mouth to keep back the rest of the sobs swelling in her chest. Her shoulders heaved silently as tears coursed down her cheeks.

Nothing compared to the pain of losing a sister to animosity and anger. Except losing the man she loved too.

❧

The night seemed eternal. But even so, Caroline still wasn't ready for it to end at the first hint of dawn.

On the one hand, she felt a measure of pride that Ryan had completed all the duties flawlessly during the night, that she hadn't needed to go up to help him. On the other hand, she wasn't ready to face the new day and all that it would bring.

In the darkness she slipped into her clothes, the coldness of the unheated bedroom filtering into her flesh all the way to her bones. Rubbing her arms through her thick knitted shawl, she tiptoed down the hallway past Sarah's closed door.

She tried not to think about the fact that this was Tessa's last night sleeping with Sarah, that from now on she'd share the bed with Ryan, that he'd wrap his arms around Tessa and bestow upon her his passionate kisses.

And she tried not to think about the fact that this was her final night staying at the lighthouse. The last night she'd be able to call it home. In a few hours she'd leave, and if she ever returned, she'd do so as a guest.

As she stepped into the dark kitchen, she was surprised to find a yellow glow already fanned to life in the stove.

"Caroline."

She jumped at the soft murmur that came from the table, followed by sniffling.

Through the dimness she saw Tessa's hunched form.

"Tessa?" Caroline whispered in surprise. "Why are you up so early?"

"I couldn't sleep." Tessa's tone was laced with misery.

"I couldn't sleep much either," she admitted. "Change is never easy. Not for any of us."

Tessa sniffled louder.

Caroline reached for the back of the nearest chair, unsure if she should go to Tessa and comfort her or pretend she didn't hear her crying. For a long moment, silence stretched between them.

"I'm sorry for getting upset at you last night," Caroline finally said. And once her words were out, a weight lifted from her chest. No matter that her relationship with Tessa was strained, at least she could try to part ways in peace. "I shouldn't have gotten angry with you—"

"You had every right to be angry with me," Tessa said, cutting her off. "I'm a horrible person!" With the declaration echoing in the quiet of the kitchen, Tessa buried her face in her hands and erupted into heartrending sobs.

Caroline knew she couldn't ignore the crying any longer. She rounded the table and didn't hesitate to put her arms around Tessa and draw her into an embrace.

Tessa held herself unyielding only an instant before collapsing against Caroline and sobbing harder.

"Shhh . . ." Caroline murmured, pressing a kiss against Tessa's wavy hair. "Everything will be all right."

"It won't be all right!" Tessa wailed into Caroline's shoulder.

Caroline hugged her sister tighter and rubbed her back in an effort to soothe her, just as she'd done when Tessa was little.

"You're just frightened," Caroline whispered. "Every girl has jitters on her wedding day. It's normal."

"I'm not frightened." Tessa pulled back and wiped at her cheeks and nose with her sleeve. "I just hate myself."

"Hate?" Caroline smoothed Tessa's hair. "That's a strong word."

"And you'll hate me too—"

"I could never hate you."

"You will once you find out what I did."

Fresh dread pummeled Caroline, and her muscles strained to pull away from Tessa. But she also needed to stand by her word. She'd promised Tessa that she would never hate her. How could she prove it if she distanced herself at the first hint of bad news?

Tessa sniffled again, then said, "I lied, Caroline."

"About what?"

"About sleeping with Ryan."

Caroline froze. She wasn't sure that she'd heard Tessa

correctly. She reached for her sister and gripped her arms. "Tell me everything."

"I didn't want him to marry you. I wanted him to marry me instead," Tessa sobbed bitterly. "So I ground up extra pain pills and put it in his birchbark tea after dinner. And then when he started to get groggy, I was the one who pulled out the bottle of whiskey. I was the one who helped him get drunk."

For a long time, Caroline was speechless, a mix of emotions running through her. "Then he didn't get drunk on his own?"

Tessa shook her head. "I kept refilling his glass. When he complained of being tired, I told him I'd help him to bed."

Caroline held her breath, hardly daring to believe what she was hearing. Ryan wasn't at fault. Tessa had been the one to get him drunk.

"Once he was in bed, he fell right to sleep."

"So you didn't share intimacies?" Just speaking the word made Caroline flush.

"I wanted to make it seem like we did, so I undressed us both." Tessa's voice was small like that of a child. "And then I crawled in next to him."

"And you did nothing more than share the bed?"

"No. He was asleep the second his head hit the pillow, and he didn't wake up until you came in the next morning."

Caroline struggled to absorb the news. She wasn't sure if she should be excited or angry.

By the faint glow of the fire in the stove, Tessa's face was pinched and pale. "He didn't so much as touch me the entire night."

Caroline stood back and folded her arms across her chest. Did this mean that Ryan was free of any obligation to Tessa? She had the sinking feeling that he'd still insist on marrying

Tessa to keep from tainting her reputation. Even if nothing had happened between them, they'd still been in bed together. And people would gossip about it regardless.

"I'm sorry, Caroline," Tessa said, her tone subdued. "After our talk last night, I realized I don't love Ryan. I don't even think I like him." Her voice dropped even more. "But I can see that you love him. And he loves you too. I could see how miserable he was last night because he had to marry me and not you."

Part of Caroline wanted to slap Tessa across the face, for getting herself into this predicament, for hurting her and Ryan so deeply. Tessa was right. It would be all too easy to hate her for what she'd done. She tried to ignore the whisper that said Tessa wasn't completely to blame, that Ryan had a part in it too.

"Why did you do it?" Caroline asked, unable to keep the hardness out of her voice.

"Because I hate this place," she cried, the passion of her words tearing at Caroline's heart. "I hate living at this lighthouse. I never want to live at another lighthouse for the rest of my life. I'd be happy never to set foot in one ever again."

"I don't understand. Why?"

Tessa gulped down a sob before responding. "The light has taken everything and everyone I've ever loved. It killed Mother. Then it killed Father. And now it's taking you from me."

"I'm still here."

"But now you're leaving too. It also almost took Hugh and Harry with their nearly drowning. Don't you see? I don't want to lose anyone else."

"You won't." But Caroline knew her words contained an empty promise. Light keeping wasn't an easy job but was fraught with all kinds of danger.

"I want to move away from here," Tessa said again, as though she hadn't heard Caroline. "I wanted Ryan to take me as far from the lighthouse as possible."

Caroline sagged, her knees almost buckling beneath her. So that was it. Tessa had believed Ryan would rescue her from an unwanted life. The girl had hoped that by marrying him, she'd have a way out. But instead she'd ended up tied to the very place she despised.

Tessa took Caroline's hand and clutched it. "Please, Caroline. Help me get out of this situation. I don't want to marry him now. I don't want to stay here."

Caroline pulled back. "You're confessing your lie because you want my help?"

Tessa started to nod.

"You don't care that you've hurt Ryan and me as a result, do you?"

"But I do care!" Tessa half sobbed. "I'm sorry I hurt you. I really am."

"Does that mean if Ryan had given in to you last night and agreed to take you away, that you still would have confessed to your lie and apologized to me this morning?"

Tessa hesitated.

Caroline pulled out of her sister's grasp altogether. "You're so selfish, Tessa."

Tessa raised both hands to her face and started crying into them again. "I told you that you'd hate me!"

Caroline was tempted to cave in to the hatred. It beckoned her to release all the frustrations and disappointments she'd had with Tessa. The girl didn't deserve her love anymore, especially after deceiving her and Ryan.

But when had any of them deserved God's love? They were constantly hurting and disappointing Him, and yet He remained patient with them. He continued to love them and call them His own. He might discipline them, but He didn't reject them or hate them.

Caroline sighed and blew out the rising anger that had wrapped around her. She reached for the kitchen chair next to Tessa and dragged it out. She plopped onto it and reached for Tessa's hand. "I told you I'd never hate you, and I meant it."

Tessa cried for a little while longer and then finally quieted. The light of dawn had been steadily increasing, with the sky outside the kitchen window turning a forget-me-not blue.

Soon Ryan would turn off the light, if he hadn't already. He would complete the morning's duties, making sure the oil was refilled and the glass prisms of the lens cleaned before he descended the tower.

What would they tell him? How could she free him of his obligation to Tessa, so that he would be free to marry her instead?

"I know I've been selfish," Tessa said, wiping the wetness from her cheeks. "And I know I've been difficult for you too."

It was true, but Caroline knew it was enough that Tessa had admitted it. She didn't need to make her feel worse by agreeing with her. "You miss having a mother, and I'm a poor substitute."

"No, you've done the best you can—all you can—to provide for us and keep us together. I should have been more grateful to you, Caroline."

"And I should have appreciated you more."

Tessa leaned forward and reached for her sister. This time, Caroline didn't hesitate. She pulled her into a fierce hug, holding her and stroking her hair, letting relief and gratefulness mingle together.

"I want you and Ryan to get married," Tessa said, pulling

back, her voice stronger. "How can we get him to change his mind? I don't want him to feel obligated to marry me."

"We need to tell him the truth, everything you just told me. He deserves to know all that happened so he can stop beating himself up."

"I'll tell him just as soon as he comes down," Tessa said. "But will that be enough? He may still think he has to marry me to save my reputation."

"He'll insist on it." Ryan's sense of honor was strong, something Caroline admired about him. But for once, she wished he wasn't so honorable.

"And what about Mr. Finick?" Tessa asked. "What if he makes Ryan marry me in order to keep the job?"

"He'll probably insist on it too." The helplessness of the situation began to creep in again.

Tessa nodded. "There must be some way to make both of them see that Ryan needs to marry you instead of me."

Caroline sat back in her chair, her mind grappling for a solution. Every option she thought of, though, ended the same—with Tessa still being left with a tainted reputation.

The patter of footsteps in the dormer room overhead told them Hugh and Harry would soon descend to the kitchen.

"I don't know what to do." Caroline stood slowly, her throat beginning to close. She was worrying again. The sensation was all too familiar, but one she didn't want to feel.

I cast my cares on you, she silently cried out. She had to cast this burden onto the Lord before it got too heavy and dragged her down. She didn't know what would happen to Tessa or to her and Ryan, but she couldn't let it consume her with worry and fear.

Whatever came her way, she had to trust that God was there with her, helping to bear her burdens.

Chapter 27

Ryan closed the tower door behind him and stepped into the charred remains of the passageway. Overhead, through the hole in the roof, a translucent patch of sky told him the morning was already half over.

And it told him he couldn't put off the inevitable any longer.

He'd completed every lighthouse duty he could possibly think of and then some. He'd even scrubbed the tower floor and steps.

But now it was past time to go down to the house, change his clothes, and take Tessa to town.

His gut ached at the thought, but after crying out to God off and on all night, he knew he couldn't take the coward's way out, not ever again.

He ducked through the blackened doorway and walked outside. Looking to the east, his eyes scanned the calm waters of Lake St. Clair. He wasn't sure how many ships had passed by the light last night, but he knew countless depended upon the beam that streamed for miles out, helping to guide them to safety.

The rocky shore and the gentle lapping of waves called to him, and he made his way to the water's edge. The whisper of the breeze that met him seemed to reach down into his soul, soothing him.

God had brought him to this lighthouse for more than just the job, he realized now. God had brought him here to begin healing. He'd taken steps in the right direction, mainly crying out his need for God. But he still had a long way to go.

And he knew what he needed to do next. He slipped his hand into his leather satchel. His fingers closed around the cold tin flask. He withdrew it, not bothering to hide the trembling in his hand. The liquid within sloshed and taunted him. His mouth watered and his throat burned, but he ignored the sensation. Instead he lifted the flask, cocked his good arm back, and heaved it with all his strength.

The flask flew far out above the water, a ray of sunlight hitting it and making it glint. For only the briefest instant did he feel any regret. And then the container plopped into the lake and disappeared beneath the surface, sinking quickly from sight.

He expelled a breath of relief. He should have done it long ago. He should have put any hint of temptation far from him. Maybe if he had, he wouldn't have brought everyone so much heartache. As it was, he'd pay for his weakness and mistakes the rest of his life.

With another sigh he turned to face the house. Smoke from the stovepipe curled into the morning air. The keeper's cottage was picturesque against the backdrop of the pale-blue sky.

It would have been beautiful, and it would have felt like home, if he'd known that Caroline was waiting inside for him instead of Tessa.

Finally, he made his way back to the house and went inside. As he closed the door quietly, pleasant chatter and the clinking of cooking utensils beckoned him to the kitchen. He moved soundlessly to the doorway and stopped at the sight of Caroline at the table, paring and chopping apples, and Tessa, standing at the stove and stirring a pot of thick sauce. Glass jars lined the sideboard. Some were already filled with the brownish liquid he guessed to be applesauce or apple butter. Other jars stood empty, awaiting their turn.

Caroline glanced up. The paring knife in her hand froze in mid-peel on a wormy apple. Her gaze sought his, and there was a hopefulness in her expression that sliced his heart as surely as the knife in the apple.

He had to avert his eyes before he strode around the table, grabbed her, and took her to town rather than Tessa.

At Caroline's silence, Tessa looked over her shoulder for just a second and then turned her attention back to the pot. "I was beginning to think you'd decided to run away."

"Nay. Just finishing up some work."

The kitchen was hot. Tessa's hair was pinned up, but strands stuck to her neck and forehead. Her sleeves were rolled up to her elbows, and her apron was splattered with brown spots.

She was clearly not ready for a wedding.

"I'll change my clothing," he offered, "and then I'll be ready to ride to town whenever you are."

He could feel Caroline's eyes upon him still, and he forced himself not to look at her.

"I won't be ready," Tessa said, stirring the pot without breaking her rhythm.

Her nonchalance took him aback. He watched her for a moment. "Well, then how about if we go once you're done here?"

She shook her head. "No. I'm not going anywhere today."

"Tessa," Caroline rebuked. Her shirt collar shifted just enough that he caught sight of the bruises Arnie had left on her neck. Once again regret fell over him like a dark shadow, that he hadn't protected her better.

Tessa lifted the spoon from the pot, blew on the brown pulp, then dipped a finger into it. She lifted it to her mouth and took a small taste before lowering the spoon again.

"Tessa," Caroline said again, "we've talked about this already. You have to go."

"I don't *have* to go."

"Yes, you do."

"You can't make me."

"What's going on?" Ryan interrupted. He stepped into the room toward the table. He stopped and faced Caroline, and this time he met her gaze head on.

The paring knife in her hand shook. "Tell Ryan everything, Tessa. He deserves to know the truth."

When Tessa turned, her young face was lined with guilt.

Ryan pulled out a chair and sat down to hide the sudden tremor in his legs.

As she relayed the story about drugging his tea with opium pills, he found that he wasn't angry with her. He couldn't be. Even if he'd been groggy and tired from the pills, he'd been alert enough to realize what he was doing when he took her offer of whiskey. He could have told her no. He could have gone straight to bed. But he hadn't. He hadn't resisted the temptation like he should have.

He was relieved, though, to discover he hadn't defiled Tessa, that he hadn't done anything in his drunken state to hurt her. But that didn't alleviate the fact that he'd fallen so quickly back into his old ways of drinking. And if he'd done it once, who was to say it wouldn't happen again?

Of course, he'd been calling out to the Lord with his needs.

346

But deep inside he knew he was still a weak man and had a lot of growing yet to do.

"So, you see, I'm not going to marry you," Tessa said with a flourish of the big stirring spoon, heedless of the applesauce that dripped onto the floor. "You and Caroline are getting married instead."

After Tessa finished her tale, Ryan turned and met Caroline's gaze. Even though there was that same tiny flicker of expectation he'd noticed earlier, she was also holding herself back.

Now he knew why. Perhaps Tessa had come forth with the truth, but would anyone else believe her? Finick had caught them in bed together, and even if they hadn't actually done anything, it sure looked like they had. Why would he believe otherwise? No one would think they were innocent, no matter how much they insisted upon it.

"Thank you for telling me the truth," he said slowly. "But even if *we* know nothing happened between us, we won't be able to convince *anyone else*."

"I'll tell them all the truth." Tessa's cheeks were flushed, and her dark eyes flashed.

"Either way, you'll ruin your reputation in this community," he said. "And I won't let you do that."

"I'll have to live with the consequences of my actions." Tessa reached for a ladle and lowered it into the pot. "People may think I'm tainted, may even consider me a loose woman. No decent man for miles around will want to marry me. But at least I won't have to make you and Caroline suffer on my account."

Caroline watched Tessa, a new kind of sadness falling over her face. "I don't know if I can let you throw away your future and your chances of a good marriage like that—"

"It's not your decision to make." Tessa lifted a ladleful of sauce and poured it into the nearest jar. "Besides, I hope I won't need to stay here forever. Maybe one day soon I'll be able to leave and start a new life someplace else, where no one knows about my reputation."

"The world is already tough enough on women," Ryan said. "Just look at Caroline and how she's been denied the keeper position because she's a woman. It will be even worse for you, Tessa. Especially if you're seen as a loose woman."

"I made the mistake." Tessa poured more sauce into the jar. "I should be the one to suffer for it, not you and Caroline."

Ryan longed to let Tessa have her way, for then he'd be free to marry Caroline. But how could he leave her to her ruin? How could he ever be happy with Caroline knowing he'd allowed Tessa to throw away her chances at having a good life?

"I can't allow you to take the blame for all that happened," he said. "I was here. I could have prevented it if I'd been more careful."

"No, Ryan, I'm the one at fault. I planned it. I did it. You had nothing to do with it."

She was so matter-of-fact that Ryan wanted to believe her. But in reality he knew he could have prevented everything if he'd only been stronger. Whatever the case, he still had to do what was right. He had to protect Tessa from a life of hardship.

The sorrow in Caroline's eyes made it clear that she agreed with him, that she didn't want Tessa to suffer either.

For a long moment, no one said anything more. Tessa busied herself filling the remainder of the jar and then moving on to the next as if the matter were settled.

A knock and a shout at the front door startled Ryan.

"Caroline?" came a woman's voice.

"It's Esther." Caroline wiped her hands on her apron and bustled around the table.

Ryan followed her into the sitting room to find Esther De-luth entering the house with her husband, the mayor. The man smiled and nodded at Ryan as he took off his tall top hat and ran a hand over his head to smooth back his hair.

Esther rushed over to Caroline and hugged her, or at least embraced her as far as her rounded belly would allow. "Caroline, I'm overwhelmed by good news," she said, pulling back and beaming. "And I made my husband drive me out here the minute I received this post."

Esther withdrew a sheet of paper from her coat pocket and unfolded it with a brisk shake of her hand. "I've finally heard back from my father and the Senate regarding your position here at the lighthouse."

Caroline drew in a shaky breath, and her face went pale.

Ryan stepped beside her and put his hand on her elbow to steady her. She glanced up at him gratefully.

Esther laughed. "Don't be afraid. It's good news!"

Caroline leaned into him as if drawing strength from him. He only wished he had more to give her.

"My father said this." Esther cleared her throat and began to read from the official-looking paper. "'The vessel men all say that she keeps a very excellent light and I think it very hard to remove this woman, who is faithful and efficient, and throw her upon the world with her siblings entirely destitute.'"

Esther glanced up with an excited smile before continuing. "'The community near her has also testified to her dedication and capability as lightkeeper. Their petition and overwhelming support indicate her competency to continue in her current position—'"

"Petition?" Caroline interrupted.

"Yes," Esther's husband interjected, patting his wife's

shoulder. "Esther worked tirelessly to get signatures from everyone in Grosse Pointe and the surrounding area on her petition to keep you on at the lighthouse."

Caroline started trembling, and Ryan moved his arm to her waist, wrapping it around her slender body.

Esther found her spot in the letter and continued reading. "'After taking this appeal before the Lighthouse Board, they have come to the agreement that Caroline Taylor shall be instated as keeper of Windmill Point Lighthouse with full duties.'"

Caroline gasped and pressed a hand to her mouth. Her eyes brimmed with tears.

Esther's eyes flooded with tears as well. "We did it. We stood up for the rights of women." Esther's normally unshakable voice wavered with emotion.

A thrill wound through Ryan. Caroline would get to keep the job she loved and deserved. He could think of nothing more he wanted for her.

Caroline broke away from Ryan and threw herself at Esther. As they hugged and cried, Ryan took a step back in time to see Tessa in the doorway with a half-filled jar of applesauce. Disappointment filled her expression.

Tessa was obviously not overjoyed by the news, probably because she didn't want to stay. She'd made that clear last night when she begged him to take her away from the lighthouse. Would she beg him again now that the keeper job officially belonged to Caroline? After all, if the Lighthouse Board was giving the job back to Caroline, that meant Tessa would have to stay and he was out of work. He wasn't needed here anymore. He would have to find a different job somewhere else.

Maybe Tessa would change her mind about marrying him once she realized he'd have to move away.

He studied her face, waiting for her to turn and beseech him for an escape.

But when Tessa finally looked at him, he saw resignation in her eyes. She pursed her lips, squared her shoulders, and then shook her head. The gesture confirmed what was written on her face. She still wouldn't marry him, and there was nothing he could do to change her mind.

He nodded at her. He couldn't force her. He'd have to accept her decision whether he liked it or not. And part of him admired her for not taking the easy way out, for her willingness to stay and accept the consequences of her mistake.

As he shifted his attention back to Caroline, to the happiness infusing her features, the other part of him was filled with a yearning sadness and resignation of his own.

He didn't stay in the sitting room to congratulate Caroline on the ruling. Instead he made his way outside and headed to the boathouse, where he began packing up the few belongings he'd left there.

"So you're leaving?" Tessa's voice came from behind him.

He spun to find her standing in the doorway. He held the driftwood cross he'd carried with him through every battle, every heartache, every step of his life for the past six years since his sister had passed it on to him.

His fingers caressed the rough wood. "I have to go." Once the words were out, he knew they were true. As much as he wanted to run inside the house, wrap his arms around Caroline, and demand that she marry him, he wasn't ready for it.

He still had to pay back the debt he owed to the family he'd hurt during the war. While he was haunted less by the death of the boy, he'd vowed to make up for what he'd done. And he couldn't forget it.

More important, all that had happened over the last couple of days had shown him that he was in need of much more healing in his life before being ready to give himself wholly to a woman the way she deserved. Even so, he had to offer to help Tessa one last time.

"Are you sure you don't want to come with me?" he asked. "Now's your chance to salvage your reputation, your chance to leave the lighthouse."

She didn't hesitate but shook her head vehemently. "Whatever may come, staying here is something I have to do."

"Then you'll understand that I have to leave every bit as much as you have to stay."

"Are you sure you can't marry Caroline?" Tessa shivered from the cold of the morning. She crossed her arms over her chest and hugged herself. "I can tell she loves you. And she'll marry you if you ask her again."

Ryan clutched the cross in his damaged hand, the rough wood digging into his two remaining fingers. "I want to marry her more than anything else in life." He was surprised by the intensity of his statement. "But I have to do a few things first before I'll be the man she needs."

Tessa nodded and then wiped a sleeve across her eyes.

He glanced down to the cross, twirled it in his palm. Just like this wooden cross, God had been there with him all along during his times of need. But he'd turned to everything else for help—to whiskey, to pain medicine, to sleep, and even to Caroline.

She'd been there for him, had accepted him and encouraged him even when he was at his worst. She hadn't condemned him but had loved him regardless of how he'd failed her. It would be all too easy to rely upon her for strength, to turn to her to help him through his difficulties. But that wouldn't be fair to her. And it wouldn't be what God wanted either.

God wanted him to go to Him with his deepest needs, to stop looking elsewhere, so that he could be made whole again. Until he could do that, he wasn't fit for marriage with Caroline or any woman.

Ryan held the driftwood cross out to Tessa. "Here. I want you to have this." He'd finally understood the hope the cross offered. Now that he grasped the message of hope, it was time to pass the cross along to someone else. After all, the letter that went with the cross urged the bearer to give the cross to a person who needed hope.

Tessa stared at it but didn't make a move to take it from him.

"My sister gave it to me. And now I'd like to give it to you."

She took it from him, turning and examining it.

"There's a story behind it," he said, and then told her about the original owner of the cross, Henry Cole, and how the wealthy young man had fashioned the cross out of driftwood left from a shipwreck that had stranded him at the Presque Isle Lighthouse. Henry had eventually fallen in love with the keeper's daughter, Isabelle Thornton. But circumstances and difficulties had thrust the two lovers apart. Through it all they'd had to learn to hope in the Lord.

By the end of the story, Tessa clutched the cross to her chest.

"Don't be a fool like me and forget God's presence in your life," he finished. "Remember that He's there every hour, every minute, every second. We just have to turn to Him with our needs."

She nodded.

He had a feeling Tessa was going to face more hardship in

the days and weeks to come as a result of her lie. And she would need to know that God had forgiven her and was still there for her, even as she had to live with the consequences.

He returned to his saddlebag and stuffed a shirt inside.

"Will you say good-bye to Caroline?" she asked.

He didn't want to. It would shatter his heart into a thousand pieces to say good-bye. More than that, it would hurt her, and he loathed the thought that he might bring her any more pain.

"Say good-bye?" Caroline's voice came from behind Tessa. "Why would you need to say good-bye, Ryan?"

Ryan's body sagged. He finished shoving the last of his things into the bag before turning to face her. She stood in the doorway now instead of Tessa. Her eyes were wide with questions. And something else . . .

Was it fear?

"Congratulations on getting the job back," he said with a smile, steeling himself for what he was about to do. "The Senate and Lighthouse Board made the right decision. I admire them for their willingness to stand up for what's right."

She reached for the frayed rope of one of the buoys hanging on the wall near the door. She didn't respond, but instead twisted and looped the rope.

Tessa had disappeared, and he was grateful to her for giving him a last few minutes alone with Caroline.

"They couldn't ask for a better lightkeeper," he added.

"Why are you leaving?" Her hands on the rope stilled, and the sharpness of her eyes stabbed him.

He had the sudden urge to hide his saddlebag behind the canoe and pretend he wasn't going anywhere. But he knew he had to face her and say his good-byes sooner or later.

"You're the keeper now," he started. "I'm out of work—"

"Tell me the truth." Her command was harsh with anguish.

His throat tightened. He picked up his saddlebag and slung it across his shoulder. "It's time for me to leave. I have to go—"

She put out her hand to stop him. "I'll let you have the job. You can be the keeper."

"No, Caroline."

She stepped into the shed, ducking under a fishnet and dodging a paddle. "I don't need to be head keeper. I'll stay as your assistant."

He shook his head. "My leaving has nothing to do with the job. I'm happy you're the keeper. You're much more qualified than me. In fact, I can't even begin to compare with your level of expertise."

"Please don't go, Ryan." In the dim light her eyes pleaded with him.

He felt his resolve begin to weaken. It would be so easy for him to stay, to rely upon her, to allow her to help him. But perhaps she needed to let go of taking care of him as much as he needed to stop relying on her for his healing.

He hung his head, hating that he had to hurt her. "There are some things I need to do," he said softly. "And God has some work to do in my life before I'll be the man you need."

"No" came her hoarse whisper.

"Aye. I have to make sure my drinking days are over."

"You did it once. You can do it again. And I'll be here to help you."

"That's just it," he said, growing more certain that he needed to go. "If I keep on looking to you for strength, then I'll never stand on my own two feet."

Thick tension hung in the air between them. For long

moments the chatter of Tessa and Esther near the house filled the silence.

"Where will you go?" Her question was strangled but resigned. It was almost as if she knew as well as he did that he wasn't ready to be in a relationship, and wouldn't be until he dealt with his inner demons.

"I don't know yet. Maybe the West."

She didn't reply except for the awful pain that radiated from her slumped body.

He started to let the saddlebag slip from his shoulder, to give in to the need to be with her. But then she looked up at him, her eyes glossy with unshed tears. "I understand."

And in the one statement he knew she accepted his choice and forgave him for the hurt he was causing her. She was as understanding as always.

He nodded and once more squared his shoulders. He had to go. Now. Before he utterly failed and gave in to temptation again.

With a heave he started forward, sidling past her. The warmth of her presence, the tiny catch of her breath, and the anguish she was desperately trying to hide all urged him to reconsider. But somehow he made it through the doorway and into the openness that led to the shore.

Any hints of sunshine he'd seen earlier had now disappeared. The clouds had closed their gaps, and the grayness had begun to spit pellets of sleet.

"I'll miss you." Her soft, almost imperceptible call followed him.

It grabbed his heart, wrenched it so painfully that he lost his breath. He stopped, tossed his bag to the ground, and spun around. Then in three long strides he stalked back inside the shed, grasped her by the arms, and dragged her against him. He dipped his head and took possession of her mouth.

He wanted her. He needed her. And he couldn't leave her.

Her lips responded to his with the same hunger. Her arms linked around his neck, and she clung to him.

The kiss deepened, and for a moment he forgot where he ended and she began. He was consumed with her. They were one. And the very thought of breaking the connection stabbed him worse than any war wound.

At the enmeshing of her fingers in his hair, he groaned, broke the seal of his mouth on hers, and brushed his lips to her cheek. His breath came in gasps.

The heat of her lips chased after his. He tilted away, trying to think straight, to remember what he needed to do. He trailed his mouth to the hollow of her ear and pressed a long, breathy kiss there.

Leave came the urgent whisper in the depths of his soul.

His fingers on her arms tightened. His breath in her ear turned heavier.

She clutched him almost desperately.

Leave now, the warning rose louder.

He closed his eyes, swallowed the desperation that swelled and threatened to drown him. "I love you," he whispered. "I'll always love you." Then he pried his fingers loose and took a step back, away from her.

Coldness filled the space between them. She shivered, but she made no move toward him.

He fought the urge to wrap his arms back around her, to comfort her and bring her warmth. He made himself do the hardest thing he'd ever done. He spun, walked through the door, and snatched up his saddlebag.

Then without looking back he strode toward his horse, his heart shattering with each step he took. He threw his meager belongings across the horse's flank.

He was leaving. And he refused to say any more good-byes.

❧

Caroline sat alone in the boathouse, leaning against the tangle of ropes and life vests hanging on the wall. Her cheeks were dry, her soul empty.

The sound of horse hooves had long since faded, and they hadn't returned. She'd sat for hours, waiting for the sound of them to grow louder again, to signal that Ryan had changed his mind, that he wouldn't leave her after all. But there was nothing.

The dismal gray had grown darker. Her fingers and toes were numb from the cold. She'd lost her appetite and thought she'd never be able to eat again, but now her stomach growled with pangs of hunger from having eaten nothing all day.

Tessa had come to check on her several times throughout the day to urge her to return to the house where it was warm. And when the boys had come home from school to find Ryan gone, they'd peeked in on her too, their sad eyes reflecting another loss in their young lives, making her want to weep from the unfairness of it all.

He wasn't coming back.

She would have to accept it. Finally.

He was gone. And no amount of wishing or crying would bring him back.

Deep inside she knew he was right, that he still needed to heal, that he wasn't whole yet. Part of her even understood why he wouldn't be able to heal here with her, that perhaps he would rely too much upon her strength so that he wouldn't regain his own.

But even if she understood, she didn't like it. In fact, at the thought of him wrenching back from their kiss and striding away from her, fresh agony ripped her again. She was tempted to lower her face into her hands and sob again, as she had so many times already.

Except that she was dry. She'd cried all the tears she could.

"Caroline," Tessa called from the doorway, "you have to come in now. You need to eat and get warmed up."

Caroline didn't move. She couldn't make herself.

Tessa waited.

At the ensuing silence, Caroline thought Tessa had left her alone, just as she had all the other times.

But after a few seconds, Tessa spoke again, this time louder and more firmly. "I know you're sad he left, but you have to get on with your life now." The rattle of a bucket and the clink of fishing lures were followed by Tessa muttering as she picked her way through the clutter in the boathouse to where Caroline sat huddled.

"This isn't the end of the world," Tessa said, planting her hands on her hips and looking down at Caroline. "Although you may not care now, you don't have much choice. You've been given a prestigious position as head keeper of a lighthouse. It's what you've always wanted. And now you have the chance to prove that women everywhere deserve the same rights as men."

Caroline shifted, letting Tessa's words seep into her, past her present grief.

"Don't throw away this opportunity," Tessa continued. "Don't give them any regrets about letting you have the job."

Caroline sighed and sat forward.

Tessa slipped a hand into the crook of her arm and tugged her upward. She stood, her frozen feet hardly able to support the weight of her body.

"And we wouldn't want Mr. Finick to have any reason to go back to the Board or the senators and make claims that he was right, would we?"

"No," Caroline agreed in a hoarse voice.

Tessa wrapped her arm around Caroline's waist to support her.

Now that Tessa mentioned Mr. Finick, Caroline was surprised he hadn't been out to the lighthouse to argue with Esther about the validity of the ruling. She supposed that meant he couldn't do anything to stop her now. The ruling was really true. The Lighthouse Board had agreed that she could keep her job.

She wished she could find the same thrill in the decision that she'd had earlier when Esther first read the letter. But there was nothing, except perhaps a small measure of obligation.

"It's getting dark, and you'll need to light the lantern soon," Tessa said. "We can't have you start your first night as official keeper without a warm meal and warm hands."

Caroline nodded and allowed Tessa to lead her out of the boathouse. Her first glance was at the empty horse pen. And then the path that led to the woods and town. Both were barren.

She stumbled. But Tessa leaned into her, holding her up once more. "He might be gone for now," the girl said gently, "but he'll be back. Someday he'll be back."

Caroline drew comfort from Tessa's reassurance. And she reminded herself that he'd told her he loved her. He loved her. He loved her.

She let the words settle deep inside.

"In the meantime, you have work to do." Tessa dropped a kiss onto Caroline's head.

Tears came again and clouded Caroline's eyes. She thought she'd cried them all out. But this time she knew the tears weren't over Ryan. They were for her sister, for the love she had for this sweet young woman who was finally growing up.

She laid her head against Tessa's shoulder and let her lead the way up the grassy knoll toward the cottage. "Who would have thought you'd ever be taking care of me?" Caroline whispered.

Tessa smiled. "Sometimes even the strongest need someone to take care of them."

Caroline's lips cracked into a small smile. She'd sacrificed so much for everyone else as long as she could remember. But maybe Tessa was right. Maybe it was time to let go of that need, to stop always having to be the strong one and let someone else take care of her for once.

Chapter 28

*C*aroline leaned against the gallery railing, peered out over the glistening water of Lake St. Clair, and drew in a breath of spring air. The monarchs had returned from Mexico. Clusters of them hovered along the lakeshore, one of the many stops in their migration north.

She caught the aroma of the peonies she'd planted around the base of the tower. It was her favorite time of year, when the flowers were in full bloom after the long winter. Of course, she didn't have quite as many blooms as in years past, for Arnie had razed most of them last fall. But with the bulbs Monsieur Poupard had planted, her flower garden was given a new start.

Monsieur Poupard came over earlier in the month with cuttings of lilies and daffodils. And now with all of them growing, the aroma mingled with the thawed lake water and brought contentment to her soul.

"God is good," she whispered into the bright morning, even as her attention strayed to a fresh mound of dirt in the small cemetery at the edge of the marsh.

Sarah, after holding on through the winter, died peacefully in her sleep in April. Caroline wasn't sure what had kept Sarah alive all winter, but she had a feeling it had to do with Monsieur Poupard's visits.

The old trapper sat with Sarah on many dark days, holding her hand and speaking to her in his strong French accent. And although Sarah had declined so that she lost her ability to speak, her eyes still shone with love, especially when Monsieur Poupard was in the room.

Caroline learned that the Frenchman had once had a little girl of his own, but that he'd been gone for long portions of the year trapping and had missed out on much of his daughter's life. He was out in the wilderness when his daughter had contracted consumption. By the time he received the news and made it back home, she'd passed away.

One stormy winter night, Monsieur Poupard had relayed the story to Caroline, and she'd understood then his need to be with Sarah and make her life as happy as possible before she died.

Caroline looked away from the grave marked by a simple cross and adorned with as many flowers as Caroline could manage to plant in the vicinity. She drew in another deep breath and moved back into the lantern room. She'd already extinguished the light, but there was something about being outside on the gallery in the early morning that nourished her.

A quick survey of the room told her everything was in order for the day. She smiled with a measure of pride in a job well done.

She'd done an excellent job—those were the exact words of the new lighthouse inspector who'd come for a visit yesterday. *Excellent job*. Her smile widened as she made her way down the winding stairway.

Last fall she'd learned that Mr. Finick had been fired, that someone had gone to the Board and reported the old inspector for taking bribes from locals. She had the suspicion that Ryan had been the one to do the reporting, not long after he'd left, although she couldn't be certain.

Someone had also filed reports about Mr. Simmons's illegal smuggling. He hadn't been caught at it, but now that the authorities had gotten involved, Caroline noticed a decline in Simmons's clandestine activities. Or at the very least, he'd moved to a different area of the lake to engage in his smuggling.

Whatever the case, she was grateful Ryan had sought justice before moving on. She guessed he'd made his reports in an effort to protect her from further harassment.

With the arrival of the new inspector, and his glowing words of praise, she felt pleased to be paving the way for women who would come after her. If she could do a job considered only suitable for men and do it equally well, then why couldn't other women do what they loved too?

At the bottom of the tower, she stepped into the restored passageway. Before the winter set in, the Lighthouse Board had sent out a crew to rebuild the connecting room. She was grateful for their swift attention and help.

With her logbooks stacked neatly on a new table and a jar of fresh-cut peonies next to them, she thought back to that fateful day when Mr. Finick had visited last fall, when he'd been disgusted with her flowers and had ordered her to leave the light. The day Ryan first arrived . . .

A quick blade of pain sliced her heart.

She crossed the small room and pushed open the door leading into the cottage, trying to just as easily push aside the pain that remembrances of Ryan elicited, even seven months after he'd left. It had gotten a little easier to stop thinking about him constantly, and it was a little less painful when she did. But not by much.

She missed him every day, every hour. She prayed that wherever he was, and whatever he was doing, that he'd finally found peace and healing.

"Is that you, Caroline?" came Tessa's voice from the kitchen.

Caroline passed by her bedroom door, wanting nothing more than to fall into her bed and sleep. She'd stayed up in the tower too long that morning to take in the fragrances and bright colors of spring.

She poked her head into the kitchen, to the sight of Tessa at the table dressing a muskrat. Her arms were covered in dark blood from the carcass lying in the roasting pan in front of her.

Caroline wrinkled her nose. "I see Monsieur Poupard has delivered another of his gifts this morning."

Tessa nodded. "He's a godsend. If not for him, our bellies would be rumbling much more often than they do now."

"True." It hadn't taken Caroline long to figure out that Monsieur Poupard was the one leaving muskrat on their doorstep all along. She'd once thought it was Arnie. But when the secret deliveries continued even after Arnie had been hauled away to prison for arson and kidnapping, they'd finally set up a lookout. One early morning, Tessa and Sarah spied Monsieur Poupard sneaking out of the woods and toward the cottage with a skinned muskrat across his shoulder.

They hadn't told Monsieur Poupard they knew he was the

one leaving the gifts. But they always invited him for dinner on the evenings Tessa roasted the meat.

"He's coming for dinner tonight." Tessa winked at Caroline. She and Tessa laughed together often over the fact that now Monsieur Poupard gave them muskrat even more regularly.

"Good," Caroline said with a return wink. "I'll warn the boys to be on their best behavior."

Of course, the twins still caused Monsieur Poupard all kinds of grief. But underneath his gruff exterior, she could tell he cared about them too.

Caroline smothered a yawn and turned to retreat to her bedroom.

"I've already pulled the curtains for you," Tessa said in a rush.

Caroline stopped at the strange statement.

"I was in there tidying up," Tessa explained, "and so I went ahead and got the room ready for you."

"Thank you." Caroline couldn't make sense of the tiny note of excitement in Tessa's voice, except that it was finally May and summer was just around the corner. And with the coming of summer she'd promised Tessa she would investigate a school for teacher's training, so that perhaps Tessa could leave the community behind her.

It had been a long, hard year for Tessa. She was shunned by most in the area, though Caroline had done her best to spread the news about what had really happened. Still, people stared at Tessa whenever she went to town, whispering behind their hands about her.

The whole experience had helped to mature Tessa, which was at least one blessing that had come out of it. But Caroline understood her sister's desire to get away from the rumors and blemishes on her reputation. And Tessa still wanted to move away from the lighthouse. While she'd allowed Caroline to teach her a few basics about the lantern, she insisted she never wanted to live in a lighthouse again.

Caroline plodded down the hallway, then paused to look into Sarah's old room. The empty bed, the smooth coverlet, the overall barrenness of the room opened the fresh wound in her heart.

She'd lost people she held dear over the past year, and she didn't want to lose Tessa too. But she had to admit that Tessa was growing up and finally ready to get married. She could only pray that one day the right man would overlook Tessa's past mistake and love her regardless.

Caroline turned to her bedroom door and opened it. Weariness drooped over her, and she shuffled inside, closing the door behind her.

Blackness surrounded her, and for a moment she was tempted to go back out into the light and skip sleeping for the day. It was this time of the morning, when she was overly tired, that she thought about Ryan the most and missed him. There were still too many mornings when she cried herself to sleep, even though she tried not to anymore.

Blindly she crossed the room until she bumped into the bed. Her fingers made contact with the warm cotton nightgown Tessa had laid there. She'd even pulled back the covers, so that Caroline's hand brushed against the coolness of the sheet.

With a sigh she sat down on the edge of the bed and crossed her ankle over her knee. She unlaced her boot and slipped it off, letting it fall to the floor. Then she shed the other and dropped it to the floor as well.

She dug her fingers into the knot at the back of her neck and fished for the hairpins, holding each one between pursed lips as she found them.

In the stillness of the room, she heard the faint *swoosh* of someone releasing a breath of air. She froze with half a dozen pins pressed between her lips, her hands deep in her hair.

Was someone in the room with her, or had she only imagined the sound?

After a moment of listening to absolute silence, she shook off the chills and resumed fishing out the remainder of the pins. She tossed her head, and her hair cascaded over her shoulders and down her back.

The bed squeaked and shifted behind her. Caroline jumped up with a scream. It was a muted scream, as she tried not to lose her hold on the pins in her mouth.

At a muttering from the opposite side of the bed, Caroline groped for her pillow. She let the hairpins drop, no longer concerned about losing them. Not when there was an intruder in her bedroom.

She lifted the pillow and brought it down with a thwack.

The intruder muttered again.

Caroline didn't stop to think. She needed to defend herself. So she brought the pillow down again, and then a third time.

A burst of laughter from the bed stopped her in mid-swing. Something about the laughter sent her pulse racing but not with fear.

"Caroline?" the one laughing said. "Are you trying to kill me again?"

"Ryan?"

"Aye."

She had to stifle a real scream this time by pressing the pillow over her mouth.

The bed squeaked again under his weight. His feet dropped to the floor and thudded as he moved away from the bed. He threw open the curtain and flooded the room with light.

Holding up a hand to shield his eyes, he gave her a full view of his injury—the puckered skin, the scars, the stumps that remained where his fingers had once been.

It really was him.

A grin lit up his face, which was covered with whiskers similar to the first time she'd seen him. His hair was long and in need of a cut. She half expected to see him in his underclothes, but thankfully he was fully attired, except for his bare feet.

She couldn't keep from drinking him in, from taking in his warm brown eyes and handsome face. His arms were thicker, his muscles bulging against his sleeves. He'd clearly filled out over the past months.

"When you're done staring," he said, his smile inching higher, "maybe you can explain why you were beating me up."

"Oh, sure." She smiled back. "And then maybe you can explain why you were in my bed."

"Unlike you, I have an excuse," he teased. "I was tired. I rode for two days almost nonstop to get here. When I arrived early this morning, Tessa told me I could sleep here, that she'd wake me when you came down."

"Looks like she woke you, all right," Caroline said wryly. She could almost see Tessa in the kitchen, giggling at the reunion she'd orchestrated.

Ryan tilted his head, and slowly he let his gaze travel over her, from the top of her head to the tips of her stockinged feet showing beneath her hem.

There was something slightly dangerous in his eyes that burned into her and twisted her belly with pleasure.

When finished, he retraced his path back to her hair and lingered there. "You're more beautiful than I remembered," he whispered, his smile fading.

She was still holding the pillow in front of her. She tossed it back onto the bed that stood between them. "I wasn't sure if you remembered me at all after so many months."

"I thought about you all the time. Every second of every day."

His admission added fuel to the fire building inside her. But the pain of the past months without him came swirling back and urged her to use caution. She didn't know why he was back and what he wanted from her. She couldn't let herself love him again if he was only going to leave her once more.

Besides, if he'd missed her so much, why hadn't he come back sooner?

"I worked laying railroad track all winter," he said, as if she'd spoken her question aloud. "I earned good money. And once I'd saved up enough earnings, I quit and rode east to Virginia."

He stood straight, without hiding his injured hand in his pocket. Had he made peace with his injury? She tried to keep her hope in check and not barrage him with a hundred questions and instead let him tell her what he wanted in his own time.

"I went back to the farm in Virginia, to the place of the murder," he said somberly. "The mother and her three other children still live there. But her husband hadn't made it out of the war alive. He was killed at Vicksburg."

She expected Ryan's shoulders to slump, for the horror of the event to weigh him down. But his eyes remained bright. "I apologized for not doing anything to try to save her son from getting shot—for being a coward that night with my comrades."

The light streaming in from the window accentuated a peace and a confidence in his demeanor she'd never noticed before, making her realize that as hard as their separation had been, it had taken him more courage and strength to leave than it would have to stay with her.

"She forgave me. And when I gave them everything I'd earned from working on the railroad, they accepted it with gratitude."

"You really surprised them, then."

He nodded. "It was the last thing they expected. Yet it was the thing they needed the most."

"I'm so glad, Ryan," she said with a joyful leap in her chest. She could see that he was better off for having done it. It was as if he'd thrown off the shackles that had bound him and was now free.

He took another step toward her but halted at the bed. He looked at her then with a forthrightness that tugged at her heart. "I've been free of drink and opium since I left here."

The joy within her expanded. "I'm proud of you."

"Not one drink in all these months. And, Lord willing, I'll not have another sip for the rest of my life."

"I knew you could do it."

"Not in my own strength, or in yours," he said gently, "but by learning to cry out my need for God every day, every hour."

She nodded, marveling at the new man before her. Maybe he was still maimed physically, but God had indeed healed his heart and mind.

"And I may have found a surgeon who's willing to take another look and see if he can remove the remaining shrapnel."

"That would be wonderful," she said.

"Even if he can't, the months of labor have strengthened my arm and hand." He flexed his arm playfully. The slight wince told her that maybe he'd never be completely free of pain, but he was learning to live with his wounds.

He dropped his arm and shook his head. "I can't believe how much I missed you. I thought I would die if I had to wait another day to see you."

She gave a soft laugh of delight at his admission.

"I'm serious." He grinned. "I about killed my poor horse on the trip back."

"I missed you too."

"Then I guess that means you won't object when I tell you I have a new job here."

"A job?"

"Aye." He started to walk slowly around the bed toward her. "Before I rode to Virginia, I met with the Lighthouse Board. I explained the mix-up with Tessa. And then I petitioned the Board to create another position here at Windmill Point."

She started in surprise.

"Don't worry," he said, drawing nearer. "They had nothing but the highest praise for you."

"I've worked hard. The inspector told me yesterday that I've done an excellent job."

"And you have. It was good for them to see you working independently these past months, to know you're just as capable as any man."

She nodded in agreement. If Ryan hadn't left, she wasn't sure the Board would have truly seen her capability like they did now. As hard as the separation from Ryan had been, it was clear that God had known it was exactly what each of them needed at the time.

"Even so, Windmill Point is a big job for one person." Ryan continued around the bed and didn't stop until he was standing directly before her. She was comforted by the strength of his presence.

"It may be a big job, but I've managed," she said, hardly able to think clearly now.

He leaned closer, lifted his hand, and stroked a strand of her hair. "Would you object to having an assistant?" he asked softly.

Again she started. "Do you want to be my assistant?"

"Would you mind?" He fingered her hair again.

"Could you be happy working under a woman head keeper?"

"Of course I could be happy. You'd be the best boss a man could ever ask for." He grinned. "And the prettiest."

"Are you sure?" She almost couldn't believe he'd be staying, that he wanted to work here alongside her. It seemed too good to be true.

"I'm certain," he said, and his expression turned serious again.

Her heart hitched a little as the humor evaporated from his face. Maybe everything had been too good to be true.

"There is one thing that would make me even happier," he whispered, and this time he grazed his knuckles along her jaw to her chin. He caressed her bottom lip with his thumb.

A breeze rippled through her, like the wind through a field of flowers. "We can't have you being an unhappy employee," she teased. "So tell me what you want, and I'll do my best to rectify the situation."

"I'd like another kiss." He traced her upper lip this time. "But only after you agree to marry me."

She sucked in a breath.

He grew motionless, his eyes fixed on her face, watching her reaction, waiting for her response. "I know I don't have the right to walk back into your life after all this time and ask you to marry me. Maybe you've found someone else . . ."

She started to shake her head, but he cut her off. "All I know is that I've wanted to marry you since I met you last fall. I haven't stopped thinking about you or loving you or praying that you'd wait for me, even though you had no obligation to do so. And I'd be the happiest man on earth if you'd marry me."

She reached up and cupped his cheek. "Yes. To both."

He smiled, the happiness brimming from his eyes and crinkling his tanned skin. "Both?"

"Yes, I'll marry you." It was her turn to trace his jaw and run a finger across his bottom lip. "And yes, you may kiss me again."

"Today?"

"Yes."

He bent in, and his nose almost touched hers. "Marry you today? Or kiss you today?"

"Both. Today. Now." She wound her fingers into his shirt and tugged him against her. "So long as it's a kiss like the one you gave me before you left." His good-bye kiss had been filled with such passion and love that even as she stood in his arms, she could feel the memory of it as if he'd kissed her only yesterday.

His lips grazed hers, and her knees nearly buckled at the sweetness of it. "I can give you kisses like that every day." His voice turned soft. "All day long."

She wrapped her arms around his neck and drew him even closer. "Then what are you waiting for?"

They smiled at each other, and when their lips finally met, they both knew that the wait had been worth all the pain, that their hearts were made whole now, and they would be able to share a lifetime of pleasure. Together.

Author's Note

*W*ith this second book in the BEACONS OF HOPE series, I hope you've enjoyed learning about another Michigan lighthouse. Windmill Point really did exist on Lake St. Clair and was in operation for over a century. It served as an important guide for the whole commerce of the Great Lakes near the Detroit River.

Today, however, if you were to visit Windmill Point, the original lighthouse and keeper's cottage are no longer in existence. Instead you would find only a small and simple unmanned electric tower in bustling metropolitan Grosse Pointe Park, a suburb of Detroit.

Caroline Taylor wasn't a real woman keeper at Windmill Point Lighthouse, but she was inspired by Caroline Litogot Antaya, a lightkeeper heroine from Michigan's history. Caroline Antaya lived at the Mamajuda Lighthouse on the Detroit River a short distance away from Windmill Point Lighthouse. Incidentally, the Mamajuda Lighthouse is no longer in existence either.

Caroline Antaya's husband served with honor in the Union Army during the Civil War, losing several fingers on his hand at Gettysburg. After returning from the war, her husband was named keeper of the Mamajuda Lighthouse, but then he fell ill with tuberculosis and passed away.

Following her husband's death, the superintendent of Detroit Lighthouses appointed Caroline as acting keeper, most likely because he felt sorry for her loss. However, six months later, Caroline was removed from her position because the superintendent wanted to replace her with a man.

The community near Caroline rose to her defense. They even enlisted the assistance of a Michigan senator to help fight for her reappointment. I quoted the senator's actual words regarding Caroline when he said, "The vessel men all say that she keeps a very excellent light and I think it very hard to remove this woman, who is faithful and efficient, and throw her upon the world."

Because of the support of her community, Caroline was reinstated as keeper with full duties. In those days, when women were regularly discriminated against because of gender, Caroline's story was inspirational and an encouragement to others to persevere in the face of injustice.

Stephen Simmons was also a real rogue from the pages of Michigan history. Though he lived in the early 1800s, in the decades before the Civil War, I used this villain as the basis for Mr. Simmons in the novel. He had a tavern outside of Detroit and was a Goliath of a man. At first he gave the impression of being cultured and educated, but once people got to know him, they realized what a brute he really was.

The community where Simmons lived grew to fear him, because when under the influence of alcohol he searched out his enemies, picked fights, and inflicted painful beatings. He later killed his wife in a drunken rage. Because he was held in such low regard, during his trial the court had a difficult time finding jurors who would be impartial. So it came as no surprise when the jury found Simmons guilty of murdering his wife.

Simmons was sentenced to death by hanging. On the day of his execution, people from as far away as fifty miles lined the streets. The makeshift grandstands and rooftops filled to overflowing with everyone who had come to witness his death.

Simmons was composed as he walked to the gallows. With dignity he delivered a speech on the evils of alcohol, repented of his sins, and pleaded for mercy. But Simmons would find no mercy that day. In front of at least two thousand people, Simmons met eternity.

Many people left the hanging feeling the punishment had been both cruel and vindictive. As a result, public sentiment against the death penalty swelled. Eventually, Michigan became the first state in the nation to abolish the death penalty.

It's my hope that through this story, like Caroline and Ryan, you will learn to turn to God with every need you have. He's there waiting for you to come to Him, every day, every hour, every minute. He wants the cry of your heart to be, *"Lord, I need you, how I need you. Every hour I need you."*

May you overflow with strength and peace as you turn to Him.

Jody Hedlund is the award-winning author of several novels, including the BEACONS OF HOPE series as well as *Captured by Love*, *Rebellious Heart*, and *The Preacher's Bride*. She holds a bachelor's degree from Taylor University and a master's degree from the University of Wisconsin, both in social work. Jody lives in Michigan with her husband and five children. Learn more at JodyHedlund.com.